Brothers of the Wind

David Weaver

PublishAmerica
Baltimore

First printing

This is a work of fiction. Names, characters, places, and incidents either are the product of the author's imagination or are used fictitiously. Any resemblance to actual persons, living or dead, events, or locales is entirely coincidental.

PublishAmerica has allowed this work to remain exactly as the author intended, verbatim, without editorial input.

ISBN: 1-60703-976-1
PUBLISHED BY PUBLISHAMERICA, LLLP
www.publishamerica.com
Baltimore

Printed in the United States of America

Violent bursts of blistering wind suddenly collided with the tranquil blue water of Lake Turkana, which created angry waves that crashed against its rocky shoreline. The brilliant stars of the Milky Way, gathered in clusters above the emerald water, appeared only as faint luminous dots through the thick swirling sand created by the wind.

Natives of the lake had little knowledge of where that fierce nightly wind came from and apparently did not care. They simply referred to it as the *upepo kali* (fierce wind) and learned to plan work and play around it. After living with that tempest for so many years they knew by instinct within hours its devastating turbulence would end and a bright, starlit sky would return.

Meteorologists had long ago theorized that a high-pressure area from somewhere around the Red Sea was responsible for the creation of that seasonal wind. They believed that at certain times of the year the gale force wind would leave the warm region of Ethiopia, pick up speed as it dashed across its parched flat lands, and then funnel its way between the jagged pinnacles of the Longondoti Hills of Kenya. After it had reached its peak velocity it would then race down the length of the lake and unleash its full fury on the southern tip. Theory or not, to the natives of that region it was a fact of life and they had to learn to live with it.

After the mournful howl of that seasonal wind had subsided to a whimper, a cacophony of strange, ominous sounds drifted across the night air filling it with pulsating baritones, staccato barks, and soprano yelps. For a few moments, the sounds dominate the remnants of the wind and then gradually faded away.

In the stillness of the cool African night an aging lioness weaved her way through the thick golden stalks of Mara grass in search of a much-needed meal; her cubs had not eaten in several days. Her sagging, emaciated belly growled loudly as it brushed across the tops of the stiff brown weed. Her once round and alert chestnut eyes were suddenly transformed into half-closed fly-infested slits above her moist, billowing nostrils. She lowered her flaxen body onto a vacant heat-hardened termite mound and out of despair dropped the massive head onto large, dusty paws.

Off in the distance, a slight movement danced across her peripheral vision. She raised her head above the tops of the Mara grass and froze in a motionless crouch. Her eyes anxiously searched the darkness. The unknown entity turned toward her, and its loud purring sound confused and frightened her. As it drew near, her nostrils picked up its acrid stench. It had come within striking distance, but she hesitated. Her indecision lasted long enough for it to disappear behind a far-off knoll.

A faint, muffled sound drifted across the hot desert sand toward her. Once again, she raised her head and scanned the horizon. An instant later, two beams of light illuminated the star-laden sky above the hill where the mysterious object had disappeared. She lowered her body back to the warmth of the mound. Through narrow openings in the field of unyielding grass, she stared hypnotically at the mysterious lights. The strange apparitions flickered several times and then went out. She lifted her head to the sky and broadcast her feelings with a guttural growl, which fractured the stillness of the night. A foraging hyena sprang from a nearby bush and raced across the barren hillside yelping staccato barks as it disappeared into the underbrush.

She struggled to her feet, shook the dust from her gaunt body, and headed in the direction of the strange prey—possibly a meal for her cubs.

Chapter One

Paul lifted his eyes to the sky and examined the endless swath of twinkling stars that hung in clusters above him. He had always been fascinated by the vastness of the universe. However, it had also troubled him; he felt small and insignificant in its presence, like an ant in the sand. He could not recall all of what the Consolata Sisters at the mission school had told him about the stars of the Milky Way, but it had something to do with his God, *Nkai*, who had created all things in the universe.

While he sat pondering the heaven's vastness, a cold wind raked its fingers across his half naked body, causing him to shiver uncontrollably. He pulled his brightly colored *kuvaa* (blanket) tightly around his shoulders, inched closer to the dying campfire, and gave the faint glowing embers a brisk stir with the tip of his spear. Multi-colored sparks sprang into the night sky, swirled upward, and then disappeared into the darkness.

For a moment, he stared at the flickering yellow flames consuming the camel-dung fuel. As he gazed into the small inferno, he could feel it was not providing the same warmth it had in the past. Even the nights were colder and longer now, and the wind much stronger. As he looked intently into its soothing glow, another burst of wind scraped its icy fingers across his bare chest and forced him to pull his blanket even tighter around his shoulders.

His eyes shifted from the glowing belly of the fire to a fallen palm frond. He picked it up and stirred the dying embers with quick, deliberate strokes. Bright red sparks spiraled into the inky sky, mingled for a moment with the stars, and then disappeared into the blackness that surrounded him. However, a few glowing bits of fire persevered and settled on top of his head. With dung-stained fingers, he combed through his shoulder length hair and knocked the fiery specks to the ground. Even so, a few flaming bits had already found his sleeping blanket. He swatted furiously at the red-hot specks until they no longer posed a threat to the only blanket he owned.

He reached across the dying coals and retrieved a long skewer with his dinner impaled on it. The aroma of the sizzling lizard made him salivate. Cooked or not, he was going to eat it anyway, he thought, he was that hungry. He slid the scorched carcass off the skewer and into his hand. Instantly, the hot flesh burned his fingers, forcing him to drop it to the ground. He stared down at the dirt-encrusted head and its bulging, lifeless eyes stared back.

When the meat had cooled, he brushed it off and slid it onto a palm frond. He slurped and smacked his lips as he bit into the juicy carcass. After devouring the accessible meat he eagerly probed the body cavity with a stick, hoping to find more.

Off in the distance he heard the faint grunts of wild camels. He thought it strange to hear them in that area; the Turkana tribe had captured most of them for food, or as beasts of burden. The raspy bleating of goats was more common. The area had always been populated by thousands of the domesticated animals; they represented the lifeblood of his tribe, the Samburu. However, essential as they were they attracted jackals, leopards and lions. His tribe had been exceptionally fortunate with their herds; the Masai had reduced the lion prides by killing them for their illegal rite-of-passage ceremonies. Even the customs of his own tribe had once dictated that a boy had to kill a lion before he could become a *lmurran*, (mu-ran) a warrior. However, with the diminishing prides, the practice had to be discontinued. Circumcised boys from his village hunted birds and small game to discharge their ancestral requirements. The elders of his village were aware of the rite-of-passage challenge for their young men, but to them it didn't matter if they killed lions with spears or small game with bows and arrows; it was unimportant; the challenge was all that mattered. Paul hung his head in thought. He was old enough to be a warrior, but the elders had not called on him, and he could not understand it, most boys his age had already been summoned.

He held the lizard's empty carcass by its bony tail and inspected it for any remaining fragments of meat. Finding none, he threw it into the bushes. He lifted a leather pouch of *saroi*, a mixture of goat milk and blood, to his lips and grimaced as the thick, bland mixture ran down his throat. "Tourists at the fishing club don't have to drink this stuff," he mumbled in Masai, his native tongue.

After he had finished eating the remnants of his sparse meal, he closed his eyes, locked his arms around his knees, and rocked back and forth on a large boulder beside the fire. In his mind's eye, he could see the 12-foot metal fence that surrounded the fishing club. He could also see images of tourists sitting beside the two mineral swimming pools, refreshing themselves with iced drinks. He had never tasted ice and had often wondered what it would be like to have a glass of water with it inside. "As long as it isn't *saroi*," he muttered, and then chuckled out loud.

A friend of his, fortunate enough to get a job at the fishing club, had once told him it was common for tourists to spend 1600 shillings a day for room and meals. That was more than he could make in a year showing them the sights of Loiyangalani.

"Paul," a voice came out of the darkness, breaking his reverie. The voice continued in Masai, "Are you all right? Is everything okay? I thought I heard you talking to somebody."

Paul turned his head toward the familiar voice. "I'm fine, Hussein," he replied, also in Masai. "How about you?"

"Were you worried I wouldn't come? The moon is almost overhead, you know." Hussein dropped a fresh pile of camel dung beside the smoldering campfire.

Paul dragged a palm frond through the nearly dead ashes, and a few dormant flames erupted. He threw several nuggets of dung onto the new flames and watched as they burst into large, yellow tentacles, which danced to the beat of the pulsing fire.

He was slow to answer. "I wasn't worried," he said. "I knew you would come." He stood up and wrapped his arm around his friend's neck. "The herd's bedded down and everything's quiet. Earlier, I thought I heard camels. Also, there was a strange whirring sound, and then a loud bang I never heard before. But that's all." He spotted Hussein's *sampur*, a pouch made from goatskin and used to carrying food and supplies. "Did you bring food?" He grinned.

"Yes. I brought *saroi*, with honey and berries in it. And maize bread."

Paul's eyes widened. "Etaira's maize bread?"

"Yes. I know how you like it." His eyes twinkled in the glow of the campfire, as he watched his friend dig into the pouch.

"Thank you. I'm never around when my mother bakes. Etaira's is better anyway. It has much more flavor. It's sweeter."

Hussein's face beamed. He sat on the abandoned warm boulder, sank the shaft of his spear into a soft spot in the sand and watched his friend devour the food.

After Paul finished the last of the sweet bread, he spread his sleeping blanket under the branches of a thorny acacia bush and dove onto it. He reached into the thicket and plucked a two-inch acacia thorn from a branch.

"Did the safari trucks come, today?" he asked, picking his teeth with the sharp spine. "Weren't they supposed to be at the oasis this afternoon?"

"Yes. They came. There were many tourists. Mostly Americans. The trucks parked in the grove, as usual."

"Was William with them?"

"Yes, he was." Hussein wrinkled his nose in mock disgust. They both giggled as images of the old Masai flashed before their eyes.

William was the person in charge of the safari trucks. He had abandoned his tribe years ago to work for the white man as a tourist guide. Because of his knowledge of the territory, and native customs, he was an indispensable asset to the safari company. He appeared to know all the answers and was not a bit reluctant to express his own opinions and points of views.

While they talked, Hussein made himself comfortable by the fire. They giggled when they remembered the many times they had crawled under the fence of the safari camp to comfort the older tourists. They would rig their tents, get safe water, and anything else to make their lives easier, if William didn't catch them.

By the time the safari trucks had reached Loiyangalani, the largest fishing village on Lake Turkana, the tourists had traveled a great distance. Although their trip was only half over at that point, most of them would have been more than willing to forfeit their money for a return trip to Nairobi and the comforts of a hotel.

If William happened to spot the boys assisting his tourists, he would yell curses at them in every language he knew. He would brandish his knotted fighting stick, his *rungu*, and chase them back under the fence. Nevertheless, the boys knew his display of anger was mostly for the benefit of the tourists.

"Did you help with any of the tents, tonight?" Paul asked.

"I didn't have time. But they're going to be here for a few days. I'm sure they'll need our help, sooner or later. Especially, when the wind blows their tents down on top of their heads." They both snickered at the thought.

Paul wrapped up in his sleeping blanket and prepared for the long, cold night. Before he closed his eyes, he glanced over at his friend and smiled; he had tucked his feet under his buttocks and resembled a bird waiting for prey.

The chill of the night air forced Hussein to wrap the warmth of his own blanket around his shoulders. He picked up his spear, pointed the blade at the sky, and pushed the butt-end deep into the sand.

Like a warrior, Paul thought. He watched his friend for several minutes, and then closed his eyes and fell asleep.

Hussein began taking a head count of the disorganized goats, mainly to ward off boredom. Halfway through the count he became aware of Paul's deep, loud breathing and knew he was asleep. "The hillside is too quiet, tonight," he mumbled under his breath. The majority of the herd was calm, but the older goats had suddenly become agitated, displayed by the rapid scurrying of their hoofs.

Off in the distance, he believed he heard the huff of a lion. At first, it was only a murmur on the wind, but a few minutes later he heard it again. With each huff the sound got closer and louder. His eyes pierced the darkness, but to no avail. He tried to reassure himself he was not afraid, that he would handle it like a man. Nevertheless, just to be on the safe side he believed it wise to recite an old Samburu proverb: "Although there are lions nearby, this is where I will rest tonight, Nkai willing."

He picked up a palm frond and swiped it back and forth through the dying coals with a desperate attempt to refresh them. They were slow to spring to life, but when they finally ignited he stared nervously into their orange and yellow hues. He leaned back on the boulder and closed his eyes. He thought it strange the fire seemed warmer now than when he was a *layeni* (pre-teen boy) tending his goats for the first time. He raised his eyes to the heavens and squinted at the stars, through particles of wind-blown sand. And there were more stars now, more than ever before. It was good to be alive. Soon, the elders would give him permission to become a *lmurran*, he was certain of it. It had been over two years and by all rights he should be one. Nevertheless, he was not worried; they would call on him in due time. He hoped it wouldn't be too much longer, though. All of his life he had dreamt of living as a warrior; to run with them when they tracked game and go with them into the mountains to search for lost goats. If the elders would only give him a chance, he knew he could prove himself.

Again, he heard the low guttural huff of a lion. However, that time it sounded like it was on the other side of the small hill behind him. He pulled his spear out of the sand and stood up straight. The sound was low and throaty at first, and then climaxed in a piercing scream.

He prodded his sleeping friend with the butt of his spear. "Paul, Paul, wake up!" he said in an anxious whisper.

Paul rubbed the sand from his burning eyes and sat upright. "Wha...what is it?" he stammered, still half asleep. He stared groggily into his friend's wide eyes.

Hussein pointed to the slope behind them. "There's a lion on the other side of the hill," he hissed.

"A lion? Are you sure?" Paul jumped to his feet, rubbed his eyes once more, and then pulled his own spear from the sand.

"Yes, it's a lion. I'm sure of it. I heard it earlier but I didn't want to wake you. At first, the sound was far off, but now it's just over the hill."

"I've never heard lions in this area before."

"You were always asleep when they were around," Hussein countered with a grin. As they waited for the sound to return, the hazy light of dawn began painting the eastern sky with a pink glow that washed most of the stars from the sky. The goats had sensed the lion, even before he had, and were on the verge of stampeding. He pointed. "See them? They know."

The lead goat had bolted down the incline of a small gully, and was soon followed by the others. The boys chased after them, trying to turn the lead goat around. Before they could reach it, they heard several loud, metallic honks on the other side of the hill. When the goats heard the sound they bolted even deeper into the ravine, making a roundup impossible.

By the anxious beeping of the horn the boys knew somebody was in trouble and raced over the hill. The silhouette of a Land Rover's bumper was barely visible in the subdued light of morning. It appeared to have been traveling where no road or goat path existed.

They rushed down the rise. As they got closer they saw the full outline of the truck. It was wedged vertically in a small gorge. They sensed the lion's presence, and approached with caution, spears held in readiness.

When they approached to the truck they heard a moan, followed by a familiar growl. Searching the area with their eyes they saw the silhouette of a lioness crouched between them and the body of a man. She had claimed her prey and would defend it with her life.

The elders had once told them that a lion would not attack if a person backed away and gave it a wide berth, unless it was hungry. Hungry or not, it was apparent that the man lying on the ground, and someone in the vehicle, were in danger and needed their help. They approached the animal with caution. She tightened her front leg muscles and twitched her tail as a warning.

Without hesitation, Paul raised his heavy spear and sent the ebony shaft sailing toward her. The long, lanceolated blade missed its target and dug deep into the sand inches from her body. With a loud roar she shrunk back, re-tensed, and prepared to charge.

Hussein hefted his spear to his shoulder, but did not throw. He stood motionless, staring into her eyes. Suddenly, with a loud snarl she lunged. He threw his spear with all his strength. The blade caught her in the forequarter and her massive body dropped to the ground, a meter in front of them.

The boys retreated to a safe distance and watched her thrash about in the sand, attempting to dislodge the blade from her chest using her paws and teeth. A few tense moments later she rolled onto her side and lay semi-motionless. Her breathing was raspy and guttural. Finally, she took one last breath and closed her eyes.

The boys remained frozen in their tracks. After several minutes, Hussein approached her lifeless body and kicked it. Her mouth was wide open, as if gasping for air. He yanked the spear from the carcass and jumped back, not fully convinced she was dead. He had heard of injured animals killing careless hunters who had mistakenly believed they were dead.

"God! Am I glad to see you guys," a man's voice called out in English. "For a minute there I thought we'd bought the farm."

"Who's there?" Hussein returned, also in English. "Are you all right?"

"Oh, you speak English?" the voice called back. "Good. My name's Eric… Eric Somerville. My arm hurts like hell and my leg is pinned under something. I can't seem to get it free. Can you boys help me?"

"We both speak English," Hussein said, proudly. He approached the truck. "I am Hussein. My friend over there is Paul." He pointed. "We will help you. Don't move. We will try to free you, and then get help from our village."

"Thanks," Eric said. "I believe William, my guide, is over there somewhere in the bushes. He might be dead, though. He was thrown from the truck and that damned animal dragged him into the bushes." He pointed to the dead lion.

Hussein followed his finger and noticed Paul crouched beside something. "I believe Paul has found him," he said. "I believe he is over there with my friend." He shouted across the clearing, "Is that William?"

"Yes," Paul replied with a grin. "It's our Masai brother, the Milika." They both giggled at the thought of him being a little devil. He looked down at William. "Are you hurt bad?" he asked in Masai. "Where are your wounds?" he continued, reverting to English. "Where are you hurt?"

Several moments passed before William could focus his eyes. Then, in a strained voice he mumbled, "I hurt all over, damn it! She took me by my ribs and dragged me here. I believe most of them are broken, on this side." Trembling fingers pointed to his right side. He began to cough in short, miniature eruptions. He looked up at Paul through half-swollen eyes, and with a painful grin, added, "And I'm no 'Milika'." Paul chuckled.

"We have killed the lion," Hussein proudly announced to the man in the truck, whose name he couldn't remember. "We will get help for you and your friend. Our village is not far. It is in the valley."

Paul looked down at the bleeding Masai. His collarless *dashikis*, which had been half-torn away from his broad shoulders, was saturated with blood. Deep gashes were visible on a balding spot on the back of his head, as if the lioness had attempted to grab him there, but was unsuccessful and took him by his ribs to drag him into the bushes. William was a stocky man, well over 200-hundred pounds and six foot tall. However, curled up in a fetal position made him appeared much smaller.

Hussein walked over to Paul, still squatted beside William, and put his hand on his shoulder. "Do you want to stay and watch over them," he asked, "or go to the village for help?"

Paul lowered his head and feigned wiping blood from William's eyes.

Hussein stared at the back of his neck, waiting for an answer. Only silence returned. He wondered what was going on in his friend's mind. He believed he knew how he felt, trying to kill the lioness, but failing. Due to a lucky throw, he would be the one honored instead of Paul.

"You go to the village," Paul finally answered. He turned his head to avoid Hussein's eyes. "I'll tend to their wounds until you get back. There's not much I can do, but maybe I can make William comfortable, or pull the white man from the truck. I'm sure I can do something."

Hussein threw him a tentative glance, turned and jogged down the path toward their village. After a short distance, he realized the sun had already crested over the tops of the mountains to the east. From the hillside that overlooked the fishing club, he could see golden shafts of light peeking through the long, green fronds of the twisted dum-palms that flourished inside the compound.

As he sped down the path in a rhythmic cadence, the hazy morning sun began to cast long, crooked shadows across his path. He darted past unattended goats, whose hoofs had over the years etched thousands of cloven hoof marks on the trail. Within a few minutes he arrived at the outskirts of the village. When he was within hailing distance, he shouted for everyone to wake up. By the time he arrived at his family's *manyatta*, a few heads had already begun peeking through the oval openings of their huts.

He bolted through the goatskin flap, and found his father still asleep. "Father, Father, wake up!" he shouted. "There's been an accident, up on the hill."

L'Umbo rolled onto his back. With a muffled groan, he looked up and squinted into the sun's rays coming through the open flap. "What's the matter?" he grunted in a hoarse voice. "Why are you waking me? What do you mean—accident?"

"A bad accident," Hussein replied in a firm voice. "We need your help." From past experiences, he knew his father would not be quick to react unless it was a matter of life or death. "Two men on the mountain need our help," he continued. "One is a Masai the other a white man. The Masai has been mauled by a lion and the white man is also injured."

"There are no lions around here, son. You must be mistaken."

"No, father, it was a lion…a lioness. We killed her."

"You killed a lion?" He cocked his head and stared up at his son in disbelief.

"Yes, Father, with our spears. Paul and me."

"The law says you don't kill lions. Why did you kill it? Were you in danger?"

Hussein detected skepticism in his father's voice. "Yes, Father. After she mauled the Masai, she attacked us. We had to throw our spears. We had no choice."

"You and Paul killed a lion in self-defense? Is that what you're saying?"

"Yes, Father." Hussein became agitated by his father's interrogation. "If there's trouble over it, I'm the one to blame not Paul. My spear killed her. Paul could not see her well enough to get a good throw."

"Then we must go to see this lion," L'Umbo said. A broad, excited grin spread across his pudgy, pockmarked face.

"We must take others with us," Hussein insisted. "Both men are injured. The white man is pinned inside the vehicle, unless Paul has freed him. I believe his arm is broken. And I think the Masai has broken ribs. We must be careful when moving them."

L'Umbo raced through the goatskin flap to an opening in the three-foot driftwood fence, and then into his brother's hut, followed closely by Hussein. With a large, deformed foot he kicked a dirty goat hide, covering a large mound in the middle of the conical room.

"G'hambi! G'hambi! Wake up," he shouted. He kicked the hide again.

Little by little the goatskin pushed aside and a large, potbellied man rolled onto his back. With squinted eyes, he stared up at them. After a few unsteady moves, he maneuvered his naked body into a crouched position in the center of the hut and with much effort stood upright. He yawned and touched the top of the hut's conical ceiling with his fingertips. He dropped his hands and began scratching his body from top to bottom, while he rocked back and forth on gnarled, calloused feet.

"What is it?" he said, irritably. "Has the earth come to an end? Did your hut burn down? What is it then?"

Although his uncle appeared angry, Hussein knew he had preserved as much civility as his sleepy disposition would allow. However, he knew from past experiences even that would soon disappear.

"You will never guess," L'Umbo cried out.

G'hambi waited patiently for his brother to continue. After a long delay, he sighed. With an edge to his voice, he answered, "I'll never guess. What must I do to get it out of you?"

"My son has killed a lion! Up on the hill," L'Umbo shouted into his face. An excited smile peeked through his wiry, salt and pepper whiskers.

G'hambi glanced over at Hussein, busy kicking pebbles back and forth across the dirt floor, embarrassed by their bantering. "Is this true, Usitani?" he said using his nephew's tribal name, which was the custom of all elders.

"My son does not lie! You know that," L'Umbo shot back.

"Shush, brother!" G'hambi hissed. "Usitani, is this true? Did you truthfully kill a lion?" His eyes widened and a smile formed at the corners of his mouth, and then spread across his whiskered face.

"Yes, uncle, it is true," Hussein replied, and kicked a small stone across the dirt floor.

G'hambi grabbed his arm. "Then we must go to see this lion," he said. "The village will have roast lion rump tonight. You will be honored as a warrior, my nephew." Still holding onto his arm, he spun the boy around. "But we mustn't let the government men know about this. They don't understand these things." He created small slits with his eyebrows.

"But it was self-defense, uncle."

"That doesn't matter to the government men. They will not try to understand, no matter what you tell them. You know that, son."

Hussein stared into the large man's dark brown eyes. He strained to free himself from his powerful grip, but of all things he didn't want to offend him. Most of all he didn't want to appear ungrateful since he would be the one performing the ceremony of manhood.

"Uncle," he said, using a somber voice. "Father didn't tell you everything."

G'hambi released his grip. "There is more?" He raised his eyebrows and stared into the boy's eyes when he was informed of the two injured men. He threw on a pair of shorts that reeked of rotted fish and rushed outside, followed by L'Umbo and Hussein.

"There will be a *lasar le ntoruto*, tonight," he shouted to no one in particular. "I will have my first ceremony as senior elder, and I will not let it go unnoticed. I will turn this ceremony of manhood into something the village will not soon forget."

Within minutes the village came alive. Men trickled into the central area, sleep still clouding their eyes, and women started their breakfast fires. G'hambi told them about the lion and the two men who needed their help. An hour later their concerted efforts had manufactured two goatskin litters for the trip up the mountain.

G'hambi noticed that Hussein was getting ready to leave with the others. "You must stay, nephew," he commanded. "You're the first of our tribe in many years to kill a lion. Tonight there will be much dancing and celebrating. You will be made a *lmurran*, son. You must stay and prepare for the ceremony."

"But I have to go with them," Hussein pleaded. "Paul will need me. We have to round up the goats. They were frightened by the lion and scattered all over the hillside."

"Don't worry son, we'll take care of them," his father assured him, beaming with pride. He looked at his brother and grinned. "G'hambi's finally right about something; you must stay and prepare for the ceremony." His brother shot him a pointed look, and then made ready for the trip up the hill.

Within minutes G'hambi had organized the villagers and sent them on their way. Hussein watched as a dozen elders and as many warriors and adolescents filed across the sparse desert toward the hillside. He held his gaze until they had started their ascent up the goat path at the bottom of the small mountain and could no longer see them, then turned his eyes back to the empty yard, sighed and kicked angrily at loose stones.

He had not asked for all the attention he was getting, but there it was. He realized he would be torn between Paul's friendship and his own desire to become a *lmurran*. If only Paul's spear had been truer, he thought. He was certain his friend was humiliated by missing the lion, as he would have been. Moreover, it was almost certain the miss was tearing him up inside. Even so, if the situation was reversed, he would be the one feeling bad, and he was not sure he could handle that. Nonetheless, it was comforting to know that Paul had once told him he never wanted to be a warrior. However, he could never understand his friend's illogical reasoning.

Lnuie carried a gourd of red ocher across the central area and placed it on the sand in front of him. With a smile, she ordered him to sit on the large boulder in the center of the compound. She giggled as she took a handful of the cool, red mud and spread it sensuously across his chest.

He stared into her light brown eyes; she had always been his desire. However, most men in the village had yearned for her, at one time or another. Her long, shining hair and slender body had always captivated them. She simply had to smile at a *lmurran* and his heart would melt. She slid her hand across his chest, placed it over his heart, and whispered in his ear, "I can touch your soul, Hussein. I can feel it flowing through your body."

Chapter Two

A small, green and gray lizard darted across the compound of the village looking for relief from the scorching sun. For a moment, it stopped, raised one front and one hind leg to cool the delicate membranes on the bottoms of its feet, and then continued on across the jagged sandstones, searching for a safe place to rest. Weaverbirds flitted about in the prickly acacia branches, trying to find cool perches in its limited shade; the morning sun had become relentless.

Hussein's body glistened with perspiration, as he sat on the hot ceremonial boulder. Tiny beads of sweat ran down his slight muscular frame and dropped to the ground where they dissolved in the hot sand. Lnuie began the long process of braiding his hair into fine, twisted strands. After each interlace, she saturated the braids with rancid fish oil. After several hours in the sweltering heat of the compound, his hairdo had been all but finished. As a final touch she slid a bright red cap made of goat leather under the short hair above his forehead, and then placed the longer braids over its small brim. Glass beads and ornaments were hung in layers around his neck. He squirmed when she tied a fish skin *shuka* (a traditional loin cloth) around his waist to cover his private parts, which were also hidden by the addition of a bright red sash pulled tightly around his waist. As a final touch, she pulled ivory earrings through previously cut slits in his ear lobes.

He rocked back and forth on the boulder, reeling from the intense heat of the afternoon sun. He was not sure being a *lmurran* was what he really wanted, but he knew he would have nothing to say about it. A grin stretched across his tightly closed lips. It was not only a tradition to be a *lmurran*, it was also an honor. Ever since he was a small *nkerai* that was what the elders had told him. Despite that, his mind was sometimes filled with doubt. Did the ceremony of manhood really bestowed respect, honor, and prestige on the young warrior? He wondered. Or, was it the desires and frustrations of the elders that were being planted in their young minds? The ceremony had once been a useful tool, passed down over many generations as a means of teaching the young men the traditions and rituals of their own tribes. However, somewhere along the way it seemed to have lost most of its merits.

He had learned about the outside world from the mission school. That knowledge had made him realize that the day of the warrior would soon disappear. A warrior could still hunt, but there was very little game to be had. He could still fight, but there were very few enemies left.

He focused his eyes on the hillside. If he squinted just right, he could make out a thin line of figures descending the goat path. His face beamed and his heartbeat grew faster when he heard the familiar hunting songs drifting across the sand. He could make out two stretchers in the middle of the column of men, but his eyes burned when he tried to follow them into the valley. Heat waves suddenly distorted his view and like magic the figures disappeared. He strained his eyes but he could no longer see them. A short time later the rescue party arrived at the village.

He spotted Paul's slender figure at the end of the procession. "Paul," he shouted. "Did everything go well on the mountain?"

"Yes," Paul answered, but did not stop or look over. "It went well. They'll bring your lion down later. I couldn't keep the vultures away, though. There are beak marks on the hide and it's somewhat torn. The elders didn't want to bring it down in that condition. They told N'guro and Natani to stay and skin it. They'll bring the carcass down when they're finished."

"Good. That was considerate," Hussein said, and gave him a sideways glance.

Paul continued down the path and disappeared in his hut. A transistor radio burst into a fast African beat and drifted across the roofs of the *manyattas*.

Hussein heard the music and turned his head and thoughts toward it. The radio had been their only possession from the outside world. Mostly, they carried it with them when they tended the herds; it made the nights shorter and soothed the animals. Nonetheless, if they had taken it they might not have heard the lion, and two men could have died.

He believed he understood what Paul was going through, and he knew he would have felt the same, under the circumstances. However, he could do nothing about what had already happened. Under his breath, he recited a Samburu proverb.

Lnuie overheard him. "What you said is true. You must live the life *Nkai* has planned for you," she said after deciphering the adage. "You cannot change that."

He turned his head and glanced at the men carrying the litters. They had stopped in front of G'hambi's hut to speak with him before continuing on to the fishing club, a half-mile away.

Lnuie jerked his head back around to add the finishing touches to his attire. He looked into her eyes, and then cocked his head and whispered a love song in her ear. She smiled, and then gave him a teasing slap on the shoulder.

G'hambi watched from a distance, as she spread more red fish oil over his slicked-back hair. A few minutes later, he walked over and gave her instructions on the proper way it should be done.

"This is a great occasion," he told her. "Everything must be perfect. It has been many years, even before Usitani's birth, since a lion has been killed by a Samburu." He was the senior elder of the village and solely responsible for making the ceremony come off without a hitch. Nonetheless, it had been a long time between ceremonies of any importance, and he was not sure what was expected of him. "Nobody else knows, either," he mumbled under his breath. For the ceremony of manhood, the *lasar le ntoruto*, the village was required to kill a bull. However, their village had very few cattle, only goats. It was a moot point, as far as he was concerned. "After all, a sacrifice is a sacrifice," he quietly commented, hoping nobody would hear. He was pleased with his reasoning and continued to mumble, "Besides, nobody will question me, I'm the senior elder."

The tinny music stopped and Paul emerged from the hut wearing his school clothes: white collared shirt, white socks and white shorts. As he slowly walked to the perimeter of the village, his well-worn sandals slapped noisily against the bottoms of his feet. He stumbled in the ebbing light, searching for the thorn-filled path that would lead him to the fishing club a half-mile away.

Hussein slid down from the boulder. "Paul, Paul," he yelled. "Where are you going? You have to be here for the feast." Paul appeared not to hear and continued on down the path. To his sorrow, he realized his friend would not be back for the feast or the ceremony.

Lnuie put her hands on his shoulders and forced him back onto the boulder. "Sit down!" she demanded. "Let Paul go. He's a nuisance, anyway." She spun her head around and her long ebony hair raked across his shoulders, sending sensuous shivers through his body. She chuckled.

The afternoon sun slowly descended behind the distant hills, but before it had completely vanished, it manufactured more beads of sweat on his back. He had the sudden urge to put on his school clothes and run after Paul, but he realized it would have been futile; the elders were settled on having the ceremony, and they didn't care how he felt about it. They took advantage of every opportunity to celebrate anything of importance: birthdays, deaths, marriages, or the simple killing of a lame goat for food.

Ataira, G'hambi's wife, walked across the central area burdened with an armload of ceremonial items that she dropped at his feet. She picked out a few strands of red, black and yellow beads and draped them around his neck over the ones he already wore. She rummaged through the pile and selected a fish skin *shuka*, which she placed over his red apron. She stared into his eyes and winked. The pungent odor of fish radiating from the apron assaulted his nostrils, but he nodded and returned the gesture.

As the sun continued its final descent behind the highest mountain, it cast long, hazy shadows across the central area. N'guro and Natani struggled with the huge skinned carcass, which had been stretched across two game poles and balanced on their shoulders. When they arrived at the outskirts of the village they straightened their frail bodies to full height, and walked in cadence into the central area, chanting a Samburu hunting song.

Dried animal dung, lake driftwood, and acacia limbs had kept the communal fire blazing for many hours. Everyone in the village had congregated in the middle of the large compound in anticipation of the upcoming feast. Women from all *manyattas* gathered around Lnuie, overwhelming her with negative comments about the final enhancements she had put on Hussein's body. She ignored them.

Gourds of *pombe*, a beer made of honey, fermented goat's milk and maize, had mysteriously arrived at the feast. Large calabashes of *saroi* were also present. On a makeshift table in the center of the clearing sat pots of mashed *dum*-palm nuts, known as *loka*. Although primarily used as baby food, Etaira had made it more enticing for the adults by adding her secret ingredients, which she would not divulge. However, everyone knew it was alcohol.

The young pole bearers stopped in front of the fire-pit, burdened by the carcass. It was hoisted from their shoulders and skewered on a long, sharp pole shoved lengthwise through its body. Four men lifted the pole onto two 'Y' shaped limbs pounded deep into the ground. The carcass was then placed several feet above the hot coals, and on G'hambi's command, two *laibartanis* rotated it with a crooked handle made of desert driftwood. Within a few hours the village would be dancing, laughing and celebrating a new *lmurran*.

As Paul stumbled toward the fishing club, his eyes filled with tears, making it difficult for him to see the path. He wiped his running nose on his arm, and then contemplated what he should do next. He knew one thing for certain; he was going to leave Loiyangalani. He would find a new life far from that hot, windy inferno. If he were to return to the village, what could he tell his friends to make them understand what he was going through? He would go to the club and find his friend Gabriel. He would understand. Maybe Gabriel could get him on the Sun Bird, the plane that brought tourists and supplies in from Nairobi several times a week. If he could, he would go to the big city and make something of himself. After a few years he would return and tell his friends all the wonderful things he had seen and done there. Moreover, he would show them his pockets full of shillings. He would bring gifts back for his mother and Nathan, and something nice for Lnuie. He might even get something for Hussein, but he was not sure about that.

"L'hari!" A voice shouted his tribal name, breaking his daydream.

He turned and faced his brother, Nathan, who was scurrying down the path toward him. As the young boy approached, he stopped and glared at him. For the first time, he realized just how small his brother really was; his frame was slight and his arms too thin. His complete wardrobe consisted of a pair of black cutoff shorts, granted by one of the countless *nkerais* that had outgrown them. The waist had been let out many times and could no longer be expanded. The beltline had dropped below his hips, which gave his belly the distended look of a starving child.

"Nathan. Where do you think you're going?" he snapped.

"I go with you," the boy replied. He looked up with large, brown, cow-like eyes that had been reddened by the late afternoon sun.

"Return to our *manyatta*!" Paul scolded. "You can't come with me you're only five years old, much too young to take care of in the big city."

"You make big mistake, L'hari," Nathan reprimanded. His eyes filled with tears and he reached for his brother's shirttail to wipe them.

Paul crouched down beside him and placed his hand on his head. "You're a nuisance," he said. "You can't come with me. I won't be back for a long time." He lifted Nathan's chin and stared into his sad, moist eyes. "They wouldn't let you in the club, anyway. That's where I'm going. You would have to stand outside the fence and freeze in the cold wind. I might be in there a long time, maybe several days, maybe a week." He could see his efforts to persuade him to return to the *manyatta* were futile.

"They no let L'hari in, either," Nathan shot back in broken English. "They no let *layenis* in club. It bad business…have Samburu boy in white man's club."

"You don't know what you're talking about," Paul said, and returned his gaze to the path. "My friend Gabriel will get me inside. You go back to our hut, they'll soon miss you. You're not supposed to be at the club anyway. You know that. I'm leaving now. Don't try to follow."

Nathan dropped his chin to his chest, and then raised his head to fix his eyes on his brother as he walked away. Through soft, wailing cries, and tear-laden sniffles, he yelled after him, "L'hari! L'hari!" He lowered his voice to a murmur, and continued. "I love you. No want you go. Come back. Come back to *manyatta*."

Paul's shoulders stiffened but he continued on down the path and didn't look back.

The red, enlarged sun had completely dropped behind the Loima Escarpment, but still had enough life left to manufacture long, eerie shadows across the mud and stick roofs of the *manyattas*.

The ceremony of manhood, the *lasar le ntoruto*, dictated that a young boy going through that right-of-passage would be forced into suffering the process of circumcision. However, Hussein had endured that operation several years earlier. For reasons he didn't fully understand, the council would not accepted him at that time, or give permission for him to become a *lmurran*, a warrior. Nevertheless, due in part to G'hambi's insistence, that element of the ceremony had been bypassed and he could become a warrior.

As he relaxed on the boulder, he watched as a procession of *lmurrans* walked by him. Most of them were in their late teens or early twenties and outfitted in their best tribal attire. Although their hair had been braided previously for their own celebration of manhood, it still hung in waves across the tops of their ochre skullcaps. Strands of blue, white and yellow beads crowned each skullcap, with a solitary mother-of-pearl shell woven into the center of each. Their ears had been pierced in two places, the tops and bottoms of each lobe. Distinctive ivory discs had been fed through the bottom slits, and the rib bones of Nile perch, wrapped with a dozen strands of colored beads, had been inserted through the top slits. Many strands of beads hung around their necks, with their personal spirit-pouches dangling from them.

Each warrior held his *mpere* (m'pair), a classic Masai spear with a long lanceolated blade, in his right hand, and in his left he clutched a *rungu* (run-goo), a knobbed fighting stick cut from the *nkoita* (koy-ta) tree, a desert bush with extremely hard limbs and a round knob at the end, making it an ideal fighting club.

The warriors gathered in the middle of the central area and began to chant, their tempo keeping in step with the warbling tongues of the virgins surrounding them. After a few minutes, they formed a circle completely around the boulder. Without warning, Ebukut, (Eh boo cut) the senior *lmurran* of the village, took Hussein by his arm, yanked him from the boulder, and threw him to the ground.

Although Hussein had witnessed the ceremony many times before, he had no idea what to expect. He remained in a prone position, waiting to see what would come next. The warriors threatened with their spears, and then formed a human barricade around him. They raised their voices in animated yells and warbled their tongues in rapid-fire staccatos. Little by little their voices shifted to soft, mesmerizing chants. On Ebukut's command, they jumped high into the air, keeping their bodies rigid and their necks straight. With each slap of their feet, the butts of their spears pounded against the hard-packed ground.

Unmarried women formed a wide circle around the *lmurrans*, attempting to clap their hands in cadence with the beat. Several frustrating minutes passed before they became synchronized. Elders squatted outside the perimeter of the central area drinking beer and stomping feet to the tempo; not the least bit interested in the ceremony, only the beer. During the fast-paced ritual, a warrior would often drop to the ground in a self-inflicted trance and would have to be dragged to the side, and then the ceremony would continue.

The warriors hoisted Hussein high into the air and raced him around the central area three times. All of a sudden, they stopped and flung him to the ground at the base of the boulder. Before he could regain his composure, his head was forced into the face of a live goat, tied to a stake behind the boulder. He scrambled to his hands and knees, attempting to avoid the goat's glassy stare. However, unseen hands on the back of his neck forced him to maintain eye contact.

He heard a sucking sound, as the goat's jugular was severed. He was aware of what was to follow; he would be forced to open the neck wound and drink the thick, warm blood. After a few seconds, he pulled his head out to catch his breath, but a warrior pushed it back into the opening. He gagged on the salty, red liquid as it trickled down his throat, but he kept on drinking until they were satisfied. Once again, they lifted him over their heads and raced him around the ring, but at a much faster pace. After a few nauseating trips, and a few incantations from G'hambi, the ceremony ended. The lion was ready to be eaten. The sacrificed goat would be taken to the local duka, a country store, and traded for firewood for the *manyattas* of the village.

Swaying from too much *pombe*, G'hambi walked across the central area toward Hussein. He placed his long fishing knife on his nephew's chest, and with a quick swipe drew blood. He moved the knife to his own chest and did the same.

"Usitani," he said, staring into the new warrior's eyes. He blinked several times, and then continued in his finest ceremonial voice. "This is the blood of our ancestors," he shouted for all to hear. He raised the knife, placed one side of the blade on his tongue, and licked it. "You have given me your young warrior's blood. Now my spirit will live forever." He turned the blade over and waited for Hussein to do the same. After he had licked the blade, G'hambi continued. "And I give my old blood of wisdom and courage to you. Our blood will mingle and we will have the best of all qualities the Samburu has to offer—courage, wisdom, and youth. This good blood will flow through our veins and our spirits will live forever." He walked to the skewer, cut off a large hunk of charred meat from the lion's hind leg, stabbed it with his knife, and brought it back to Hussein. "Eat this earthly queen's flesh, young *lmurran*, and you will gain her cunning, stealth, fearlessness, and knowledge of the land. Those traits will join your new spirits and live with you forever."

Hussein readily accepted the meat and started eating. It was good, he thought, nothing like goat meat.

When he had finished half his share, G'hambi gave the order for everyone in the village to eat. He staggered back across the compound and demanded a gourd of *pombe* from the elders, which he brought back to the young warrior.

Hussein lifted the gourd to his lips and drank several gulps before coming up for air. With a contented sigh, and a loud burp, he headed back to the spit for more meat.

G'hambi went after him. "Usitani," he snapped. "It is forbidden. You must not have more of the lion. It is for the village. You've had your spirit food, that should be enough."

"But, uncle, it's my kill. Why can't I have more?" the boy slurred.

"Usitani, the lion is no longer yours," G'hambi insisted. "It belongs to the village. Your body is now filled with many wonderful spirits. You should be satisfied with that. Let the spirits be your food."

Dejected, Hussein returned to his beer and sat down on the boulder.

Ebukut wobbled across the compound, chewing on a large piece of meat. He stopped a few feet from the young warrior and wiped his mouth on his forearm. He took a long swig from the gourd of *pombe* that hung from his shoulder, and then moved closer and belched into the boy's face. With a swipe of his knife, he cut another large piece from the massive hock in his hand and forced it into his mouth, along with the other half chewed pieces. He swayed back and forth, attempting to focus his eyes on Hussein.

Ebukut was the oldest *lmurran* in the village. Although he stood over six feet tall, to the children he appeared much taller. He demanded respect and most of the time got it. His face was leathery and long and housed a set of dark, piercing eyes above high painted cheekbones.

"Hussein," he said, after finally focusing on him. "So, you're now a *lmurran*." His loud chewing all but drowned out his words.

Hussein glanced down at the large hunk of meat in the warrior's hand, and then at the half-chewed pieces still rolling around in his mouth. He tried to avoid his stare, but with no success. He could not remember the last time the warrior had spoken to him, or even confronted him. He had always been intimidated by his demeanor, and had avoided him whenever possible.

"Yes," he said. "But I was a *lmugit-of-the-arrows* for over two years."

The warrior glared at him with piercing black eyes. He walked back and forth in front of him, while continuing to cut off meat to stuff into his mouth. After several minutes, he gagged and was forced to relieve himself. When he had finished vomiting, he looked up with a scowl.

"You say you killed the simba?" he questioned in Masai, and pointed to the skewer. "Look at her, she was dying of old age anyway." He taunted the boy with a sneer.

"Yes, I killed her. She attacked us," Hussein replied, aware that the warrior had detected his nervousness.

"Attacked you?" Ebukut raised his voice. Several warriors glanced in their direction. "Ha! I hear she could barely walk. What happened, did she fall on your spear? Did you wait for her to collapse, before you speared her?"

Hussein had never seen the warrior act this way, especially in front of the entire village. Nonetheless, it didn't seem to bother him. Most of the time he was not in the village anyway. He and his friends would be up on the mountain hunting lost goats, at least that was what the villagers believed. Most warriors looked up to him for advice and guidance; he was their hero. Now, they appeared embarrassed by his actions. He was conducting himself like a fool in front of them and the entire village.

He didn't know what to do. After much deliberation, he decided to stay and listen to the insults. Then again, maybe he should walk away; he didn't know how much longer he could take the abuse. No matter what he decided, it would probably be the wrong choice. Out of respect, he decided to stay and listen to the drunken warrior attack the age of the lion, his inability to throw his spear, and his own lust for Lnuie. Hussein had never been insulted before, and didn't know how to react to it. However, his face was flushed by anger.

He would stay and take the warrior's insults, but he would not let his emotions get the best of him. He believed he should go across the compound and speak to his uncle about the situation. But he would endure the insults a while longer. After a few minutes, he stood up. As he did, he brushed hard against the drunken warrior and sent him sprawling backwards onto the ground.

The big warrior shook his head, attempting to clear it. He got to your feet, and with dark, menacing eyes stared into emptiness.

Hussein was halfway across the compound before Ebukut spotted him. The warrior let out a savage cry and charged him from behind. Hussein turned in time to see him coming, and with the agility of a gazelle he stepped aside.

The warrior dove headlong onto the hard-packed dirt. For a few seconds, he remained in a prone position. After several deep breaths, he staggered to his feet. He squinted his eyes and turned to look for Hussein. After spotting him, he yelled over the silence of the crowd, "He's not a *lmurran*, he's a *layeni.* He didn't spear the lion. His spear was not true. She died of old age. He lied to us."

Hussein turned to face him. His eyes were narrow slits, and his face was flushed. He walked over to a young warrior standing at the edge of the compound and yanked the spear from his hand. He pointed it at the big warrior. "Do you want to be the lion, great warrior?" he yelled. "We'll see if my aim is true." He hurled the heavy spear. It sailed between the warrior's legs, missing his groin by inches.

Ebukut showed no fear. He faced the boy with his hands on his hips and a smirk on his face. "You want me to be the lion?" He roared with laughter. Hussein didn't reply. "All right. I'll be the lion, you be the hunter. We leave first thing in the morning. Do you agree?" He threw a contemptuous sneer at the young *lmurran*. "Do you agree? Do you agree?" He repeated his demand and waited for an answer. He finally reached for the spear, still stuck in the sand between his legs, and raised it over his head. With a powerful downward thrust across his knee, he broke it into two pieces.

"Be quiet, both of you," G'hambi shouted, and rushed toward them. "It is forbidden. A Samburu no longer fights to the death. Those were the days of our ancestors. It has no place here." He positioned his huge body between them.

Ebukut ignored the elder. With fire in his eyes, he glared at Hussein. "Tomorrow! Agreed, *layani*?" he shouted. "You come with your spear. I won't take mine. You see if you can do to me what you say you did to the old, toothless lion. I'll take your spear away and hurt you—bad!"

"Agreed!" Hussein shouted back. "Tomorrow. In the morning."

The central area suddenly became silent. There was a broad grin on Ebukut's face, as he walked across the compound for more beer.

Hussein remained at the far end of the compound deep in thought. Why had he accepted the challenge? What had come over him? What had made him even consider fighting for his life with the leading warrior of the village? His face flushed and a sick feeling gnawed at his stomach. He walked over to the broken spear, pulled the blade end out of the sand, and out of frustration rammed it back into the ground.

Many years ago, to settle an argument or disagreement, two Samburu warriors would hunt each other with only one spear between them. The one who had accused the other of a wrongdoing would not be allowed to take his spear. Even so, he would be given a two-hour head start. In order to be proven right, he had to take the spear from the person he had accused. If successful, he could then punish him any way he saw fit.

However, if he was unable to take the spear away, he would not only suffer the humiliation of being wrong but the one he had accused would have the right to punish him.

Ebukut walked to the other side of the compound and searched out Lnuie. After finding her, he bared his teeth in a broad smile and draped his muscular arm around her shoulder.

To add to Hussein's frustration Lnuie looked into the big warrior's eyes and returned the smile. Now, more than ever, he wanted to punish the big warrior. On the other hand, he was only 14 and Ebukut 25 and much larger and stronger. Nevertheless, he realized he had to go through with the challenge; everyone in the compound had heard him accept. Moreover, they were more than anxious for the hunt to begin. "Lnuie," he murmured softly, and then sighed. "She's a devil. Why do I get so upset when I see her with him?" He looked around to see if anyone had overheard. Even when they were little children he had wanted her. Paul had also sought for her affections. Half the men in the village had, at one time or another. Due to his friendship with Paul and the others, he had done nothing to encourage her. However, she was now responding to the advances of Ebukut, the one person who had paid no attention to her, in the past.

The moon had climbed halfway up the inky sky, and the Milky Way had painted a swath of stars across the heavens. It was time for the villagers to return to their huts.

"Tomorrow will come soon enough," he mumbled, and hunched his shoulders as if to vomit. "I feel sick, tonight."

Chapter Three

Paul peeked out from the corner of his blanket and squinted into the early morning sun. He had arrived at the fishing club too late the previous night to see Gabriel, who had already gone to bed, and Kirinyaga, the old Kikuyu standing guard at the gate would not wake him. He had pleaded with him, but had only received a blank stare for his efforts. He had no way of knowing if the old man understood him, but he would not answer. He had tried Samburu, English, Swahili, and Masai, with the same results. He didn't speak the old man's tongue; there were too many differences between Kikuyu and his language. Therefore, it was a standoff.

He stood up and the blanket the purser had thrown over the fence the previous night dropped from his shoulders. He looked over at the gate and saw the old Kikuyu talking to one of his friends. As he watched their animated conversation, he flapped his arms to regain circulation. Several times during the night he had gotten up to get relief from the hard ground and had noticed the old man still standing guard at the gate. Apparently, he had been there all night without sleep.

He had been told the old man came from Nairobi, where the Kikuyus cohabited with a much larger Bantu tribe, which were predominant in that area. How he had managed to travel the 600-kilometers to the club, nobody seemed to know. One day, he walked into the fishing club, and never left. Paul found out later the owner of the club had asked him to stay and guard the entrance to the club. After several days standing at the gate as stiff as a sentinel, and without food or water, the employees had been instructed to give him whatever he needed to survive.

Young boys from the village would gather around the outside of the gate to mimic him. He ate only a small amount and spoke even less. When anyone approached the gate, native or tourist, he would ring the bell to summon a porter, and then return to his post. The manager of the fishing club, Kurt Versteeg, had let him stay on, mostly as a conversation piece; it was good for the tourist trade, he had said. The old man was quite popular with the tourists. However, they soon discovered he wouldn't answer their questions. For the most part, he wouldn't even acknowledge their presence, unless he believed they were important to the club. He was totally aware of what went on around him, and if he didn't like what he saw he would make threatening gestures with his seven-foot spear.

Paul had always felt uneasy around the old man and gave him a wide berth. The previous night, when he had asked to see Gabriel, without saying a word the old man pointed to a spot on the ground, indicating he was to wait there; he had no idea how he understood the request. When the old man left to get Anthony to bring him a blanket, he realized he would be spending the night on the hard ground.

The people of the village considered the old man the embodiment of the Kikuyu tribe. He could have been in his 80s, but his stature was that of a 20-year old. He stood like a sentinel at the gate. His bright red blanket was always wrapped around his body and flung over his left shoulder with its trailing end tied in a knot behind his back.

His seven-foot spear had been banded with many long pieces of black leather and adorned with colored strips of cloth, suggesting he was once a Kikuyu warrior. The spear's two-foot blade was always spotless and honed to perfection. The remaining hair on his balding head was curly, white and fluffy, but over the years, tobacco had stained his gray-white beard at the corners of his mouth. When Paul looked into his eyes, all he could see were two black disks, surrounded by pure white.

"Paul," came a cheerful greeting from the other side of the fence. He recognized Gabriel's voice. The young boy had flanked him on the other side of the fence. "Did you sleep well?" he said with a grin, and then burst into laughter. The porter had told him about Paul's night on the cold, hard ground.

"You're funny, my friend," Paul said with a grin, and then rubbed his butt. "The ground is okay if there's a blanket to wrap yourself in, and one for your bottom, too." He hesitated long enough to rub his behind. "I'm afraid the acacia thorns won out, last night."

The boys bantered back and forth, as they walked along their respective sides of the fence. When they arrived at the gate, Gabriel motioned for Kirinyaga to open it. The old man complied, but stood in their path and scowled. After several pensive moments, and a detailed inspection of Paul, he stepped aside.

They walked up the red brick path toward the main building. "Are you hungry?" Gabriel asked, as they approached the first of two large kidney shaped swimming pools.

Paul stopped beside the larger of the two. He had seen them many times before, but from the other side of the fence. "A little," he said, as he held his hand in front of his face to ward off a frond loaded with brown *loka* nuts.

As they continued up the sidewalk toward the second pool, he noticed his friend's slight stature, for the first time. His white, Guru-style jacket that hung to his knees nearly covered his black, silk shorts, the proper attire for all waiters at the club. The oversized uniform emphasized his thinness; his butt was slender and his legs were skinny. His nimble body appeared to glide down the path without his feet touching the redbrick sidewalk. His face was smooth and youthful; its bronze color made it appear much lighter than the other waiters. Paul had been told he came from somewhere around Ethiopia.

"Okay," Gabriel said. "First, let's eat,." He gave Paul a comical glance. "Then, you can tell me why you came to see me. Not that I mind, of course."

The tourists were not awake, and it was too early for the general help to start their daily chores. However, the cook and his helpers had arrived at the break of dawn.

"Sit by the pool and relax," Gabriel said. He turned to leave for the main building that housed the restaurant. "I'll be right back."

"If someone comes, what should I tell them?" Paul yelled after him.

"Don't worry, nobody is up yet. If someone happens along, tell him you're helping me with my chores today. Nobody will bother you."

A large hand shook Hussein's shoulder. "Wake up, son," L'Umbo said in a soft voice. "It's time to go. Ebukut has been gone for two hours now. Have some breakfast, ask Nkai for his blessings, and go."

Hussein opened his eyes and focused them on the hut's conical ceiling. "Is this really happening?" he muttered. "Why didn't somebody stop us from making fools of ourselves last night?" He rose to his feet and trudged to the center of the yard, where his nose had picked up the scent of sweet tea and maize bread.

His father joined him at the fireplace and repositioned a pot of tea over the flames.

"Why didn't you stop me last night, Father? I'll probably be killed today. Doesn't that bother you?"

"Of course it does, son," his father replied, as he poured two cups of tea. "But you accepted the challenge. You didn't have to. You know very well it would have been useless to try to talk sense into either of you, last night."

"Yes, I know. Not only did you hear me accept the challenge, but the whole village did."

"That's the problem, son, the whole village was aware of the challenge. If they hadn't been, you two might have been able to work something out this morning, when he was sober. I doubt if he wanted this any more than you. But now it's too late. He's waiting for you, somewhere out there." He pointed to the hills.

"Which way did he go, Father?"

"You know I can't tell you that, son."

"But Father, if I go in the wrong direction I may never find him. Can't you tell me if he went north or south? I don't want to be made a fool of by not finding him."

L'Umbo hesitated long enough to pour another cup of tea. "He went west, toward your lion kill, son. Maybe it had some significance for him." He stirred his tea with a charred stick from the fireplace and continued. "He had his fighting stick with him. He wasn't supposed to take it, but he did. Beware, my son, he's an experienced warrior. He'll stop at nothing to win. He looks at you as a young and foolish *layeni.* Nevertheless, I have confidence in you. If you stay to the high ground and never approach an outcropping or boulder, you should be fine."

"I don't understand him, Father, he's not my enemy. He has always been pleasant to me, up to now. Why did he challenge me? Was it the beer?"

"It wasn't just the beer, son," L'Umbo said with a sigh. "Although, I'm sure that didn't help matters." He glanced up at the sky and recited an old Samburu parable: "Those who don't drink much soon get drunk. No, he was also jealous. You're the one that killed the lion. If it had been Paul, he would probably be going on this hunt, instead of you. That is, if he had accepted the challenge. Do you understand? It has nothing to do with you personally. It's what you stand for; a young man who killed the lion, instead of him."

Hussein took his spear from the side of the hut. He strapped a hunting knife to his hip, picked up his *rungu*, and joined his father at the fireplace. "I feel sick at my stomach, Father. I believe I had too much *pombe* last night."

L'Umbo looked up at his son. "You must not take your knife or *rungu*. It's forbidden. Take only your spear."

"But you said he took his. Who knows what else he took?"

"This is true. Nevertheless, wouldn't it be better to go on the hunt knowing you played fair, regardless of what he does?"

"I suppose you're right, Father. Even so, I should have some advantage. He has been a *lmurran* for many years. Not only that, he's much bigger and stronger."

"You do have an advantage he doesn't have, son."

"What could that possibly be?"

"You not only have the knowledge and skills of the Samburu, which he also has, but you have the intelligence and education given to you by the sisters at the school, which he does not have." L'Umbo smiled at being so profound.

Hussein smiled, but it was weak. "You could be right, Father," he said. "I never thought of it that way. He hasn't been around the white man much, and has little knowledge of their deceitful ways. I suppose that could be used to my advantage." He glanced toward the distant hills, trying to catch a transitory glimpse of the warrior. He said goodbye to his father, took a deep breath, and walked through the thorn gate. As if an unknown force had rejuvenated him, he burst into a fast run and headed north.

"Hussein," his father called after him. "I said he went west. Didn't you hear me?"

"Yes, Father, I heard," he yelled back. "But I'll use the white man's cunning and unpredictability. With that, and Nkai on my side, I might stand a chance."

L'Umbo stood at the thorn gate and watched his son race toward a small rise to the north. "Don't forget," he shouted after the vanishing figure, "you have until this time tomorrow to find him. If you don't, you'll have to come back as a defeated warrior and face the village." Hussein did not acknowledge.

Gabriel rushed down the red brick sidewalk, his arms overloaded with food. Paul's eyes widened when he saw the items being placed on the glass-topped table in front of him. He had not seen that much food since the last religious feast at the mission school. After his eyes scanned the table, he reached for a brown biscuit and a pat of butter wrapped in silver foil. He unwrapped the cover and sniffed the soft, yellow mixture.

"Eat, my friend," Gabriel said. "Then we will talk about your problem."

"What makes you think I have a problem?" Paul grinned.

Gabriel slapped him playfully on the shoulder. "Why else would you come to see me in the middle of the night?"

"I was hungry," Paul said, chuckling through a mouthful of biscuit. "I knew you would feed me."

Gabriel smiled and leaned forward in a deck chair close to the pool's edge. He flipped off his leather *kiatus* and dipped his feet in the hot mineral water. "I'm sure you've come with at least one problem," he said. "How can I help you?"

"I want to leave Loiyangalani, as soon as possible."

"What's the hurry? All of a sudden, you have to leave? Are you in trouble? Is that your problem?"

"No, nothing like that." Paul swallowed another mouthful of soda biscuit and continued. "I want to live with the white man for a while. I don't want to live for the rest of my life as a goat herder. I want to have things, like you. Now, I can't give my mother or little Nathan anything. I want to leave my tribe behind. They're not a real tribe, anyway. They're not like our brothers the Masai. The Samburus were once great cattle herders and warriors, but now they're shepherds, goat herders. I'm afraid they'll stay that way forever. Their days are numbered. You know that. That's even what the sisters at the school told us."

"All tribes' days are numbered, not just yours," Gabriel said. "Everybody knows that. I've heard of people from our village going to the city, and most of them starved. They couldn't get work, because they had no education. Furthermore, without a job they couldn't survive. They had to beg for food. If you went to the city you would be begging from those as bad off as you." He lifted his feet from the water and swung around. His dark brown eyes opened wide and his face turned somber. While examining Paul's face, he brushed his slender fingers through his straight, black hair, and then continued. "You say you want to be like me? Let me tell you something, I was sold by my parents and taken from my home, a small village in Somalia. They were starving and had to make money the best they could to feed themselves and my brothers and sisters. You have your *manyatta,* over there." He pointed. "All your friends and relatives are there. What about your mother? Does she know you want to leave? Hussein, your best friend, does he know?"

"Hussein is now a *lmurran,*" Paul said, cutting him off. "He's no longer interested in our friendship. He killed a lion and now he's a warrior."

"He killed a lion?" Gabriel said in disbelief. "But I thought you no longer had to kill lions to become warriors. I heard all you had to do was kill a few birds." He grinned, hoping he had not offended him.

Paul shot him a quick glance. "That's only for three months after circumcision," he said, with a tinge of sarcasm. "You can then become a *lmurran,* if the elders call on you." He exhaled a long sigh. "It's been two years and they still haven't called for me." He cocked his head and shrugged his shoulders. "But I don't much care." He paused and gazed across the jade-colored water of the pool. He looked back at Gabriel. "It took the accidental killing of a lion, before they would even acknowledge Hussein."

"Accidental killing of a lion?"

"Well," Paul began to explain, "it wasn't exactly an accident, but we didn't go looking for it. Hussein killed it; his spear was luckier than mine. That's all."

"Luckier than yours?" Gabriel said with a snicker. The corners of his mouth curled up in a grin. "You mean if your spear had killed it you would be a *lmurran* instead of him?"

Paul shrugged. "I guess so. But it doesn't matter to me, I never wanted to be a warrior anyway."

"I believe I sense a little jealousy here," Gabriel said. He reached over and nudged his friend's knee.

"I'm not jealous," Paul shot back. He slid the empty plate across the table and leaned back in the deck chair. "It's a matter of pride. They could have made me a warrior, too." He looked over at Gabriel and quickly added, "Even though I never wanted to be one." He stared across the pool, deep in thought. "After all, I was there, too," he continued. "There was as much danger for me as for him. Besides, I helped rescue the two men. That should count for something."

"Two men?" Gabriel questioned, and leaned forward in his chair. "This is getting more interesting by the minute."

"There were two men, in a Rover—" Paul started to say, and then stopped. "I'll explain it all later. First, I have to ask if you'll help me get to Nairobi." Before Gabriel could answer, Paul continued. "I understand what you said about your family, and I appreciate what you're telling me, but I have to learn what only the white man can teach. Can you understand that?"

"Paul, no matter what it looks like, my life here isn't as good as you believe it is. I've been with the white man for several years now, and it isn't that great. Trust me."

Paul slid from his chair, sat on the edge of the pool, and swished his feet in the 80-degree water. "But look at you. Here, you have everything. You have lots of food to eat and your clothes are new and clean, and I imagine they pay you many shillings."

"Most of that's true. I have plenty to eat and my clothes are clean, but I don't make that much money. Most of it comes as tips from the tourists."

"Tips? What do you mean?"

"It's money you get when you do things for people above and beyond what you're supposed to do. Like keeping their glasses filled with ice water, and always being at the table when you're needed. Those things will bring you a few extra shillings." He hesitated for a moment, and then added, "It's like when you and Hussein assist the tourists with their tents down at the safari grove."

"Oh," Paul said. "You keep their glasses filled with ice water?"

"What? Oh, yes, ice water. Things like that."

"What does it taste like?"

"What? Ice water? It tastes like water. What do you think? It's only water with ice in it." He cocked his head to one side and giggled. "You've never had ice water?"

"No." Paul blushed. "Of course I know what water tastes like. There can't be that much difference."

Gabriel got to his feet. "Wait here," he said, and started up the sidewalk. "I'll be back in a few minutes." Paul knew what he was going after and found it difficult to wait for his return.

A few minutes later, Gabriel raced back down the sidewalk holding a glass of water with three ice cubes inside. Paul held the glass between his hands and felt its coldness. He put it to his lips, took a short sip, and jerked his head back when the ice hit his teeth. After a short hesitation, he took a more deliberate drink. When all the water was gone, he put a cube on his tongue and rolled it around in his mouth. He took Gabriel's hand and shook it up and down, like a pump handle.

"Mmmm, it's cold, but good," he said with a beaming face.

"I'm glad you liked it, my friend. Now we must talk about your problem." Once again his face turned serious. "Or, do you still have one?"

"Yes, I have the same one I had when I came to see you last night. But now I have it with a full stomach and a cold tongue." He hesitated for several moments, attempting to find the right words to express his feelings. "My friend, I thank you for your kindness." He pointed to the empty plate. "That was a happy surprise. But I suppose you know why I came to see you. I'd like to know if you could get me on the Sun Bird."

"I figured that. You've so much as told me. I tried my best to talk you out of it, but I can see it's useless, so I guess I'll have to help you."

Paul's face glowed with happiness. "You are indeed a friend. Thank you." Then he frowned. "But how can you do that? How can you get me on the plane? I have no money."

"The boy who carries the mail to Nairobi in the Sun Bird is a friend of mine," Gabriel said. "The plane's due in tomorrow, as if you didn't know." He threw Paul a quick grin. "I'll speak to him. I'm sure we can work something out. Also, I believe Mr. Versteeg will let you go in his place."

Paul stared into his friend's eyes. "I know nothing about mail," he said. He turned his head and looked back at the shimmering pool. "What if I'm caught?"

"I assumed you wanted to go to Nairobi?"

"Yes, I do. But I don't want to end up in the white man's jail when I arrive."

"Don't worry, you won't. You don't have to know anything about mail. All you do is carry the mail pouch onto the plane. When you arrive, you give it to someone at the airport. That's all there is to it."

"It all seems too easy," Paul said, after considering it. "You're sure they'll let me on the plane, instead of your friend?"

"You worry too much. When I work out the details with Kimbi, we'll know more. In the meantime you can stay in my room."

"You have a room? All to yourself?"

"Yes. I have my own room. I got it not long ago. It's small but big enough for the two of us. I'll take you there in a few minutes. I believe you should stay there until tomorrow. Don't worry, I'll bring you food."

The hut had been built on a small rise behind the compound. On their way up the hill they passed a hot water spring bubbling out of the ground. The waterway had been lined with stone ductwork, which directed its flow into two kidney-shaped swimming pools. The overflow from the pools was filtered and used by the tourists for showers and other uses.

A wooden partition divided the hut into two halves. Gabriel lived in one side and another waiter in the other. The floor was completely covered by gleaming, blue linoleum. A single bunk bed sat in one corner, and a small toilet enclosure with a shower and sink in the other. A small clothes closet was nestled neatly in the same corner as the toilet.

When Gabriel first arrived in Loiyangalani, Paul had befriended him by carrying his bags to the main gate of the club, and he had never forgotten that act of kindness. In the months that followed, they would occasionally meet at the main gate and walked into the village, where Gabriel would buy them soft drinks or something to eat from the only duka in the village that had small amounts of western goods.

As Hussein raced away from the village, his long strides fell into a rhythmic cadence. He was familiar with that particular trail; he had used it many times when hunting lost goats. However, he was now on the trail of something larger and smarter than goats, a Samburu warrior. His feet soon became sore from the constant pounding on the hard-packed sand, and the muscles in his legs began to knot, forcing him to stop and massage them. Sweat ran down his arms and onto his hands, making the shaft of his spear slippery. He knew his feet and legs would soon adapt to the pain, and when the sun got higher in the sky the moisture on his skin would evaporate to cool his body.

One of the many things he worried about was the small amount of water he had taken with him. His goatskin bag would last for a short while, but the water would eventually seep through its seams and evaporate. He wondered if Ebukut was having the same problem.

He had traveled for about an hour, when he arrived at one of the few umbrella trees along the path. He stopped in its shade long enough to survey his surroundings. At that point, he figured he would turn west and travel for several more hours. After that, he would go south until the sun had dropped onto the peaks of the western horizon, and then turn east. If all went well, he would arrive at Ebukut's suspected hiding place by late afternoon, when the sun was in the warrior's eyes. If he was right, his prey would be at a particular hiding place, one he knew well.

His father had told him Ebukut set out on a course to the west. After years tending goats in that direction, he knew he had limited hiding places. He believed he had the advantage, but he had no idea what was going on in the warrior's mind. Ebukut was clever, but he was also arrogant, and a show-off. He was concerned that if he were spotted too soon, he would be challenged to hand-to-hand combat. If that were to happen, he would not stand a chance. His only hope would be to catch him off guard.

He tried to imagine what it would be like to meet him, face-to-face. Would the warrior kill him, if given the chance? Moreover, if he managed to take his spear away, would he use it on him? If he did, would he die instantly, or would it take a long time? Would he writhe in pain and plead for mercy? Sourness invaded his throat and dryness formed on his lips, as he envisioned the steel blade being thrust into his body. He tried to shake the image from his mind, but it persisted. After resting a few minutes, he left the shade of the umbrella tree and headed west at a deliberate pace.

Ebukut had been at his hiding place for several hours between two large boulders on the eastern side of a hill overlooking Loiyangalani. Where was the boy, he wondered? Had he changed his mind about the hunt, and returned to the village? In a way, he hoped he had. If he had, he could go back to the village and brag that the *layeni* was not man enough to confront him. If he was coming, where was he? He wanted to get the hunt over as soon as possible and return to the village to celebrate his victory. He was anxious to accept the praises that were certain to fall on him. Hussein would cower like a little *layeni*, when he met this *lmurrans*, he thought. Maybe he should stand on top of the boulder and search the area. But that would be foolish; the boy could be right outside. If he were not ready for the challenge when Hussein arrived, the boy would have the upper hand. Surprise was the only sure way to take the spear away from him.

He leaned back against the boulder's warmth, closed his eyes, and considered his options. He knew Hussein was no coward. After all, he did kill the lion. Another *layeni* would have fled in panic, but not him. He had been told the boy looked the lion straight in the eye and threw his spear. His stomach fluttered, when he envisioned the boy's spear in his chest. However, he knew that was foolish. He simply had to take his spear away, and that should not be difficult. He opened his eyes and stared up at the sky, in deep thought. If he did get the spear, would he use it on the boy? He didn't know.

He heard a sound on the other side of the boulder and his heart skipped several beats. Using the stealth of a lion, he slithered to the top of the boulder and peeked over. He chuckled when he saw a wild camel feeding below him. Relieved at the sight, he slid back down the incline and returned to his hiding place behind the boulder.

Before he left his *manyatta* that morning, he had made certain everyone knew he was heading west. He even told everyone where he would be, hoping the young boy would get the word. He counted on him falling prey to his clever trap, and the possibility of a one-on-one confrontation.

When Hussein arrived at the suspected hiding place, he noticed a camel grazing in front of two large boulders. He was too far from the animal for it to hear him, but it did appear nervous and ready to bolt. Knowing the area, he believed the warrior would be hiding behind the first of two large boulders, slightly up the incline.

Quietly, he approached the animal. When it looked up, he stood perfectly motionless, until it had lowered its head to take another mouthful of the dry grass. He crept closer, until he was within a few feet. Cautiously, he reached out and touched the animal's hind leg, hoping it would not bolt. It turned its head and looked at him, but did not shy away.

He had learned from the teachings of the elders that if a wild animal allowed you to touch it, it would more than likely remain docile. He counted on that to get closer to the boulder. By applying a slight pressure on either leg, he steered the animal toward the opening between the two large boulders; the path connecting them was big enough for it to pass through.

He was familiar with the trails that led into the suspected hiding place; there were two large boulders at the left of the entrance and a cluster of smaller ones on the right. He was convinced the warrior would be hiding behind the larger one, facing east, and overlooking the village. From there he could survey the valley.

After a few attempts, and much resolve, he steered the camel down the path between the two boulders. After it had committed itself to the opening, he gave it a slap on its rump.

The warrior heard the footsteps and spun around like a leopard ready to strike. However, the only thing he saw was the camel he spotted earlier. As the lanky beast ambled by, he realized there was no danger. He returned to his vantage point and continued to scan the valley.

Hussein sneaked through the passage and stuck his head around the corner of the first boulder. The big warrior had leaned up against the larger of the two boulders, and was staring down into the valley. He continued down the path in step with the animal, but a few feet behind. The characteristic clumping of its padded feet were the only sounds on the hill.

When Hussein was parallel to the boulder, he charged out from behind the animal and placed the tip of his spear against the warrior's spine. Ebukut's face turned ashen and his body stiffened. He applied more pressure to the spear, and its honed tip drew blood.

"The great warrior," he hissed, "has been defeated by a *layeni*…a goat herder." He applied even more pressure and the spear went deeper into the warrior's back.

Ebukut's face winced in pain and he cried out. He turned his head until their eyes met. "I'm ready to die. Push harder," he said through clenched teeth. His eyes narrowed and he glared at the young warrior. "Why do you sneak up behind me? Fight like the *lmurran* you say you are."

Hussein pushed on the spear until the warrior's head was forced back around. "I'll fight you the way you cannot, with my mind," he whispered, hoarsely. "It would be stupid to fight you, I'd lose to your strength and size. However, you don't use your head. That makes it easy to outsmart you. I learned that from the white men. There are many things you could learn from them. Most of them are common sense, anyway."

"I would die, first."

"That depends on you," the boy snapped back, and applied more pressure. "But you can save your pride, and your life, if you do as I say."

"What does the *layeni* ask?" Ebukut said with a sneer. "Not that I would do it."

Again, pressure was applied and the warrior cried out. "There's a way both of us can stay alive," Hussein replied. "And you won't lose your honor." He eased his grip on the spear.

The big warrior took advantage of his relaxation and spun around to face him. Hussein was caught off guard, by his swiftness. The warrior yanked the illegal *rungu* from his waistband and struck him alongside his head. The boy staggered backwards, and as he started to fall Ebukut wrenched the spear from his hand. As he lay prone, the warrior put the tip of the spear against his chest and applied pressure. Hussein bit his lip from the pain, but didn't cry out. The warrior stared into his defiant eyes and pushed harder, but he still refused to make a sound.

He knew Hussein had won the hunt legally and fairly. If he hadn't used the illegal *rungu*, the boy could have killed him, easily. Nonetheless, he believed if he killed the boy, the wrath of L'Umbo and G'hambi would be upon him. On the other hand, if he let him live, there would always be the risk of a confrontation in front of the others, because the boy knew he won.

"I don't want to kill you, layeni," he said. "But I don't know why I should let you go. If I do, you will return to the village and tell them you won. I have a tiger by the tail, I believe."

Instead of answering, Hussein chanted an old tribal song that was supposed to ward off pain. G'hambi had taught it to him, when he was a laibartani barely old enough to tend goats.

The chant unnerved Ebukut. He pulled the spear from the boy's bloody chest and flung it to the ground. "What am I to do with you, *layeni*?" he said with a frown. "I'm lost for words." He leaned against the boulder and winced when his injured back touched it. "What plan do you have? The village must never know you won the hunt…this way. It's a matter of pride, you know. Is that clear?"

Hussein stopped chanting, but remained submissive on his back. His chest wound was shallow and the bleeding had all but stopped. "I'll tell them I couldn't find you," he said, and looked into the warrior's eyes.

"But they said I had to find you and take the spear away," Ebukut said. Then he added, "And what do I tell them about the *rungu*?"

"Tell them you hunted for me, but you couldn't find me because I hid from you," Hussein said with a puckered brow. "They'll believe you, you're the leading warrior." He considered it for a moment, and then added, "Another thing, the hunt is for a whole day, and it's only been a few hours. We can't remain enemies for the rest of the time. Our people know nothing, if we tell them nothing. If you say you couldn't find me, you will keep your honor. They will believe that because I'm young I hid instead of hunting for you. In time, they'll forget. It doesn't bother me."

"I'm surprised," Ebukut said, after considering what the boy had said. "You are a wise *layeni*." He corrected his statement, with a broad grin. "I meant to say, *lmurran*."

As the young boy picked up his *sampur*, which had fallen from his shoulder during the struggle, he began to feel the pain from his wound.

"Turn around," he told the warrior. "I'll clean your wound, then you do mine." He opened his leather bag and took out a piece of white linen. After stuffing one end into the warrior's wound, he cut strips from the other end with the blade of his spear and tied it around his chest. "How do we explain these wounds?"

"You'll think of something," the warrior said, with a toothy grin. "That, I'm sure of."

They moved behind the boulders, where they could not be seen by the curious eyes of the village, and hunted for camel dung to build a fire. It would be dark soon and without a fire the cold wind would penetrate their bare skins.

They took turns spearing lizards, as they darted from rock to rock. After many attempts, they stabbed two fat ones. They laid the carcasses on the red-hot coals and watched attentively, as the intense heat ruptured their hides and exposed the white meat of their bodies. Their mouths drooled, as they listened to the sizzling and snapping of the dripping juices.

Hussein broke the silence. "And Lnuie?" he said.

Ebukut gave the impression he had not heard. He fixed his eyes on the campfire, and then picked up a stick and rapidly stirred the coals. After a long pause, he said, "What do you mean? She's not important to me, if that's what you're getting at." He was silent for a few more moments, and then added, "She's too young anyway. She's your age." He forced a grin.

The night had been long and cold and the raging desert wind had blown sand across the hillside, tormenting their aching bodies with the miniature projectiles. The icy wind had chilled their bodies, plagued their wounds, and had kept them from a peaceful night's sleep. After several hours, the wind had subsided and the remainder of the night was almost bearable.

The cold, dew-laden morning found their semi-naked bodies huddled together for warmth. With a great deal of effort, they untangled their limbs and stretched. The fire had died hours earlier and no dung in the area to light another. It was time to return to the village.

"I'll go now," Ebukut said. "I'll tell them I couldn't find you. You come in an hour."

"I'll tell them I went in the wrong direction to look for you," Hussein said. "My father saw me go north, anyway. They wouldn't be surprised if I couldn't find you."

"Hussein," Ebukut said. His face turned somber. "I'm sorry I said those bad things at your ceremony of manhood." He paused for a moment, trying to find the right words. "On the day that belonged to you, I made a fool of myself. I'm proud of this scar. It punishes me, forever."

"What will you tell them about the scar?" Hussein asked.

"I will tell them nothing, and they will not ask. To them, I'm still a bad ass. They're afraid of me. What will you tell them about yours, little brother?"

"I'll tell them I fell on my spear, they'll believe that." They both laughed.

"Good luck in the village, little *lmurran*," Ebukut said, as he turned to leave.

Hussein watched the warrior trot down the hill and out of sight. He would wait until he had reached the village to spread his lies, and then enter with a sad face. Ebukut had warned that he would be taunted when he arrived at the village, but he was not to worry. At least not until the next time he gets drunk.

Chapter Four

Gabriel woke Paul by a gentle tug on his blanket. "It's time to get up," he said.

Paul tossed the blanket aside and jumped to his feet. "Did you find out anything?" he asked. "Am I still going to take the mail to Nairobi?"

"Yes. I even got permission from the manager. He said it would be all right if you went in Kimbi's place. It'll work out well. He needs him at the club today, anyway." He peeked between the louvers of the window. "And he won't have to pay you," he added with a snicker. "Are you hungry?"

Paul shrugged.

"I guess that means yes. You stay here. I'll bring you something from the restaurant. The plane doesn't land for another two hours. There's plenty of time."

Paul was ecstatic. Soon, he would be riding in the plane that flew over his village several times a week and excited his goats and shook his hut. What would it be like? He wondered. How does it stay in the sky? The sisters at the school had tried to explain it, but he didn't understand. However, he would find out soon enough. He sat on the edge of the bed, propped his elbows on the windowsill, and looked out over the short runway.

Minutes later, the door flew open and Gabriel walked in, his arms laden with food. "I brought you some bacon and eggs," he said. "The cook fixed them especially for you."

Paul had never eaten a cooked egg. He had always looted flamingo eggs at the lake's edge and sucked their juices. Bacon was also alien; there were only a few pigs in and around Turkana and most were pets and not to be butchered and sold. After eying the contents of the plate, he picked up a fork and stabbed at the yolks. He put the fork down, puzzled by its function, scooped up the eggs in his hand and brought them to his nose. When he touched the yellow mass to his tongue his eyes lit up. They didn't at all taste like flamingo eggs. He wondered if they would taste the same, if they were cooked.

He finished his food and washed it down with a cup of strong Kenyan coffee. Before he could slide the back of his hand across his mouth to put the greasy remnants on his white shorts, Gabriel threw him a napkin.

"Did you like it?" Gabriel asked.

Paul's face beamed. He nodded and rubbed his stomach.

"I have to go back to work now," Gabriel said, and walked toward the door. "As soon as the plane lands, I'll come and get you. The only thing you'll have to do is go by the mailroom and pick up the bag. Then you can board the plane."

Paul's face filled with anxiety, as he listened. He didn't want to miss a word. "Gabriel," he said, before he closed the door, "you're trusting me with something important, and I won't let you down. You're doing me a big favor, and I'll never forget it."

Gabriel walked back across the room and put his hand on his friend's shoulder. He reached into his pocket and pulled out a packet of folded bills. "Take these," he said. "There's not much here, but you must have money when you get to Nairobi. At least you'll be able to eat, until you can find work." Paul looked down at the brown shilling notes. "Please, take them," he insisted, and held the bills in front of his friend's eyes. "You can call it a loan. Pay me back when you're rich." He smiled, displaying an even row of white teeth, between copper-toned lips. He knew he would not voluntarily take them, so he forced them into his hand.

"Thank you," Paul said in Masai, and stuck the wad into his pocket. "I will pay you back, I promise."

"There's one more thing, you'd better get used to speaking English. Don't speak Masai or Swahili in Nairobi, or you'll never get a job. The shops hire only those who can speak several foreign languages. Usually English, Japanese or French."

"I'll remember that, my friend," Paul came back in English.

Gabriel grinned and left.

The hut sat high on a hill behind the fishing club. From its small window, Paul could see all of Loiyangalani and the southern-most tip of the lake. With a little effort he could scan the entire length of the main street. He watched as his friends, Ebukati and Emanuel, entered the duka beside the butcher shop, the only store in the village that sold small quantities of western goods. In front of the shop was a makeshift counter covered with empty maize bags. Behind the counter, attached to the stucco wall by long steel wires, a long shelf displayed several-dozen grocery items. When tourists came to the market they were always surprised that they could not buy toilet paper, soap, candy, or most other western items. Even so, they could buy soft drinks. A sign on the front of the store read: Cold Soft Drinks. The storekeeper had put warm soda in a deep hole in the shop's dirt floor, filled it with lake water, and covered it with palm fronds. The drinks were cooler than off the shelf, but not much.

He strained his eyes to see through the side of the window. "N'guro, Natani," he mouthed their names and watched as they walked past the cyclone fence and headed into the village. Each day a small group of boys from the many *manyattas* would meet at the fence and go to the lake a half-mile away to swim and wash in its warm mineral water. The lake was fed by many natural springs, which were loaded with mineral deposits from the nearby mountains. The minerals made the water silky and pleasant to the skin. He watched until they had disappeared behind the last building. The heat of the morning had already made the barren land unbearable, and a swim in the lake would have felt good.

He moved his head to the corner of the small window and turned his eyes west toward his *manyatta*. He could see the smoke from many breakfast fires, as they hovered over the huts, like the curved crowns of umbrella trees. Then, little by little, it drifted up and vanished into the stark blue morning sky. He could not make out his own hut, but he knew where it was and what his family would be doing that morning. His stomach fluttered.

He glanced at the clock on Gabriel's nightstand. The Sun Bird would land soon. He sat on the edge of the bed and stared through the window, waiting impatiently for its arrival.

A few minutes later he heard a faint purring sound. He squinted through the louvered slats and caught sight of the plane, which seemed to hover above the desert floor. It circled the village once, and then settled onto the short runway.

The door of the hut swung open and Gabriel motioned with his finger. They ran down the long, red sidewalk to the billeting office in the main building, where the mail pouch was waiting. As they raced by the door, a wide-eyed orderly tossed Paul the mailbag.

Kirinyaga could not read, but he held out his hand for identification papers. Paul had no papers and the old man complained loudly. Gabriel rushed down the path and intervened. With his best sign language and modified Swahili, which he knew the old man could not understand anyway, he attempted to explain that Paul had taken Kimbi's place on the mail run. Confused, the old man motioned for him to board the plane.

Paul held the pouch tightly under his arm and waved goodbye to his friend. He dashed across the tarmac, while the pilot was checking the plane's magnetos. After he boarded, he was directed to the back of the small plane to allow room up front for paying passengers.

As the plane sat idling in the sun heat flooded its interior, making it nearly unbearable. After a long wait in the stifling cabin, a safari truck pulled beside the plane with two passengers, a white man with his arm in a sling, and a black man in a stretcher. Paul recognized them from the wrecked Land Rover. He didn't want to be seen, but the last seat in the back of the plane was as far as he could retreat.

When everyone was strapped into their seats, the engines revved to a thunderous roar and the plane turned onto the short macadam runway. As soon as the nose wheel was lined up with the centerline, full power was applied and the plane sped down the strip. Paul placed both hands over his ears and closed his eyes. Within minutes, the plane had reached its circling altitude and the power cut back. He clutched the armrests on both sides of his seat and opened one eye to look out the window.

Regulations dictated that the plane had to make one full circle over the landing strip, before heading south. As it started its turn, Paul opened both eyes and focused on the lake far below. He believed the flamingos must see Turkana, the way he now sees it. He cocked his head toward the El Molo village and discovered hundreds of the magnificent birds standing at the water's edge. As the drone of the engines passed over them, they took to the wing and formed a pink cloud, which appeared to drift with the wind. He could see his village directly below, and tried to find his hut in one of the many *manyattas*, but they all looked the same.

The surroundings he had been so familiar with soon disappeared and a land he had never seen before came into view. His heart pounded and his hands sweated, but he loved every bounce and air pocket of the ride. If only Hussein could have been there to share the experience. However, he was certain he was having his own thrills back at the village, now that he had become a *lmurran*. For a brief moment, his heart fluttered, but the feeling soon disappeared; there were too many new and strange things for his eyes to behold through his window.

Paul's thoughts were transported to the plush valley below them. It was hard to believe his eyes; there were so many vivid colors; he had only known the browns and grays of Turkana. As he stared in awe at the scene below, he saw a multitude of farmhouses with red roofs, surrounded by triangular fields, bordered by white fences. There were large patches of yellow, brown and green vegetation, a stark contrast to the lava-rock Loima Hills of Turkana. He tried to envision what it would be like to live in such a place, but he could not.

"Paul!" a voice rang out above the din of the plane.

Paul snapped out of his daydream and glanced to the front of the plane. William was staring at him from a stretcher strung across two window seats. He smiled and waved, and then motioned for Paul to come closer. However, the boy folded his arms across his chest and shrugged like an animal in submission. William motioned again, but this time he cupped his hands around his ears to suggest he could not hear, due to the noise from the plane. Not knowing what to do, Paul turned and looked out his window. The passengers had already trained their eyes on him, making it even more difficult to react to William's gestures. Uncomfortable with the situation, Paul squirmed in his seat. When he finally noticed all eyes were on him, he got up and moved slowly to the front of the plane. William smiled and thrust out a large hand.

Paul could not help but notice his teeth, they were as white as pieces of cut ivory and even as the teeth of a saw.

William's eyes twinkled as he held out his hand, waiting for acceptance. Paul hesitated for a brief moment then grasped it.

"I thought I recognized you when we came aboard, but I wasn't sure," William said with a broad grin. He pointed his stubby finger at the man sitting beside the stretcher. "You remember Eric Somerville, don't you? The man stuck in the Rover."

Paul nodded and held out his hand.

Eric shook it firmly. "I never got a chance to thank you or your friend," he shouted over the roar of the engine. "What was his name?"

"Hussein."

"Hussein? Well, both William and I probably owe our lives to you two."

Paul was fascinated by his red hair and stared at it for several moments. The Masai warriors also had red hair, but theirs were painted with red ocher. This man's hair was not painted; at least he didn't think so. He glanced at it once more, and then lowered his eyes to his long, chiseled face. Uneasy over Paul's inspection, Eric combed his fingers through his bushy hair and turned his eyes back to the window.

"Where you going, son?" William asked, and propped his head up with his hands. He hesitated for a moment, and then added, "That was a stupid question, wasn't it? I guess you're going to Nairobi." They all chuckled at his blunder. "What I meant was, why are you going to Nairobi?"

Paul held up the mail-pouch, which he had not deserted since he boarded the plane. "I must take this to Nairobi for the fishing club. I will remain there. I will not return to Loiyangalani," he said in one breath.

"You won't be coming back on the plane, when it returns in a few days? You're going to stay in Nairobi?" William questioned. His eyes widened.

Paul nodded, but said nothing. He held the zippered pouch tight against his chest and stared at the tattered carpet that ran down the aisle.

"Eric's a photographer from New York," William said. "He's been in Kenya off and on for years taking pictures of animals. He'll shoot anything that moves." He stared into Paul's eyes. He was determined to get him into the conversation. "Is the master of the house in?" he said in Masai. He reached over and tapped Paul on top of his head.

Paul grinned, when he realized he had asked if he was paying attention. With a broad grin, he answered in Masai, "Yes, the master of the house is in."

"I thought I could get to you with that one." William grinned and lowered his head back to the softness of his pillow.

Eric turned and looked at the boy. "Where is Hussein?" he asked with noticeable concern.

Paul hesitated for a moment and then looked away, as if he were not interested. "He's back at the village. The elders have made him a warrior…a *lmurran*. It was his spear that killed the lion, if you remember."

Eric glanced over at William and winked. "What about you? Didn't they make you a warrior, too? You were there. You certainly helped us out of a barrel of pickles."

Again, Paul looked down at the purple runner on the aisle, and then turned his eyes to the window. "No. He's the one who killed it. It was his spear that pierced the lion's heart, not mine." He hesitated for a moment, and continued to look out the window. "I don't want what he's been given, anyway."

"Hogwash!" Eric erupted. "Regardless of what you say, you should be honored too."

William propped his head up with his hand. "Hogwash?" he mimicked. A broad smile spread over his face. "I don't believe you understand the Samburus, Eric." He lowered his head back to the pillow. "Years ago the lion was a symbol of strength and hunting prowess. The Samburus believed that if you pitted your hunting skills against it and won, you would gain its spirit and strength." He put his hand on Paul's shoulder. "But, if I'm reading you correctly you don't want what the killing of a lion has to offer. Is that correct, Paul?" He stared into the boy's eyes, and then looked at Eric. "I believe he would rather live in a world where all spirits are his own, not the lion's. I don't believe he wants to be a warrior just to prove something to somebody. Am I right?"

Before Paul could answer, Eric leaned over and touched his arm. "Then you want to be like William," he said. "He's a good man, you know. He's been with me for many years. Did you know he was once a great warrior?" He leaned closer to be heard above the drone of the plane. "When I met him, he was wearing a loincloth and had lion's teeth in his ears. He could throw the spear better than any man I've ever known. Nevertheless, after many years as a warrior I guess he felt the same as you do now; he didn't want to go the way of the Masai. He saw the changes coming and decided to make a new life for himself, before he got too involved in the ancient customs and couldn't leave them." He scanned Paul's eyes for a sign of comprehension. "Then instead of being like

Hussein, you want to be more like William? Is that right?"

Paul didn't answer right away; he appeared to be absorbed in what Eric had said. A worker on one of the safari trucks had also told him William had been a Masai warrior. The thought of him leaving his tribe for the white man's ways, after having been a warrior for so many years, was hard for him to understand. To take advantage of what the white man had to offer before he became a warrior was one thing; *layenis* had not yet experienced that life. Even so, to abandon one's tribe after being one for so long was highly unusual.

"Paul," William said. "Are you unhappy because your friend was made a *lmurran*, and you were not, although you say you don't care?" His smile faded. He placed his large hand on the boy's shoulder. "It's true, to kill a lion and be accepted by the elders is indeed an honor." He hesitated long enough for the boy to digest his words, then took his hand off his shoulder and continued. "But it's only an honor for those who wish to be dictated to by the elders. Those who look ahead at progress do not see the advantage of being a *lmurran*. Not anymore at least. The days of the warriors are numbered. They cannot live on tradition alone. Soon, there will be no more hunting, not even as a *lmugit-of-the-arrows*. All tribal customs and ceremonies will cease to exist. It's sad but inevitable. You have to be ready for the change when it comes."

It was difficult for Paul to accept, let alone comprehend, the fact that after so many years the Samburu way of life might come to an end. However, he knew it was true. He saw it coming when the fishing club came at his village. There were many big changes: Land Rovers, airplanes, tourists, and a mission school.

"What will you do in Nairobi, Paul?" Eric asked. "Do you have a place to stay? Do you have money? You must have money to survive in

Nairobi. You do realize that, don't you?"

Paul's face flushed and there was a gnawing in the pit of his stomach. "I have money," he said. He reached into his pocket and pulled out the shillings Gabriel had given him, and waved them in the air. "I will find a place to sleep and a place to work."

Eric eyed the bills. He reached into his pocket, pulled out his hand full of folded shilling notes and held them out to Paul. "Here, this is all I have with me," he said. "I believe this is about a thousand shillings. Take it, you'll need it. Believe me. When I leave the doctor's office, I'm going to the New Stanley Hotel. I'd like for you to stay with me until you can get situated."

Paul looked at the folded bills, but made no attempt to take them.

"Take the money, son," William insisted. "Mister Somerville wants you to have it. And I have an apartment in the eastern section of Nairobi where you can stay for a while, if you'd like to." Paul still did not take the bills. William continued. "Paul, listen to me, money is not as important as a man's life. Agreed?"

Paul turned his eyes toward the window and looked out, but still refused to take the money.

"It's almost certain both of us would be dead if it hadn't been for you and Hussein," William said, and looked sternly at the boy. "If we were dead money wouldn't be important to us. Now would it?" Both men smiled. Again, Eric held out the notes.

Paul hesitated for a moment, then reached over and took the folded shillings. "I'll take the money as a loan," he said. "I'll pay you back. That's the only way I'll take it."

"Okay," Eric said. "You pay me back when you've made ten times this amount. Agreed?"

"*Absante.*"

"He said—" William started to interpret, but was cut off.

"Yes, William, I know what '*absante*' means," Eric replied with a grin.

The plane landed on an auxiliary runway at the far end of the Nairobi International Airport and taxied to a parking tarmac in front of a long Quonset hut. The customs office was located at the end of the building. Passengers from all flights, even those returning from short side trips, were required to stop and check in at the office.

A large black man in a white tropical suit approached the plane to check the passenger's papers and passports, before he would allow them to disembark. Two porters in blue uniforms came alongside the plane and carried William into the building on a stretcher. Everyone left the plane except Paul, who had been instructed to remain. The man in white escorted the passengers into the building, and then returned to the plane. He stuck his head through the door and glared at the boy. Wide eyed and frightened, Paul pulled the mail pouch close to his chest.

"Who are you?" the man asked in Swahili. "What is your name? Where are your papers?"

Paul fixed his eyes on the man, anxiously, and then pulled the pouch even closer.

The big man entered the cabin, yanked the mail pouch from his hands and read the tag on the zipper. "Okay," he said. He handed it back and ordered him out of the plane.

"I cannot come with you, I must stay here," Paul replied in English. "I must give this mail to somebody."

"The plane won't be going back for several days, son," he said in a firm but fatherly voice. "You can't stay in the plane. Besides, I'm the one who'll take care of the mail." The man reached for the pouch. Paul hesitated, but when he saw the resolve on the man's face, he handed it over. "Don't you have someplace to go?" he said. Without waiting for an answer he turned and started to walk across the tarmac. Halfway to the Quonset hut he looked back and noticed the boy was not following. "Come on, boy," he shouted. "You can't stay there. You'll have to come with me to the customs office."

Paul had no idea what he meant by customs office. He didn't know what to do. He had no papers, like the other passengers. He had nothing but a sick stomach and a fire in his head.

The man stormed back to the plane. "Come on, boy," he shouted in a gruff voice. "I haven't got all day."

Gabriel had told him there wouldn't be any problems. Nevertheless, sensing the man's growing impatience, he jumped out of the plane and followed him across the tarmac.

They headed for the metal building with a white sign on top that read: Customs Office—Local Flights Only. As they approached the door, the man stopped to talk to another official. Paul saw his opportunity and rushed around the corner of the building. When he believed he had gone far enough to avoid pursuit, he slowed to a trot and then a fast walk. He glanced over his shoulder every few seconds to make sure he was not being followed. After a few minutes he stopped to rest. He noticed a tall sign on a metal pole directly in front of him. One of the pointed boards read: Nairobi 22 km. "Twenty two kilometers to Nairobi," he mouthed the words. He had no idea how he would get there. He knew it was much too far to walk.

Dejected, he leaned up against the signpost. Gabriel had once told him about a vehicle in Nairobi called a taxi. He had said it took people where they wanted to go, for money. He had money; perhaps he could find a taxi to take him into Nairobi. But did he have enough? He wondered. He had no idea how much money he had. He pulled the bills out and began counting. Halfway through, a Land Rover slid to a stop beside him and a window rolled down.

"Paul," came a voice from inside. "Where are you going? I thought you'd wait for us. We planned on driving into town together."

Paul was startled by the voice and assumed he had been caught. He glanced in the back and saw William lying on a stretcher laid across two back seats. Eric motioned for the driver to open the back door for him. The driver was a white man he had never seen before. "Thank you, Mr. Somerville. Thank you, William," he said. He got in and sat beside the stretcher.

"You're welcome, Paul," Eric said, and pointed to the driver. "This is Dan. He's a good friend of mine from South Africa." Dan slid back behind the wheel, looked in the rear view mirror, and nodded. When their eyes met, Paul returned the nod.

Eric turned to Paul, and said, "Dan flew in from the Zululand in South Africa. He was looking for the burial ground of King Chaka of the Zulu tribe. He was to take pictures of it for me. Do you know about King Chaka, Paul?"

Paul considered it for a moment. "Yes, we learned about him in school. He was an evil person, I believe…a *tsotsi* (sot see) (thug)." He frowned, and then continued. "He killed many warriors, and even more who were not warriors."

"That's the guy. He was a mean dude," Eric said, grinning.

As they drove the long, straight stretch into Nairobi, Paul noticed the sullen expressions on all their faces. He stared at the back of Eric's head. The man appeared to be deep in thought, never taking his eyes off the road. From their conversation on the plane, and the wreck site, Paul had learned that one of his problems, in addition to his injured arm, was that he had lost his expensive camera, and other photographic equipment in the accident. He had told him he had other cameras at the hotel, but none could compare to his Canon. When he and William were carried from the wreck site, Eric had asked N'guro and Natani to keep their eyes open for them. They said they would come back and look for them. He knew they would, because he had offered them a great deal of money to find them. He shifted his eyes to William, staring out the side window. Gabriel had told Paul the safari company that William worked for had to bring people in from Nairobi to take his place on the safari trucks; he had left 22 people stranded in the grove, without an English-speaking guide. In addition, he was in hot water for the loss of the Land Rover. The fishing club would retrieve the vehicle, sooner or later, but Turkana was 600 kilometers from Nairobi, the only place where they could get another one.

To add to the company's woes, no telephones or cell phones were available at the club. For some unknown reason cell phones rarely worked around Loiyangalani. The club had a transceiver, but it was difficult to send a message; it was used primarily for emergencies. Furthermore, it was on what they had called a time-sharing network. Due to the accident, William's company discovered what he had been doing in the foothills of Loiyangalani. They had not known about his photographic safaris, in the past. Gabriel had also told him that as soon as William parked the stake trucks in the palm grove, and settled the tourists in for the night, he and Eric would travel deep into the desert to take night pictures.

Paul shifted his eyes to Dan. He was staring straight ahead at the long lines of cars and trucks in front of him, seemingly hypnotized by their erratic behavior. Paul was surprised at the man's prowess, as he watched him manhandle the large Land Rover between the never-ending rows of honking vehicles. Other than the fact he was a photographer for Eric, he knew nothing about the fair-haired man from South Africa. He would have to find out more.

The excitement of the morning made him hungry. He reached into his *sampur* and pulled out several sandwiches that Gabriel had given him. All heads turned when they heard the crinkling of foil. He offered them around, but to his delight no one accepted. By the time they had reached the outskirts of the city he had finished off two sandwiches, a banana, and a large piece of cake.

"We'll be there soon," Dan said, to no one in particular. "It's down the next boulevard. I'll drop you two off at the doc's office and take Paul to the hotel."

"That'll be fine," Eric replied. "Come back in a couple hours. It shouldn't take any longer than that to patch us up."

William propped his head up in his hand. "Dan, maybe it would be wise for you and Paul to stay in the truck," he stated. "At least until we're finished. I don't think they'll let Paul into the hotel without Eric." Paul stared at William's mouth, attempting to hear what he was saying over the roar of traffic.

"Good point," Dan said.

The four-wheeler stopped at a shabby, gray building off Kenyatta Boulevard. Both Dan and Eric helped William hobble into the doctor's office. As soon as he was comfortable in the waiting room, Dan rushed back and pulled the vehicle into an adjacent alley.

Paul slouched down in the back seat and stared at the nape of Dan's neck. He had overheard one of his subtle comments to Eric, while driving in from the airport. He recalled the words "*Afrikaner*" and "*apartheid*", which he had mentioned several times. The sisters at his school had told them the word *apartheid* meant, "being apart" or "segregated". However, that was all he knew about it.

Dan turned around and looked at Paul. "What do you want to talk about, son?" he said, forcing a smile. "Women? Politics? Religion?"

After a few moments, Paul said, almost too quiet to be heard, "South Africa."

Dan pulled an American cigarette from his soiled khaki shirt and lit it. He pursed his lips and blew a smoke ring into the windshield, where it burst into tiny fragments as it collided with the dirty glass. "South Africa? What do you want to know about her, kid?"

"What made you come here?" Paul asked. "Was it only because of the pictures you took of King Chaka's grave for Mr. Somerville?"

"It's a long story, kid," Dan said. "That's part of it. But I never did find the guy's grave. Nobody down there really knew where it was. The truth is, I'm here because I don't dare go back to Johannesburg, or anyplace else in the south. It's not safe for me to return. At least not 'til things settle down a bit."

"You can't go back to your home? Did you do something against the law?"

"Depends on whose law you're talking about. The ones for *apartheid*, or against."

"I don't understand this *apartheid* you keep talking about. Does it have to do with the black man and the white man living together?"

Dan thought for a moment. "Yeah, I guess it does. You don't have it here in Kenya as much as we do in the south, but you have it here, too."

"We have *apartheid* here, in Kenya?" Paul asked. He thought for a moment, and then added, "But we have no problems with the white man."

Dan took several long drags on his cigarette, and then flipped it out the window. "It's not just a matter of living together, it's more complicated than that."

"Then what?" Paul was confused. "*Apartheid* means to be apart, doesn't it? Does it not mean that they want the black man and the white man to live apart, to have separate lives?"

"Yes, it does. But it's not only that. If the white man had his way down there he would have the black man living without a vote or even legislation that would affect his livelihood."

"I don't understand," Paul said, with a long sigh.

Dan reached back, tapped him on the knee, and grinned. "Don't they teach you anything in that school of yours?"

"They taught us about voting. But I still don't understand why the black men of South Africa are not allowed to vote in their own country."

"They did get a chance to vote…a few years back," Dan said. "For the first time in their lives the black man was allowed that opportunity. In the past, the real problem had been the one-man-one-vote philosophy." He noticed the bewilderment on the boy's face. "For example, in the south there are more blacks than whites. Of those blacks, there are more Zulus than all other tribes put together. The whites knew that if every black man voted for a president a Zulu would always win. The whites didn't like that, and neither did the other tribes. There would always be a Zulu president. Understand?"

Paul thought for a moment. "Yes, I believe so. But didn't you say they *had* an election? Did a Zulu win?"

"No. Fortunate for them it was a man from the ANC, the African National Congress, who won. It was a sympathetic vote; the man spent over twenty years in prison for his beliefs."

"Kenya has a black president," Paul said, matter-of-factly. "He was voted in by the black man. And he's a good president. I don't believe it's a problem here." As an afterthought he added, "You can never go back to South Africa, even though this ANC man won the election?"

"Maybe one day," Dan reflected. "When they get their act together. Maybe when they get a government that's organized better than the one they now have. Maybe when I can say my piece when and where I want without being thrown in jail. Maybe when they stop having race riots. Maybe then."

"Get their act together?" Again, Paul was confused.

"What I'm trying to say is that the ANC is a political body of both blacks and whites. They've attempted to take control of the government for some time. They had hopes of solving the problems of the south, but of course that's almost impossible. But at least they're trying. It's a start. They're doing their best but they're being blocked at every turn by many factors." He lit another cigarette and blew another smoke ring against the windshield. "For many years the ANC had been an outlawed organization. Nevertheless, eventually the government recognized them...for what it was worth. Do you understand what I mean by outlawed?"

"Yes, I think so. It means it was not legal for anyone to be in the ANC."

"Well, in a way," Dan agreed. "It used to be that way, but now you can be a member. However, it will still be some time before the blacks know if they truly have a say in their own government. Before, the members of the ANC, both blacks and whites, were never allowed to have legal meetings. That's why many went into exile. Some went to Zimbabwe, some to Zambia, Zaire, and Tanzania. Others came here to Kenya."

"The word 'exile' means they were forced to leave their country," Paul stated, pleased for knowing its meaning. "But I thought you said you were exiled years ago. If that's the case, why are you still running? If the ANC won the election, why can't you go home?"

"I can't go home because I did a few things the government didn't like," Dan said, and then chuckled. "I did more than just talk and have meetings. Do you understand?"

"Yes, I think so. But what can you do here in Kenya to make it possible for you to return to your own country?"

"That's a good question. Maybe nothing. But at least here in Kenya I'm a free man. And, hopefully here I won't get thrown in jail."

Paul's eyes widened. "You could go to jail in your country for what you did there?"

"With this new government, I'm not sure. But I'm not about to take any chances." Dan thought for a moment, and then added, "South Africa isn't the only country where you can get into trouble with your mouth. Even here in Kenya you can go to jail if you say the wrong thing to the wrong person."

"I didn't know that," Paul said. "But you were not trying to take over your government down there, were you?"

"No, of course not," Dan said. "We were merely trying to come up with some viable solution so the blacks and whites could live together in peace without having the bloodshed we've had in the past."

"They have had much bloodshed?"

"Yes. Too much, I'm afraid. But it used to be worse. The terrible thing though, a large percentage of those who shed their blood were blacks trying to fight off their own sadistic black police."

"Do they not have spears to defend themselves against the police?"

Dan laughed. "Well, for one thing they're fighting against a dominant black police force, made up of their own brothers. Besides, what good are spears against machine guns and pistols?"

"But can't the ones with spears also get guns?" Paul said. He felt sick at his stomach, but he continued. "The tribesmen here in Kenya have guns. I have seen them. I'm sure they would loan them to your country, until they were no longer needed."

A smile spread across Dan's ruddy, sunburned face. "I hope it never comes to that, son," he replied. "Can you imagine what would happen if all Zulus had guns? You can be sure there would be a massive blood bath. You know what I mean?"

"But, what's the difference? If they all had guns, it would be even."

"You've got a point. But first let's see what we can do with the government we have."

Paul was still confused, but said nothing.

Eric's damaged leg and slung arm forced him to move at a snail's pace down the alley toward the truck. When he arrived, he stuck his face up against the window.

Dan rolled the window down and a cloud of smoke rushed into Eric's face. "You guys finished?" he asked.

"I am, but the doc's keeping William," Eric said, fanning the smoke from his face. "Seems he has a punctured lung, on top of everything else. The doc is going to do more tests after he wraps his ribs. They might take him to the hospital, but they're not sure. Let's go to the hotel." The door was unlocked and Eric slid into the passenger seat. He looked back at Paul. "You okay, son?" Paul shrugged.

The Rover backed out of the alley and headed for the New Stanley Hotel. It was only a few blocks away but in the noon traffic of Kenyatta

Boulevard it took longer than expected to even get close to it. It appeared that every person in Nairobi had congregated at the downtown crossing in front of the hotel. Vendors had set up their stands in the parking lots of all major hotels and the Stanley was no exception.

The towering facade had been visible for well over half an hour, but the truck had made little progress toward it. Every beggar and vendor in Nairobi appeared to be crossing the boulevard at the same time. The ones not taking up spaces in the parking lots to sell goods were opportunists looking for easy marks at the windows of stalled cars.

Dan finally found an opening the length of a car between two slow moving trucks and dashed the Rover across the street to the half-moon driveway of the hotel. He pulled up to the front entrance and waited for the parking attendant. After several minutes, a husky black man knocked on the window and motioned for him to move. Dan pulled a *kumi*, a ten-shilling note, from his shirt pocket and waved it in front of the man's face. He pointed to his passengers, indicating they wanted to go into the hotel. The attendant accepted the money with a smile. He opened the back door for Paul, and then raced around to the passenger side. Dan pulled up, allowing another vehicle to discharge its passengers. He pulled another *kumi* from his pocket and waved it at the same attendant. The man saw the note and ran to a spot some ten meters in front of them, where a taxi had blocked the hotel entrance. After several moments of animated Swahili, the cab left and Dan pulled into the vacant space.

Eric and Paul walked up the marble steps and into the hotel lobby. As they moved across the gleaming floor to the purser's desk Paul looked down, and then jumped back, startled by his reflection in the polished stone. While Eric talked to the man at the desk, Paul wandered around the spacious lobby, eyeing everything that moved and touching everything that glittered.

The manager, surrounded by a massive mahogany desk, frowned at Paul's antics, but said nothing. "Mister Somerville," he finally said in flawless King's English. "How nice to see you again, sir. Did you just arrive back from Turkana?"

"Yes, I did, Carl. That's Paul over there." He pointed across the room where he was standing in front of the door eyeing the restaurant. "He'll be with me a few days. If that's okay."

"But of course," Carl replied with a counterfeit smile. "We are honored to have a friend of yours with us." He pulled a slip of paper from underneath a file folder and held it in front of him. "Mister Somerville, about your last week's bill, do you wish to carry it over into this week?"

Eric took the invoice and held it up to the light. "Yes, Carl, finish the week out on this and I'll take care of it this weekend. Okay?"

"Very well, sir." His smile melted away.

"Paul." Eric raised his voice to carry across the lobby. Paul looked over. "We're going up to the room now. We'll come down in a bit and have something to eat in that room you're so fascinated with." Paul slid across the marble floor on the heels of his sandals. Carl frowned.

They entered the elevator and Eric pushed the button for the fifth floor. He looked over at Paul and winked. As the elevator started to ascend, Paul clutched the walnut railing with all his strength. He fixed his eyes on the floor and opened his mouth as if to scream, but nothing came out.

Chapter Five

Hussein slid from the warm boulder and searched the area for more dung to reactivate the dying coals. His mind was not on the herd or fire it was 600-kilometers to the south, in Nairobi. He wondered what Paul was doing in the big city.

He wanted to believe things had changed since becoming a *lmurrans,* but they hadn't. He still looked after the same goats, drank the same *saroi,* ate the same maize bread, and roasted lizards for most of his meals. His physical appearance was the only thing that had changed. He now had braided and slicked-back hair, beads around his neck, a red wrap around his groin, and two ivory discs dangling from his ear lobes.

He sat back down on the boulder, tilted his head to the sky, and gazed at the stars. How bright they were that night, he thought. He extended his arms and recounted a verse he had once heard the elders chant: "I will reach for the stars, hold in my hands as many as I can, and let the rest fall at my feet" He wondered if Paul could see the same stars.

The excitement of being a *lmurran* was all too short-lived. He had been informed that the Park Rangers found out about the slain lioness and were investigating. He knew they would not have far to look. They would pursue him to no end they were that persistent. What would happen when they caught him? And he knew they would. He leaned back to ponder his situation. If he couldn't avoid the rangers, and he didn't believe he could, maybe the best thing would be to go to Nairobi and join Paul.

He had heard stories about a man who had poached lions and was caught by the rangers; it was not a reassuring story, by any means. The man had been taken to a small jail in Maralal 100-kilometers to the south and locked up for a year before going to trial. He had never heard the outcome, but the story alone had been enough to deter him and his friends from poaching. However, he and Paul had not been poaching; it was a matter of life and death. Nonetheless, he realized anyone caught in the act would use that same scenario as his defense.

The constant bleating of a young goat caught Hussein's attention. It had wedged its hind legs between two boulders and could not get free. He jumped down from the boulder and pulled the stones apart. The kid bleated loudly, and then scurried back to its mother.

On his way back to the boulder, he noticed a slight movement behind one of the many acacia bushes on the hillside. He picked up his spear and the subtle movement stopped. He squinted into the semi-darkness and saw a pair of glowing eyes staring at him. After a few seconds they drew back and disappeared behind a large bush. He slowly approached the campfire, trying not to make any sudden moves. He picked up a burning limb from the coals and blew on it until it had burst into brilliant, orange flames. He held the torch in one hand and his spear in the other and moved cautiously across the thorn-infested sand toward the acacia bush where he had last seen the eyes.

The shining orbs reappeared, narrowed, and again drew back behind the bush. He slowly raised his spear to his shoulder. He could not mistake the deep, gurgling sound of a lion. His heart pounded in his ears and his knees weakened and shook. The lion slithered out from behind the acacia bush and crawled toward him on its belly.

He stared hypnotically into its eyes. "Are you the mate to the one I killed?" he whispered in Masai. "I didn't mean to kill her, you know. Really, I didn't." How stupid this would have sounded if some one overheard, he thought. "Nice lion. Be good, now. Go away and I won't tell your friends you didn't eat me. I'm in trouble enough as it is. Please, don't make me kill you."

The lion crawled on its stomach to the front of the large bush and stopped, but continued to gargle with a low, muffled growl. Frantically, Hussein waved the torch out in front of him. The lion's rumbles turned to snarls, and then into high-pitched screams. Its ears lay flat against its head and saliva dripped from its two-inch fangs. He knew one of them had to back off or one would die. As he stood staring into its eyes, his intense fear suddenly turned to stubborn pride.

"Are you stalking me, a *lmurran*?" he asked the lion. "I will not be the one to retreat. You're the one in danger, not me. See my spear?" He waved it in short circles above his head. "This is the same spear that killed your mate. Did you know that?"

He had learned from the elders that a lion would not attack if one stayed close to a campfire; they have a natural aversion to fire. And they would not be the aggressors unless cornered, wounded, or hungry. It could be wounded, he thought. But it definitely was not cornered, he was certain of that.

There could be cubs in the area, he thought. If they were in danger, a lioness would attack. However, he was certain this was a male, although he couldn't see it clearly in the shadows. Only its eyes and part of its head were in front of the acacia. Often, males would protect their cubs, but they were also known to kill and eat them.

He worked his way around to the opposite side of the bush, where the lion would be between him and the flickering campfire. There was little light left in the dying embers, but enough to see its outline lying beside the large shrub.

Without warning, and with the speed of a gazelle, the lion charged. Hussein froze in his tracks. Retribution for killing its mate, he rationalized. The attack came with such ferocity he didn't have time to aim his spear, or even think about it. He closed his eyes and waited for the inevitable.

The 300-pound body knocked him off his feet and hurled him to the hard-packed ground. He closed his eyes and waited for the dripping fangs to take their revenge. Several anxious moments passed and he felt nothing but the agonizing pain of his fall. He opened his eyes. The lion lay on the ground several feet behind him, a spear protruding from its side. He jumped to his feet and searched for its owner. At first, he saw no one. Moments passed, before a shadowy figure skirted a large boulder and walked toward him.

"Who's there? Who are you?" he called out. The figure didn't answer but kept coming toward the faint light of the campfire. "Ebukut?" A broad smile spread across his flushed face, when he recognized him. "Ebukut!" he repeated. "What are you doing here?"

"Looking for you," the warrior said with a grin. "Is it not good that I found you?" There was a trace of sarcasm in his voice.

"Did you know the lion was here?" Hussein queried.

"I tracked him for many hours. I knew he had to be on this hill." The big warrior yanked his spear from the lion's rib cage, put his foot against the lifeless carcass, and rocked it back and forth several times. "Where there's a lioness a lion is sure to come. All *lmurrans* know this."

Hussein had not considered that, but he was right. Lions travel in small prides; the female is the hunter and when she makes a kill she either brings it back to the male or he follows to get his share. Without a doubt he was looking for his mate to get a reward.

"I'm happy you're here," Hussein said. "If your spear had not been true I'd be lying there instead of him."

The tall warrior smiled. "You didn't kill me the other day when you had your chance." He dropped his eyes in thought. "I killed him to save you. Now we're even."

"I didn't kill you the other day because I didn't hate you," Hussein returned.

"I didn't kill this lion because I hated him," the warrior said, wryly. "I killed him because I don't hate you."

The two warriors squatted beside the dying campfire. Hussein stirred the coals with the tip of his spear, until they had erupted into flickering tentacles. "It's been several days since I killed the lioness," Hussein said, and looked up. "What made you look for her mate, now?"

"I was not after him, I was searching for her cubs. I knew they would come looking for her, sooner or later."

"Do you think she had the cubs with her when I killed her?"

"No. But they were close at hand. I guess they got hungry and started to search for her. Her cubs are hidden under those rocks, over there." He pointed past the carcass.

Hussein's eyes followed his finger. He walked over, moved a boulder from the top of a hand-made stone cage, and four brown eyes stared up at him. The frightened cubs sidled backwards and hissed, displaying their quarter-inch fangs. "When did you put them there?" he asked. "I've been here for several hours. I didn't know they were there. What shall we do with them?"

"We do nothing. They live or they die," Ebukut said. "I came here earlier and found them. I knew he would come looking for them, so I waited."

"Don't you think we should take them back to the village and at least feed them?"

"No!" Ebukut snapped. "We don't dare take them back. The tribe would be in great danger; the cubs would bring lions into our village." He saw the disappointment in the boy's eyes, but knew he understood.

"Earlier, before I left my *manyatta*," Hussein began, "I heard the wardens were asking questions about the lioness. Is that true? Did you hear anything?"

Ebukut swished the tip of his spear through the hot coals and watched as a few diffused sparks hovered, twirled in small circles, and than disappeared into the night. "Yes," he affirmed. "It's true, they're hunting for you. Now, they'll hunt for both of us."

Hussein opened his eyes wide. "They're hunting for me, now?"

"Yes. That's another reason I came. I wanted to warn you not to go back to the village. The gray men will be back in the morning to continue their search. If you stay with your goats, they will find you. You can be sure of that."

Hussein thought for a moment. What could he do to avoid the rangers here in the open desert? They had vehicles and guns and it was a well-known fact they would use them at the slightest provocation.

"The moon is sinking fast," Ebukut said, and pointed to the star-laden sky. "We must go before it gets light. But first, we have to hide the *simba*; it will take the gray men longer to find him. It will also give us the time to escape."

"Us?" Hussein said, puzzled by his remark. "Then you'll help me get away? You'll come with me?"

"You're my brother. I have concerns for you. I'll help you…we'll help each other." Ebukut extended his hand. Hussein grasped it and squeezed until the warrior winced.

Hussein's mind raced, as they walked toward the cage. He had never known gray men personally, only of their hostility toward his people. He had known of Samburus who had been detained by them and for no apparent reason beaten to the brink of death. Most of all, he had heard they enjoyed torturing younger tribesmen. However, they were careful when it came to harassing *lmurrans*; they risked getting spears in their backs. They also gave the *shamans* a wide berth. Their tribal upbringing had made them fearful of their powers. Even after living with the white men for years, they still believed the *shamans* had control over *Milika*, the spirit God of everything evil.

It was common knowledge that the gray men were given short courses in local law enforcement and then issued guns. The moment they exchanged their spears for guns, and cast aside their tribal customs for the white man's ways, they became rude and arrogant toward their own people. They had been instructed, at the risk of severe punishment, to be courteous to all whites, tourists in particular. He still couldn't believe all gray men were bad. But he didn't know which would be hunting for him, the sadistic or the considerate ones.

"We can't dig here, the ground is too hard," Ebukut said. "We'll put the lion with the cubs in the rock pen. When the little ones get hungry they can eat its meat, and drink its blood when they're thirsty. It will save their lives. We'll put smaller rocks on top of the big ones. They won't be harmed, and they can push them aside when they get a little bigger. It will give us time to hide from the rangers."

"You said you'll help both of us escape?" Hussein asked.

"Yes, that's what I said. When they hunt for you, they will also hunt for me." As an afterthought, he added, "They will probably find the carcass when the vultures fly in the morning. It isn't safe for us here. Others know I went hunting for the lion…and for you. We will go to the northern desert together."

"What about the goats?" Hussein said. "I can't let them run wild."

"What about them? What's more important your life or your goats?"

"Even if they do find us," Hussein said, "they can't put us in jail for killing the lions. We've done nothing wrong. We killed them both in self-defense. Some tribes kill them for sport…and food."

"That doesn't mean anything," the big warrior said. He took the lion's legs and started pulling the carcass toward the rock cage. "If we are caught we will go to the ranger's jail. Do you understand?"

Hussein shook his head.

It took half an hour to pull the heavy carcass to the boulder cage, which had been fashioned into a small, circular corral. They were careful not to harm the cubs when they stacked stones and dead palm fronds on top of the pen. Ebukut cut a long slit in the lion's stomach to make it easier for the cubs when they got hungry. He explained that within a few days they would have no trouble pushing the boulders aside…if the rangers didn't find them first.

The first light of dawn had by then faded the stars to a dim glow on the eastern sky. From Hussein's vantage point on the hillside overlooking the fishing club, he could make out silhouettes of the club's *dum*-palms against the gray backdrop of morning.

Any other time he would have remained at his campfire for hours marveling at the beauty of the sunrise, but not that morning. He could not stop wondering what would happen if they were caught. Where could they go where the rangers couldn't find them? If they were spotted, without a doubt they would be captured; they could not outrun the Land Rovers. Nor could they last in the scorching heat of the desert without water, and the oasis at the fishing club was the only good source for miles. The lake water was drinkable but silt and minerals had to be boiled out to avoid getting sick. Even so, they didn't dare go to the lake; it would be the first place the rangers would look.

"We'll go to our *manyattas*," Ebukut said. "Get all the food and water you can carry. But only take the things you can use in the desert." When he had finished camouflaging the stone cage, he added, "Do you still have your bow and arrows?"

Hussein grinned. "Yes, the ones I had when I was a *layeni*...several days ago." The big warrior's lips curled up in a grin.

As they approached the village a few bragging roosters began to salute the morning, but everything else appeared to be asleep. Long, finger-like shadows, manufactured by the domes of the huts, climbed the thorn fence that surrounded their *manyattas*, and then moved slowly across the central area.

Hussein rushed to his father's sleeping hut and found him lying on his back close to the entrance. His blanket had dropped to one side and exposed a nude, rotund body. Hussein picked up a dirty blanket from the dirt floor and tied it around his shoulders. He searched for his spare *sampur* and finally found it hanging on the wall. He stuffed a hunting knife, a box of matches, and a few strips of smoked goat meat inside it. He needed more food, but when he went to the storage hut he found nothing. He crept into his brother's hut to hunt for anything edible. He remembered the bag of hard candy he had given him some time ago, but the boy had concealed it well. He finally found it stuffed inside a smaller *sampur,* under some old shorts. He put the brown bag into his own *sampur* and turned to leave.

"Brother," came a whisper. "What are you doing? Are you stealing from me?"

Hussein looked down at the small boy knotted up in his blanket. "I'm not stealing, I'm borrowing your candy. I'll replace it when I return. I must go little brother. I have to hide in the hills so the gray men can't find me."

"Are you in trouble with them?" N'turi said, with half-closed eyes. Not waiting for an answer, but rolled over and went back to sleep.

Hussein took a half-full goatskin water bag from the wall and hung it around his shoulder. He didn't want to take the full one; his brother would be forced to walk over a kilometer to get more. His hard-soled mountain sandals, given to him by the mission school, finished filling his *sampur*. He was ready to meet Ebukut at the edge of the village.

He left the hut as quietly as possible. If his father woke up he would try to talk him into staying. "Meet your problems head-on," he would say. Then his uncle would get involved. If that were to happen it would be too late to escape and he would be captured.

When he arrived at the edge of the village he noticed Ebukut pointing in the direction of the club. Two vehicles were racing toward them. Clouds of dust, churned up by knobby tires, drifted across the valley, and the metallic screams of their engines shattered the morning calm.

The warriors raced toward the sloping hills, but before they could make the first knoll the vehicles were upon them, and they had no place else to run. The first vehicle slid to a dusty stop no more than 20-meters from them.

A ranger lowered his window and stuck a gray, conical device through it. "Stop!" a tinny voice said. "We want to talk to you."

The second Rover pulled up beside the first. The dust was allowed to settle, and then the doors were opened.

A tall man in a khaki uniform stumbled across the rocky slope toward them. He wore a golf-style cap, pulled down over his ears, with a Park Ranger's logo embossed on its bill. His face was dark, slender and leathery and had two long warrior marks carved down both sides of his cheeks. He took off his sunglasses and squinted into the morning sun, which made his eyes appear malevolent. His uniform, shoes, and hat were spotless.

"Why do you boys run?" he asked in English. He put his sunglasses back on and gave them a sinister smirk. "We only want to talk to you. We saw you running and chased after you. Don't be afraid, we only want to ask some questions."

Still gasping for air from the run, Ebukut stared into the man's eyes. "We go to mountain, hunt lost goats," he said in broken English.

"You hunt goats with bows and arrows, and a spear?" the tall man asked, with a smirk. A threatening smile appeared on his menacing face. "And enough food and water for a week?" He pointed to their *sampurs* and water skins.

"We use arrows to hunt lizards for food," Hussein told him, nervously.

"I see," the tall ranger returned. He walked up to Hussein, stopped several feet from him and glared into his eyes. "I am Sergeant Mandeli. I am in charge of all rangers in this sector." He paused for a moment for effect. "Are you from that village, down there?" He pointed.

Hussein nodded.

A short, chubby ranger with large, moist sores on his face moved up close to Hussein. His uniform was torn, and he reeked from too many days without bathing. "We're looking for someone named Usitani!" he bellowed into the boy's face. "You know him? He's from the village down there." He pointed toward the *manyattas*.

Ebukut approached Mandeli, stopping when their eyes met. "Me, Ebukut...him Hussein," he said in broken English. "We not know name, Usitani."

The fat man glanced down at Hussein's fresh ceremonial paint, still visible on his stomach and chest, and then at his braided hair. "You're a new *lmurran*?" he asked with a contemptuous grin.

Hussein's face flushed. It was the end of the line, he thought. All the rangers had to do was put the pieces together and it would be easy for them to figure out who killed the lioness. They could not get away by telling lies, and he knew it. There was no escape. If they attempted to run, in the end they would be caught and the rangers would be twice as hard on them.

"I am Usitani," Hussein volunteered, with an audible sigh. "I'm the one you're looking for. I killed the lioness. But I killed her in self-defense." His eyes burned, as they stared unblinking at his reflection in the sergeant's dark glasses. "She mauled a Masai warrior and attacked me. I threw my spear and killed her. I had no choice."

The ranger looked down at the boy. "You're only a boy. How old are you, thirteen...fourteen?"

"I am a *lmurran*!" Hussein stated, proudly. "I killed the lioness. I will go with you for punishment, if that is what you wish."

The fat ranger reached out to take his arm, but was held back by the sergeant's strong hand. "Wait," Mandeli said. "This is a mere child. He can't be the one we're after. He couldn't kill a lion. He's protecting somebody." His voice reflected contempt for the fat ranger. "You get back in the truck. I'll handle this."

"I killed the lioness," Hussein insisted. "Do not look for another to blame. I'm the one you're after."

"I killed a *simba*, too," Ebukut announced arrogantly in Masai. "It was the mate to the one he killed. He attacked Usitani while he was looking after his goats. If I had not killed the lion, it would have killed him."

The tall ranger glared at the warrior. His dark lips formed a sneer, and then he snickered. "Oh, you want to be a hero, too?" he came back in Swahili, which was close enough to Masai that the warrior understood. "You might want to think twice, before you confess to killing a lion, when you see what's in store for your friend here. If in fact this is Usitani. Now be off with you." He pointed a crooked finger at him. "Go back to your village. We're taking this boy to the fishing club for questioning."

Ebukut's expression told Hussein that he had evaluated the situation—two men were in the second Rover and Mandeli's driver had returned to the first. The warrior had calculated his odds and found they were not in his favor. Nonetheless, it didn't matter to him; he would do what he must.

The second Rover backed up, making ready to depart. Ebukut turned toward the hill, as if leaving. The first truck sat idling, while waiting for the sergeant. A ranger from the second truck jumped out to assist the sergeant with his charge. Ebukut spun around, raised his spear, and rushed the man when he opened the door to the Rover. Mandeli turned in time to see the spear penetrate the ranger's lower back. The man screamed, fell against the Rover, and slumped to the ground.

Mandeli grabbed Hussein's arm, rushed him down the few feet to the open door of his vehicle, pushed him into the back seat, and locked the door from the outside. He pulled out his revolver and pointed it at

Ebukut. The warrior saw it in time and jumped behind the second Rover. A loud explosion sent shock waves across the quiet valley, and a bullet ricocheted off the fender. The driver of the second truck jumped out and began firing in all directions.

The big warrior could see the futility of his situation. He turned and zigzagged up the rocky hillside. As he raced up the slope he kept boulders between himself and the firing game warden. Halfway up the hill he glanced over his shoulder and saw Hussein's face pressed up against the inside of the window. He realized then it was too late to help him.

Mandeli's driver jumped out of his truck, and along with the other ranger continued to fire up the slope. Mandeli yanked the spear from the wounded ranger's back, flung it to the ground, and helped him into the second truck. When the rangers could no longer see the warrior, they jumped into their vehicles and sped down the rock-strewn trail toward the club.

As the Rover approached the club, Hussein slumped down in the back seat, attempting to stay out of sight. He knew right then Ebukut's performance had not helped matters. As a result of his actions his own punishment would now be more severe. He could count on that. He wanted to believe he would have done the same, given the opportunity, but he doubted if he had that kind of courage.

It was difficult for him to understand his friend's vicious attack. Was it because he was a *lmurran*? Most warriors would have done the same, if injustices had been done to them or their brothers. Sister Emanuella would have called it instinct for survival. However, the one thing the big warrior had not considered was the consequences his actions might bring on them. Even so, his friend got away without being captured or killed. He smiled.

The bumpy, pitted goat trail the Rovers had been traveling on smoothed out as soon as it turned to gravel in front of the club. Kirinyaga opened the gate, and with a long, crooked finger waved them through. They pulled up to the admissions building and rushed the injured man inside.

The village had no doctors, but several porters had limited medical knowledge, which had been acquired from the nuns at the mission school. The school also kept the rangers and fishing club supplied with most of their medical needs.

Hussein remained locked in the back seat, but the rush of activity outside his window made him extremely uneasy. Children from the nine tribes of the village had lined up outside the cyclone fence to see what all the commotion was about. Some were more agile than others and had climbed to the top of the fence to get a better look. He slouched down in the corner of his seat, embarrassed by his sudden notoriety; word of his troubles had already spread throughout the village

Mandeli came back to the truck and escorted him up the steep walkway to the lounge area of the club and instructed him to sit in a wicker chair while he spoke to Kurt Versteeg, the club manager.

After several minutes of animated conversation, the sergeant shouted across the room, “Come with me, boy! We’ll put you in a safe place, while we get medical attention for my friend. Don’t try to escape, there’s no place to go.” Slowly, Hussein trudged across the room. The sergeant grabbed him by the arm and dragged him forcefully to the back section of the restaurant.

At the same moment Hussein and the sergeant arrived at the back door of the kitchen, Gabriel entered the dining room with a tray of food. He followed them with his eyes, until they disappeared through the door and left the restaurant. He put his tray down, rushed to the screened door and watched as Mandeli pushed the boy toward an abandoned half-ton truck. The truck had once been used for transporting supplies, but now it was a rusty derelict. Hussein was hoisted onto its tailgate and shoved into a large aluminum box on the bed of the truck. He was thrown onto a pile of rancid hay and the door was slammed shut and padlocked.

Kurt Versteeg sat at the bar drinking a cup of coffee. When the sergeant returned he set his cup down and eyed him, contemptuously. The tall ranger went across the room toward him.

The sergeant addressed him with a threatening voice. "I put the boy in the abandoned truck in the back field. He's to stay there until I return from Maralal. Is that clear, Versteeg?"

"For Christ's sake, you can't leave him there!" Kurt blurted out. "He'll suffocate in all this heat. Let me put him in one of my rooms and lock the door. At least he'll survive."

"No!" Mandeli's face reddened in anger. "He must not be removed from the box! Do you understand me? We'll be back soon. Until then he's to stay put." His eyes ignited. "I repeat, do not take him from the box!"

Kurt gave him a glassy stare. He remembered one other incident when the box was used as a jail. Mandeli had been sitting at the bar when he overheard a French tourist speak out against the Kenyan government. The man believed that because he was within the confines of the club he had nothing to worry about. He was mistaken.

In the darkness of night the man had been taken from his room and thrown into the box. Kurt had been instructed to keep him there until arrangements could be made to transport him back to Nairobi. The man remained there for over two weeks with little water and even less food, barely enough to keep him alive. A guard was posted at the box to make sure nobody fed, watered, or freed him.

Kurt's face flushed. "Are we allowed to give him water once in a while?" he barked, as the sergeant turned to leave.

The sergeant understood Kurt's inference. Without turning he shouted across the room, "There will be a guard. He will take care of his needs. Don't bother yourself with details. The issue is closed."

Kurt's knuckles formed white fists. He knew just how far he could go with this big man, and he figured he had reached that limit. Several years earlier, he had suffered severe financial losses because of him. He was certain it was for his political views. Mandeli had instructed travel agencies not to book tourists to the fishing club, and had all landing rights canceled for those wanting to fly in from outside the country. As much as he hated it, he thought it prudent to keep further comments to himself. After the sergeant left, he made himself a stiff martini and retired to his room.

When Gabriel returned to the dining area a boy in a white uniform came up behind him and whispered that the breakfast guests at his table were looking for him. He had been absorbed in the situation and had forgot all about them. He ran into the kitchen, picked up his cold order of scrambled eggs and poached Nile perch, and delivered them to their table. With a large wooden spatula, he slid the food onto their plates. He poured chicory coffee into their porcelain cups, and then stood back and waited for them to begin eating.

The fat man sitting at one end of the table, wearing an undersized tropical shirt that hung over an unbuckled belt, took a tiny bite of the perch. He spit it back onto his plate and glared up at the boy.

"Is something wrong, sir?" Gabriel asked.

"You damn right there's somethin' wrong, boy," the obese man said in a deep southern drawl. "This food's cold as hell, boy. I can't eat this crap." The two women at the table blushed.

Gabriel looked down at the food. "But, sir," he said, trying to force a smile, "that is the way it's supposed to be eaten. You told me when you came to the table you wanted a native breakfast. This is the breakfast of the El Molos. It's supposed to be eaten cold."

The man turned his eyes on the uneaten food. With a flushed temple, he glanced sheepishly across the table. Both women smiled and nodded.

"That's right, Charles," said the woman with a pair of oversized, rhinestone-studded glasses resting low on her nose. "You did say you wanted something with a local flavor. Don't mind him, son," she continued. "You did good. You never mind him."

Gabriel turned and eyed several chuckling bus boys that had been watching the episode from across the room. As soon as they were discovered, they turned their faces to the dining room wall and whispered amongst themselves. Although their voices were low, they were loud enough to be heard by the *maître d'hôtel'*. With a long, crooked finger and a stern look, he pointed threateningly toward the kitchen. The boys rushed from the dining area, sniggering.

The middle-aged woman sitting beside the fat man took a small bite of her fish and looked over at the other woman. "Gladys, this is good," she said in a high-pitched voice. "Try some. You too, Charles. Try it again. It has a definite local taste. Like the green stuff we had back in Nairobi. You remember, the stuff made with peas and potatoes and such."

Charles took another bite and rolled it around in his fat jowls. Not wanting to be outdone by the ladies, he forked more into his mouth. "Well, maybe it ain't so bad, after all," he said, and scooped up another large portion of eggs and cold perch. "So this is the crap they eat down by the lake, huh? That right, boy?"

"Yes, sir. The El Molo tribe," Gabriel said, and smiled at the two women. "Would you excuse me, please? I'll be right back. Enjoy the local meal while I'm gone. When I return I'll bring you a delightful breakfast drink called *saroi*."

He rushed through the swinging door of the kitchen and bumped into the waiters, who were still laughing. He stopped in the back of the kitchen and stared through the window that overlooked Hussein's jail. No guard was at the truck, but he figured one would be there soon. He put food and several bottles of purified water in a small bag and rushed through the screen door. As he approached the box, he whispered, "Hussein! Quick! Come to the window!"

Hussein looked through the bars at the same moment his friend forced the bag through them. "Is that you, Gabriel?" he whispered back.

"Yes, but I must go. Hide the food and water. It may be all you get for a long time. Be careful not to spill any. I don't think I'll be able to come back…at lease not for a while." He turned his head from side to side to see if anyone was coming. He knew if he were caught he would be put in the box with him.

"Gabriel," Hussein said. "What about Paul? Do you know if he made it to Nairobi?"

Gabriel jumped down from the flatbed and glanced up at the iron bars. "Yes, he's in Nairobi. He made it. I can't talk right now, I've got to get back inside before they discover I'm gone." After he had traveled a few feet from the truck, he turned and whispered, "I'll see what I can do about getting you more food and water, later. However, I can't promise."

"Thank you," Hussein said. "I'll be right here." He smiled, and then stuck his hand through the bars and waved.

Gabriel acknowledged his wave, and then disappeared into the kitchen.

By the angle of the sun, Hussein figured it to be about 10 o'clock. The morning air had already begun to heat the inside of the cab, which made it nearly unbearable inside. He had heard of the French tourist Mandeli had locked in the box for two weeks. The man had lived for only a short time after his release, and then died of dehydration. The one who had told him about it may have exaggerated, it wasn't that bad inside the box. Nevertheless, he had also heard that the man had been given no food or water in all that time. Nonetheless, he knew that in order for the man to live for two weeks they would have had to give him water. Without food he could have survived, but not water.

He placed his back against the sweltering side of the metal box and slid into a squatting position on the straw-laden floor. He realized he had to take good care of the water Gabriel had given him. Even if they didn't release him for two weeks, he could survive.

He rested his arms on his knees, closed his eyes, and evaluated his situation. If they did this to him for killing a lion in self-defense, he wondered what they would do to Ebukut for spearing the ranger.

He opened his eyes and discovered his sampur, half exposed under the straw. To his delight the rangers had not taken it. He opened it and found his food still wrapped in wax paper. He poked around in the straw and also found his water skin, still half full. He could not believe they had not taken them.

He examined the six-foot square enclosure, searching for a place to hide the items. He found a pile of putrid straw in a corner and slid them under it. He knew he could survive.

Ebukut had received a slight injury to his arm, when a ranger's bullet ricocheted off a rock. He had heard they were bad shots, now he knew it. His arm throbbed, as he trudged up the rock-strewn hill, and he stopped to inspect the wound. It did not appear to be bleeding, but as a precaution, he wrapped it in a strip of cloth from his sampur.

He waited in the foothills until he was certain the rangers would not return. After an hour, he retraced his footsteps to where he had left his spear, hoping it would still be there. "After all, a lmurran is nothing without his spear," he muttered in Masai.

He was familiar with the gray men and knew they would only use their Land Rovers to track him; they would not get out of the air-conditioned vehicles, unless forced to do so. He figured he had the advantage; they would stay in their vehicles while they looked for him. They would not drive the Rovers far off the mountain paths. He had positioned himself where he could see all trails leading into the valley. He could see them from miles away, but they couldn't see him.

He knew that if the rangers found him, they would try to capture or kill him. Nevertheless, should he kill them, if given the chance? He had already wounded one, and as far as they were concerned that was the same as murder. He knew they would come after him in droves, like the Flamingos of the lake.

Images of his manhunt with Hussein flashed through his mind. However, this would be much easier, the rangers were stupid and Hussein was not. The gray men had been away from their tribes too many years and were no longer a threat to most lmurrans. He figured they would be easy pickings for a warrior like him. He didn't believe they would return that day; they would go back to Maralal to get more rangers. If they did, it would give him more time to find Hussein. When he was restrained at the trucks, he believed he heard the rangers say they were taking the young warrior to the fishing club, but his comprehension of English was limited. They could have said anything and he may not have understood.

At that moment, he realized he had to do something fast. They would surely capture him, if he remained in the mountains. A thought came to him...the fishing club was where they would not expect him to go. He must have picked up some of Hussein's white man's ways, after all. In the past, he would have stayed in the mountains and wandered without direction. However, something intrinsic told him he should be the hunter and not the prey. In the past, he had taken on several rangers and had won, but this was different; he had seriously injured one of them. He realized he had a desperate situation on his hands, but he didn't know what to do.

From his vantage point on a large boulder, he had a good view of the fishing club with all its dum-palms and small luxurious huts. He squinted, trying to locate the two Land Rovers that had taken Hussein away, but was unsuccessful. He guessed this would be a long night.

Chapter Six

Paul had noticed a magazine on the nightstand and began thumbing through it. His eyes widened and his face flushed, when nude figures leaped from its pages. Just as he started to get pleasure from its pages, there was a loud knock on the door. He closed the magazine quickly and flung it back onto the stand.

The locking bolt turned and Eric entered. "Hi, kid," he said with a grin. "You getting hungry?"

Paul's face beamed, and he shook his head.

They left the room and took the elevator to the lobby. When they entered the restaurant a young native boy escorted them to a table, handed them menus, and left. Paul glanced over at Eric who was busy reading the long cardboard. He held the folded page in front of him and tried to read its strange words, but they were confusing.

Eric put his menu down and looked across the table. "Do you see anything you like?"

Paul hid his face behind the menu. "I don't understand these words, they're not English."

Eric reached across the table and flipped it over. "Try it now. I don't believe you read French, do you?" he said with a grin. "That side's in English."

Paul looked at the now familiar words, but there were still many he didn't recognize. The waiter returned, stood behind them, and tapped his pencil impatiently on the order pad.

At the club, Paul had heard tourists from the safari trucks say they sure could go for a good old American hamburger. "I'll have the American hamburger, please," he said, looking up and smiling at the tall waiter.

"Good choice," Eric said. "I'll have the same." The waiter wrote down the order and left.

"You were gone long. Is everything all right?"

"Yes, all's well. I'm sorry it took so long, but I had to make arrangements for Dan and me to go back to Turkana."

There was a lull in the conversation while they waited for their food. When it arrived, they wasted no time devouring it.

Eric waited for the boy to finish, and then slid his chair back from the table. "I have to go out again, Paul," he said. "I'm sorry, but it'll only be for a short while. Get whatever else you want. I'll tell the waiter to put it on my bill. I'll be back around five or five-thirty. When I get back, we'll figure out what we're going to do with you. Okay? Here's a key to the room in case you want to watch TV."

Without answering, Paul took the key and stuck it in his shirt pocket. He wondered what Somerville meant when he said, "We'll figure out what we're going to do with you?" He didn't want anything to be done with him. All he wanted was to be left alone and on his own. It wasn't that he didn't appreciate what Eric was doing for him, but he wanted to do things the way he had planned when he arrived in Nairobi.

Eric left the table and motioned the young waiter to the side, and spoke to him. The boy looked over at Paul and nodded. Eric slid several bills into his hand and left.

After finishing his second hamburger, Paul clasped his hands behind his head and leaned back in the chair. The waiter brought an ice-cold soft drink and a piece of pie and placed them in front of him. Paul stuck his finger in the cold drink and stirred the ice. He picked up the sliver of pie, held it in his hand, and started to shove it into his mouth. The waiter leaned over, picked up a fork and put it in his other hand. Paul looked up and smiled. He thought it was a strange way to eat such a small piece of pie.

After he had finished the pie, he walked through the front door of the hotel and onto the ramp that overlooked the street in front of the Stanley. As he gawked up and down Kenyata Boulevard, he was awestruck by the wide variety of people: blacks, whites, Orientals, and copper-skinned people with white towels twisted around their heads. He was accustomed to blacks and whites and a few Orientals, but he had never seen copper skinned people before.

From the steps of the hotel, he looked out over the heads of the bustling crowd, and the tops of cars as they darted up and down the street. He was amazed at what he saw. A porter roughly pushed him aside to let tourists enter the lobby. It was difficult to imagine there were that many people in all of Kenya. Everywhere he looked, they were walking, running, talking, bartering, smiling, screaming, and begging.

He put his hand in his pocket, clutched the folded shilling notes, and left the steps. He turned the corner at the end of the hotel and strolled casually down the sidewalk. The store windows were crammed with items for sale to tourists. Sister Emanuella had told his class about the tourists in Nairobi and how they bought anything relating to native folklore or wild life. He was shocked by the massive amounts of carved ivory pieces displayed in the windows. Elephant hair bracelets, worn on the arms of boys his age, were also being sold to tourists. He walked up to one of the boys and inspected them. They were not real, he could tell by looking at them; they were the tail hairs of water buffalos. In addition, most of the carvings were made from the bones of other mammals or fish, not elephant tusks. He wondered why they were cheating the tourists. After a few more inspections of goods, he backed up against the wall of the hotel, in an attempt to get away from the traffic on the over-crowded sidewalk.

A black man in a dirty, white shirt sidled up to him. "Jambo," the man said in Swahili. "What do you say, little brother? How are you?"

Paul eyed the man up suspiciously, before answering. The first thing he noticed was his hairline; a scar ran for several inches across his upper temple. It was matted down, dirty and sprinkled with tufts of white. His shoes were run-down at the heels, and the laces had been knotted several times. The pupils of his eyes were dark, almost black, and the whites had small blood vessels running at irregular angles through them. However, when he smiled, his teeth were straight and white.

After a long pause, he answered in Masai, which was close enough to Swahili that the man understood. He volunteered his tribal name, and Lake Turkana as the locality of his people.

"Ndiyo," the man acknowledged. He then switched to English. "I know of Lake Turkana," he said. "It's not far from my country, Uganda."

"You are from Uganda?" Paul questioned, also reverting to English. "I have never met anyone from there."

"I'm afraid there aren't too many of us outside the country," the man answered, and then displayed a bitter grin. "I walked all the way here to escape the government soldiers."

"The soldiers were after you?" Paul said. A deep frown furrowed his temple. "Why were they after you? What did you do?"

"I did nothing, my little friend." The man glanced down at the sidewalk. "In Uganda you do not have to do anything to be picked up by the soldiers, they can come for you at any time."

Paul figured the man to be in his forties. He spoke intelligently, pronouncing his words as if he was educated in England. "My Christian name is Paul. What is yours?" he told him.

"I am Christopher. Christopher Banderi," the man answered, and then held out his hand in friendship. "I'm from the Luo tribe of eastern Uganda. What brings you to Nairobi, Paul? Do you have a job here?"

Paul hesitated for a moment, not knowing how sociable he should get with this stranger. "No, but I have friends," he answered. "And I will soon get a job."

Christopher eyed him with amusement, and snickered. "You are filled with confidence and optimism my little friend," he said. "How long have you been in Nairobi?"

"I just arrived. I came here in an airplane, the Sun Bird."

"Do you have a place to stay?"

"Yes, for now," Paul said. "I'm with a friend, here at this hotel." He pointed to the wall behind him.

"You are staying at this hotel?" Christopher spoke as if he didn't believe him. "Your friend must have lots of money for you to stay here."

"I don't know about his money. He's a friend from Turkana…a white man. I helped save him from a lion."

Christopher's eyes widened. "You saved him from a lion? He must truly be grateful."

"I do not know that word."

"It means he would give you almost anything for saving his life. He's indebted to you. Do you understand what I'm saying?" He leaned his elbow against the wall beside Paul's head and pressed his body close. "Did he give you anything for saving his life? In addition to allowing you to stay at this hotel, of course."

Paul pulled the folded shilling notes from his pocket. "He gave me money. But it's a loan. I will repay him."

Christopher moved his arm from the brick wall and reached over to feel the money. He raised his eyebrows. "That's a lot of money, Paul," he said. "You say it's only a loan? And you plan to pay him back for saving his life?"

"Yes. I will pay him back," Paul replied, slightly agitated by his comment. "I will not take money for saving someone's life. It's not right." He put the money back in his pocket.

"I'm sure he meant for you to keep it, Paul, and not as a loan," Christopher said with a wry smile. "I'll bet it was your idea to pay him back. Wasn't it?"

Paul dropped his head and stared at the dirt-filled rutted lines in the sidewalk. "Yes, it was my thought that it should be a loan," he said. "But I'm right in thinking that."

"Of course you are. It's an honorable thing to want to pay back a debt…if in fact it is a debt. Look at it this way, my friend, wouldn't that same man pay a doctor for saving his life, if he was sick?"

Paul stared into his dark eyes. "I guess so. But that's different."

"Of course it's the same. If he was dying of a disease and the doctor gave him a cure, he would pay the doctor…and pay him well. Would he not?"

Paul started to feel uncomfortable with the man's questions. Without a doubt, he was up to something. Why else would he talk that way? What did he want? Was he trying to get his money?

Christopher continued. "Paul, let me tell you something. Is that okay?"

Paul shrugged, and looked back down at the sidewalk.

"Paul, we are friends, are we not?" he said, and stared into Paul's eyes. "Oh, I realize we have only known each other for a few minutes, but we are friends because we are tribesmen. Granted, we are from different tribes and countries, but we are still tribesmen." He put his hands behind his back and glanced up in the afternoon sky. "What I'm saying is, the black man is entitled to take advantage of any opportunity given him."

Paul looked into his eyes, then again stared down at the sidewalk, but said nothing.

"We are not as fortunate as the white man," Christopher continued. "We must take advantage of whatever is thrust our way; opportunity, money, or what have you." He put his head close to Paul's ear and whispered, "Don't let your friendship with the white man cloud your business sense. The man intended for you to have that money for saving his life, and you would insult him by repaying it. He doesn't expect you to give it back. In fact, I'm sure he would offer much more if only you would let him. Isn't that true?"

Paul looked at him for a few seconds, and then back down at the grooves in the sidewalk. "He did offer me more money," he said, "but I'm not going to take it."

"Ah," Christopher said with a smile, which again revealed the whiteness of his teeth. "That's what I thought. He does want you to have more money, he the same as said so." He bent over and stared into Paul's eyes. "Are you going to take the money, or insult him by refusing it?"

Paul considered it for a moment. The man was confusing him with words. He didn't know how to react to so many questions. He had to get away, but he didn't know how.

"Tell me, Paul," the man continued. "What did you come to Nairobi for? Did you come here to work and make lots of money, or did you come to borrow and spend all your time paying it back? I'll tell you right now there's little money to be had by the black man here in Nairobi. It's almost impossible to get a loan. You would have to have a good job before anyone would even consider lending you money." He paused and waited for a reaction.

Paul fondled the bills in his pocket. He tried to understand what Christopher had said, but he became even more confused. He could not think straight. He desperately wanted to be rid of this man, but he couldn't just walk away. He was trying to be a friend to the man. After all, he was a tribal brother. Maybe he could give him some of his money that might get rid of him. He had said the blacks could not make money or get loans in Nairobi.

"Do you have a job, Christopher?" he asked.

The Ugandan remained silent for several moments, swaying back and forth on his run-down heels. "No, my friend," he said with a sigh. "I do not have a job. I must make money the best way I can, for my little brother and me. I humble myself by asking the white tourists here on the streets for money. It's degrading, you know." He stared into Paul's eyes. "You will be doing the same if you stay here, my little friend. You will not be able to get a job. Trust me on this."

"You have a brother here, too?" Paul queried, paying no attention to his answer.

"Yes, we both walked here from Uganda. The soldiers were looking for both of us."

"Where is he now? I don't see him." Paul glanced up and down the sidewalk.

"Oh, he isn't here. Not right here. It would be too dangerous. Besides, he isn't well. I left him at the railroad station, about two kilometers from here. He's hidden under the station platform, where I hope nobody will find him. If they do they will turn him over to the government men, here in Nairobi." He glanced up and down the street, trying to appear nervous. "We have no passports, you see. No papers at all. If they stop us they will either throw us in jail or send us back to Uganda." His face turned somber.

"What can you do here in Nairobi without these papers?" Paul asked.

"Nothing. However, we are not staying here. We are on our way to Mombasa. We've been trying to get there for about a month." Again, he nervously glanced up and down both sides of the street. "We are getting close to having enough shillings, but asking tourists for a few at a time is difficult, and not the least bit profitable."

"But why are you going to Mombasa?" Paul asked. "You can get caught there as easily as here. Can't you?"

"That's true." Christopher looked down at his tattered shoes. He lifted one foot at a time and polished the tops on the back of his trouser legs. "But when we do get to Mombasa, I have already made arrangements for a cargo ship to take my sick little brother and me to America." His face beamed. "The ship's expenses are taken care of. All we need is the money to get us to Mombasa. However, we are running out on time. The captain of the ship said we must be there by the day after tomorrow. It's a long trip by train. It would take us many hours, even if we left tonight."

"You are going to America? Where in America?"

"We will go to Los Angeles, California," Christopher said, exhaling a deep sigh. "There I will work, it has been arranged. But it doesn't look good, my little friend." A well-dressed white man came out of a shop a few steps from them. He glanced at the man and said, "Paul, please wait here while I see what I can do."

He walked up to the man, and with a broad smile began his spiel in English. The man held out his hand in friendship. He had been with the man briefly when a woman came out of the shop and joined them. He started a one-sided conversation. They both laughed and the man warmly placed his hand on Christopher's shoulder. Several minutes later, the woman's expression changed from a smile to a grin, but she continued to listen. Suddenly, her face flushed and her lips tightened. She tugged at the man's arm, attempting to pull him down the sidewalk. He yanked his arm free and reached into his pocket, but the woman persisted by a firm grip on his coat sleeve. With a fierce tug, she spun him around and forced him down the sidewalk.

Christopher returned where Paul had been watching. "See, it's not easy asking for money," he said with a dejected look. "The men will often help, but when the little woman comes...poof, it's all over. They will not try to understand what I'm asking of them. They believe I'm being less than honest with them. They don't believe I have a brother who needs medicine. They believe if they gave me money, I would not use it for medicine, or to get us to Mombasa."

"Then your brother is quite ill?"

"Yes. It was a long journey from Uganda, and extremely hot. He was almost dehydrated when we arrived. He came close to dying. He's getting better, though. However, every shilling I make during the day must go for medicine and food. When I use it for medicine, I can't use it for the trip to Mombasa."

"I do not know that word, 'dehydrated'."

"Dehydrated means he lost most of his body fluids," Christopher explained. "He did not get enough water to drink. The sun was extremely hot and it drained much liquid from his body. Your body needs a lot of liquid for you to stay alive. Do you understand?" He gave Paul an impatient smile.

"Yes, I believe so. When you buy medicine for your brother you might not be able to meet the ship because of that?"

"That's right. Every shilling I get my hands on goes for medicine and food for Nathan."

Paul's face beamed. "Your brother's name is Nathan? That's my brother's name, too."

"You're kidding," Christopher said, his face aglow. He put both hands on Paul's shoulders and squeezed. "What a coincidence, we have something in common."

Paul pulled away, embarrassed by the man's overt friendliness. "Yes, I guess we do," he said, and shrugged uneasily.

Christopher reached into his pocket and pulled out a small glass cylinder that had a prescription typed on its side. A small amount of yellow liquid was visible at the bottom.

"See, this is what I must get for Nathan every other day," he said. "And it's expensive." He held it up for Paul's inspection. "As you can see, it's almost empty. I need more tonight, before I go back." He studied Paul's face.

"How much does this medicine cost?"

Christopher cleared his throat. "Well, It's not cheap, I can tell you that."

"How much?" Paul fingered the bills in his pocket.

"Well, two days ago when I bought this," Christopher said, holding up the container, "it cost me two hundred and sixty shillings."

Paul pursed his lips.

"I said it was expensive. I doubt if I can make that much by tonight."

Once again, Paul wrapped his fingers around the shilling notes. He had received 1000 from Eric and 150 from Gabriel. Altogether he had 1,150-shillings. He was certain he could spare 260 for the medicine. After all, it was a small boy, much like his own brother, who needed it. He pulled the money out of his pocket.

"I will give you the money you need for the medicine," he told him. "But I would like to see Nathan. Can I come to the station with you?"

The expression on the man's face changed to a scowl. "Paul, I would love to have you come with me, but I don't believe it's wise. What if the police stop us and ask for our papers? I don't have any. Do you have papers to show them? I doubt if you do. No, my friend, you must trust me." With a shocked expression on his face, he stared into the boy's eyes. "You do believe I'm telling you the truth, don't you?"

"Of course. Why would you lie?" Paul replied. He held the shillings in his hand and started counting. He could not get far with the count before he lost concentration and had to start over.

Christopher reached over and took the notes. "Please, allow me," he said. "I have had much more experience in these matters." After he had finished counting, tears swelled in the corners of his eyes. He stared at Paul intently and waved the handful of bills in his face. "My friend," he continued. "Do you know how much money you have here?"

Paul backed up against the rough, brick wall. "Yes, I believe so."

"This is exactly what I need to get my sick brother and me to Mombasa?" Christopher said. "And there would be enough left for his medicine, too." He stopped long enough to wipe the tears on his dirty shirtsleeve. "This could save our lives, you know. This little wad of brown paper could save our lives." An expression of despair came over his face. He dropped his arms to his sides and forced the money back into Paul's hand. "But of course it's not mine. Therefore, things are as they were." He took Paul's hand, pried it open, and pulled out 300-shillings. "But I will take the money you offered for the medicine, with my deepest gratitude. I only wish I could do more for my little brother. He's such a wonderful little boy."

Paul glanced at the dejected figure, and a queasy feeling invaded his stomach. Something didn't seem right, but he believed he could be wrong. He shoved the remainder of the money into Christopher's hand. "I don't know if you're trying to trick me or not," he said. "But I'll take my chances. If you're telling me the truth I want to do something for little Nathan. I want him to go to America. I only wish my little brother had the same opportunity." He pushed his body away from the brick wall, turned and headed toward the hotel entrance. "That's all the money I have," he said, loudly, and then continued up the sidewalk. "You can keep it because we are brothers." I know the kind of person I am, I only hope you know who you are."

He arrived at the hotel lobby, as a porter was about to get into the elevator. Before the door closed, he rushed in beside him.

"What room do you want, boy?" the man asked. Paul held up the key.

When the elevator stopped, Paul walked down the corridor to the room number on the key. He entered and found a note pinned to the bed with several 500-shilling notes wrapped around it. The note read: "Paul, something came up. I have to leave Nairobi for a short time. You're welcome to use the room until I return. For food, go where we went for lunch. It's all been arranged. See you soon, Eric." He sat on the edge of the bed and sobbed.

Chapter Seven

The late afternoon sun was balanced on top of the craggy Saw Tooth Mountains, and resembled a huge egg yolk about to be ruptured by its highest peak. Camels began their slow ascents up the mountains in search of grass, and doves darted to the lake's edge for one last drink and bath, before settling in for the night among the nut palm trees that lined the periphery of the club's compound.

Ebukut sat on the top of a large flat boulder, examining the valley far below. After his eyes had adjusted to the darkness, he studied each building on the dark streets of Loiyangalani. He could make out a large portion of the club, except for the shadowy areas behind the main buildings. He knew his friend was somewhere in the compound, but didn't know exactly where. Nevertheless, as soon as the moonlight flooded the area he would go down and search for him. He was not afraid to go into the compound; he had been there many times before with the small children of the village, when they slid under the fence and watched the white man drink his beer and swim in the warm water of the pools.

He lowered his back to the coolness of the boulder and closed his eyes. The peace and tranquility of the last few minutes before total darkness allowed him time to reflect on his role as a *lmurran*. For many warriors, ceremonies of any kind were the only things they lived for. But to him it meant power, power over the village, over its children, and over its women. In addition, prestige accompanied that power.

Many years ago, he had accepted the honor and respect that went along with the title of *lmurran,* without question. Nevertheless, over the years there had been many changes. Honor and respect for the warrior had all but disappeared. Now, a *lmurran* was given as much respect as a fat goat ready to slaughter.

The one thing of any significance left was for him to select a wife and be a married man, a *lpayan* (elpayan*)*. If he were to decide on that title, there would be a nice endowment, at least a small tribe of goats. In addition, he would get more respect from the elders.

Hussein's desire to become a *lmurran* was beyond his comprehension. What was going on inside the boy's head? He wondered. What could make him want to be what he himself had become? He knew *layenis* and *laibartanis* needed someone to look up to, but they should not pattern themselves after him, or other warriors in the village. They should look to the elders for guidance; they were the true warriors of the past, the real *lmurrans.*

His mind returned to Hussein's ceremony of manhood, and the near tragedy of their forbidden hunt. He believed if he had not been drinking *pombe* he would not have challenged the boy. However, in the end it had turned out for the best. He had discovered something he never realized before; he was not the warrior everyone believed him to be. Moreover, the fact that being a *lmurran* was not all that important. He also found out, to his astonishment, he had compassion for his fellow tribesmen. Such a trait had never surfaced before. He had always played the part of the leading *lmurran*, but that time it had backfired. It was fortunate the children and elders of the village could not read his mind.

Long shadows slid across the desert floor, as the dark orange sun slowly sank out of sight behind the horizon. Ebukut glanced down at the darkness in the village. It was time to go.

It took the better part of an hour to get to the fishing club, and when he arrived at the fence-line it was difficult to see it. Even so, he knew exactly where the break in the fence was located.

Once inside he inched his way around the many buildings, peeking into each louvered window as he went by. He crouched under drooping nut-palm trees, and used their fronds as camouflage. Hussein was nowhere to be found. He wondered if they had taken him from the compound while he made his way down the mountain. If they had moved him to another location, he realized he would never find him.

The slapping of bare feet on the red brick walkway got his attention, and he peeked through the fronds. In the dim overhead lights of the sidewalk, he could make out a small, slender figure walking toward him. It was a young native boy. When he got closer, the warrior jumped out from his hiding place and pulled him into the foliage. He put his arm around the boy's neck, and with his free hand covered his mouth.

The boy yanked Ebukut's hand free. With a squeaky voice, he stuttered in Masai, "Who is it? What do you want?"

"What have they done with Hussein?" the warrior said in a throaty whisper.

"I don't understand," the boy said, in a trembling voice.

"Where have they taken Hussein? What have they done with him?"

The warrior released his grip when the boy pointed to the rear of the compound, where the old truck was parked. As he turned to look, the boy backed out of the bushes and disappeared. The warrior turned and sped in the direction the boy had indicated.

Winded, the native boy raced up the steps to the restaurant. As he entered the lounge, he and spotted the ranger that was supposed to be guarding Hussein, sitting at the bar with a drink in his hand. He rushed past him and into the restaurant. A small, slender waiter came out of the kitchen weighed down with a heavy tray of food. The panting boy waited until he had served his customers, then met him in the middle of the room.

"Mathew," the breathless boy whispered. "Where is Gabriel? I must see him."

"What's wrong?"

"Nothing, maybe," the boy said, gasping for air. "But I must see him right away. Is he still here? Do you know?"

Mathew took the boy by the arm and escorted him to the back of the room where they could talk without being overheard. "He must be in his room," he said. "He's not on duty now."

Without acknowledging, the boy raced out the back door of the restaurant, up the incline to Gabriel's hut, and bolted through the door.

"Gabriel, Gabriel," he shouted.

Startled by the boy's sudden appearance, Gabriel nearly fell off the bed. "Jonathan? What is it?" he said. "What's wrong?"

The boy stopped for a moment to catch his breath, then took him by the arm and attempted to pull him toward the door.

Gabriel yanked his arm free. "What's wrong, Jonathan?" he repeated, a frown furrowing his forehead.

"You must come!" the excited boy cried out between gulps of air. "There's a fierce looking warrior trying to find Hussein! I had to tell him where he was. He said he would kill me if I didn't!"

"Slow down, Jonathan. Tell me what's going on."

"I told you," the boy hissed. "There's a warrior, a *lmurran*, looking for Hussein. I think he's going to kill him, or something. He's real mean looking. He has a painted body, a spear, and everything."

Gabriel raced from the hut to where he could see the box on the truck. The guard was nowhere to be seen. He ran down the hill to the kitchen, with Jonathan on his heels.

"Did you see the guard, Jonathan?" he asked.

"Yes. He's in the lounge getting drunk."

"Good." Gabriel peeked around the corner of the dining room into the bar. The guard sat in front of a drink, having a rowdy conversation with a tourist. "I want you to do something for me," he whispered.

"What?"

He took the boy by the arm and spun him around. "Give me a few minutes," Gabriel said. "If the guard starts to get up, for any reason at all, I want you to spill a drink on his uniform, so he'll have to go wash up. Do anything to make him stay in the restaurant. Can I count on you to do that?"

The boy smiled. "I'm good at spilling drinks. You know that."

Gabriel turned, left the restaurant, and dashed across the backyard to the box. As he approached, off to his right he heard bushes rustling. He ignored the sound and jumped onto the ramp of the truck. He whispered through the bars, "Hussein, we have to talk."

Hussein peeked through the only window in the box. "Gabriel? It's nice to see you. What's wrong? Is there a problem?"

"There could be. There's someone looking for you. I think it's one of your friends, but I'm not sure."

"That must be Ebukut."

"Is he a friend?"

"Yes. At least I think so. Where's the guard? He must not come if he's here."

"I think I've taken care of that little matter. He's in the lounge drinking, but he could be here at any time." He glanced at the bushes beside the truck and pointed. "I think your friend is over there." Without warning, a tall figure jumped onto the ramp and put a knife to his throat.

"No! Ebukut!" Hussein shouted. "He's a friend! *Umekosa*! You have made a mistake!"

The big warrior sheathed his hunting knife, shoved Gabriel aside, and moved quickly to the window. "I will free you," he said.

Gabriel reached over and touched his arm, cautiously. "You won't have time to free him," he said. "The guard will be here at any moment. He has a gun and he'll use it if he sees you."

"He won't see me. I'm not afraid," the warrior said confidently.

"Why not wait until he comes back?" Gabriel suggested. "Then you can surprise him. We'll tie him up and use his key on the lock." He pointed to the rusty padlock.

Again, Ebukut pushed him aside. He put the tip of his spear under the clasp and with one quick turn of the blade dropped the lock to one side. He swung the door open and grabbed Hussein by his arm.

Hussein yanked free and ran back into the box to retrieve his food and water. He swept his hands through the putrid straw until he found them, then raced back to the open door, thanked Gabriel, jumped down from the platform, and with Ebukut leading the way, darted into the bushes.

Gabriel heard the thrashing of underbrush, as the two warriors raced toward the cyclone fence. Several minutes later the metallic creaking of the fence broke the silence. When all was quiet he dropped to his knees, looked at the stars, and gave thanks to *N'kai.*

"Gabriel," came a youthful whisper from across the field. "Did they get away?"

"Jonathan, I asked you to stay with the guard," Gabriel whispered back.

The boy raced across the field and dropped to his knees beside him. "But I didn't have to spill a drink on his uniform," he said, with a mischievous grin. "He did that all by himself. He's totally drunk. The tourists bought him many drinks. He'll be useless the rest of the night."

"I don't think I'd like to be in that man's shoes when the tall ranger returns and finds out he's not standing guard over Hussein," Gabriel said with a grin.

The two boys walked back to the restaurant and sat at a vacant table on the lounge patio.

"Was the *lmurran* going to hurt Hussein?" Jonathan asked.

"No, he was a friend…at least enough to break him out of the box. I'd say that's a pretty good friend, wouldn't you?" Jonathan shrugged.

The boys went to the outside railing of the patio and found two vacant chairs that overlooked the lake. As they sat looking up at the Milky Way, they heard rustling at the bottom of the banister, a concrete railing at the edge of the deck, with shrubs at its base that had grown within a few inches of its flat top.

"Gabriel," came a familiar voice.

Gabriel looked over the edge of the railing and saw Hussein half-hidden behind one of the larger shrubs.

"I thought you left with your friend. Is something wrong?" he said. He turned his head and inspected the lounge. The guard still sat at the bar, tottering back and forth on his stool, attempting to finish his drink.

"No. There's nothing wrong," Hussein said. "But there is something you could do for me, if you wouldn't mind."

"Anything, if I can."

"Will you see if you can get a message to Paul in Nairobi? I would like for him to know what's happening, and where I will be. It's quite possible I may never see him again."

"I thought he went to Nairobi to start a new life," Gabriel said with a chuckle. "He said he wouldn't come back until he had made his fortune."

"He'll be back," Hussein said, confidently. "He'll find that his friends are more important than he thinks." He stood upright and peeked through the concrete columns of the banister. "Will you try to get a message to him? Tell him we're on our way to Koobi Fora. We know a friend at the diggings who will hide us and perhaps get us a job. However, we may stop at Illah on the way up. My stepmother has relatives at the El Molo village. We'll be safe there, if we make it that far."

"Do you think the rangers will go that far to search for you?"

"Yes. Ebukut wounded one of them. They'll come, all right."

"Of course I'll get the message to Paul, if at all possible," Gabriel assured him. "You know I'll try my best."

"I must go. Thank you," Hussein said, and then disappeared into the bushes. The shrubs swished back and forth noisily, as he rushed to the fence for the second time.

"I wonder why they're headed to Koobi Fora?" Gabriel said to the young boy seated beside him.

"Why do you wonder that?" Jonathan replied. "It seems like it would be a good place to hide. Besides, there are many caves along the way. I think it's a wise choice."

"But Koobi is many kilometers from here," Gabriel said. "It will take them days to get there. After they arrive, what then?" He glanced over at the young boy swinging his legs back and forth under the rattan chair.

Jonathan ignored his question and returned with one of his own. "The people at Koobi hunt bones, don't they?" He stopped swinging his legs long enough to stir an ample supply of cream into a newly acquired cup of coffee.

"You mean the ones who dig for the bones of our ancestors?"

"Yes, I think so," the boy said, cocking his head to one side. "What's the other name they call that place?"

"The tree where man was born…I think," Gabriel said.

"That's strange." A comical frown spread across the boy's forehead. "There aren't that many trees up there, you know. I was up there once with my father. It was hotter than blazes, and dry. Why do they call it by such a funny name?"

"I was told by a man that works at the diggings they believe it's where monkeys first came down from the trees and walked upright," Gabriel told the boy.

Jonathan thought for a moment. "There's no monkeys at Koobi. At least I don't think so."

Gabriel laughed. "They don't mean it literally."

"I don't know that word," Jonathan said, and gave him another sideways glance.

"They were not talking about real monkeys." Gabriel thought for a moment, and then continued. "How can I put it so you can understand? It's difficult to explain something I don't fully understand myself to a boy who's barely twelve years old, and not one of the brightest on the waiting staff." He grinned, and then with an open hand swatted the boy on the shoulder. "I guess they found bones of people who died two or three million years ago. From that they figured man, as we know him, stopped acting like a monkey and started life as a man, at Koobi. In other words, he stopped acting *like* a monkey and became a man. Do you understand now?"

"I think I understand what you said, but I don't understand what you mean. Do you mean the first *real* man on earth was born at Koobi?"

"I guess you could put it that way. You see, Jonathan, many people believe man evolved from the monkey or ape. The tree the ape lived in is symbolic, and that's the tree they're talking about. From that tree the ape was supposed to have climbed down and started walking on two legs. Man is the only animal who walks upright on two legs. Do you understand now?"

Jonathan's turned his head and looked up at the thatched ceiling of the patio. He opened his mouth and pursed his lips. "Ah. . .yes." He looked over and grinned. "But apes don't live in trees. How can they come down from them?"

Gabriel slapped his shoulder, again. "You're making fun of me." Jonathan sniggered.

The night wind of Turkana had arrived on schedule, and the two warriors bent their bodies against its gale force. With each step forward they seemed to move one step backwards. They were slowed down even more by razor sharp lava dust blowing in their eyes with the fury of a hurricane, and tiny sand projectiles that ate away at their skin. The only protection they had was their blankets. They knew the wind would soon stop, but they were still too close to Loiyangalani to rest. They would have to travel well into the night, to put enough distance between them and the sergeant. Without a doubt, he would be coming for them in the morning. The rangers would be there at first light; therefore, they would have to be as far from their village as possible. Even after they reached the caves they would still have to find a suitable one to hide in; the daylight hours were not far off.

Hussein raised his head to look up at the sky, but it was forced back into the security of his blanket. The elders had once said that if one could see the stars in the Milky Way the wind would soon diminish. He had used that technique many times before while tending his goats, and it had always worked. Now, when he looked up all he could see were sheets of tan and white sand across his field of vision. He knew several hours of the stinging wind still remained.

Koobi Fora was due north of Loiyangalani, and a few miles from the eastern bank of the lake. They would have to travel around a large bay, before they could head in that direction. It would take them many hours to get there, but the rangers only a fraction of that in their Rovers, once they got started. They had to travel as far and fast as possible, before first light.

If they made it around the bay before morning without getting caught, they could hide in one of the many caves above the shoreline. However, they could only travel at night; it was too easy to be spotted during daylight hours, especially in that barren wasteland.

As if someone had closed a door, the wind suddenly died to a whisper. Hussein had always been amazed at its abruptness—one minute a gale, the next a warm summer breeze. He couldn't understand why it was so fierce around Turkana, but he guessed it had something to do with hot days and cold nights. His uncle, G'hambi, had told him it was the work of *laidetidetani* (lay-deti-de-tani), the diviner and maker of all small miracles. But he didn't believe it had anything to do with the divine or supernatural. The sisters at his school had once tried to explain their theory about the wind, but he still didn't understood. It would have been difficult to separate years of tradition from the sister's modern viewpoints, anyway.

They stopped for a few minutes to rest. Ebukut slumped down on a boulder, uncovered his head, and looked up at the stars to verify that the wind had left the area. As he waited for Hussein to catch up, he pulled the water skin from his shoulder. "Do you want a drink?" he said.

Hussein took the bag and squirted a long stream into his mouth. "I must have been thirstier than I thought."

"We'll make the cave at dove's cove by early morning," the warrior said. "There, we can rest while the rangers burn in the sun."

Hussein reached down and dislodged a stone from one of his sandal. "The cave is still several kilometers away. We may not make it before morning light. It's past midnight now."

"We'll make it," the warrior assured him. "But if not, we have our bow arrows." He patted his quiver. "And our spears."

"Arrows and spears against guns?" Hussein laughed. He could not believe he was serious. It would be foolish to fight the rangers. They would have to hide or they wouldn't stand a chance. If they were caught they would be taken back to the box and transported to jail in Nairobi, or Maralal. He realized he would also be an accomplice to the wounding of the ranger, and if caught whatever punishment Ebukut got he would also get. "We don't have any options," he told the big warrior. "We have to be at the caves by morning. There's no question about it."

Ebukut adjusted his pack, stretched his bowstring across his chest for easy access, and then honed his spear tip with a pumice stone until he could cut an acacia thorn in half.

As Hussein watched him work the stone, he started to have second thoughts. He might have been better off staying in the box. At least he wouldn't be racing across the desert in search of a place to hide, and the possibility of being caught, again.

He had known Ebukut for a long time and was fully aware of his wild streaks. The warrior would take his tribe of goats to pasture and lose some so he could go back later and search for them. It would take him and his buddies several days to track them down.

It was a rarity when Ebukut's father stayed at his hut. He spent most of his time in the village drinking with whatever he could win from the transient tribes by playing the local stick and rock game. His mother seldom scolded or reprimanded him. He was allowed to do almost anything he wanted, which was usually the opposite of what his parents and the elders wanted. He realized he would have to be careful around this warrior; he could easily get them killed.

The big warrior stood up and began trotting down the well-worn goat path. After he had traveled a few yards, he turned and motioned for Hussein to catch up. They raced down the rocky path, unmindful of the sharp turns and inclines that made it even more difficult.

The full moon had already ascended halfway across the sky and lit the path in front of them with a soft, dull glow. It was difficult for Hussein to keep up with the *lmurran's* long strides, and he would occasionally trip on sandstone ridges and fall to the ground. He would glance ahead to see if he had been noticed, then force himself back onto his feet and continue.

As the sun slowly snuck out from behind the distant crags of the Rift Valley, the horizon took on a soft glow. It rose above the earth's cool crust, and its subdued glow turned into a soft, yellow hue that made the pale, purple cast of the mountains disappear.

As he trotted beside the tall warrior, he looked up and caught a fleeting glimpse of hundreds of chalk-white doves on their way for their morning bath on the lake. He knew it was going to be another hot day. He was glad they had brought plenty of water, it would be difficult, if not impossible, to get more; they would be several hundred feet up a steep, sandy cliff.

As the sun rose above the horizon, he could see the brownish gray of the tallest sandstone wall, 500-meters away. They would be within the security of the cave soon, hidden from the rangers' searching eyes.

He had not been to the largest cave in several years and didn't know if it was still inhabitable. All caves on the cliff had been carved millions of years ago by the wind, when the lake was filled to capacity. At that time caves dotted the lake's edge, but now most were high above the waterline. He remembered the path to one particular cave; it had been extremely difficult to climb and only the strongest and healthiest would attempt it.

Ebukut broke the silence. "I'll go up first to make sure everything is all right," he said, pointing to the cave entrance high above them. "Sometimes hyenas use them as lairs, and they're not happy to share them."

Hussein watched the warrior scurry up the almost vertical incline. At first he moved with speed and agility, but as he reached the halfway point he had slowed to a snail's pace. When he finally reached the top, he was panting furiously, trying to catch his breath. After resting for a few minutes at its mouth he inspected the cave, and then motioned to Hussein.

Hussein knew he would have trouble climbing the path, the same as the last time he was there. He had trouble climbing it then, and he knew it wouldn't be any easier. By the time he started his climb the sun had already heated the sand stones beneath his hands. When he reached the top his fingers were split and bleeding from the sharp, lava rocks. It had taken him twice as long as the big warrior, but he was proud of himself for even finishing the climb.

Before going inside, he sat on an outcropping at the mouth of the cave and rested. At the entrance was a small cavern that ran at an angle 20-meters inside the cliff. There, it expanded into a much larger room; their hiding place for the day. In the center of the room lay a ring of stones forming a fireplace, which had obviously been used many times before. The stones were positioned in such a way where the flames could not be seen from the outside.

The walls of the cave had many paintings of giraffes, lions and camels. Some of the other figures were indistinguishable. He didn't believe it was the work of modern man; the ocher and blacks were too old and scarcely visible. When the reflected light of the morning sun struck the walls at the right angle, some drawings were more vivid than others.

As he strolled around the cave looking at the drawings, he said, "I have been here before, but I don't remember these paintings."

Ebukut dropped his spear and *sampur* to the uneven floor and followed his gaze. "You must have been here at night," he said.

"Yes. I remember now, it was night time," Hussein said, and kicked a few loose stones back into the fireplace. "Should we light a fire?"

"Do you want to be captured, again? The smoke might be seen."

Hussein's half-naked body shivered from the dampness in the cave. To ward off the chill he walked around the cave and looked closer at the drawings. He strolled to the mouth of the cave, looked out over the lake, and stretched his arms over his head in a yawn.

"I think you should come back inside," Ebukut yelled to him. "If the rangers are out there they might know about this cave and look for movement or smoke. They're too lazy to climb up here but they do have sharp eyes."

Hussein returned to the center of the cave and sat next to the long-dead fireplace. He opened the leather flap of his *sampur* and foraged until he had found his brother's candy. He tossed a piece into his mouth and sucked on its sweetness. He offered a piece to the warrior, but after a close inspection he refused it.

Ebukut rested his head on his *sampur*, clasped his hands behind his braided hair, and closed his eyes. "Hussein?" he said. He waited for a response that never came. "Why do you want to be a *lmurran*?" he continued. "Because you killed a lion?"

The boy glanced over. After considering the question, he answered, "All *layenis* want to be *lmurrans*. I'm no exception." He was not satisfied with his answer, but he didn't understand what the warrior really meant. It was a stupid question anyway, he thought. "You're a *lmurran*," he continued. "And I was told when you were my age you couldn't wait to be one."

The warrior hesitated. He rolled onto his side into a more comfortable position. "It's been a long time since I was your age. But in those days it was the thing to do." He took in a deep breath and exhaled. "But today…today there are many other things for you to do with your life…better things."

"Such as?"

"Such as finishing the white man's school. After that you could leave Loiyangalani to make something of yourself, like your friend Paul did." He propped his head up on his hand and stared across the fire pit at the boy. "Do you really want to be a warrior? Tell me truthfully."

Hussein couldn't believe what he was hearing. All the years he had known Ebukut he had been the personification of a warrior to all children of the village. They looked up to him because of his bravery, tenacity and fearlessness. But now he nearly sounded envious.

"I don't know," he answered. "I guess I thought if I became a *lmurran* it would automatically make me like you and the other warriors. Every young boy in the village wants to be like you. Especially when we see you go into the desert to hunt. We know you're using the skills taught by our ancestors." He picked up a stick and stirred the dead ashes.

Ebukut looked over and grinned. "So, you envy us when we go into the great desert to hunt the ferocious lion, the cunning jackal, the fleeting deer, and the wild pig?" He tilted his head back in raucous laughter. Puzzled, Hussein stared at him,. "Do you know what we do when we go on our hunting trips? You didn't know this but we find a nice spot in the hills where nobody will find us and get drunk. Drunk as *milikas*." He roared with laughter until it was difficult to catch his breath, and then lowered his head onto his *sampur*. "So you see, young *lmurran*, it isn't always as it seems."

Hussein frowned. It was hard to believe what he had just heard. Nonetheless, his lips fashioned a grin. "You really did that? You're not joking?" Without answering, the big warrior rolled onto his back, still snickering.

Chapter Eight

Gabriel cleared his breakfast tables and tossed the remaining breadcrumbs to the weaverbirds nested in the nearby acacia bushes. On his way to the kitchen he glanced into the lounge and saw Eric Somerville having coffee at the bar. He thought it strange he had not been at his breakfast table, but he dismissed it as unimportant. He had seen him board the same plane as Paul, when it left for Nairobi. He must know where his friend is, he thought. He might deliver Hussein's message. He would ask.

"Mister Somerville, could I please speak to you for a moment," he said, walking across the lounge toward him. He scanned the room for anyone who might overhear him.

Dan had been sitting next to Eric and moved down to the end of the bar. He eyed the boy and then returned to sipping his coffee.

"Yes, of course," Eric said. "Is something wrong?" He hesitated, indicating he could not remember the boy's name.

"Gabriel, sir."

"Of course, forgive me. It's been some time since you were my waiter. What can I do for you, son?" Sensing the boy wanted privacy he took him by the arm and walked him from the bar to a secluded spot on the small patio.

Gabriel scrutinized the lounge again, and then said, "It's Paul, sir. I have to get a message to him. Do you know where he is in Nairobi?"

Eric gave him a blank stare. "Yes. I know exactly where he is. At least I think he's still there. Why? What's so important that you have to get a message to him? It's difficult from here, you know."

"Yes sir, I know how hard it is. But please try." He looked down at the floor and kicked the tufting of the aging Persian rug that ran under several rattan chairs. "His friend, Hussein, is in trouble. I think he should know."

"Hussein?" Eric said, suddenly becoming interested. "Isn't that the boy who killed the lion?"

"Yes, sir. His friend broke him out of the box last night...the one who speared the ranger. Now, they're both on the run and need help. The rangers are after them and they don't know what to do except run." He took in a long, deep breath and exhaled.

"Freed him from the box?" Eric questioned with a scowl. "What box? Who speared a ranger? What are you talking about, son?" He walked back to the bar to get his coffee. When he returned he said, "Where are the boys now? Maybe I can help."

Gabriel thought for a moment. He didn't believe they had arrived at the destination Hussein told him, at least not yet. It would take them several days to get there. But he believed he knew where they would be hiding. He had no other choice but to trust the man.

"I'll explain everything later, sir," he said, almost inaudibly. He didn't want to be overheard in the lounge. "But I think they're on their way to Koobi Fora."

"Koobi Fora!" Eric said, loud enough for Dan to turn and look at him. "Do you know how far that is from here? Do you have any idea how long it would take them to get there on foot?" He stared into the boy's eyes and took a sip from his cup. "They *are* on foot, aren't they?"

"Yes, sir. They left last night, about eight or nine."

"Where do you think they are now?" Eric held his wristwatch up to the dim light. "It's almost eight now. How far can they get in twelve hours?"

"Will you try to get the message to Paul, sir?" Gabriel asked, an edge to his voice.

"Do you want me to help your friends or not?" Eric shot back. His face flushed. He stared angrily into the boy's eyes, shifted his weight, and continued. "Let's suppose I could get a message to him. What then? He couldn't get here from Nairobi. And even if he could, what could he do? He might join them and be hunted along with them. Is that what you want?"

Gabriel could see the anger in Somerville's face and regretted getting him involved. But it was too late. He would have to tell him everything and hope for the best for his friends.

Eric took a deep breath and the redness on his face vanished. He took Gabriel by the arm. "Look, son," he said. "I know you want to do what you think is best, but believe me I can be of more help to your friends than Paul. Please, tell me where they are."

Again, Gabriel looked around the bar. "Have you seen any rangers in here this morning, sir?" he asked.

"No!" Eric returned in a firm voice. "Will you please tell me where the boys are, and what's going on? Or do I have to look for them myself without your help?"

Ignoring the question, Gabriel said, "The rangers will be here soon and they'll be hunting for them."

"Gabriel!" Eric shouted. His face again turned crimson. "Why don't you tell me the whole story? What happened here yesterday? I think I'm entitled to know everything, if I'm getting myself involved in something I might regret."

Gabriel shifted his weight from one foot to the other, as he relayed everything he knew about the events leading up to the present. The moment he had finished his account, Kurt Versteeg walked into the bar. The boy's body immediately stiffened. Kurt smiled and winked at Eric as he went by. Gabriel glanced into the dining room where he knew he should be.

"I must go back to work, Mr. Somerville," he whispered. "I will talk to you more when Mr. Versteeg is not around."

As Gabriel turned to leave, Eric caught him by the arm and pulled him back. His rubber-soled sandals squeaked noisily on the parquet tiles and Kurt and Dan both turned around when they heard the sound.

"Not so fast, damn it!" he shouted into the boy's face. He glanced over at Kurt, and then continued in a whisper. "Tell me where you think they might be. I can help. Trust me."

"I believe they're in one of the caves on the east side of the lake," the boy whispered. "Straight across the lake from here."

"But which cave? There must be a hundred over there."

"I don't know which one, sir," Gabriel said. "I'm just guessing that's where they are, anyway. It's logical they would go there."

Eric released his grip. "We'll find them, don't worry," he said. "I won't let anything happen to Hussein, that's for sure. I owe him that much." He patted the boy on the shoulder as he started to leave, and then called after him loud enough for Kurt to hear, "I'll take your luncheon suggestion, Gabriel, the Nile perch steamed in curry sounds good to me." The boy turned and grinned.

"What was that all about?" Dan asked, as he took a sip of the robust

Kenyan coffee and made a face. "And don't tell me it was about the luncheon menu."

Eric watched Gabriel until he had disappeared into the kitchen, and then joined Dan at the bar and ordered a full pot of coffee. He turned his eyes on Kurt, sitting in his favorite seat at the end of the bar stirring coffee. "Hey Kurt, hear you had some excitement here yesterday," he said with a grin.

"What do you mean? What did you hear? Nothing much happened."

"Oh, come on," Somerville came back, "the grapevine has it the rangers put a boy in the box out back, last night. Is that right?" He poured a cup of coffee and set it down on the counter. "Grapevine also has it somebody broke him out." He poured half a can of condensed milk into his cup and stirred it.

"That so?" Kurt replied with smugness in his voice. "Did the grapevine also tell you those boys killed a couple lions? Which happens to be against the law in Kenya. And did it tell you one of them speared a ranger and that he might die?"

"Come on, Kurt. Sure, it's against the law to kill lions if you're going to capitalize on it, but I know of at least one killed in self-defense. And I'll bet the boy who speared the ranger did it in self-defense, too. Besides, I imagine he had it coming, knowing the rangers as I do. I'm sure both boys had good reasons for their actions."

Dan's eyes darted back and forth as the two men fenced. "What the hell's going on, Eric?" he said, when there was a break in the conversation. "Where did you pick up that stuff? The boy there?" He pointed to the dining room.

"Did Gabriel tell you about the boys?" Kurt asked in a commanding tone.

"Keep him out of this," Eric said, raising his voice. "I did ask him. But I also asked some of the other boys. All of them were aware of what went on here last night." He took a sip of coffee, made a face, and stirred in three lumps of sugar. He had lied about speaking to the other boys, but he didn't want to get Gabriel in trouble with Kurt. "Have there been any rangers here since last night?" he continued. "And oh, by the way, how did Mandeli take it when he found out his guard let somebody break the kid out of the box?"

Kurt grinned. "He doesn't know yet. I told the guard he better not hang around and wait for old skinny to get back, if he knows what's good for him. He left in a hurry. Don't think we'll be seeing much of him anymore."

"What the hell's going on, Eric?" Dan demanded. "You going to fill me in or what?"

"I'll tell you all about it later, on our way to Koobi For a. You've got just enough time to finish your coffee."

"Koobi Fora!" Dan protested. "There's nothing in that neck of the woods but camels and lizards. And oh, by the way, it's hot as hell up there, you know."

"I know. Life's a bitch, ain't it?" Eric slid his empty cup across the counter and turned to face Kurt. "You'll keep this under your hat, won't you? I mean about Koobi Fora. Wouldn't want the wrong people to get wind of it. You know what I mean?"

"Certainly."

"By the way, may I use your transceiver for a few minutes? I understand cell phones won't work up here."

"Of course. But I must warn you it's on a secure network and monitored by the park and game. I'd be careful what I said, if I were you."

"You're a peach," Eric said with a grin. He patted him on the back and left with Dan.

Paul raised his head from the blanket he had thrown on the floor for the night. He looked around the room, yawned, and threw it back on the bed. He had tried to use the bed but it was too soft. Also, his head sank too deep in the large pillow and made it difficult to breathe.

The window on the fifth floor overlooked one of the main boulevards of Nairobi. He walked out onto the iron balcony and surveyed the street far below. Although it was still early, the city swarmed with traffic. Aromas from a multitude of food vendors wafted up from the street, adding to his hunger. He thought about the food he had eaten in the restaurant the previous day and was anxious to return.

He took the key from the nightstand, left the room and slammed the door behind him. He walked down the hallway to the elevator and waited for the door to open. He noticed colored buttons on a panel beside the door but didn't associate them with anything of any importance. He stood waiting anxiously for it to open, not knowing what else to do.

A white couple came down the hallway and stopped beside him. They noticed none of the buttons had been pushed so the tall man reached over and hit the down button. Paul glanced up at him and smiled.

The man smiled back. "You going down, son?"

"Yes, sir," Paul replied. "I'm going to the restaurant."

"Oh, that's nice," the woman said with a smile and a quick peek over the tops of her jewel-studded glasses.

Paul glanced at her silver-blue hair. She must belong to a tribe in America that dyes their hair blue like some of their chiefs, he thought. Several strands of colored glass beads hung around her neck and from her ears dangled elongated slivers of glass that swayed back and forth when she moved. She must be of nobility, to wear so many beads and jewels. The elevator door slid open and they entered and the downward plunge began.

After a brief, stomach-lurching ride, the elevator stopped at the lobby floor and the door swished open. Paul remained in the back of the pod while the Americans exited. After they had left he made his way to the open door, but before he could get through it slid shut, trapping him inside. His mind raced with thoughts of being swallowed alive by that metal monster. He tapped on the door but nothing happened. He threw his fists against it, still nothing.

The monster made a sucking sound and shot upwards. He threw his body flat against the wall and closed his eyes. Where was it taking him now? He wondered. Who was in control of this thing? Without warning, it stopped and the door slid open. Before he could dash through, two people entered and pushed one of the buttons on the lighted panel in front of him. The monster raced back down. Once again, his stomach was being forced into his throat. With a sudden lurch the elevator stopped and his knees buckled.

The door opened and the couple walked into the lobby. The restaurant was visible from inside the monster but he was afraid to walk through its mouth and be caught in its gaping lips. He edged toward the door, desperate to get out before it closed again. Halfway through, the door closed pinning him between its rubber lips. He opened his mouth to yell, but nothing would come out. Without warning, it slid open and he lunged for the safety of the marble floor.

Carl caught Paul's dilemma out of the corner of his eye and his lips curled up in a slight grin. "Hey, boy," he shouted across the vast, glittering lobby.

Paul turned and looked over. When he noticed Carl staring at him, he pointed his finger at his chest, raised his eyebrows, and placed an animated question mark on his face.

"Yes, you, boy," Carl barked. "Come here, I have a message for you." His face was stern and unsmiling. Paul skated across the polished floor on the heels of his *kiatus*. Carl glared at him, shoved an envelope across the counter, and then returned to his duties.

Paul opened the envelope and read: "Paul, Gabriel wants you to know that Hussein and another of your friends are in trouble with the rangers. They are all right for the time being, but Dan and I are on our way to help them. Don't worry they will be okay. Eric."

He walked to a nearby chair and sat down to read the message again. He had learned to speak English well but his reading ability left a lot to be desired. Furthermore, it looked as if someone who could not write any better than he could read had written it. He returned to the counter where Carl was busy thumbing through some papers.

"Sir," he said.

Carl didn't look up.

He repeated his query even louder, "Sir!"

Carl looked up. When he saw Paul he lowered his eyes back to his paperwork. "Yes, boy. What is it?"

Paul detected irritation in his voice, but continued. "Sir, when did you get this message?"

The manager paused for a moment. "It was here when I came on duty, about an hour ago. I don't know how long it's been here. Why?" He lifted his eyes to stare at Paul.

"I was just wondering, sir. Do you think it came in this morning…or last night?"

"Why do I have to answer so many questions, boy?" the manager said, irritably. "I'm busy. Don't bother me with questions I can't answer. Now please go away, I have work to do."

Sensing the shortness in the man's voice, Paul walked across the gleaming floor to the restaurant. It might help him think if he had food in his stomach, he rationalized.

The waiter he had the night before met him at the door. "Hi there," he said, with a smile. "Where is your American friend?" He took Paul by the arm. "Come on, I'll get you a good seat over by the window."

"Thank you," Paul replied. "Mister Somerville is at Lake Turkana. He will return soon."

"Turkana?" the waiter questioned. "There's nothing up there but goats, acacia trees, and old bones."

"Yes, I know. That's where I live," Paul said, with a comical grin.

The waiter smiled. "Sorry, I didn't mean anything bad." He pulled the chair back from the table.

"It doesn't bother me," Paul returned. "You're right though, there is nothing up there but desert and goats." As an afterthought, he added, "And lions."

"Lions?" the young boy questioned. "I've never heard of lions that far north." He turned and left. Moments later he returned with a glass of ice water. "You *are* joking about the lions, right?"

Paul picked up the menu and turned it over to the English side. "I do not lie," he said. "We killed one close to my *manyatta*. Don't tell me there are no lions at Turkana."

"Sorry, I didn't mean you were lying," the boy said. "I only meant it's the first time I ever heard of a lion being that far north. Like the leopard on Mount Kilimanjaro."

Paul thought for a moment. "I do not know about this leopard." He knew of Kilimanjaro, but he didn't know how it could possibly have anything to do with a leopard, or a lion at Turkana. He would have to find out about it, later. But he could have been joking, he thought.

"That's all right," the boy said with a snicker. "What do you want to eat? You can go up to the breakfast bar or I can bring you something. Whatever you want." He stood beside him and waited; there were only a few people in the restaurant at that early hour.

"I will have the American hamburger with the long potatoes," Paul said and handed him the menu.

"For breakfast you want a hamburger?" the waiter questioned with a grin. He shook his head and left for the kitchen.

Paul leaned back in his chair and looked out the window. He glanced up and down the same sidewalk he had been on before and saw what looked like the same people. It was hard to believe there were so many people in Nairobi; he had not seen that many in all his life.

Yesterday, his mind had reeled at the number of items displayed in the shops and the prices being asked for them. Back in his village he could have bartered for the same things with a goatskin. He stood up to get a better look at the people on the street below him. He noticed a man with a long, deep scar at his hairline. "Christopher!" he said aloud. He reached over to tap on the window, then thought against it and drew back. What was he doing here? He wondered. He had said he and his brother were leaving for Mombasa, since he now had enough money.

Paul watched as Christopher approached two tourists. His mouth worked fast and his facial expressions changed every few seconds. His hands thrashed the air as he spoke. After a few minutes he pulled out a small, empty vial. The woman took it in her hand and inspected it. Paul could see the expressions on her face, as he continued his plea. The older man put his hand in his pocket, as if debating whether to give him money. The woman fumbled around in an embossed shopping bag, apparently searching for something. The man put a hand on Christopher's shoulder, pulled several bills from his pocket and handed them to him. The woman retrieved a handkerchief from her bag and wiped tears from her eyes. They shook hands and the couple left. Halfway down the sidewalk they turned and waved as they crossed the street.

Christopher pulled out a thick roll of shillings, wrapped the new bills around them, and tied the wad with a rubber band. He smiled and continued on down the sidewalk.

"Hey, kid. Here's your burger," the waiter said, tapping him on the shoulder. "What were you looking at?"

Paul seemed startled by his voice and spun around. When he saw it was the waiter, he said, "That man with the scar on his forehead. See him there?" He pointed.

The boy strained his eyes. "Oh, him," he said with a grin and a giggle. "The man with the scar on his head? Yes, he's out there every day. He sure takes the tourists for a shilling or two." He put the food down and stood beside Paul. "By the way, if you're going to be around for a while, my name's Hectar. What's yours?"

"Hectar?" Paul mouthed the letters in an attempt to pronounce the name. "That is a strange name." He looked up and added, "But I like it. My Christian name is Paul, but my tribal name is L'hari."

"I don't have a tribal name," Hectar said and looked up thoughtfully at the ceiling. "I guess I was born into too much civilization. But my tribe is Kikuyu, if that means anything, anymore."

Paul glanced up, puzzled at his comment. "You don't have a tribal name?"

"No, I was born here in Nairobi, and so was my father. I guess they gave up years ago on tribal names." His looked out the window. "Sometimes I wish I had a tribal name…or something I could associate with. My tribe is still here, but they're too civilized. There's nothing of the 'old' left…unless you go way back into the hills. There, you might find a few people who still live the way they used to. I've often wondered what it would be like to live in a hut, hunt for your food…live off the fat of the land, so to speak." He stared out the window, deep in thought, then glanced down at the table. "So, you're from Turkana? Which tribe, the Turkana?"

"No. My tribe is Samburu. We are brothers of the Masai."

"Yes, I know of your tribe. They're from up north, somewhere around—"

"Turkana," they both said in unison.

While Hectar waited on another customer, Paul devoured his hamburger. He had discovered what he suspected all along; Christopher had taken his money by deception. He must have lied about everything, he thought. There was nothing he could do about it now, but he had learned a hard lesson, one he would not soon forget.

His thoughts shifted to Hussein and Loiyangalani. Even if he wanted to return to that parched land to help him, he didn't have the slightest idea how to get there. In the first place, the airport was too far from Nairobi. Even if he could get to the airport, he didn't know how he could get back on the plane. If Hussein was in trouble he wanted to help. But there was no way he could do anything from Nairobi. Mister Somerville had said in the message he would help Hussein, but he also wanted to help.

Maybe coming to Nairobi wasn't such a good idea after all. He should have waited until he was a little older. By then he would have learned more about the people who lived there.

Mister Somerville had told him he could stay at the hotel as long as he wanted, but that was no good, he would not be on his own, as he had planned. Moreover, after talking to Christopher it was apparent he would not find a job. He would have to depend on Somerville, and he didn't like that thought at all. He would not try to look for a job here the people were too deceitful. After being disillusioned by Christopher, he felt that others would cheat him if he worked for them. Nothing seemed bearable to him.

He closed his eyes and his mind transported him high above the clouds. His thoughts took him over the fields of maize and sugar cane, and the vegetable gardens he had been so impressed with on his way to Nairobi. His mind's eye delivered him to the northern desert of Turkana where he could see his village and the palm trees of the fishing club. It took him to the hot, mineral pools where Gabriel brought him food and drink.

He realized he might have been too impulsive. He should not have left his *manyatta* and his friends. Was the killing of the lion the real reason he left? Maybe he only used that as an excuse. He was not certain. He could not forget the weight his heart had carried that day in the village.

"Paul. Paul," Hectar repeated several times. "Where are your thoughts? You seem miles away."

Paul looked up. "They're in Turkana, where I wish I was right now."

"How long will you be in Nairobi? You never did say."

"I must wait for Mr. Somerville to return," Paul said. "I have no other way to get home." He looked down at the empty plate. Suddenly, a thought came over him and his eyes widened. "I have a friend here in

Nairobi named William. He's at a doctor's office. He was hurt."

"Do you know which doctor?"

Paul moved his hand back and forth across his forehead, trying to remember the name. "It was something like. . .Singer. . .or Kissinger, or—" He put both hands on his forehead.

"Was it Kensinger?" Hectar interrupted his thoughts. "He treats people in trouble." Then he added, quickly, "Of course, I'm not saying your friend is in trouble, but they would take him there if he were."

"Do you know how to get to that doctor's place?" Paul asked.

"Yes. I'll take you there when I get off work, in about an hour," the boy said. He put his hand on Paul's shoulder. "His office isn't far. Do you think this friend will help you get home?"

"I don't know, I can only hope." Paul got up from the table, and before he walked away, he added, "I can see now Nairobi is not such a good place for me. I guess I didn't give it much of a chance, but I've seen enough. I couldn't live here. I must go back to my village and live like a Samburu. My friend is in trouble and I wouldn't be a good friend if I didn't try to help him." He held out his hand. "I'll be back in one hour. I would like you to help me find this doctor."

"You got it, pal," Hectar said, slapping his outstretched palm.

Chapter Nine

Dan pulled the Rover to the side of the road, grabbed a pair of binoculars from the glove compartment, and jumped to the ground. As he surveyed the route they had traveled earlier, he noticed a thin line of dust billowing from behind a fast moving vehicle. It veered off the road and headed toward them. He tossed the glasses onto the dash and swung back behind the wheel.

"I think we've got company," he said. He put the Rover in low and pressed down hard on the gas.

"Rangers?" Eric asked.

"I think so, it's a blue truck. Besides, who else would be out here in all this damned heat?"

"Us. Is there only one?"

"As far as I can tell. But that doesn't mean there won't be more coming."

"Can you tell how many men are in it?"

"No, it's just a blur from here."

Dan remained silent, while he manhandled the truck down the rutted path. An occasional boulder prompted Eric to wince and grab his injured arm. Ten minutes later, Dan stopped again and jumped onto the hood to check on the progress of the blue truck. "They're catching up," he said.

"God, they must have soft seats in that thing!"

Eric grabbed the binoculars and trained them on the path ahead of them. About a kilometer away, he spotted two figures dressed in tribal red. From that distance he could not tell if they were the boys, however it was obvious to him they were warriors. He reached around the windshield and tugged on Dan's pant leg.

"Let's go. I got an idea," he said. "Get closer to those two men."

Dan started the Rover and headed toward the two figures. When they got closer they discovered it was not the boys but two other warriors dressed in their traditional attire. Dan stopped the truck and the two men approached.

"*Jambo*," said the toothless one, and leaned up against the side of the Rover.

"*Habari gani*?" said the taller one, and then moved into the shade of the truck.

Eric opened the door and with a forced smile, said, "*Jambo sana*." After the salutations, he took two 10-shilling notes from his pocket and dangled them in front of their faces. "This fellow have two *kumis*," he said in English. "You ride in Rover...two *kumis*? One for you." He pointed at the toothless man, and then moved his finger to the taller man. "And one for you."

They eyed the shillings with interest, and then turned from the truck and babbled back and forth in Swahili. With a tobacco-stained grin, the toothless one held up two fingers.

"You got twenty more shillings on you, Dan?" Eric asked.

Dan handed the bills to the warriors. "*Karibu. Ketini*," he said. The warriors hopped in and they sped down the goat path. "What do you have in mind, Eric?"

"Let's have a little fun with the rangers. Slow down and let them get to within a couple kilometers, to where they can barely make us out with their binoculars. Then, we'll lead them on a wild goose chase."

The truck dodged boulder after boulder, and forced Eric and the warriors to hold onto the handles above the doors.

Dan's eyes widened. "Of course," he shouted over the noise of the road. "It finally sunk into this thick head of mine. That's clever. Make 'em think these are the boys they're after. Right?" He drove to the highest point that overlooked the lake and stopped. After instructing the warriors to sit tight, he picked up his binoculars and searched for the ranger's vehicle. He caught sight of the truck several kilometers back, but coming on strong.

"We'll wait here for a couple minutes," he said. "Here, they can see us with their binoculars." He jumped down from the truck and pulled out a pack of cigarettes. "Have an American smoke," he told Eric, holding them out in front of him.

Eric refused, but joined him outside the truck.

The morning sun had become nearly unbearable in the cab, but the warriors didn't seem to mind. Nonetheless, within a few minutes the heat got too intense and they climbed out.

Dan kept his glasses trained on the fast approaching vehicle. After he had finished his cigarette, he swung back into the driver's seat.

Eric followed but not before he had an animated chat with the warriors to make them return to the truck.

"I'm sure they saw us," Dan said. "They stopped and pointed their glasses in our direction, then took off like a bat out of hell. Now for some fun."

From their vantage point on the crest of a hill, they could see the caves no more than two or three kilometers to the north. Dan turned the vehicle around and headed south. He made as much dust as possible; to make sure the rangers saw them.

He continued south for about five kilometers, and then turned west toward the club. He figured the rangers would anticipate their move and take a shortcut to cut them off before they got there. When the rangers went south on the anticipated ambush course, Dan turned around and headed back up north. By the time the rangers had discovered Dan's ploy, and stopped to turn around, their prey was too far away for them to chase it.

Mandeli leaped onto the hood of the canvas-topped truck and trained his binoculars on the distant Rover. He could do no more than watch, as it increased its distance between them. In a fit of rage, he cursed and stomped up and down on the heavy metal hood, forcing it down to the engine compartment. His prey was several kilometers away and moving fast. He jumped down from the hood and watched, as it disappeared in a cloud of dust. He squinted into the subdued light. He had lost this round, but he knew there would be others.

He was now convinced Somerville had something to do with the escape of the two boys. He had no choice but to go back to the club and wait. He was certain the American could not take the boys any place he did not know about. Again he stared into the distance but saw no more than a thin trail of dust.

"When I catch him, a few days in the box will soften him up," he mumbled angrily. At that point, he wanted the American even more than the boys. That time he lost the opportunity, but he figured it would come again.

He had no idea where Somerville was taking the boys, but he thought it strange they were headed north. Nothing was up there but heat, lizards and dryness. He figured the American had to have a plan, or he would not be taking them in that direction.

He swung back into the truck and turned a pair of menacing eyes on his driver. "Go back to the fishing club," he bellowed. "We'll wait for them there."

Within an hour, they had arrived back at the compound. After a brief but fruitless conversation with Kirinyaga, the driver parked the truck, and Mandeli hurried into the lounge.

When he entered, Kurt was chatting with one of his guests. He glanced over briefly, and then continued his conversation.

"I want to speak to you, Versteeg," Mandeli interrupted, using Kurt's last name to add emphasis to his demand.

Kurt looked over but didn't acknowledge him. He turned his back on the sergeant and continued with his conversation.

Mandeli threw him a contemptuous glare. "Now! If you please!" he shouted across the room filled with tourists.

Kurt excused himself and walked over. "What is it?" he snapped. "Couldn't you have at least waited until I finished my conversation with my guests?"

"No!" the ranger shot back. "I'm afraid I couldn't. This is important…it's official business." Kurt took a deep breath and released it in a long sigh.

Mandeli turned and whispered to his driver, a small, pudgy man outfitted in a uniform too small for his body. The man shook his head and left. He turned around and eyed Kurt.

"It appears there was an escape here last night," he said with a voice loud enough to be heard across the room. "What do you know about it?"

"No more than you," Kurt replied. "Your guard was in the bar getting drunk, and the kid got out. That's all I know."

"Where's the guard now?"

"I haven't the faintest. But I don't think I'd have stuck around either, if I were him."

"Why didn't you inform me of the boy's escape, last night?"

"If you didn't already know," Kurt said with a smirk, "why were you on the other side of the lake this afternoon trying to track him down?" He thought for a moment and then added, "Also, if you didn't know, how did you know which direction to go?"

"Don't get yourself involved, Versteeg," the sergeant fired back. "It's no concern of yours."

Kurt's face flushed red. His eyes narrowed and his jaws tightened. "And another thing, sergeant," he shouted in his face, "you have no authority in this club, and you know it. You're not the police, so get off my case!"

Mandeli glared at him. "I have the right," he snarled. "If I find someone doing harm to our wildlife, I have the authority to do whatever is necessary to resolve the situation, and that includes jail. And you could go there yourself for letting the boy escape. They call it obstruction of justice."

"You stupid ass!" Kurt bellowed. "You know very well your man is responsible for his escape. Don't try to pin that crap on me…or Somerville." The bar drew silent, as the two men sparred back and forth.

Mandeli's driver returned. He hesitated for a moment at the end of the bar, as if mustering enough courage to intervene. After a few moments, he gently pushed the two men apart and stepped between them. He stood on his toes and whispered into the sergeant's ear.

Mandeli lowered his stare long enough to acknowledge. "Is that what he said? The caves?" He said it loud enough to be overheard. He shoved his driver toward the door. "Get back in the truck. I'll be there in a minute." The driver turned and left.

Kurt didn't know how far he could push the sergeant; there was no set rule. On a few occasions, Mandeli had been given full authority over everything, including criminal justice. But the power had never been permanent and he knew he resented it. His main function was to keep poaching at a minimum.

However, not knowing the rule-of-the-day, he figured he better think twice about pressing his luck. Not too long ago the sergeant had been authorized to go onto the fishing club's property whenever he deemed it necessary, and that annoyed Kurt to no end. He was forced to bring his grievances to the officials in Nairobi. But it did no good, it never had.

Mandeli shot him a formidable look and unlocked his set jaws. "I'm going now," he said, with a sneer, "but I won't forget this conversation." He glared at him once more, spun his tall frame around, and headed for the door. When he arrived at the truck, he questioned his driver. "Did the boy say which cave?"

"No, sir. But he did say there was another warrior with him, one who used to go to the highest caves all the time. That should pin it down."

"That may explain why we saw two *lmurrans* in Somerville's Rover today," Mandeli said, as he slid his tall frame onto the seat. "However, I think it was a trick. I'm sure of it now. The ones we saw in his truck were not the ones we're after." He looked through the windshield at the stars that had just become visible, then back at Joseph. "I went to those caves myself, when I was young. There are as many high ones as there are low. Too many!" He distorted his face in disgust.

"Are we going out there, tonight?" Joseph asked.

"Why not? Are you afraid of the dark?"

"No, sir, it's not that. But how can we search for them at night?"

"Have you ever heard of flashlights?" Mandeli snapped. "Of course we're not going out there tonight, you idiot. Head for the barracks. We'll leave first thing in the morning." Joseph didn't answer, as he swung the truck around and headed for the main gate of the compound.

Mandeli glanced over at his driver. He knew Joseph no longer had a stomach for this job. Years ago, when there were many poachers, he seemed to enjoy what they were doing. But not long ago he had confessed to him that all they did now was chase kids and harass tribesmen who shot an occasional animal to put food on their tables. He should have been mad at him for thinking that way but he was not, it was true.

Joseph had also told him he didn't like the idea of following him around when he went on his personal vendettas. He said he didn't relish the thought of getting a spear in his back. He knew Joseph was only driving for him because it meant a few extra shillings in his paycheck. He smiled, knowing no one else would have even considered the job.

As the cape of darkness spread out across the land, the moon's glow manufactured millions of white caps across the lake. The Milky Way suddenly appeared and spread its trillions of stars in a swath across the ebony sky. However, the night had come too soon for the warriors. They would only have a brief respite, before they would have to move farther north.

Realizing that flames and smoke were not visible in the high caves at night, Hussein lit a fire deep within the cave, where he knew it would be safe from prying eyes; the rangers would not look for them at night.

Nonetheless, to be on the safe side they would travel when it was darkest.

Hussein rested his head on his *sampur,* and eyed the smoky ceiling. His mind became flooded with images of their dilemma. For one thing, he could not figure out why Ebukut had rescued him from the box. He would have been more than willing to stay and let the officials pass judgment on him. Now, because of his escape, they would treat him even worse when they caught him, and he knew they would. Nevertheless, he had no one to blame but himself. In addition, it was too late to turn back.

A few desert bats flitted about in the darkness of the cave, trying to find places to suspend themselves that was far enough from the fire for safety but close enough for warmth. Their red eyes, highlighted by the flickering flames, made the blackness of the cave appear demonic.

Ebukut had found a spot far enough from the eye-smarting smoke that it would not bother him. His occasional grunts indicated he was asleep and oblivious to the problems they faced.

Hussein knew there was nothing to worry about that night, but there were not many places to hide going north. If they traveled at night they would have to find places to hide during the day to get relief from the heat and avoid detection. That would not be easy in the desert.

As tired as he was, he could not close his eyes. He got up, walked to the cave's entrance and glanced up at the heavens. The brilliant moon had spread a soft blanket across the desert to the south, and the brightness of the Milky Way was reflected off the calm, emerald water of the lake. It was time to go. Although the moon was exceptionally bright, it was dark enough to travel. They would have six or seven hours, before the sun came up and forced them to find another hiding place.

As he turned to go back into the cave, he bumped into the warrior's large frame. He had his spear in his hand and his *sampur* slung over his shoulder.

"It's time to go," Ebukut said. "We've been here too long. It's late. We can cover much distance in the moonlight."

Hussein rushed back into the bowels of the cave, picked up his belongings, and followed him over the lip of the cliff. He watched with envy as the warrior scampered down the steep incline ahead of him. He had only made it halfway down, by the time the warrior had reached the bottom.

As he slid down the steep slope, the jagged rocks and course sandstones cut into his hands. He had nearly made it down when he wrenched his ankle under a flat rock and slid the rest of the way down on his butt. He landed at Ebukut's feet, with a sheepish grin on his face.

"You okay?" the warrior asked. "You didn't break anything?"

"No. I don't think anything's broken," Hussein said, and felt his ankle. "Maybe somewhat bent. But I can walk." When he stood and put pressure on the injury, he winced. He found a nearby boulder and sat. "It'll be all right. Give me a couple minutes."

"A minute. No longer," Ebukut said and walked behind a mound to relieve his bladder. From his privacy he called out, "If you need a stick to help you walk I'll get you one."

"No. I think it would be better if I walked it off. Give me another minute." After several minutes he put pressure on his ankle by standing and walking on it. It felt better and they continued their final descent to the desert floor.

They had traveled less than a mile when they noticed headlights in the distance. Their hearts pounded. They darted from boulder to boulder to avoid being seen, but the vehicle was quickly shortening the distance between them. They had no place to run. They couldn't go back the way they had come, and they couldn't go north without being seen; the terrain was wide open. The only direction left was toward the lake, but they didn't want to be cornered by the cliffs and have no way to escape. They cowered behind a large sandstone boulder.

The vehicle came within 50-meters of their hiding place and stopped. A voice rang out, "Hussein!" It was clear and loud.

Hussein squinted his eyes, but was unable to penetrate the darkness. All he could see were two beams of light pointed directly at them.

"Who is it?" Ebukut whispered.

"It must be the rangers." Hussein's face turned ashen and his heart skipped. "But the voice did say Hussein, not Usitani."

The loud, metallic buzz of a horn sounded. The same voice rang out, "Hussein, do you hear me? I know you're out there somewhere. This is Eric, Eric Somerville. I have to talk to you. I can help you guys. Please answer." He honked the horn several more times, but only silence prevailed.

Eric was about to ask Dan to turn the truck around and head north to continue their search, when in the glare of the headlights he spotted a slight movement behind one of the boulders. He called out, "Hussein, is that you? If it is, come toward the lights. We want to help you and your friend. Trust us. We know what happened and we're on your side." The clucking of a night-foraging desert grouse was the only sound in the darkness.

Several minutes past, before the headlights picked up two figures with hunting spears walking toward them, the ocher in their headdresses reflecting the light of the sealed-beams.

"Hussein," Eric shouted, and walked toward them. "I didn't think I was ever going to get a chance to thank you for saving my life." He held out his hand and smiled.

"Mister Somerville," Hussein said, and reached for his hand. "We thought you were rangers." He smiled and released his grip. "I thought you were in Nairobi. How is your arm? I hope it's better."

When Ebukut was introduced he looked into Eric's eyes then down at his outstretched hand, but made no effort to shake it. He shifted his weight and leaned on the shaft of his spear.

"Ebukut saved my life from a lion, too," Hussein said.

"Is that true?" Eric said. He glanced over at the warrior. "Then I'm honored to have not one but two great warriors with me."

Hussein started to translate but stopped when he realized the warrior understood. To his knowledge, Ebukut had never been complimented by a white man and didn't know how to react to it. He had told him before that all white men's words were insincere. Although he didn't understand English well, he could pick out the main topic of a conversation, and from that draw his own conclusion. Hussein believed he would weigh Eric's words and if they rang true he would be his friend.

As they walked back to the Rover, Eric relayed everything that had happened. When they arrived the boys were introduced to Dan. Hussein laughed when they told him about the warriors they bartered with to fool the rangers. After recounting the events of the day, everyone got into the truck and Dan pointed it north toward Koobi Fora.

"I have friends at the diggings," Eric told them. "You'll be safe there. The rangers won't bother you. They know the diggings are sanctioned by the government."

"I do not know that word," Hussein said with a frown.

"The government gave them permission to dig for bones," Eric explained.

Hussein's eyes widened. "I have heard it is human bones they are digging for," he said. "Maybe my ancestors."

"Yes, it is," Eric said, and looked over at Dan and winked. "They've found bones at the site that are millions of years old. It's possible they're the bones of the first humans on earth. Koobi could be where our ancestors came from."

Hussein thought for a moment. "Then because we also live here," he said, carefully analyzing his statement, "it could have been my ancestors that were the first people on earth?"

"I'm afraid it's not quite that simple, but yes, I guess you could say that," Eric replied.

Hussein frowned. "If this is true, and we *all* came from here, why am I black and you are white?"

Dan looked over at Eric and grinned. "Yes, professor, why is that?"

Eric turned and looked at the boys. "Well, some people believe that in the beginning all people were black. But, when some left Africa and went to other parts of the world, not this hot and dry, their pigments were altered."

Hussein interrupted. "Pigments? What is that?"

"Pigments are the little things that color our skin…more or less. You have black ones and mine are white. The Indians have brown and the Chinese yellow. Do you understand?"

Hussein shrugged and nodded his head. "I guess so. But how can you lose your pigments? I can't lose mine." He took his thumb, wetted it in his mouth, and rubbed it up and down on his arm. "See."

"You can't rub them off, if that's what you mean," Dan said, and glanced in the rearview mirror. "They won't come off. It's what they call evolution. Over a period of hundreds, maybe thousands, of years if something is not needed on an animal it disappears, or changes into something it needs more."

"What do you mean 'disappears'? Like what?" Hussein said.

Dan thought for a moment. "For example, it's believed that thousands of years ago monkeys came down from the trees and began to walk on two legs." He looked in the mirror, saw no reaction, and continued. "As soon as he walked upright, he no longer needed a long tail; it was there in the first place to allow him to swing through the trees. After thousands of years of evolution his tail slowly disappeared, because he didn't need one. After many more thousands of years man, who more than likely evolved from the monkey, has no tail at all. That's the way with pigments. People in the cold climates don't need black pigments to protect them from the sun; the sun's rays are not that strong where it's cold."

Hussein translated the information to Ebukut. The warrior remained silent for several moments to absorb what he had just heard. All of a sudden, he exploded in animated laughter. He turned to Hussein and through chortles, responded in Masai.

Hussein nodded and smiled. "He's not sure he believes everything you said about the monkey becoming a man," he told them. "But he said his uncle might have been one, because he still has a tail. On the other hand he himself has never had one. except the one hanging between his legs." Everyone roared in laughter.

Chapter Ten

At 3 o'clock in the morning Dan pulled the Rover onto a gravel road that ran north to south, and parallel to the lake. He cut the engine and pulled out a pack of cigarettes.

Eric had been catnapping. He opened his eyes and squinted into the darkness. "What's the matter? Why are we stopping?"

Dan took a long drag on the cigarette dangling from the corner of his mouth. "I don't know about you but I don't think we should go any farther 'til we decide what we're going to do," he said, and blew a smoke ring through the half-open window.

"What do you mean? I thought it was all settled," Eric said. "We're going to take the boys to Koobi to see if John will hide them. If he won't, at that time we can make other arrangements."

"Do you think that's a good idea?" Dan said. "Let's face it, the rangers aren't stupid. In time they'll think of that. Personally, I'd hate to put that burden on John. He'd be in a hell of a lot of trouble if he was caught hiding them. He might even lose his license to dig. The sergeant would see to it."

"What do you think, Hussein?" Eric said, and turned to face the boys. "Do either of you have any other suggestions? After all, you should have something to say about it." While they mulled over the situation, he continued. "I said I'd help you boys, and I meant it. I thought under the circumstances taking you to Koobi would be your best bet. But if you've got a better idea, let's have it."

Hussein explained the circumstances to Ebukut, and then leaned forward. "We have spoken about this problem," he said. "We think my uncle's village in Illah is best for us. We had planned on stopping there anyway, before going on to Koobi."

"Then you really were on your way to Koobi?" Eric asked.

"Yes. We have a friend that works there. I think he would help…at least hide us."

"Illah? What's an Illah?" Dan questioned.

"Illah is the name of the second village of the El Molos, on this side of the lake. It's not far from here," Hussein explained. "I'm sure we could stay with my relatives. They would be pleased to see us. It's been a long time, but I believe they would remember me."

"Which way do we go, left or right?" Dan asked.

"It's to the right. You will see a large termite mound several meters high. There, you will turn left and go down to the lake's edge; the village is there. Nevertheless, before we enter we must wait until they are awake and moving about in the village. They don't receive visitors until the sun has been in the sky for at least two hours. It's their custom and we must obey it."

"Terrific," was Dan's sarcastic remark.

"That's okay, it'll be light in another hour or so," Eric assured him. "Until then we can drive down to the lake and wait in the truck. What are another couple hours, anyway?" He adjusted the sling on his arm and winced when it touched the window.

"For one thing," Dan countered, "the rangers will have two extra hours to hunt for us. And I'm sure they'll take advantage of every minute of it. They're either going to leave from the club, which I doubt, or from the barracks, which is more plausible. Either way, it doesn't give us much time." His face turned serious, and he added, "And what if they use a spotter plane? That'll get them here long before the boys can get settled in the village."

Eric shifted in his seat, and again adjusted his sling. "Oh, come on, Dan," he said, with a sideward glance. "You know they wouldn't waste the taxpayer's money on a plane just to hunt down a couple boys. Not unless they had killed somebody. Besides they couldn't land up here."

"Yeah, in all probability you're right," Dan said with a sigh. "But didn't you tell me Mandeli was more than a little pissed when his buddy got speared?"

"That's what somebody told me. But where's that adventurous spirit you're supposed to have? I thought you were once a member of the ANC. Didn't they ever take chances?"

Dan laughed. "Yes, but they were calculated. However, you've made your point. What I'd like to know is what are we going to do after we drop off the boys? Have you thought about that? You know we don't dare go back to the club, at least not yet. And we're too damned far out in the desert to get back to Nairobi on this tank of gas."

"Let's take it one step at a time. Shall we?" Eric said. "First, let's make sure the boys are settled in and safe. After that we can work on getting ourselves out of this mess. Okay?"

"If there is a way out," Dan mumbled under his breath. "All the photographic equipment I own is back at the club. And you didn't give me a chance to get it."

"Stop worrying, so is mine. I'm sure Kurt will take good care of it."

Dan started the truck, turned on the headlights, and slipped it into gear. The tires dug into the soft sand, and they headed north.

"Sure hope he don't have to keep the stuff long," he muttered.

A half hour later, they had located the termite mound. Dan turned down a well-worn path, barely wide enough for the truck, and headed toward the lake. Several minutes later they stopped at the edge of a small village on the waterfront. Dan killed the lights and turned off the engine. The faint lapping of waves breaking against the rocky shoreline was the only sound heard.

"Hussein," Eric said, and turned to face him. "From here it's about a day's walk to Koobi. If anything goes wrong, like the rangers get too close, or you don't feel comfortable in this village, I want you to get to the campsite. I'm sure John will hide you until this blows over. After we get you settled in here, we'll go on ahead and explain the situation to him. Okay?"

Hussein nodded and turned to Ebukut to explain.

"We'll also have to hole up for a while at the site," Eric continued. "They'll be looking for us, too. Nevertheless, it wouldn't be difficult to hide an entire army in there; it's spread out over a number of acres. There're lots of places to hide."

"What about our truck, after we get there?" Dan said.

"What about it? They have a few trucks just like ours. That shouldn't be a problem."

"Hope you're right."

"When have I steered you wrong?"

"When you took me from Nairobi and got me involved in all this crap," Dan said with a comical snort.

As they sat in the coolness of the truck, the sky on the eastern horizon began to take on a subtle glow, which produced long, dim shadows on the western sides of the huts. Within minutes, the sun's brilliance struck the lake and produced millions of whitecaps that shimmered like diamonds on its surface.

Dan pulled out his ever-present pack of cigarettes and offered them around, but nobody accepted. Eric made a comment about him smoking too much but Dan shrugged it off with a grunt and a smoke ring in his face.

The truck had been pulled under sandstone outcroppings at the far end of the village, but a portion of the cab was still exposed to the rising sun. Although the windows were open, within minutes they could feel the penetrating heat of the morning sun.

Eric rested his head on the door casing and focused his eyes on the rippling water. His peripheral vision caught movement in the village. Four tribesmen, followed closely by two women, walked from a hut to the water's edge carrying what appeared to be a stretcher about the same length and width as the ones used to cart him and William off the hill after their accident. As he followed the activity, his interest deepened. Within minutes, the entire village had joined the procession. He turned to wake the boys but they were already alert.

"What do you make of that, Hussein?" he said.

When Dan heard his voice he opened his eyes and locked them on the activity.

Hussein leaned forward and scanned the shoreline. "I think someone has gone to see *Wacq* (Wok)," he answered.

"*Wacq*? What's a *Wacq*?" Dan asked.

"It's the name the El Molos have given their God," Hussein explained. "The name of my God is *Nkai*, theirs is *Wacq*."

"What does it mean?" Eric asked.

"Someone has died," Hussein explained. "They're taking the body to the edge of the water. There, they will bury it under a mound of stones. It's their way."

"They don't bury people in the ground?" Dan asked.

Hussein bared his teeth in a smile. "Have you ever tried to dig in the soil of Turkana?"

Eric didn't consider the response important enough to take his eyes off the activity on the beach.

The procession marched to the water's edge and stopped at the bottom of a huge formation of rocks that jutted out into the lake. The stretcher was placed on the sand beside the stones, and within minutes large mounds of rocks had been piled on top of it.

After the burial the villagers returned to their huts, tore the palm fronds from their roofs, and carried them a few dozen yards down the beach. When the roofs were bare of all fronds, the men returned, gathered the driftwood frames, and lugged them to the new location. After many trips they had transported all their belongings and started to reassemble their huts.

"What's going on?" Eric asked, puzzled.

"It is their way," Hussein replied. "I don't fully understand why they move their huts every time someone dies, but they do. Years ago they moved them a kilometer or two, but now only a few meters. I suppose over the years they discovered it didn't matter how far, as long as they were moved."

"Strange custom," Dan said.

Ebukut nudged Hussein for a translation. When he was certain he understood, he answered in Masai, which was accompanied by lively gestures.

After several minutes, Hussein nodded, slid forward in his seat, and tapped Eric on his shoulder. "My friend told me something about the El Molos even I didn't know," he said. "It is stranger than what you have just witnessed."

"What's that?" Eric said. "It'd have to be awfully strange to beat what I just saw."

"Once a year the people of this village travel to a place called *Moitá* (Moy-tay)," Hussein began. He leaned back in his seat and glanced over at Ebukut for confirmation. "It's a village a few kilometers from here, but still on the lake. There, they perform a ceremony called *Ngwere* (gwere). Every warrior must hunt the great *kiboko*, the hippopotamus. If a man refuses to hunt, or shows fear, he's punished by the tip of a spear. They slash him once on the chest so all may see his scar of cowardice. After that, he is commanded to hunt again. If he still refuses or hesitates he's slashed again. Soon, he either shows no fear…or he's close to death. You must understand the hippo is one of their primary foods.

"They spear the animal until it's weak. When it's tired and ready to be sacrificed for *Wacq*, the elders select one warrior to kill it. After he has killed it, he's not allowed to eat the flesh; it is taboo, for he has killed one of their sacred beasts. Nevertheless, he's honored in other ways. He's allowed to sit at the head of the counsel of elders for a day and is given an earring cut from the tailbone of the animal he has killed."

"That's strange," Dan said. "You mean these people hunt the hippo like we hunt deer and antelope? That's kind of death-defying, isn't it?"

"Yes, it is. But that isn't the most dangerous thing they do." He looked over and spoke to Ebukut in Masai. The warrior nodded. Hussein turned back to Eric. "I asked my friend if he had ever seen them hunt from their rafts. He said he had…in this village."

"What do you mean?" Dan asked.

"They take two or three dum-palm logs and tie them together," Hussein said, and pointed to the shoreline. "See them lined up on the beach? The men paddle the narrow rafts to the other side of the lake where the *kibokos* and *mambas* live. The *mamba* is what you call the crocodile. They hunt them with hand-held harpoons."

"They must be brave people," Eric remarked, staring at the slender rafts. "Or nuts."

"No. It's not bravery, it's hunger," Hussein said. "The El Molos believe *Wacq* put the *kiboko*, the *mamba*, the *tylapia*, and the perch in the lake just for them, and they consider them sacred. When they are eaten their spirits are also consumed."

"But I thought all tribes believed if something was sacred it shouldn't be killed and eaten," Dan said with a frown.

"That's true if the tribes are not hungry," Hussein said with a grin. "If you had a sacred cow and you were hungry, would you not find a way to change the tribal laws so you could sacrifice it for food and still remain within the graces of your God?"

"Good point," Eric said. "I never thought of it that way."

The sun had ascended two hours above the horizon and it was time to enter the village, but Ebukut hesitated. He leaned over to Hussein and said in Masai, "The villagers have not completed their huts, and until they do we must not enter. Only after the last hut is finished can we enter without fear of reprisal. Even then, we must wait to be accepted by the elders."

Hussein conveyed the information to Eric and Dan.

When the sun finally broke over the horizon, the ranger barracks at

Maralal bustled with activity. A line of hungry men had formed in front of the mess building waiting to be fed, and men with towels and shaving gear patiently waited in front of the only bathhouse in the compound. Smoke from the cooking fires, reeking of greasy fish oil, hung low over the tops of the barracks.

A door in one of the far barracks flung open and Sergeant Mandeli stomped through. He stopped for a moment and waited for Joseph, who was scurrying to catch up. He gave him a condescending sneer, and then continued down the weed-infested path.

"What's wrong?" Joseph asked, and turned to face him. "Where are we going?"

"We're not going to take the truck this morning," the sergeant answered.

Joseph frowned. "What do you mean, sir?"

Without answering the sergeant turned his head and glared disgustedly at the stocky man. They had traveled only a short distance when the sergeant turned onto another path, one that led to a small isolated airstrip.

Joseph ran to catch up. "Sir," he said, panting to catch his breath. "You're not going to do what I think you're going to do, are you?"

"And what might that be?"

"They won't give us an airplane. If that's where we're headed."

"No. They won't."

Joseph stopped in his tracks. "I don't understand, sir. Then why are we going to the airfield? We have to be on the road soon if we're going to Turkana. It's a four-hour drive just to get where we were yesterday. After that, we'll have to drive north for several more hours. It'll take us all day just to get where the boys are supposed to be. And we'll still have to search for them."

"Do you think I don't know that?"

"No, sir. I mean *yes*, sir."

"Will you stop talking and follow me?"

"Yes, sir," Joseph said, flying down the path on his short, sturdy legs trying to keep pace.

A fuel truck had just driven away from a blue and white Cessna. A tall, heavy-set white man was busy taking off the tie-downs that secured the plane. He never noticed the sergeant's arrival and went to the wing tank to check on the tightness of the gas cap. When he turned around he bumped into Mandeli.

"Sergeant," the man said, with a smile. "What brings you way out here? You going to join our little air force?"

The man was as tall as Mandeli, but outweighed him by at least 30-pounds. His face and nose were covered with pockmarks and reddened by too much whiskey. A pair of sky-blue, blood-shot eyes stared at the sergeant from beneath a Yankee baseball cap.

"We want you to fly us to Koobi Fora, Keith," Mandeli said.

"Do you now? Where are your flight orders? You know I can't fly without them."

Mandeli pulled out a roll of bills with a rubber band wrapped tightly around them and stuck them into the pilot's shirt pocket. "These are my flight orders," he said.

Keith pulled them out, stared at the thick roll, and then gave the ranger a piercing glare. "You should know I can't take this. I can't help you. All the men in camp know of your obsession with those boys. I don't want any part of it. I *won't* be a part of it. I've got to have a signed set of orders before I can even take off. And you know that. Put this damn money back in your pocket it's no good to me." He took the packet of bills and flung it in the sergeant's face.

Mandeli turned his back toward the camp and pulled out his revolver. He pointed it at Keith's stomach. "I have to get to Koobi!" he shouted. "I want those two boys at any cost! My friend might lose his life because of those two. They've broken the law in many other ways, too. As you know."

Keith grimaced, as he looked down at the barrel of the gun pointed at his groin and stepped back several feet. "You stupid idiot!" he exploded. "Do you know what you're doing?"

"I know exactly what I'm doing," Mandeli replied with a calm, restrained voice. A sneer formed on the sergeant's lips, as he cocked the hammer.

Joseph looked in the direction of the camp to see if anyone had spotted them. "Sir," he yelled. "You can't do this. I won't be a part of it."

Mandeli turned the gun on him. "You have no choice," he barked. "You'll come and you'll help me track down those boys. They have to be punished for what they've done. I'll make an example of them."

"You're definitely crazy," Keith said, with a nervous sigh. "You know they won't let me take off without a clearance. Those trigger-happy goons in the tower would shoot first and ask questions later. You know that."

"They won't shoot if we go now…this minute," Mandeli snarled. "They're all at breakfast. We have time, but we have to leave now." He nudged Keith into the plane with the barrel of the gun.

Keith knew from previous experiences that the sergeant was fanatical enough to do something stupid. He took his place in the pilot's seat, followed by Joseph who scrunched himself into the small back seat.

Mandeli got in last and strapped himself into the co-pilot's seat. He waved the pistol in Keith's face. "Hurry," he demanded. "We don't have much time."

"You know you'll be finished as a ranger," Keith shouted over the noise of the turning prop. The engine caught. With a push of the throttle the small plane jumped forward and headed for the down-wind end of the runway. "You'll end up in jail, you know." Mandeli's eyes glazed over and he glared at him.

After a short take-off the plane lifted into the stark, blue sky. Mandeli gave Keith another warning glance, and then looked down at the ground. He saw a few curious rangers pointing at them as the plane flew low over the camp.

The radio in the cockpit crackled. Over the din of the engine a tinny voice said, "Cap two this is Cap one, over."

Mandeli jerked the mike out of Keith's hand. "Don't answer!" he commanded. He reached over and turned off the radio. "We don't need that."

"Of course you realize they have a chopper up north," Keith said, in a feeble attempt to intimidate. "I'm sure they'll be interested in what we're doing up there."

Mandeli stuffed the gun into his belt and glared at Keith, daring him with his eyes. He glanced back at Joseph, whose eyes were glued to the sights on the ground. This was his first plane ride and the sick expression on his face proved to the sergeant he didn't like it one bit. His knuckles had turned white from gripping the armrests and he had tightened his seat belt to the point where it was difficult for him to breathe.

The engine strained until the plane had reached its cruising altitude, and then it fell into a rhythmic purr. The air was smooth and warm making the wings of the small plane appear stationary against the distant hills, as they cut through the cloudless sky. Except for the monotonous drone of the engine, silence prevailed in the cabin.

"I think it's safe to go into the village now," Hussein said.

The two warriors walked toward the newly erected huts. They turned and waved to Eric on their way to the sandy beach in front of the village. After finding a likely spot on the outskirts where they could wait for recognition, they squatted on the blistering sand and leaned their backs against each other for support. They pushed their spears into the sand and committed themselves to a long wait. When they were finally settled in, Dan pulled the truck back onto the goat trail and headed for Koobi.

The bright morning sun had a peculiar haze to it. Hussein had seen it many times before and knew it was going to be another sweltering day. He hoped they would be accepted into the village before it got too hot. He could remember temperatures well over 45 centigrade (113 Fahrenheit) in that area. Furthermore, there was little shade to be had: some conifer bushes and several umbrella trees that were too far away, and a few *sokotei* cherry trees that dotted the lake's edge. There was nothing close enough that could afford them relief from the boiling sun.

If they didn't get accepted soon, they would be forced to move elsewhere to seek any shade they could find. The only possible relief from the sun was an overhang on the shoreline a 100-meters away. The sun was bad enough but sitting in one position for several hours with leg cramps was not pleasant, either. Nevertheless, they had to abide by tribal customs or they would not be allowed into the village.

Soon after one of Hussein's more severe leg cramps, he noticed a young man walking toward them. His hair was braided in tight strands and saturated with dark red ocher. He could have mistaken him for a Samburu warrior, except for the lack of ivory earrings. He had nothing on but a red loincloth and a few strands of polished beads hanging around his neck.

He had been told that the El Molos copied traditions and customs from other tribes, but he never thought he would see a warrior from any tribe that looked as much like a young Samburu as the boy did. His spear was long and thin, but did not have the same style blade as the Samburu *mpere*. It was no more than an inch wide and came to an abrupt point, making it much better for spearing fish and crocodile.

"Hello," the young warrior said in El Molo, a derivative of Swahili. He walked around them, admiring their garments and spears. "You are Samburus."

"Yes. We're from Loiyangalani, where your first village of Anderi is," Hussein said with a smile.

The young boy thought for a moment. "That is a long way to travel. How did you get here?"

"We came by—" Hussein started to explain.

"We are Samburu warriors," Ebukut interrupted. "We have come all the way across the desert to be here. Is that not enough?"

Warriors from all tribes admired *lmurrans* who did great deeds, and Ebukut had set the scene. In the young boy's mind they would be great warriors because they had traveled a considerable distance across the burning desert.

The boy walked closer, fondling his spear like a seasoned *lmurran*. "You have come a very long way," he said. "It is over fifty kilometers. You must be tired."

"Yes, it is far. But it is not too far for Samburu *lmurrans*," Ebukut said. "Are we welcome in your village, young warrior?"

"I will get the elder," the boy said. "He is the one who must welcome you." As he turned to leave he took the water bag from his shoulder and handed it to Ebukut. "Drink my water while you wait. I will not be long."

Although they had their own water it would have been an insult to refuse his. They knew it would be warm and reek of brine, but they accepted it with displayed gratitude. As soon as the boy had disappeared behind one of the huts, Ebukut put the plug back in the goatskin bag and made a gagging sound.

"This is bad water," he said, and repositioned his legs to avoid a cramp. "I wonder if this is the only water they have?"

Hussein ignored the question and started to stand up.

Ebukut caught his wrap, forcing him back onto the sand. "Don't get up," he said. "Wait until we have been accepted, unless you want a spear in your back. If the elders don't accept us we'll be considered taboo and thrown out of the village. You should know these things. You have been here before. These are your half-people."

"Yes, but it's been many years," Hussein said. "How do you know so much about the El Molos? I should be the one who knows these things, my stepmother is one."

"Yes, you should. It pays to know your brothers ways. Some day it could help you."

Two aging tribesmen, two warriors, and several women walked across the sandy beach toward them. They circled the warriors several times, and then motioned for them to stand. Although eager to accept their offer, getting to their feet was not an easy task. They had been sitting with their knees bent for over two hours and it took several minutes before they could stand erect.

A short, pot-bellied elder with a craggy, bearded face and missing front teeth did all the talking. The women in the welcoming party circled the boys, moved their sweating bodies closer, touched their clothes, and felt their braided hair.

Several young boys came onto the scene. One tried to force the spear from Hussein's hand to look at its long blade, but he was pushed away.

The elder spoke in what seemed to be a mixture of all tribal languages. When he had finished welcoming them, he and his entourage turned and walked away, leaving them standing alone with the young El Molo warrior.

"You have been accepted into our village," the boy said.

"What did the old, toothless one say," Ebukut asked, rubbing his legs to get circulation.

"I don't know," the boy said. "He spoke the ancient tongue. He's the only one who knows it, anymore. It is no longer used. The old man is to be humored, anyway."

"I am known as Ebukut and this is Hussein…Usitani," Ebukut told the boy and held out his hand for a traditional limp shake. "What do they call you, young warrior?"

"I am Kibbi," the boy said, and shook his hand. "I will take you into the village." He turned and headed for the new central area. "Why do you come this far when there is so little to see?" he added, turning his head to look at them.

"There is much to see here, Kibbi," Hussein said. "But we have come for another reason, to see my stepmother's relatives. It's been a long time but I believe they will remember me."

"What are their names, Hussein Usitani?" he asked, using the two names Ebukut had given him.

"They are known as Akahlal," Hussein answered. "I don't know their first names…I have forgotten. They have lived in Illah for many years. They are my step-aunt and uncle."

Kibbi stopped and turned to face them. "Then your aunt's name is

K'eti," he stated. "But your uncle went to see *Wacq* this morning." He stared into Hussein's eyes, waiting for a reaction. "I am sorry, Hussein…Usitani. He was a good hunter of the *kiboko*."

Hussein looked over at Ebukut and shrugged. "You mean my uncle was the one they buried under the stones this morning? What happened?"

"We were hunting the *kibobo* last night, by the island-of-no-return," Kibbi began. "Your uncle was a fourth man on a three man raft. There wasn't enough room and he fell into the lake in front of a *kiboko.* He was attacked before we could get him. It crushed his chest with its teeth."

Hussein had never hunted hippo but he had heard of them charging and crushing men with their strong jaws and eight inch teeth. He had been told they were docile on land, but when they returned to the water they were extremely aggressive. He believed it had something to do with them guarding their territory. Even so, to be hunted by the El Molos every day was in itself a good enough reason for them to attack. A hippo was no different than any other animal, when hunted or cornered. Over the years they had learned to sense man's violent behavior and instincts told them they were not safe around him.

"My aunt," Hussein said, "is she well? Did she take the news badly?"

"She understands the facts of life," Kibbi explained. "He who hunts the *kiboko* is also hunted by him. The *kiboko* won this time. Your aunt realizes this. It is our way. Your aunt is in one of those huts, over there." He pointed to an unfinished hut beside two others that were also incomplete. The huts formed a triangle around a small sandy area, which had been dug out to make a fireplace. "My hut is over there by the large group." He pointed a few degrees to the left. "It is the big one with the drying racks beside it. If I can help, call me. Anyone will know where to find me." He left them standing beside the first of K'eti's three huts.

Hussein lifted the goatskin flap that covered the doorway and looked inside. A frail, gray haired woman, clothed only in a loincloth, sat on a blanket in the center of the hard-packed floor. He opened the flap wider and she looked up with a vacant stare.

"Who is it? Who is there?" she demanded in a shrill voice, and then spun around to face them. The bright morning sun through the doorway forced her to squint and look away.

"It is Usitani, aunt K'eti," he said in a soft voice, "from Loiyangalani. Do you remember me? I am your sister Etaira's stepson."

The old woman put her feet under her buttocks and attempted to stand, but fell back onto the blanket. She tried again. After several attempts she managed to get onto her hands and knees. With uncertain stability she stood upright and placed her hands on her hips. Her bloodshot eyes narrowed into a squint, as they searched for recognition.

After a few moments she gave him a toothless smile. "Is it really Usitani?" she screeched. "It has been many years, boy. You have grown much. Why have you come? If you are here to see your uncle you are too late, he has gone to see *Wacq*."

"Yes. I know, aunt K'eti. I heard. I'm sorry."

"Do not be sorry, nephew," she said with sadness in her voice. "Many times he had wished to see *Wacq*, but I do not think he wanted to see him so soon and in such a way."

"Aunt K'eti, this is my friend, Ebukut. He's a Samburu warrior."

Ebukut held out his hand and she accepted.

"He's a fine looking warrior, nephew," she said, studying him up and down. "He reminds me of your uncle when he was young. He was strong too, and stood without a bend to his body. He was a great warrior, at one time." She hesitated for a moment, and then added as an afterthought, "I wish he could be here to see you, nephew." Without another word she rushed past them and darted through the goatskin flap.

They stared at each other, taken back by the abruptness of her exit. After several confusing moments they followed her into the central area where she had stopped in front of a half-finished fireplace.

"Nephew, put paper and kindling wood…right there," she said, and pointed at the center of the fire pit. She reached down with a long, crooked finger and marked a cross in the sandy center of the ring of stones. "I will make sweet *sokotei* tea. It was your uncle's favorite."

After searching for several minutes, he found a bundle of small, dried branches and folded paper in a goatskin bag that hung on the outside of the main hut. He took a handful of twigs and placed them on the paper in the fireplace.

"Do you have matches, aunt K'eti?" he asked. "I have some, but they're somewhere in my *sampur*."

Without answering, she squatted beside the fireplace and slid more small pieces of paper under the twigs. She reached into her *selah* (apron) and pulled out a half-round piece of glass. She held it over the paper and within several minutes smoke began to billow from the pit.

Hussein smiled his approval. He had seen fire made this way by the elders but they would only speak of it in secrecy and would not say how it was done. He knew it had something to do with the sun's rays through the glass, but he didn't know how it made the fire.

She took a cast-iron kettle and put it on an iron grate above the blazing twigs.

"You have come from Loiyangalani?" she asked. "And how is my sister? Is she well? Is she tired of the ways of your father?"

"She died several years ago," Hussein answered. "I thought you knew.

Even before, it was no concern of mine how they felt about each other."

K'eti stared at him for a long moment. "Tell me, nephew, what brings you here? It is much too far for just a visit."

He glanced nervously at Ebukut. "We are being chased by the rangers, aunt K'eti." He saw no reason to lie. "We would like to stay with you for a while, if you don't mind."

She picked up a stick and tossed it onto the flames. "Are you in bad trouble with them, nephew? What did you do to make them angry?"

"We have done nothing but kill two lions, aunt K'eti." He didn't think it wise to say anything about the wounded ranger. "We killed them in self-defense, but the rangers would not listen."

"I know about the rangers," she said, and repositioned the hot kettle over the flames with her bare hand. "You are right they will not listen to reason. They are always here when we go hunting. They try to catch us when we bring the meat back to the village." She stared into the fire. "They are gray men you know. They are our brothers who have been changed by the white man. Have you heard them called 'gray' men, nephew?"

"Yes, aunt K'eti, I have."

Her long, leathery face turned somber. "They have no sympathy for us when we hunt the *kiboko* and the *mamba*," she said. "They do not realize we are simply trying to feed ourselves." She paused for a few seconds, and then added, "They were once tribesmen like us. Why won't they leave us alone and let us hunt in peace? That's all we ask. We have nothing left but our *tylapia*, *mamba*, and *kibobo*." She attempted to rise from her crouched position, but without success. She finally held out her hand for support. "Of course, you can stay as long as you wish, nephew. Do not worry, the rangers will not come to this hut. They are afraid of me." She laughed with a piercing screech. “They are afraid of this old woman. I have the evil eye, which they do not understand. They have become too gray…too white.” She giggled. “That is why they are afraid of this old woman.”

“What do you mean, ‘evil eye’?” Ebukut asked.

Without answering, she turned and stared into his eyes. Her pupils rotated slowly in their sockets and the warrior’s face flushed. All of a sudden, he raised his spear and hurled it at the shoreline, 50-meters away, where it plunged deep into the sand short of the waterline. She returned her gaze for a few more seconds and all emotion seemed to drain from his face. He reached down, picked up a stick from the fireplace, and held it by its blazing end. Instantly, he let out a painful cry and dropped it back into the fireplace. Confusion replaced his shocked expression. With a furrowed frown, he rubbed his burned hand against his wrap.

She smiled. “Now do you understand the evil eye? Do you see why they are afraid of me, nephew?” For a fleeting moment she stared into his eyes. Instantly, his mind became confused. It felt to him like his mind had been cut off from the rest of his body and taken into another realm of existence. He could not look away from her eyes. After a few seconds she dropped her head and looked down at the fireplace. Hussein shook his head several times and backed away.

“Don’t be afraid, nephew,” she told him. “I will not give you more of the evil eye.” A grin enveloped her face, as she bent down and stirred the tea. “I wanted you to understand.”

Hussein looked at Ebukut. “Did she make you do those things?” he asked.

The big warrior’s eyes had acquired a vacant stare and he shook his head several times. “What do you mean,” he said. He looked down at his throbbing hand and blew on it to ease the pain. “Where my spear?” he said. "I lost spear. You see spear?" His words were scrambled and he could not think straight. His simplest words and sentences were garbled.

Hussein pointed down the beach to where the warrior's spear had landed. "You don't remember throwing your spear?" he asked.

Without answering the warrior walked down the beach and inspected the spear. He looked back with a blank stare. "How this happen? I had spear in hand. Then I don't have it," he mumbled. He tried to be coherent but his mind had trouble functioning.

"He won't remember about the spear," K'eti said. "And he will always wonder how he burned his hand, if you do not tell him."

"How can you do this, aunt K'eti?"

She was in no hurry to reply. The teapot whistled, spewing steam from its spout. She took the wire handle in her bare hand and poured the hot, sweet liquid into two cups. She reached into the netting of her *selah* and pulled out a fragile china teacup that had a delicate curved handle and paintings of bright colored flowers on its side. She held it up for their inspection, and then poured it half full of tea.

"I have always had this evil eye," she said, and handed them the cups. "I did not use it much, long ago…it got me into trouble. But now I'm an old woman and can control it." She took a sip. "I cannot explain it so you can understand, I do not understand much of it myself. It has always been there." She stared into the dying embers. "At times I wish I did not have it. But I can do nothing about it, so I use it." She smiled, exposing two rotting teeth on her lower jaw.

With no shade or wind, heat from the late morning sun began to overwhelm the boys. She invited them into the larger of the two unfinished huts, where a few palm fronds had been placed on its conical roof as a semi-protection from the searing sun. She lifted a bag of warm goat milk from a nail on the wall and offered it to them, but they refused.

"When the sun is at its hottest, the men of the village hunt the great *mamba*," she said. "Do you warriors wish to go?"

"We don't know how to hunt them, aunt K'eti," Hussein said.

"You would be shown," she assured him. She sensed his nervousness. With a grin, she added, "But I will understand if you do not wish to hunt the great one."

"We will go," Ebukut announced. "They are not as ferocious as the lion."

"That may be true," she said with a smile, again displaying her two teeth. "But you are not standing on a small raft bobbing up and down on the water when you hunt lions."

Ebukut tried not to show his anxiety but the tapping of his fingers on the side of his cup gave him away. "We will go," he repeated. He looked over at Hussein for reassurance. "Is this not true, my friend?" Hussein nodded, but did not answer or smile.

Chapter Eleven

Eric leaned back in the canvas chair, sipping his third lemonade. Dan had already finished his third and had retreated to the shade of the sorting tent. They sat watching diggers go about their chores in the heat of the early afternoon sun.

John Anderson, the camp manager, approached them. "Hi, boys," he said. "I see you've finally quenched your thirsts after that long, dusty ride."

Eric lifted his glass. "Elixir of the Gods," he said with a smile. "How do you get your ice way out here?"

"We have an old generator on the other side of the clearing for that purpose, and to keep our food fresh," John said, and then pointed across the digging fields. "We keep it over there for peace and quiet's sake."

"Have you thought anymore about our problem?" Dan asked. "With the boys, I mean."

John sat down in a vacant chair and poured himself a glass from the ever-present insulated container.

"That's what I wanted to talk to you about," he said. He took a long swig and wiped his mouth on his sleeve. "You said the boys *might* make it here?"

Dan nodded.

"Before we make any decisions, I think we'd better wait 'til they *do* arrive. It's not that I'd hesitate for a minute to help, it's just that I have my doubts whether they'll show up at all."

"What do you mean?" Eric said. "Do you know something we don't?"

John took another long drink. "I suppose you could say that. We heard on the transceiver that a ranger had swiped a piper from Maralal and they figure it's headed in this direction. It could be here at any time."

"Mandeli!" Dan snorted. "That idiot isn't going to give up 'til he gets those boys."

Eric tilted his chair forward. "Can he land the thing here, John?"

"Unfortunately, yes. There's an area we cleared for small supply planes…on the other side of the hill…over there." He pointed to a clearing on a section of semi-flat terrain. "They could land a plane there and there wouldn't be a hell of a lot we could do about it."

"Is that the only place he could land around here?" Dan asked. A smug look spread across his tanned face.

John got up from his chair, drained the rest of his glass of lemonade, and stretched his arms in a yawn. "Yes, I believe so. Not too many level spots around. That little strip took us a week of hard labor just to clear it of rocks and brush. Why? What do you have in mind?" He returned Dan's impish grin.

"It may have taken you a week to clear that spot, but I'll bet we could push a couple big boulders out there with our Rovers in no time at all," Dan said.

Both Eric and John understood his meaning and ran from the shade of the tent into the 100-degree temperature to their vehicles. Dan took a last swallow of his lemonade and joined them. Within minutes, they had pushed four large boulders onto the landing strip, which made it virtually impossible to land a plane without serious consequences.

They had barely finished when they heard the drone of an engine over the chugging of the diesel generator. They drove back across the strip and parked under the tent flaps, where it was a few degrees cooler.

Several minutes later, they spotted the blue fuselage of a plane coming in low over the *Karari Escarpment*, a low chain of ridges running northwest to southeast, five kilometers from the site. They filled their glasses once more with the sweet cold drink, and then relaxed.

The plane circled once over the airstrip, and then returned to the campsite. As it flew over the pilot waved and pointed at the boulders. John and the others waved back, and held their glasses up in a salute. The plane made several more passes, and then headed north.

John said it might be headed for Ileret, a small fishing village due north and several kilometers from the site. It had a small flat area where planes had landed in the past. However, to his knowledge it was inaccessible, due to the many deep ruts caused by seasonal rain run-off.

They were celebrating their victory over the rangers, when the plane returned. It came in low over the camp and dropped an object onto one of the tents. A camp worker retrieved it and gave it to John. A note had been written on the back of a navigation chart, and then wrapped around a crescent wrench. It said: "This is Sergeant Mandeli! You are ordered to remove those boulders at once! This is an official order! I command you!"

John handed the note to Eric. "What do you think? Should we?" he said, with a derisive grin.

"How much fuel would you say that baby holds, John?" Eric asked, pointing to the plane.

John thought for a moment, then said,. "Enough to take them about five hundred kilometers, I would think. Why?"

"Let's see," Eric mumbled to himself, computing in his head. "It's about four hundred kilometers round trip from Maralal. Assuming they had a full tank when they left, they would barely have enough to get here and back. If we could detain them by not allowing them to land, they would have no choice but to head back."

"Okay," said John. "Get your trucks, we'll head out to the runway and make believe we're trying to clear the strip."

After feigning several unsuccessful attempts, John brought the trucks together in the middle of the strip. He stood on one of the hoods and indicated their futility to the pilot by shrugging his shoulders and extending the palms of his hands upward.

After watching their fruitless attempts to remove the boulders, Keith turned to Mandeli. "We can't land down there," he complained. "They can't get those damn rocks out of the way. We won't have enough gas to make it home, if we don't leave right away."

"Land!" Mandeli commanded. "Land this instant! You can land over there." He pointed to what appeared to be a smooth area paralleling the strip.

Keith surveyed the spot and frowned. "You gotta be kidding. I can't land there, it's too damn rocky."

"Did you hear me? I said land!" Mandeli stuck the pistol under his chin and pushed.

"Okay, okay!" Keith shouted. "If that's what you want. But tighten your seat belts."

With no wind, it made little difference which direction the tiny four-passenger Cessna came in from. As it lost altitude it began to floated inches above the long, coarse elephant grass and barbed desert rose bushes. Its wings wobbled and its fuselage bobbed up and down in the hot air currents, which threatened to keep it aloft. As the plane came in for a final pass, its nose pointed upward and it shuddered in an imminent stall. As it headed for the ground, and one of its wheels caught a large boulder and flipped it onto its back.

John was the first to arrive at the scene. As he jumped out of the truck, he discovered the pilot hanging upside down from his shoulder harness. He crawled into the cockpit to check him for a pulse. It was weak, but detectable. However, from the attitude of his head it appeared it had been badly twisted, if not broken. Mandeli was nowhere to be seen. Joseph was thrashing about in the back, still attached to his belt. John forced the door open; at the same time, Joseph released his belt buckle. He tumbled head first onto the hot sand, muttering endless strings of Swahili on his way down.

"Where's Mandeli?" John demanded.

Before Joseph could answer, the sergeant emerged from behind the broken fuselage and pointed his pistol at him. "I'm right here," he said. "Don't do anything foolish."

John's eyes narrowed, when he saw the gun. He turned and started inching his way back to the jeep. The sights of the gun followed him.

"What the hell is this?" he yelled at the sergeant.

"This is a pistol," Mandeli said with a smirk. "And I fully intend to use it, if you don't do exactly as I say."

A red Rover pulled up to the crash site and Eric and Dan jumped out. Mandeli eyed them for a few seconds, but said nothing. They started to approach him, and then saw the gun and backed off.

Mandeli walked over to John's truck. "I'll take your vehicle," he said. "I'm commandeering it. It's official business." He held the gun on John, while he climbed into the passenger seat. He then motioned for Joseph to get behind the wheel. The aide hesitated, but he was quickly convinced by the discharge of a round over his head.

The sound of the shot brought workers out to the camp's communal area. They were just in time to watch the Jeep speed down the camp's peripheral road. They knew something was wrong, but from where they were they could not tell what.

When Mandeli had finally left the confines of the camp, the men rushed to the plane to assist the pilot. They unbuckled him, placed him in Dan's truck, and drove back to the tent area.

John went to the radio tent and called the ranger station at Maralal to tell them about their situation. They informed him they would send a helicopter from Marsabit to pick up the wounded pilot. They also apologized for any trouble the sergeant had caused. They asked which direction the sergeant went, repeated their apology, and signed off.

After making the call, John returned to the sorting tent to check on the pilot. By the time he had returned, Dan and Eric had already downed several glasses of lemonade from the bottomless container.

"I guess Mandeli won't stop at anything to get those two boys," he said, and reached for a glass.

"Kind of looks that way," Eric said, squinting into the bright sun. "Do you have any weapons? Maybe some hunting rifles?"

John appeared startled by the question. Nonetheless, after thinking about it for a moment, he told them he had an old .22 caliber rifle, used for hunting snakes and lizards. He didn't know if it still worked, but at least he wanted them to know about it.

"Any ammo?" Eric asked.

"Several boxes, I think. But I'll have to look for them."

"Would you, please?" Dan asked. He took his canteen from the truck and replenished it from the fresh water barrel.

"Is this your way of telling me you're going after that mad man?" John said.

"Yes, we are," Eric replied. "But first, we've got to get to the boys. They'll need our help, if that bastard shows up at Illah." He followed Dan to the water barrel. "At least we know where the boys are, and the sergeant doesn't."

"We think he doesn't," Dan said, and tightened his jaws. "I'd believe anything about that asshole. I think he got help from somebody at the club. Somebody there has been feeding him information. I'd bank on it. I'm sure he knows where the boys are. If not, why didn't he look for them when he was here? He saw us but didn't give us the time of day. I'll bet he knows exactly where they are."

"You don't think Gabriel's behind it, do you?" Eric said with a frown.

"I don't think so, he's too much of a friend. I'd really be surprised."

"Well, I'd sure like to find out who it is," Eric said with a sigh. "But it's too late now. If he knows the boys are at Illah nobody there will be safe…including the El Molos."

"You got that right. Come on, let's go," Dan said. He jumped into the Rover and started the engine. "We'll see you later, John. Thanks for everything. Sorry about the mess on your runway."

John stopped them long enough to hand them the .22 rifle and several boxes of ammunition, then waved them off.

"We're going to Illah, right?" Eric said.

"Right. But we're not going to follow that crazy man's route," Dan said with an impish grin. "We'll go our own way, the way we came in this morning. Remember?"

"You're kidding. We're not really going back over that same damned road, are we?" Eric remembered the goat path they had taken on their way to the site and was not a bit happy about returning on it.

"It's not the freeway," Dan said, "but it's a hell of a lot closer, and faster. We'll beat him there by at least half an hour."

The sergeant's confiscated jeep bounced and swerved down the small, rutted road on its way to Illah. Joseph tightened his hands on the wheel, to avoid any mishaps from the speed they were traveling. When they had reached a smooth stretch of road, he glanced over at the tall ranger. He wondered what had turned this man into the vengeful person he had become. The sergeant's silence triggered a curiosity he could not shake.

"Sir," he said, fretfully. "May I ask you a question?"

The sergeant turned his head and glared at him. Without answering, he put his hands on top of the windshield for stability, and then stared at the road ahead.

Joseph figured that the sergeant's silence gave him permission to speak. "Sir, why do you hate your brothers?" he asked, and then swallowed hard. "You go out of your way to bring pain and suffering on them." He realized he could have brought the man's wrath down upon him by questioning him, but he had to know.

Mandeli looked over. "What do you mean?" he said. "I don't hate my brothers. I only hate Samburus."

Joseph reached into his memory and put bits of information together. He was right. The times he had been with him Samburus, more than others, had taken the brunt of his persecution. He had never realized it before, but the sergeant had just been confirmed it. Again, he pressed his luck. "Why only Samburus, sir?" he asked. "I thought you were Samburu. You live in the area."

"Ha!" Mandeli exploded. "It would be a day in hell, if I were a Samburu! They are vicious, lowlife scum! They are swine! They're as close to non-persons as is possible, *Ndorobos*, (Low-life people—scum of the earth). I spit on them!" He turned his head and spit out the window.

"Do you mind if I ask what tribe you do come from?" Joseph asked, hoping he would not say Pokot, which was his tribe.

"I am Kikuyu," Mandeli's voice thundered, loud enough to be heard over the rattling of the truck. He hesitated for a moment, swallowed hard, and then added, "I am Kikuyu, from the nine tribes of Gikuyu, our great father. I was once a Kikuyu warrior. In my village, our *nyumbas* (numba) (Family huts within a village, similar to *manyattas*) had many great warriors." He looked down at his uniform. "Now, look at me, I'm a gray man...half Kikuyu...half white. There's nothing left in my life except to hunt down my enemies, the Samburus."

Joseph became even more perplexed. He had asked a direct question, but had only received a partial answer. He had not found out what he wanted to know, regarding the sergeant's hostility toward the Samburus. His questioning thus far had gone without resolution. He continued the interrogation.

"I don't understand," he said. "Why do you hate the Samburus more than other tribes? What have they done to make you so angry?"

Mandeli trained his bloodshot eyes toward him. He leaned back in his seat and breathed a long sigh. He hesitated for a moment, as if pondering his answer, then said, "I once had a wife, N'umbi," he began, "and three children that I loved with all my heart." He swallowed hard and stared out the side window. "We lived in a large *nyumba* with my father and mother in a village north of Nairobi, near Maralal. It is in Samburu territory, as you know. Our *nyumba* had many fine cows. The Samburus had none. One night they raided my village and took six of our finest head. My father discovered who the men were and the next morning went after them. He killed several of the thieves, but he was also killed." He shifted uneasily in his seat, which gave Joseph the impression he wanted to get it off his chest, possibly for the first time. "The Samburus did not let it go at that," he continued. "One night, while I was away hunting, they came back to the village and set fire to our *nyumba*. My wife and children were killed in the fire, as was my mother. I tried to find those murdering Samburus, the ones responsible, but I could not. The only way I could get revenge was to become a ranger and use the white man's tools. I won't rest until I've made all Samburus pay for what they did to my family."

"But these boys from Turkana had nothing to do with your sorrow," Joseph said. "They're young warriors who got caught up in a situation."

"That's enough," Mandeli shouted, and then gnashed his teeth. "I don't wish to speak of this any longer." He turned his head back to the road and stared at the mountainous ruts ahead of them. "Go faster! I want to get there before it gets too late to catch them."

Joseph's concentration returned to the treacherous road, but more questions lingered. He was sad for Mandeli's unhappiness, but his misery did not give him the right to inflict pain and suffering on all Samburus, he thought. The ones who did those terrible things were the ones to blame and not the two boys, or the many other Samburus who had suffered from his vendetta.

He believed he would ask for a transfer when he returned to the barracks. He could no longer drive for a man so obsessed with revenge. He was sorry he had asked him for an explanation, but by the same token, he was glad he had discovered what had been troubling him. The one good thing about their conversation, he believed, was that he now had a legitimate reason to ask for a transfer. Under the circumstances, he figured the sergeant would give it to him, since he had bared his feelings to him.

Paul stepped off the plane at the fishing club and Gabriel was there to meet him. They greeted each other as if he had been gone forever. Paul put his arm around his friend's neck and squeezed it.

"It's good to be home," he said, as they walked toward the club.

When they arrived at the gate, Kirinyaga's eyes scanned Paul for recognition. A feeble grin spread across his ancient face, and he opened the gate. He made a sweeping motion with his spear and they walked by him.

"You said it was good to be home?" Gabriel said, as they walked up the sidewalk to the dining room. "You've been gone only a couple days, you know."

Paul grinned, and then unwrapped his arm from around his friend's neck. "Yes, I know, but here I have a much better life. There are no friends in Nairobi, only people who take advantage of you."

"It didn't take you long to find that out."

"It didn't take long…only a few hours," Paul said. "I was ready to return the first night." He reached into his pocket and handed Gabriel a small envelope. "Here's the money you loaned me. Thank you."

Gabriel took the money, knowing it would do no good to argue; he was an honorable person and had his pride to contend with. "Thank you," he said. "Are you sure you don't need it for anything?"

Paul put his hand on Gabriel's shoulder. "No. Thank you. I even got Nathan and my mother presents," he said, beaming. "I got Nathan a pocket knife. And I got my mother a pair of shoes made of real rubber and leather." He handed Gabriel a small package. "And this is for a very special friend. It is also a pocketknife, which I know you will enjoy."

"That was very thoughtful," Gabriel said. "We will enjoy them, I'm sure." They stopped in the lounge long enough to get Paul a glass of ice water. "Tell me, how were you able to come back on the airplane?" he continued. "You didn't have that kind of money."

Paul gulped down the water and placed an ice cube on his tongue. "You remember William from the safari trucks, the ones that comes every week or two and park down in the grove?"

Gabriel nodded.

"You remember I told you he was one of the men injured by the lion Hussein killed? And that he was going to Nairobi to have his wounds tended to?"

"Yes, I remember." Gabriel paused, trying to understand what his friend was trying to tell him. "But how does he have anything to do with you getting on the plane?"

"When I got the message at the hotel that Hussein was in trouble, there was only one way to get back," Paul said. "And that was to ask William to loan me enough money to get on the special tourist plane."

"But that's a lot of money," Gabriel said. "How are you going to pay him back?"

"He said he wouldn't take the money back," Paul said. "I insisted, but he refused." He hung his head in obvious shame. His face turned sad and his eyes moistened. "I know what you must think, but I had no idea he wouldn't take the money back. I never would have asked, if I had known. I thought when I returned I would sell some of my goats to pay him back. I felt ashamed for taking his money, but I had no other way to get back. He was my only hope. I couldn't have returned if it weren't for him. Can you understand that?"

"Yes, of course," Gabriel said. He put his arm around his friend's shoulder and squeezed. "But it is not my business. It doesn't matter how you got back, it's enough that you're here." He refilled Paul's glass with ice water. "What are your plans…about Hussein?" he continued. "There isn't much you can do. Mister Somerville and his friend are searching for him. I don't know if they have found him yet."

"They will not find him unless he wants to be found," Paul told him with a grin. "He's now a warrior. He's at home in the desert." He snickered, and then paused long enough to take a drink and put another ice cube in his mouth. "But I think I know where he is."

"So do I," Gabriel said. "I believe he's at Illah."

Paul looked up, surprised. "How do you know this? It wasn't in the message I received in Nairobi."

"I know Hussein has relatives at Illah. I figured it out. That's right, isn't it?"

"Does anyone else know about this?"

"I told little Jonathan about my thoughts, but nobody else. Why?"

"If anybody knows it might get back to the rangers and then they would know."

Gabriel frowned. "I didn't think by telling Jonathan there would be a problem. After all he's an employee…a friend. I'm certain he wouldn't tell the rangers."

Paul looked down at the ground and shrugged.

"I don't believe the rangers know anything or we would have heard by now," Gabriel said, trying to justify his questionable action. He glanced over at Paul's grave expression. "I'm sorry I told Jonathan, but he's the only one. Believe me."

"Is there a quick way to get to Illah?" Paul asked.

"I don't know of any. Why, do you want to go? There's nothing you can do up there. Let Mr. Somerville take care of it. I trust him. I think he's a good friend."

"I have a bad feeling about this," Paul said.

Gabriel hung his head in thought. "It will be dark in a few hours. It would be impossible to get to Illah before nightfall."

"I must try," Paul said. "My friend needs me. I will not sit here and do nothing. I have to try." He looked into Gabriel's unblinking eyes. "It's only a couple hours by Rover." He reached over and touched his arm. "Do you think Mr. Versteeg would loan me one of his Rovers?"

"You must be joking," Gabriel said, laughing. "He would never do that. Besides, you can't drive and neither can I."

"There must be someone who will take me."

Gabriel looked at the ground and shook his head in despair.

Paul jumped to his feet and dug into his pocket. "How much do tourists pay to hire the Rovers?"

Gabriel was silent for a few moments, and then said, "I think the club gets a hundred shillings an hour, plus gasoline, which is another twenty." His eyes widened with excitement, when he looked down and saw Paul's fist filled with brown notes. He pulled out the money Paul had returned to him, along with some of his own, and handed it to him. "Now, we have enough for a five hour drive," he said, smiling. He nudged Paul in the ribs. "But do you want to spend all your money to get to Illah? We don't even know he's there."

"I have no need for money here in Turkana, you know that," Paul said. "There's nothing to spend it on, anyway. But I do have a friend who might need my help. I must at least try."

"Stay here for a few minutes. I'll be right back," Gabriel said, and rushed from the lounge. He raced down the sidewalk where the Rovers were parked. Ten minutes later he returned with a broad grin on his olive-colored face.

"Have you found someone?" Paul asked, wide eyed.

"I think so," Gabriel said in a whisper. "But we must not let anyone know we are going. They might not approve."

"You're not coming, Gabriel," Paul said, firmly. "You have done too much for me, already."

"I don't know Ebukut well, but Hussein is also my friend."

"Ebukut? What do you mean? Is he with him?"

Gabriel's eyes widened. "Yes. You didn't know?"

"No. How could I have known?"

"He's the one who broke Hussein out of the box."

"The box?" Paul frowned.

"The box on the back of the old truck, out back," Gabriel said. "The one they used as a jail a long time ago. You remember that, don't you?"

"Oh, yes. I heard about the box," Paul said. "But what does that have to—"

"I'll explain it all, later," Gabriel interrupted. "Let's get down to the parking lot."

An impatient black man sat in a bright red Land Rover. When the boys got closer, he leaned out the window so he could see their money. He counted out the shillings needed for the round trip and put it in his right hand. Without hesitating he counted out another 200-shillings and put it in his left. He held up his right hand, and said, "This is for the round trip to Illah." Then, he held up his left. "And this two hundred is for my time waiting up there. Get in, we don't have much daylight left, and it's a long trip."

The Land Rover swung through the gate, past Kirinyaga, and down the dusty main street of Loiyangalani. They sped past the one room hotel, the butcher shop, and the provisions store and disappeared down the only road out of the small village.

The Samburu warriors had tried to rest while waiting for the hunt to begin, which was supposed to have taken place several hours earlier. However, they kept hearing a cackling voice outside their hut reciting constant barrages of El Molo rituals, mixed with mass quantities of Swahili gibberish.

"Warriors! It is time to hunt," K'eti yelled at them. She lifted the flap of the half-finished hut and the afternoon sun pierced the semi-darkness. It blinded them for a few moments, but their eyes adjusted in time to see the old woman ready to prod them with a long stick. "You have slept long enough. It is time to see who is the smartest, the Samburu warriors or the *mambas*." She cackled and dropped the flap back across the opening.

Hussein got up and retrieved his spear, which had been leaning against the inner-wall of the hut. He was in no hurry to go on the hunt. Maybe the fishermen would forget about them, he thought. Maybe they should take their time going down to the beach.

By the time they arrived at the shoreline, a small group of men had already launched several *dum*-palm rafts. After one had been launched, another was made ready. The boys sent nervous glances to each other. The rafts were no more than a meter and a half wide and six meters long. The boys were directed to the last raft.

As they poled away from the shoreline, they glanced over their shoulders at K'eti, who stood by the water's edge smiling and waving, her two teeth glistening in the subdued evening sunlight.

"Did you agree to this?" Ebukut asked, with a nervous grin.

Hussein did not reply.

The man in the front of the raft was obviously a professional; he swept his long, narrow spear through the placid water using a skilled stroke. He looked back and motioned for them to do the same. Before long, their raft had caught up with the others and they headed for a small island several kilometers away. The sun seemed less severe, as they skimmed across the water toward the middle of the lake; a constant spray from their paddles cooled their bodies and quenched their thirsts. After a half hour, they had arrived at the mid-point between the island and the village and could no longer see the figures on the shoreline.

"What do we do if we catch a *kiboko*?" Ebukut asked.

Hussein laughed. "They put him on the raft with us, I guess."

Each rock-strewn mile they traveled, Eric's arm hurt even more. He was certain Dan had found every rut and boulder in the goat path he called a road. By protecting his injured arm with his free hand he could not hold onto the truck's safety handle. He thought about asking him to pull over and rest, but it was crucial they get to Illah before the rangers. If Mandeli got there first the boys would be in deep trouble, and he wanted to avoid that at all costs.

He leaned back and closed his eyes in thought, trying to figure out how he had been caught up in this situation. He had not known Hussein long but he had saved his life and that alone made him want to develop a more amiable relationship with the boy. He didn't know the tall warrior, but something deep inside told him he was committed to helping him, also. He held onto his shoulder the best he could, as the truck continued to careen down the rutted path.

An hour after they left Koobi, he had spotted the termite mound. They would be in the village within minutes. He had no idea what to expect when they arrived. Moreover, he didn't know what they would do when the rangers got there. He didn't believe they would shoot them; that would not be in their best interest. Nevertheless, they had to stop Mandeli, or at least slow him down. They had to prevent him from getting into the village, if at all possible. They could ask the El Molos for help, but he didn't believe they would. Even so, it was worth a try. An old cliché came to mind: nothing ventured, nothing gained.

When they arrived in the village the toothless elder, who was already weaving from too much *pombe*, came to chant his greetings. After several minutes of gibberish, he allowed them to enter. It was not often white men came to their village and when they did they were usually considered a curiosity…or trouble.

A young, slender warrior came to the truck. "I am Kibbi," he said in English. "Are you lost?"

Eric stepped from the truck and wiped his brow on his shirtsleeve. "No, we're not lost, son," he said. "We're looking for two Samburu warriors. Do you know where we can find them?" He figured the boy did know, but didn't believe he would tell.

Kibbi eyed them. "Yes, they're out on the lake hunting the *kiboko*," he said. "Why do you ask for them?"

"We're friends," Dan said. He got out of the truck and stretched his legs. "We have to warn them about the rangers. They're coming here. We have to get in touch with the boys, right away."

"You can not, they are out there," Kibbi replied, and pointed toward the island.

"There must be some way to bring them back," Eric said. He took the boy by the arm. "They're in great danger."

Kibbi pulled free. "Why? What have they done?"

"Nothing serious," Eric said, and then changed the subject. "One of the boys named Hussein has relatives here. Do you know where I can find them?"

"Yes. I will take you to Hussein...Usitani's aunt." He took them to K'eti's hut and introduced them.

After a brief session of handshakes, K'eti said, "The hunters will not be back before sunset." Her eyes sparkled and a nearly toothless smile spread across her thin, haggard face. "The village has only one raft left but you are welcome to use it, if you want to go to the island to search for the boys." They looked at the log raft pulled up to the shoreline and declined.

In the distance they heard the unmistakable whine of a Land Rover. They raced to their truck at the edge of the village and drove it behind the largest mound they could find and waited.

Chapter Twelve

Sergeant Mandeli's jeep grazed the side of a tall anthill, as it hurtled down the steep slope of the rutted road into the village, and came to a sliding stop between two sandstone mounds. The sergeant jumped out of the cab, drew his revolver and pointed it at the sky. As he scanned the area, with bloodshot eyes, he saw there was no opposition. He searched each hut, but the boys were nowhere to be found.

He saw an opportunity to take his frustrations out on somebody and stomped over to Kibbi, who stood at the edge of the central area leaning against his spear. "I'm looking for two Samburu *lmurrans*," he shouted into the boy's face. "Where are they?"

The boy leaned harder on his spear and glared at him. "This is an El Molo village," he replied. "We have no Samburus here."

"I know where I am, boy!" Mandeli roared. "I know they're here, somewhere. Take me to them." He waved his gun in the boy's face. "You are ordered to take me to them! Do you understand, boy?" His shouts drew a few curious men from their huts, but when he waved his gun at them they rushed back inside.

"Sir," Kibbi asserted, "there are no Samburu warriors in this village."

The ranger fired a shot over his head and he jumped back, frightened by the explosion.

Joseph leaped out of the truck and sprinted to Mandeli's side. He pulled the sergeant's arm down and pointed the barrel at the sand.

Mandeli's eyes ignited and his face flushed. He jerked his arm free and shoved his driver to the ground. "What are you doing?" he demanded, his voice filled with anger. "You stay out of this! I'll call if I need your help!"

"But these people are frightened," Joseph said, as he got up from the sand. "They won't tell you anything if you terrify them." He stepped back several paces, out of the reach of Mandeli's long arms.

"Mind your business! That's an order!" the sergeant bellowed in his face.

Joseph returned to the jeep and leaned up against it. Out of harm's way, he folded his arms and glared at him.

Mandeli took the young warrior by the arm and spun him around. He moved up close to his face and snarled in his ear, "Tell me where they are, boy!"

From his hiding place at the edge of the village, Dan saw that a dangerous situation developing and raised the single shot rifle to his shoulder.

Eric put his hand on the barrel and pushed it down. "Not yet," he said. "He's not going to do anything but yell, at least for a while. Let's see what happens next." Dan lowered the rifle.

The ranger fired two more shots into the air. "I want everyone in this village to go down to the lake. Now!" he shouted at Kibbi's. "If they don't I'll shoot you! And that's a promise." Revulsion spread across his face, as he glared at the boy.

"Go to the water's edge," Kibbi yelled to the villagers. "Do you hear? Go down to the beach. The ranger has threatened my life, if you don't do as he says."

One at a time, the villagers left their huts and trudged down to the shoreline. After they arrived, they milled about the water's edge, confused and angry.

In the past, the rangers had always taken a percentage of the village's meat, when the hunters returned with their kills. For that donation they were told they would not be prosecuted as poachers. However, that time they had no meat to donate and it confused them even more.

Mandeli took the young warrior's arm and pulled him along while he double-checked each hut. When he discovered there was no one left inside, he released the boy's arm.

"You make sure they understand me, boy," he snarled. "You tell them to tell me where the Samburus are or I will place them all under arrest for hiding them. I might even burn their village down."

"They don't know," Kibbi said, emphatically.

Disgusted, Mandeli pushed the boy to the ground and walked over to a toothless elder, weaving from too much *pombi*. He stood in front of the staggering old man for several moments eying him. All of a sudden, he grabbed his throat and shoved the pistol into his ribs.

"Old man," he shouted into his weathered face. "Tell me where they are."

Kibbi got up from the sand and rushed to the elder's aide. "Sir," he pleaded. "The old man is drunk from too much beer. He can't tell you anything. He doesn't know anything. He's old and doesn't speak your tongue. He doesn't understand what you're saying or what you want."

The ranger spun his gun hand around and caught Kibbi alongside his head, dropping him to the sand. "Shut up, boy! I'm not talking to you," he snarled. "I'm talking to this old, toothless *ndorobo* (dorobo)."

A bright red Land Rover silently coasted to a stop outside the village, and remained hidden from the action on the beach. Dan looked up from his cover behind a sand dune and noticed Paul sitting in the front seat. He nudged Eric, and then motioned with his finger.

From Paul's vantage point, 50-meters away and overlooking the village, he could see something happening on the beach, but could not make out what. He motioned for Gabriel to stay in the truck, and with a nod indicated he was going down to the beach to take a closer look. As he approached the fringe of the village he noticed Mandeli holding the gun against the old man's stomach.

When he crept closer, he saw a blue truck with a Site 51 logo on its side, no more than 30-meters away. A short, squatty ranger was leaning up against it with his arms folded and his eyes fixed on the sergeant. He ducked behind a nearby hut to avoid detection.

After a brutal twist of his hand, Mandeli let go of the old man's throat. The elder's eyes rolled up and he started to collapse. As he leaned forward he fell against the sergeant's gun hand and a loud explosion shattered the silence. The old man screamed and dropped to the sand. The village was suddenly filled with the screams of women and angry words from the men.

Mandeli spun around in time to witness a body sailing through the air, directly at him. It collided with his tall frame and sent him sprawling onto the sand. Before he could get his footing, the figure got up and landed on top of him. It twisted his arms behind his back and wrestled the weapon from his hand. When he pulled his head out of the sand to breathe, he caught sight of a hunting knife being held high above his head.

Joseph was caught off guard by the suddenness of the attack. His mind had not yet fully grasped the impact of the situation. He hesitated, and then reached for his holstered gun.

Again, Mandeli's head was pushed into the blistering sand. However, he managed to turn it enough to plead with Joseph.

"Shoot him, you stupid idiot!" he screamed. "Shoot him! Don't stand there like a fool."

The stocky ranger pointed his gun at Paul, but did not pull the trigger. His hand jerked in nervous twitches.

"Shoot him! That's an order! You stupid fool! Do something!" Mandeli shrieked.

Sweat ran down Joseph's forehead and into his fear-filled eyes. Frustration and apprehension spread across his face, as he cocked the hammer.

Gabriel had been watching from the truck. The instant he saw the ranger point his gun at Paul he bolted down the embankment toward him. When he made contact with the ranger's arm the revolver discharged, sending a bullet ricocheting off the frame of a hut. Although he was much smaller than the ranger, he had the advantage of surprise. Before the man could get up, he was sitting on top of him. Dan raced to his side and within seconds they had Joseph's hands tied behind his back, using his own belt.

Paul still held the knife over the ranger's head and was glaring down at him. It appeared he didn't know whether he should use it, or not. When Eric saw the situation had become dangerous, he raced to Paul's side. He grabbed his arm, before he could do any harm to the sergeant. Paul held the knife for a few seconds, and then let it drop to the sand. Eric picked it up, handed it back to him, and told him to cut a strip of cloth from his sling to tie Mandeli's hands behind his back. After the sergeant's hands were secured, they maneuvered him into a sitting position.

"You're in serious trouble, Somerville," Mandeli hissed. He tried to break the cloth handcuffs, but found it was impossible. "You'll end up in the box, along with all your friends."

"I don't think so, Mandeli," Eric said with a contented smile. "You're the one who's in over your head. You and your partner there." He pointed to Joseph.

Joseph squirmed in the sand. "I did nothing," he pleaded. His eyes filled with tears. "It was all his doing. He forced me to go with him. He also forced the pilot to land at Koobi. Don't blame me. I had nothing to do with it."

"Is that true, Mandeli?" Dan asked. He walked over and looked down at him. "Did you force the pilot to land at Koobi?" He waited for a response, but it never came. "That could make you a murderer, too. The pilot might die...he had a broken neck." He flipped Mandeli's cap off his head, with his finger.

Mandeli cocked his head and glared up at Dan. "He was all right when I left him," he retorted with a snarl. "He was only injured. I know you, you'll let him die and blame it on me." His blank expression turned into a contemptuous sneer.

Eric gave Mandeli an equally condescending look. "What about the old man lying on the beach, over there? What if he dies, too? You'll have a double murder on your hands. You have no way out." The sergeant remained silent, as he glanced over at the elder being treated by the women.

K'eti approached Eric and looked into his eyes. Her pupils slowly rolled around in their sockets. "Untie him," she whispered. "Give him his weapon and let him go after the boys. We will give him the last raft."

She approached Mandeli, bent down, and stared into his eyes. No matter how he tried to avoid her stare, he could not. His face flushed and his eyes rolled up in their sockets.

"The Samburu warriors are on the little island out there," she told him, and with an arthritic finger pointed across the lake.

"Please, do what she says," Kibbi pleaded with Eric. "Untie him. She knows what she is doing."

Within seconds, Mandeli's hands were untied and he tossed off the bindings. Eric handed him his pistol, which he holstered. He turned and walked down to the beech to the remaining raft. Not looking back, he picked up a long fishing spear and mounted the raft. Several men pushed it onto the lake and he began rowing toward the small island. As he paddled farther out, the villagers lined the shore and cheered.

"Now, I've seen everything," Dan told Eric, as he shielded his eyes against the brightness of the evening sun reflecting off the water. "What did she whisper to make you give him his gun and let him go?"

"She told me things would be balanced, and that I shouldn't worry," Eric replied with a snicker. "And for some unknown reason I was compelled to believe her. As a matter of fact I don't think I had much of a choice in the matter."

Kibbi walked over to Eric and Dan. "She also said he would be punished for what he did to the old man," he told them. "And that his punishment would be by his own hands, not ours." While staring out over the lake, he added, "While he hunts for the warriors…the *mamba* hunts for him. Things will be balanced."

Dan turned to Eric. "Does that mean what I think it does?" he asked. "Did she send him out there knowing he probably wouldn't come back?"

"I think that's the general idea," Eric replied. "These people know he doesn't stand much of a chance to make it to the other side, let alone capture the boys. I guess this is their way of retribution for what he did to the old man, and many other things out of the past."

As they watched the raft get smaller and smaller, the unmistakable flapping sound of a helicopter broke the silence. The villager's eyes widened as the huge, metallic object approached, and then hovered directly over their huts. They ran to their huts and tried to throw their arms around the palm fronds on their roofs to keep them from blowing away.

The helicopter hovered for several minutes over the village, floating back and forth, toppling drying racks and showering the insides of the huts with clouds of sand. At the edge of the village, it found a large clearing where it could land, and with a measured descent settled to the ground. The pilot waved but remained in the cockpit until the blades had come to a full stop.

A huge black man in a lieutenant's uniform stepped from the open doorway. His hat was pulled down over his sun-glassed eyes to shield them from the incessant glare of the sun.

"*Jambo*. Hello," he said to Eric, and extended his hand.

"Hi. How are you?" Eric replied. "I'm Eric Somerville. And that's Dan, over there." He pointed. "What brings you rangers way out here? You lost?"

The pilot smiled, displaying a perfect set of pearl-white teeth. "No, Mr. Somerville, we couldn't get lost out here if we wanted to," he said with a broad grin. "We don't even carry maps, that's how sure we are." He hesitated long enough to pull a long, thin cigar from his vest pocket and light it. "No, we landed at Koobi to pick up our wounded pilot, but they told us we should get to Illah right away, if we wanted the sergeant. The pilot wasn't as bad off as first believed, that's why we came here right away." His dark, piercing eyes inspected the village and noticed several roofs had been blown off. "Sorry about the turbulence." A sheepish grin spread across his face. "We're looking for—" He stopped when he noticed Joseph sitting on the sand with his hands bound. He pointed a chubby finger. "May I ask why he's tied up?" Before anyone could answer, he added, "And where *is* the sergeant?"

Eric motioned for Gabriel to untie Joseph's hands. After his bonds were cut, he was helped to his feet. He leaned against the truck while circulation returned to his legs. When he could stand upright, he walked over to the pilot.

"Mandeli is on his way to the island to search for those two Samburu boys," he said.

"What do you mean?" the pilot answered with a frown. "Why is he after *them*?"

"He has this foolish notion they're poachers, or something," Joseph said, and bowed his head. "He's determined to capture and prosecute them, at all costs."

The pilot looked over at Eric, who was on his way to the Rover. "Is that true?" he said.

"I'm afraid it is," Eric replied, and turned to face him. "He's obsessed with it. On top of that he's responsible for the pilot's injury…and also the old man's." He pointed to the elder. The women had surrounded the old man and were busy feeding him more *pombe*. "They didn't tell you about the boys when you were at the diggings?"

"Not really," the lieutenant said. "They said if I wanted Mandeli I should come here right away. There was nothing mentioned about two boys. Of course I wasn't there very long." He paused long enough to take an extended drag on his cigar. "Will somebody please let me know what's going on here?" Before anyone could answer, he instructed his copilot to get the medical kit and help the women with the wounded elder. He glanced over at Joseph. "Sorry, Joseph, but until I can figure things out I'll have to take you into custody. You can stay in the chopper for the time being." He took him by the arm and escorted him to the door, where another ranger helped him inside. After Joseph was secured in the back of the plane, the pilot joined Eric at the Rover. Eric offered him a seat and explained everything he knew about the situation up to the present.

After the pilot's questions had been answered, he slid from the Rover's hot leather seat and stretched. He lifted his cap and ran his stubby fingers through his short, salt and pepper hair. He took several long drags on his cigar, adjusted his sunglasses, and turned to face Eric.

"It's about time we did something about the sergeant, anyway," he said. "This is the last straw. We've waited too long. The least we can do is prosecute him for what he's done to the pilot…and the plane. And possibly for what he's done to everybody else, with this little vendetta everyone keeps talking about." He walked to the helicopter and opened the door. Before entering, he called back, "We're not all bad guys, you know." He waved and climbed aboard. While waiting for the blades to turn up to speed, he slid the window open and yelled from the cockpit, "We'll go to the island and pick up Mandeli. We'll keep our eyes open for your friends. If we find them, and they don't give us too much trouble, we'll bring them back."

"Thanks," Eric shouted, and gave him a salute.

The helicopter rose above the village and again tore fronds from roofs and uprooted drying racks. The natives knew what to expect and were prepared, that time. They watched until the huge machine had all but disappeared across the lake, and then returned to the task of replacing roofs and reconstructing drying racks.

When the excitement was over the women turned their attentions back to the wounded elder. It was obvious his injury had not been life threatening; he savored the attention of the women, too much. Several young girls bandaged his wound with the newly acquired supplies from the helicopter, while others poured more *pombe* down his throat.

"Mister Somerville," Paul said. "Do you think the rangers will find our friends and bring them back? They won't take them to jail, will they?"

Eric placed a reassuring hand on the boy's shoulder. "No, they won't put either of them in jail," he said. "The lieutenant from the helicopter, who is Mandeli's superior, said they'll probably put the sergeant there, instead."

"That Sergeant Mandeli is a terrible person," Paul said. "I don't understand why he does those bad things to my people."

"I don't understand either. Only he knows, I guess. Maybe someday we'll find out what he's all about." He squeezed Paul's shoulder and returned to the truck.

"What's happening, buddy?" Dan asked, as he lit a cigarette and blew a smoke ring into the hot, still air. "What was that all about...you and Paul?"

"He's confused. I guess he doesn't understand his own people. But, neither do I." Eric leaned back against the truck and sighed.

Before the soft orange glow of the sun had completely disappeared behind the Loima hills, it had cast long, finger-like shadows across the tranquil water of the lake. Doves glided down in pairs for a last drink, before nesting in the branches of the thorny bushes that flourished near the water's edge. Carnivorous night creatures came out of hiding places and started searching for food.

Paul sat at the water's edge looking out over the lake. He suddenly heard the faint popping sound of the helicopter returning, and his heart quickened.

The huge craft came in low over the village and headed for its landing site. Once again, prop-wash upended fish racks and ripped palm-fronds from the hut's roofs. The moment it landed its powerful engine shuddered and died. However, the sound of the swishing blades prevailed over the lapping sound of the lake. The entire village rushed to the landing site; its weird sound and destructive force was no longer an intimidation.

The door of the plane opened and a ranger jumped out to pull the metal staircase down. Paul's eyes searched the doorway, but they could not penetrate the darkness inside.

Without warning, Hussein charged through the door, knocking Paul headlong onto the sand. After spitting out a mouthful of hot sand, he looked over and saw Paul lying beside him.

"Paul! Paul!" he shouted. "How did you get here? I thought you were in Nairobi. You must tell me all about your adventures in the big city."

They got to their feet and Paul wrapped his arm around his friend's neck. "I'll tell you all about it later," he said with a smile and a poke in the ribs. "There's not much to tell. I didn't have an adventure like you. That's for sure." He raised an eyebrow. "Was Ebukut really with you?"

"Yes, he's with me now. He rescued me from the ranger's jail."

Paul's eyes widened. "You must tell me everything."

"I will, my friend," Hussein assured him. "First, we have to find out what's going to happen to us, now that we're prisoners of the rangers, again." They walked to the door of the helicopter and sat on the hot, metal steps.

Before Ebukut left the plane, he had made his way to the cockpit to speak to the pilot, whom he felt comfortable and at ease with. After they had finished their conversation, he walked to the stairs, where the boys were still sitting, and relayed what he had learned.

"The pilot told me we might have to go in front of a board in Maralal and tell them our story," he told them. "He said they will do nothing to us, if we tell them the truth...which we will. He said he would speak in our behalf, and that it might be helpful if the white men came."

Hussein walked across the sand to the truck and relayed the information to Dan and Eric.

"Of course we'll come," Eric said. "We'd be glad to speak against Mandeli." He followed Hussein back to the plane and listened as Hussein relayed the message back to Ebukut.

The pilot maneuvered his massive body around the boys on the steps and planted his huge feet on the sand. "That may not be necessary, Mr. Somerville," he said. Sweat dripped from his ebony face, ran down the front of his khaki shirt, and formed large moist rings below its pockets. "We have all the proof we need to put him in jail for a long time. However, there is one problem...we can't find him. We've searched the entire island, and the water in between, but with no luck. I think the crocs may have gotten him. It would be a terrible price to pay, but no worse than he deserved, I guess. I understand it was common knowledge, at least in Maralal, that over the years he had been responsible for many Samburu deaths. We all had our suspicions but nobody would speak out...fear of reprisal, I guess. He was a mad man, no question about it."

"Let me know if you need us," Eric said. "I'll make certain everybody gets to Maralal." He reached for the pilot's hand.

"It all depends on whether we find the sergeant," the pilot answered. "If we don't, we can assume he's dead. If that's the case, there will be no investigation and you won't be needed. I don't think the headquarters in Maralal knew about the two boys...only the rangers in the field. I guess Mandeli kept it a secret from the officials. If they had known, it wouldn't have gone this far. I can assure you of that. There's no law that says you can't kill an animal in self-defense. Mandeli was using those boys to justify his hatred for the Samburus. At least that's the impression I got after speaking with Joseph." He pointed to the back seat of the helicopter, where Joseph sat with his head bowed.

Wide-eyed and trembling, Joseph leaned forward in his seat and looked at them. "I'm sorry for all the suffering he's caused all of you," he told them. "I wish it had never happened. I wish I hadn't been involved at all. Even so, I was only following the orders of my superior. I didn't know or want to know what was happening, until recently. I hope you can understand that. I should have put my foot down on several occasions, but I was afraid and did nothing." After he had finished he leaned back and stared out the window.

The pilot started the engine and engaged the blades. Once again the village was enveloped in a thunderous roar and a severe windstorm. He yelled over the sound of the fluttering blades, "We'll make one last sweep over the island, before it gets too dark. If we still can't find him we'll go back to Koobi and pick up the pilot. I might see you in Maralal. You'll be informed. Good bye, good luck." The helicopter hovered for a few seconds, to make certain the blades were clear, and then lifted up and over the tops of the huts.

After the village had returned to normal, the natives went about the business of racking fish for the next day's relentless sun.

A young boy ran down the beach, waving his arms and pointing in the direction of the island. Everyone looked out on the lake. A low, rhythmic chant drifted out over the dark water. The hunters had returned with their kills.

The sun had all but disappeared behind the hills, but its pastel rays had lingered on the horizon long enough to give the lake one last, triumphant salute, before plunging out of sight.

Soon, the brilliance of the Milky Way would be obscured by the strong nightly wind. Campfires would dot the village and send their eerie, wind-blown shadows up and down the beach. Women would cook at their fire pits, and men would gather around them to swap tales of hunting crocodiles and hippos.

Eric told the boys it would be foolish to head back to the fishing club that late at night, over that rough terrain. They would sleep in the trucks and depart at first light in the morning.

The driver Paul had hired to bring them to the village said he could not stay, he had to check into the club by a certain hour every night, but he would not charge them for his time while spent in the village. He said it was the best adventure he ever had. He returned 200-shillings.

Eric and Dan had been invited to sit by the fire and listen to the hunter's tales about *mambas* and *kibokos* they had brought back from other hunting trips, but they refused. They could have told stories too, but the natives would not have understood their English any better than they understood the El Molo language. Instead, they sat in silence at the edge of the campfires helping them drink their *pombe*.

Paul and Hussein walked to the edge of the village, gathered small pieces of broken limbs and elephant grass, and started a fire to ward off the chill of the impending wind. Flames erupted into long, orange fingers, which pierced the semi-darkness around them. They found a sandstone boulder to sit on and stared up at the Milky Way, as they had so many times before. Ebukut and Gabriel joined them. Kibbi soon arrived and asked if he could join them.

"Paul," Hussein said, breaking the silence. "You didn't care for Nairobi?"

Paul threw a small-knotted limb from a flower-bearing *nkoita* tree onto the flames. He thought for a moment, and then replied, "It wasn't what I expected."

"What did you expect?"

"I'm not sure. When I saw the tourists at the club, how they appeared to have everything, I thought all I had to do was go where they were and I would be like them and have everything they have. It was a foolish thought."

Ebukut cleared his throat. "It's not foolish to want to live like the white man," he began in Masai, "but it's unwise to do so. No doubt they have many shillings and other things we do not have, but there are things we have that they don't have." He picked up a smoldering twig and blew on it until it burst into flame.

A puzzled expression came over Paul's face. "But we have nothing," he replied. "We don't even have a table to put our food on…and no food to put on it, even if we did."

The conversation was confusing Kibbi. He leaned on his spear and wrapped one leg around it like a stork waiting for prey. "I don't understand," he said. "What is a table?"

Paul gave him a disgruntled look, and continued. "I saw many things in Nairobi. Things I never saw before. Things we could surely use in Loiyangalani."

"If that is true, why did you come back?" Ebukut asked. "If you had stayed, those things might have meant something to you. But you didn't stay, so now they mean nothing. They're only memories in your head."

Paul thought for a moment. "That is true," he said. "If a person doesn't know about something, he doesn't desire it. That's what a wise old elder once told me." He stirred the ashes until they had erupted into flaming tentacles, and then continued. "Nevertheless, I saw things in Nairobi and desired them. But to have them I would have had to go through too much to get them. I realize now it was my selfishness and lust for what the white man has that made me go to Nairobi in the first place. I used my friend's good fortune to fuel my own greed." He looked over at Hussein and put his arm around his shoulder. "I am ashamed for almost losing your friendship, over such a childish thing…the white man's lifestyle."

"So, did you come back out of guilt?" Ebukut asked.

"I came back to see if I could help my friend," Paul said with a frown. "I received a message he was in trouble and I wanted to help."

Ebukut stirred the flaming coals and again sparks sprang into the night sky. "Isn't it true," he began, "that you came back because you couldn't live like the city people? Hussein was just a convenient excuse for you to return." He added, quickly, "Don't take this wrong, but I believe you found out the hard way that the white man's things didn't mean as much to you as you thought they would. I believe, down deep, you would just as soon have nothing the white man has to offer, than to lose what you have as a Samburu. And you have many things." He lifted his eyes and watched as the sparks swirled in little circles above the fire, and then disappeared. For several moments, complete silence prevailed. He continued. "You have the friendship of your brothers. There is no true friendship between the white man and us. He is sometimes friendly, but there is no true friendship."

For a long moment, Paul dwelled on what the warrior had said. It was true, the white man could be friendly, but he could never be a true friend.

He believed it was because the white man didn't have the desire to understand the Samburu's ways, and the fact that material things were unimportant to them.

He then realized the bonding river of friendship and honor that flowed through the veins of all tribes had more intrinsic value than anything material could ever have. The natives of Africa, the aborigines of Australia, and those who had survived for eons without the material things of life were possibly the only ones who *could* understand that.

Paul took off his white shirt, white shorts, white socks, and the white tennis shoes he had purchased in Nairobi, and dropped them onto the sand. He turned to Hussein, reached for his hand and placed it against his own heart. "Can you feel my soul, Hussein?" he said. "Can you feel it flowing through my body?"

Chapter Thirteen

On a thorn-infested path outside his village, Nathan squatted on his haunches nursing an injured leg of a black and gray lizard. Off in the distance, he believed he heard a faint sound and jerked his head around to investigate. He cocked it to one side, trained wax-encrusted ears on the expanse of desert, and then surveyed the landscape. Satisfied that nothing out of the ordinary needed his immediate attention he returned to nursing the lizard's limp leg. After probing the tiny creature's wound with his fingers, he realized he could do nothing more and dropped it to the ground. He watched the tiny creature hobble into the bushes, dragging its injured leg behind.

He sat down in the middle of the path and a bloody toe captured his attention. He had stumbled on one of the many low acacia bushes that lined the path, and a one-inch thorn had found its way under his big toenail. With jagged, dirt filled fingernails and much effort, he managed to extract the thorn. He scrubbed the wound with hot sand, and then lifted his foot to admire his handiwork. He turned his chubby frame around and walked toward the thorn fence that surrounded his family's *manyatta*.

He heard the sound again and snapped his head up to check the desert out. He cupped his hands over his eyes to protect them from the intense rays of the morning sun and saw a fast moving column of dust headed toward his village. When he could see through the billowing dust, he saw an object that had the shape of a Land Rover. Was it one of the ranger's trucks? He wondered. After watching it for a few minutes he realized it was not the right color; it was red and theirs were blue. Furthermore, it didn't have men hanging from its sides, like the ones that frequent the village to check for illegal game. He stood motionless, straining his burning brown eyes like the captain of a ship in search of sea monsters. His heart pounded excitedly, making it difficult to breathe. Could it be his brother coming back from Nairobi? That would be too much to hope for. Although he had been gone only two days, to him it had seemed an eternity.

He would never forget the day his brother flew away in the silver machine. After it had taken off it circled the village, flew out over the lake, and stirred up hundreds of pink-winged flamingos. He recalled how his heart had fluttered when the silver bird had crested the tops of the hills and kept on going until it was out of sight.

As the Rover drew near, he spotted a figure hanging halfway out the door waving at him. "L'hari?" he shouted, and rushed to meet the slow moving truck. He waited until it came closer, and then shouted in Masai, "My brother, my brother, you have come home." He performed a miniature war dance in the middle of the dusty path, jumping up and down as high as his stubby legs and injured toe would allow. When the truck slid to a complete stop, he waited for the cloud of dust to settle.

Clad in white shirt and shorts, Paul jumped from the truck and raced toward him. "Nathan!" he yelled. He picked the small boy up in his arms, swung him between his legs, and then pulled him close to his chest and hugged him. "Look at you, you've not grown a bit, my little brother.

You're no bigger now than when I left."

Nathan swatted him on the shoulder and frowned. "You no joke with me, L'hari," he came back in abbreviated English. "You only gone short time. No joke with me, brother. I big enough." He formed a fist and hit his brother a glancing blow on the side of his chin. Paul put his hand to his jaw and swayed back and forth, feigning injury. Nathan appeared apprehensive, but after a few moments, he grinned exhibiting two empty spaces where front teeth had once been.

Two young men in full tribal attire clambered out of the truck. Ebukut plucked Nathan out of Paul's arms and straddled the young boy's legs around his neck. "What's your name, little warrior?" he asked in Masai. He turned his head and looked up at him.

"Nathan. You know my name," the boy came back, also in Masai. "And I know yours."

"Speak English, Nathan," his brother scolded. "What will I do with you? You never speak English, anymore. And stop calling me L'hari my Christian name is Paul. I call you Nathan don't I? I don't call you N'Gwani."

"But this warrior know Masai better," Nathan replied in English and patted Ebukut on top of his head.

"This true, small friend," Ebukut said in broken English. "But brother right, you speak white man talk…some day you be rich like him…but strong like Samburu. You speak white man talk you get much money and food." He winked at Paul.

"I no want to be like white man. He not friend," Nathan replied. He looked down at the top of the warrior's head and again patted him on his ocher hairpiece. "Someday I be like you, great warrior. I be rich…and strong too." They all laughed.

"Little brother, I have a present for you," Paul said, as they walked toward their *manyatta*, which was set off to one side in the village.

Nathan's eyes widened. "A present? For me? What is it? Something to eat?"

"You'll see," Paul said. He patted his *sampur*, which held all of his possessions. "But you must wait until we get to our hut. I have something for *mama mzazi*, too. I want you and mother to be happy together."

"Something to wear?" Nathan asked, excited by the thought. His face beamed. "It must be clothes. I no have good pants, they too short. And I no have *kiatus* for bleeding toe." He jabbered all the way to the thorn fence that surrounded their *manyatta*. "I hope is food. I hungry."

Hussein lingered a few moments by the truck, and then ran to catch up with the others. He glanced up at the dirt-encrusted boy bouncing up and down on the warrior's shoulders, and giggled. His own brother, N'turi, was about his age. All children in the village were the same; their minds forever on food, play, or sleep. A thought flashed through his mind. He remembered the day he crept into his brother's sleeping hut to look for a bag of candy he needed for himself and Ebukut, when they were running from the rangers. N'turi had opened his eyes and asked if he was stealing his candy. He told him he was not stealing only borrowing, and that he would pay him back when he returned. Satisfied with the response the boy turned on his side and went back to sleep.

As they approached the stockade fence, a young girl strolled across the dusty central area toward them. She hesitated briefly in front of the boulder that had played a major role in Hussein's ceremony of manhood, and then continued her sensuous walk toward them. Her fish-skin apron flapped against her long, slender legs as she walked, and her muscular body glistened with sweat from the morning sun. She acknowledged the others by a casual glance, and then fixed her eyes on Paul.

"I didn't think you would be back so soon," she said in Masai "Did you make your fortune, already? Are you now rich?" She smiled, displaying a row of pearl-white teeth, surrounded by full, moist lips.

He grinned. "Yes, I made my fortune…my riches," he said, and put his arms around the two warrior's necks. "These are my friends…they are my riches."

She put her finger above his heart and let it slide down his chest. "I'm glad you came to your senses…about coming back, I mean." She stared into his eyes, leaned forward, and pressed her multi-beaded ear lobe next to her finger. "I feel your soul, Paul," she whispered. "I can feel it flowing through your body."

His heart raced. She had never spoken to him like that, before. A friend at the fishing club had told him she had said those same words to Hussein when she guided him through his ceremony of manhood. Which made him wonder why she had said them to him. Maybe she had changed her feelings toward him. He was confused.

Years ago, when they were all much younger, both he and Hussein had vied for her attention. Nonetheless, she had never favored one over the other. Because of that indifference he believed she must have had feelings for someone older, perhaps a warrior.

Lnuie had always been the ceremonial maiden for the young boys of the village, when they had reached the age of circumcision, and then manhood. By tribal tradition, she had been required to recite certain phrases as part of the ritual. However, they were only incantations and had no special meaning. Any significance the words may have had was lost over the years by the many changing formats of the ceremony. However, what she whispered could not have anything to do with tribal tradition; he was not a warrior. He could only hope she had said it because she was happy to see him. It didn't matter to him why she had said them, it was enough that she had.

She lowered her finger from his chest, turned to the others, and gave each a limp handshake. "I thought the ranger as tall as a giraffe had captured you two," she said to them.

"Yes, he did find us," Hussein said. "But now everything's fine. I don't think we'll have any more trouble with him, or the other rangers." Embarrassed by her eye contact, he glanced down at a small child munching on a fist full of maize bread. He watched him until she had turned her head and looked away.

"Do you really think we have nothing to worry about from the rangers?" Ebukut said. "They *are* gray men, you know. It's almost certain we'll have more encounters with them." His expression turned grave and a frown formed above his dark, piercing eyes. "They'll find ways to make our lives miserable, you can count on it. They will always be gray men and we will always be Samburus. They treat us like wild dogs, and nothing will change that." They all nodded in agreement.

When the village discovered that Paul and the others had arrival, dozens of sweating, foul-smelling bodies swarmed around them. L'Umbo, Hussein's father and tribal leader, approached them. Before greeting them, he placed his hand on each child's head who had been circumcised and patted them several times, which was the custom. After the last boy had been greeted, he turned to the warriors and shook their hands with a single pump of his arm.

Paul's mother raced across the central area to greet them, her arms flailing over her head in excitement. Spouting a barrage of Masai, she threw her arms around his neck. After the short welcome, she abruptly turned and rushed back to her hut. Several minutes later she returned with her arms full of maize bread and *saroi*. She dropped them beside him, and then returned to the hut for more food.

G'hambi, Hussein's uncle, heard the commotion and arrived with a large gourd of *pombe* beer; which he dispensed only on special occasions. His wife, Etaira, who had never liked *pombe*, shoved him and the gourd aside. Small children ran up to the warriors, fondled their bright red wraps, and attempted to force their grubby fingers into their *sampurs*.

Nathan walked over to Paul and tugged on his shirt. "My brother," he said in English. "Is it time?"

Paul looked into his large, cow-like eyes. "Time? Time for what?" he asked. It took several moments before he remembered the gifts. "Oh, yes. It's time. But first, get *mama mzazi*." He didn't have to say it twice. Nathan's short, bowed legs spun his chubby body around and propelled it like a rocket across the compound. Several minutes later, his mother arrived with more food and stood at his side.

He un-strapped his *sampur* and sat it on the ground. Nathan tried to sneak his hands into the bag, but they were slapped away. He extracted a small, brown package, no larger than Nathan's fist, and handed it to him. The boy looked at it and hesitated. Paul saw his dejected face and realized he was waiting for something more, something bigger. However, he had nothing more.

Nathan turned the package over and over in his stubby fingers, while eying the *sampur*. When he finally realized nothing more was coming, he untied the course manila twine and tore off the brown wrapper. Every sweaty body in the compound moved closer. The ones in back jumped high into the air to see over the heads of the ones in front. As the wrapper settled to the ground, his hand exposed a small, red object with a silver crown embossed on one side. Even after a close inspection he could not identify it. On one side were appendages, which he also did not recognize. After several minutes of fondling the object, his face beamed and his eyes widened, forcing his forehead up to his black, curly hair. He let out a shout of joy, and then threw his arms around his brother's neck.

"L'hari! L'hari!" he screamed into his ear. He put his fingers across his mouth, realizing his verbal mistake. "Paul! Paul!" he shrieked again. "Thank you. Thank you. Thank you." He released his grip from around Paul's neck and raced up and down the compound holding the knife high above his head for all to see. The children of the village chased after him shouting and reaching for the knife.

Paul yelled after him, "Be careful the blades are sharp."

"It will do no good to tell him to be careful," Ebukut said. "He will do what he must." He watched Nathan and his entourage race through the thorn gate and out into the desert. "He will learn later what a knife is really for."

Like a nervous sentinel, L'empi stood silent and tense at her son's side. Her excitement grew with each moment that passed. It was obvious her son had taken his time searching the *sampur* for her gift. She wondered what it could possibly be. Maybe it was something to sew with. Maybe store-bought needles, like the ones she had seen in the village *duka*. Maybe a real dress, like the ones the tourists wear at the fishing club. But that would be too expensive, she thought. Besides, the *sampur* was not large enough to hold a dress. She could not guess. An anxious smile spread across her long, toothless face, and then disappeared.

Paul continued to fumble about in his bag. "Ah, here it is," he said. He looked up at his mother, but did not pull it out of the bag.

She tried not to look apprehensive. She knew the tribal custom; a person should not covet something they did not work for. She folded her arms across her bare breasts, glanced off into the distance, and tried not to look nonchalant. The women of the village crowded around teasing and nudging her closer to the *sampur*. She unfolded her arms and turned on them. With a few unsavory words and gestures she shoved them back into the crowd.

With a magician's swoop of his arm, he extracted a brown package from the *sampur* and handed it to her. Her dirt-stained fingers tore into the brown cover. Several women tried to help but their hands were slapped away. When she had finally ripped through the wrapper, two black and white rubber-soled shoes were exposed. It took several pensive moments, then a sign of recognition spread across her face. With a broad smile, she pulled the price tag off one shoe, and then dropped them both to the ground. She placed her hands on two adjacent shoulders for support and slid her feet into their soft, foamy comfort. For a long moment she stood motionless, admiring them. At the coaxing of the women she walked amongst them, one cautious step after the other. After a few moments she began to leap up and down like a springbok deer. The women had to move out of her way to avoid a collision. They formed a line behind her, warbled their tongues, jumped high into the air, and chased after her.

CHAPTER FOURTEEN

Far to the west of the lake, the sun had descended to the tops of the highest peaks on the Loima Hills. As it came to rest on the ridgeline, it resembled a large orange about to be impaled by the highest peaks. For a few minutes it appeared to teeter precariously, then slowly descended down the other side. Before it completely disappeared it manufactured long, dark shadows that zigzagged across the rock-strewn desert to the east. Its feeble, reddish haze sent dull swaths of amber to the highest pinnacles of Mt. Kulal, and then projected its cone-shaped image far into the eastern desert. After the soft glow on the horizon faded, the landscape was once again overwhelmed with brilliant moonlight.

A single engine Cessna darted low over the tops of large rocky protrusions, a few kilometers west of Loiyangalani. Strong air currents had forced it down to within a few meters of the warm desert floor, and then strong updrafts sent it careening toward another craggy hilltop. Its engine sputtered and spit, coughed and popped, and its wings trembled against the strong air turbulence.

"Didn't you check the engine before we left?" the pilot asked the young co-pilot, in a gruff voice.

The co-pilot reached to the dashboard and turned the magneto lever to one side. The engine coughed. He swung it in the opposite direction and found no discernible difference.

"Yes, I did," he returned. "Something's happened to one of the mags." He glared at the pilot, and then added, "That was your job anyway, you're the friggin' pilot."

"I thought you wanted to learn something about flyin', kid," the pilot came back. He reached over to double-check the mags. "Can't get any elevation out of this damn thing, either." He pulled back hard on the yoke and the plane skimmed over the top of a solitary umbrella tree on the crest of a rise. Unexpectedly, the engine caught and smoothed out to a purr. With a sudden burst of power, and the assistance of an updraft, the plane nosed higher. Both men heaved a sigh of relief. "I got a sick feelin' in my gut, kid," he added.

"Yeah, I know what you mean, Jack," the co-pilot said. "I got one, too. But I did check the mags in Nakuru." The young man glanced over at the grumpy old pilot, hoping for a sign of assurance.

Jack didn't answer right away. After a few moments, he said, "I know you checked 'em, kid. But there's somethin' else ailing this baby. I can feel it in my bones. I only hope she makes it to Koobi, before she wets the bed."

"God! I hope so, too," the young man said through a nervous sigh. As he looked out his window, he could see the tops of rocky ridges and the flat, bushy limbs of acacia trees dart by. "I'd hate like hell to put her down in that stuff. We wouldn't stand a chance." Jack glanced out his side window and nodded.

They took their eyes off the dark, threatening objects, a few meters below, long enough to listen for signs of pending trouble. Their breathing became taxed and their hearts pounded.

Without warning, the plane caught a fierce, turbulent wind, which made it dart toward an obscure hillside. Another gust came out of nowhere and forced the plane over the crest, which allowed it to straighten out and gain altitude.

When it had leveled off, Jack loosened his grip on the yoke and flapped his hands to regain circulation. "Son-of-a-bitch!" he blurted out. "That was too damned close!"

The young co-pilot eyed him with a cynical grin. "We could have flown over Baringo, or Pokot, you know. We didn't have to go over these damned saw-tooth mountains."

"With the cargo we're carryin'?" Jack said, taken back by his comment. "Hell," he continued, "the shortest distance is still a straight line. If we took your route and crash landed with this cargo over Pokot, we might get down all right but there'd be cops all over the place." He considered it for a moment, and then added, "At least if we went down here in the Turkana area we'd stand a good chance of *not* gettin' caught."

"Yeah, if we survived," the kid said, with a mocking sneer. "Look at the crap down there…nothin' but rocks and trees."

"George," Jack said. A smile spread across his tobacco-stained, whiskered face. "You don't have faith in my flyin' ability? Is that what you're sayin'?"

"Could you dodge those rocks down there?" George said, and pointed into the darkness.

"No problem," Jack came back with a smirk.

George stared through the windshield, mesmerized by what he could and could not see. He wondered why he had gotten himself involved in this mess. Nevertheless, this trip would give him a nice nest egg, if he lived to take advantage of it. Jack, an old retired Viet pilot, had approached him several days earlier and caught him at a weak moment; he needed the money. There was no question about that. For a long time he had wanted to put a down payment on a 20-foot fishing boat he saw in Nakuru, and this seemed an easy way to get the money. Jack had assured him no one would get hurt. He had said it was only a few hours flying time, and then he would have all the money he needed. It sounded too good to be true, or to pass up. No problems, no worries, just fast bucks.

Nothing had prepared him for the possibility that the 40-year old Cessna might not make it. Jack had also neglected to tell him they would be flying over the worst terrain in east Africa. He had heard about the area, known for its thermals, downdrafts and severe air currents. In addition, he had not told him the compass didn't work and they would be flying "seat-of-the-pants".

A veteran of the Viet war, Jack Emerson had well over 10,000 hours logged. With that in mind, George was confident the man could handle any situation that might come up. Quite to the contrary, he had received his pilot's license only a few months earlier. Therefore, their predicament bothered the hell out of him.

"You want a beer, kid?" Jack asked.

A disgusted look flashed across the young co-pilot's face. He shook his head and looked back out his window.

"What's the matter, you don't approve?" Jack said, raising his voice an octave. "You not old enough or what?" He grinned and popped the top off a bottle of strong local beer he retrieved from an ice chest behind his seat. He guzzled half of it down, before coming up for air. He waved the bottle in front of the young pilot's face, and said, "Sure you won't have one, kid? It's ice cold."

George had fixed his mind and eyes on the darkness outside. "Thanks, but no thanks, I drink *after* work," he said, sarcastically.

Jack's eyes twinkled, as he leaned back in the pilot's seat. "Oh, pardon the hell out of me," he shot back. "I didn't know you were so damned 'company'."

Although the sun had disappeared, at their altitude its soft glow lingered on the horizon. Except for an occasional popping of the sick engine, silence permeated the small cockpit.

George looked over to say something, and then noticed Jack's head bobbing up and down, as if he were asleep. For a few moments he held his gaze on the bear-like figure. He didn't know why, but he admired that aging hulk of a man. He had thought of him as the epitome of a bush pilot, at least until he had acquired that extended beer gut and started wearing that stupid Smilin' Jack hat. His face was red and pockmarked from too many years of hard, fast living and too much booze. His upper lip supported a thin, well-trimmed mustache that had turned silver-gray over the years. His salt and pepper hair hung in greasy strands down the back of his neck, and then cascaded over the top of his soiled dark blue collar where it ended up in a tangled mass on his shoulders.

Over the years, law enforcement officials from all territories had become aware of Jack's mischievous antics, but they turned their heads the other way and treated him like a favorite uncle. For the most part, he was easy-going with not too many serious vices. His six foot four, 240-pound frame made him an imposing figure that intimidated most men. Of course he knew this and took advantage of it. No one could say "no" to him. He knew he couldn't. There was something about the old bastard that made him want to emulate him. God forbid, he thought.

He took his mind off Jack long enough to strain his eyes into the darkness, in a futile attempt to find a spot to land, but without success.

He turned his head and again looked at the bent-over figure. He wondered what had made him transport this stuff. He didn't believe it was like him to be this far out in left field. To his knowledge he had never been in serious trouble with the law. As far as he knew he had been thrown in jail only once, and that was for a friendly bar room brawl. Maybe his age made him do stupid things, he rationalized. Maybe he was in financial trouble. Whatever the case, he had been running around with the wrong crowd…the big boys played for keeps around here. He figured he would tell him that, later.

He was only going to make this one trip, he was certain of that. Then, he would get out of the business and stay out. Wasn't that was what they always said in the movies? He snickered.

At the very moment his mind returned from his analysis of Jack to the business of flying the plane, the engine sputtered and died.

Jack's eyes popped open and he quickly scanned the instrument panel. "Christ!" he yelled. "Look at the damn cylinder head temp! It's off the friggin' scale! What the hell you been doin'? Haven't you been watchin' anything?"

Flustered and embarrassed, George jerked his hands off the yoke. He leaned back, took a deep breath, scanned the instrument panel, and then clamped his hands back on the wheel.

"Christ!" Jack roared, and threw the empty bottle in the back.

George's face turned beet-red and he looked over. "Don't Christ me!" he shot back. "It's not my fault this piece of crap's fallin' apart!"

"Piece of crap? Piece of crap?" Jack bellowed. "This 'piece of crap', as you call her, has more hours in the air than you got on the ground, sonny."

"I can believe that."

"You believe any damn thing you want!" Jack erupted. "Hold onto the goddamn wheel while I look for the problem."

"Yes, sir! I have been," the young co-pilot snapped back, and gave him a quick salute.

Jack crawled halfway under the dash and aimed his flashlight around "Ah ha!" he shouted.

"Find something?"

Jack didn't answer. After a few seconds, he pulled an oil-laden hand out from beneath the instrument panel and held it up to George's eyes.

"Oh, crap!" George mumbled. A pained expression spread across his face.

"Does that answer your question? Does that tell you anything?"

George looked over with a nervous grin. "Yeah, it tells me I should have stayed home."

"Funny," Jack replied. He turned upside down, rested the calves of his legs on the back of his seat, and slid deeper under the dash to look for a damaged line, or anything that might have caused the problem. Several minutes later he stuck his head out. "We got big problems, kid. The oil's comin' from the engine compartment and I can't get at it. Got to land to do anything about it."

It took George several seconds to grasp the gravity of their situation. He looked down at Jacks grubby face, still half buried, and said, "Land? What do you mean, land? Where the hell we goin' to land?" He pointed out his window.

"Hell, I don't know, improvise," Jack said in a calm voice. "We can cut the engine and ride these updrafts for a while...let the engine cool down. Maybe she'll restart...and maybe she won't."

"You're awfully damned composed for a man about to meet his maker," George said with a nervous snicker.

"Hell," Jack bellowed, above the hiss of the wind through the ill-fitting doors. "I've been in worse predicaments than this and lived through it. Gotta have faith, baby. That's all it takes…a little faith. And lots of gonads."

George's stomach churned. He could never find those antacids when he needed them. Whenever he was in a tight spot or excited his stomach flared up. He glanced out his window at the craggy hills and dark images of umbrella trees a few meters below, and then turned his eyes back to the instrument panel.

"My God! Where *can* we land?" he shouted. "There's no place to set this thing down. There's no valley down there, no meadow…not even a level spot." He looked over at Jack, still upside down in the pilot's seat. "How can you be so damned calm?" He was surprised that Jack had not opened another beer.

Jack pulled himself upright and reached into the cooler, as if he had read the kid's mind. "Want one now?" he asked, and held a bottle in front of his face. "You could probably use one about now." He popped the cap and continued. "It might be your last, you know." A twinkle formed in his eye.

"Damn it!" George roared. He glared at Jack with malevolent eyes. "No! I don't want one. I've got more important things to do. Would it be asking too goddamn much to give me a hand with this problem of ours?"

"Problem? What problem?" Jack replied, unruffled. "What do you want me to do? You want me to climb out on the wing, open the cowl, and fix the damned leak? Is that what you want?"

"Don't be a wise-ass!"

"Well, then tell me. What should I do?" Jack looked at the kid with a blank expression.

The hot air currents they had been riding to maintain altitude had suddenly vanished, which forced the plane to descend. It could no longer sustain enough air speed or elevation to hunt for new ones. They were less than 20-meters above the jagged hills, and descending at a perilous rate.

George pulled back hard on the yoke. The plane reared back ready to stall. "Dammit! Jack, do something," he screamed. "I can't hold this stupid thing any longer. She's about to stall." A moment later the shrill sound of the indicator filled the cockpit.

Jack wedged the beer between his legs and grabbed the yoke. With the skill of a surgeon, his hands flew from one control to the other. The stationary wheels were barely clearing the tops of trees, a few meters below. The engine sputtered, coughed and died, and the propeller spun in the wind. Nonetheless, an experienced yank on the throttle and a careful adjustment of the choke restarted it. The plane lurched forward, gaining altitude with each revolution of the prop. By the time the engine had smoothed out, they were directly over a small meadow. By the light of the moon they could make out a steep but smooth incline in front of them. However, as they approached it, they discovered the area was seeded with large rocks and tall shrubs; too many to attempt a landing.

Jack pulled back on the yoke, twisted it all the way counter-clockwise and banked to the left. He pushed hard on the left rudder pedal and shoved the throttle to the dash. The Cessna lurched to the left in a severe turn, missing a tall umbrella tree by inches. The prop-wash churned its spiny boughs as the plane sailed over it. The engine whined and the plane's metal skin rippled under the strain of his command.

"Jesus Christ! Jesus Christ! Jesus Christ!" George kept repeating, and put his hands in front of his face to shield it. He glanced over at the subtle look on Jack's face and tightened his jaws in anger. How he could be so damn calm, so mechanical, was beyond him.

After the severe 180-degree bank, the plane glided back down the incline, paralleling the meadow it had flown over a few seconds earlier. As it regained power and mobility, it headed for the crest of the previous hill. The Cessna finally reached its cruising speed and climbed to the top of the rise at the end of the meadow. When it had reached the crestm Jack cut the power in half and allowed it to glide down the other side. Halfway down the slope the engine sputtered and popped, stuttered and died.

From out of the darkness, a large boulder loomed in front of them. The plane dove toward it at a 45-degree angle and crashed into its base. Shattered pieces of wing and landing gear remained at the bottom of the boulder, but the bulk of the fuselage sailed over the top of the mountainous rock and into the darkness. The cabin came to rest against the trunk of a large umbrella tree, nose down, its tail assembly balanced vertically in the air. It teetered for a few seconds, then toppled over and landed upright.

Jack looked over at George. His head had been smashed against the windshield and blood oozed from his forehead and ran down the front of his white, open-neck shirt. He checked for a pulse, but found none. He could tell by the attitude of his head that his neck had been broken.

"Crap," he muttered. The word seemed to echo in the quietness of the cockpit. "Goddamn you kid! Why the hell didn't you have your belt fastened? You stupid ass!" He held a one-sided conversation with his dead friend. "Now, what are we going to do, George?" he continued. He reached over and slapped him on the shoulder. "Goddamn it, kid! This is one helluva time to get yourself killed. Son-of-a-bitch!"

He dropped his hands in his lap and sighed. He didn't have the faintest idea where they were. He hadn't noticed a thing while George was flying.

He had not even looked at the map, not that it would have done any good; the navigation chart he picked up in Nakuru before the flight was useless. There was nothing on it he could have used as a reference point. Only the highest mountains and largest lakes were pinpointed, and to his knowledge there were none of those around.

Lake Turkana was on the map, but where the hell was it? He wondered. He didn't have the slightest idea. Was he north of the lake, south, east? Where the hell was he? He would have to wait until first light of morning. He definitely didn't want to get out of the plane at night, not in that area, there were too many critters and they were all hungry.

He stared into the blackness through the shattered side window, attempting to find a landmark he could associate with on the faintly lit horizon. He heard a low moan. It sounded like it came from inside the plane. On the other hand, it could have come from outside, possibly an animal. He heard it again. This time it appeared to be directly behind him. He turned his head and looked into the back of the plane, where the seats had been removed to make room for his cargo. He heard it again, but this time it was a low, almost inaudible moan, like somebody in pain. He knew that was impossible, he was the only one there, except George, and he knew it wasn't him.

He heard the moan again. He loosened his seat belt and crawled into the back. It appeared to be coming from a pile of plastic bags that had been torn loose from their bindings. He put his ear close to the packages and listened. In the silence of the cockpit, he detected breathing. With a tug on a retaining strap, he pulled the rest of the bundles free.

Under the array of white bags sat a young black boy. His eyes were wide open and filled with fear, and his shoulders shook, uncontrollably.

Jack brought his face close to the boy's. "What do we have here?" he said, raising his eyebrows.

The boy stared at him, but said nothing.

Jack moved closer, forcing the boy up against a metal retaining wall that had been moved back to make room for maximum cargo.

"Hey, relax, boy," he said. "I'm not gonna hurt you. "But I'd like to know what the hell you're doin' in my plane. That's a fair question, isn't it?" He moved back to give the boy room. "You do speak English, don't you?"

"Hey, man, get outta my face," the boy shot back. "Hell yes, I speak English. What the hell do you take me for, one of those spear-throwing zambuzzies…or whatever the hell they are?"

His colloquial English amused Jack. "New York?" he asked with a grin. "Do I hear the Bronx in there somewhere? That's where I'm from, originally."

"So, big stinkin' deal, pop, lots of people are from New York. You ain't got a corner on the market, you know."

"No, I guess I don't," Jack said. The boy's dark brown eyes glared at him. "Will you relax, son?" he continued. "I ain't gonna hurt you. I don't bite…I promise. I only want to know what the hell you're doin' here. That's all. It ain't every day I get a stowaway."

"I ain't your 'son', pop," the boy said, glaring at him.

"And I ain't your 'pop'," Jack countered. "Now, are you gonna tell me what you're doin' here? Where'd you come from, anyway?"

The boy relaxed his shoulders, and then slid across the bulkhead as far away from Jack as was possible in the small confines of the cabin. He took in a deep breath and exhaled into the cool night air.

"I had to get someplace, fast," he said, quickly. It appeared to Jack that he wanted to get it out before he changed his mind. For a few seconds there was silence, and then he said, "They took my old man away. Now, they're prob'ly after me."

"Whoa, boy, slow down." Jack raised his eyebrows. "What do you mean, 'they took your old man away'? Who took him? You in some kinda trouble, son?"

"Hell yes, I am," the boy shot back. "The other day we were fishin' on Lake Nakuru and when we got back to the hotel some goons came and got my dad. He told me to run like hell and not to stop 'til I got to Koobi Fora…wherever the hell that is." He hesitated long enough to catch his breath, then glanced at George's body. "Is that guy really dead?"

Jack looked over at his co-pilot, his head still forced up against the windshield. "Yes, he is. Now go on with your story, it's getting interesting."

"Nothin' else to tell."

"Come on, damn it! There's got to be more," Jack said. He was starting to get aggravated with the boy. "Why are you supposed to go to Koobi? And how did you know I was going there?"

"I was hiding behind a desk at the terminal, when you came in. You told those guys you wanted to go there. Did they have to give you permission or something?"

"That's right, or something. Now, why did your father want you to go there? He must have had a reason."

The boy didn't answer.

Jack was getting nowhere with him, and he knew it. Maybe he wasn't asking the right questions. Maybe he should start over, using another approach. "What's your name, son? Mine's Jack…like in Smilin' Jack."

"Smilin' who?" came a confused response.

"Smilin'…never mind, you had to be there, I guess."

"I'm Anthony…Tony. Tony O'Brien."

Jack snickered. "You Irish?"

Tony's jaws tightened. He looked away, ignoring the comment. "I'm supposed to find somebody named John up at Koobi Fora," he said. "Or something like that. He's a big shot up there, I guess."

Jack realized the boy was not about to tell him anything more, at least for the moment, so he decided his best course of action would be to drop his query and concentrate personally on him.

"How old are you, Tony O'Brien?" he said.

The boy cocked his head to one side and stared at him. "I'm old enough," he said, defiantly. "Why are you makin' fun of my name? There's lots of blacks in New York with Irish names…and Italian, and French, and Jewish. What's the big deal anyway, pop?"

Jack grinned. "No big deal. Anybody who can stow away on my plane and get away with it has gotta have lots of balls, Irish or not," he said, as he eyed the boy. "And to have that many balls you gotta be old enough." Jack hesitated for a moment, and then added, "It takes a mighty big fellow to go on a trip all by himself, especially as far as Koobi. That's rough territory up there, you know."

Tony grinned. "Hell, it can't be any rougher than that stupid landing you made."

Jack smiled. His mind drifted into the past. He had been flying small planes in Kenya for 15 years and never once had to make an emergency landing. He was proud of that. Not many bush pilots could say that with a straight face.

He remembered with fondness his first instructional flight over the Maasi Mara in southwest Kenya. His instructor had been a woman. As a young girl she had been raised in a small college town in Connecticut. But, out of boredom, she moved her entire world to Kenya. At least that's what she told him.

Although he had many more flying hours, in her eyes he could do nothing right; his banks were too lazy, his climbs too calculated, and his landings too "seat-of-the-pants". With her reports going to safari headquarters in Nairobi, he was surprised he got hired.

"Is he *really* dead?" a concerned voice interrupted his thoughts.

Jack turned and looked at the boy. "Think so," he said. He reached over and shook the motionless figure. "Hey George, you dead? See, he's dead all right."

The boy chuckled. "What are you gonna do with him?"

"Don't rightly know. Think we'll have to bury him right here."

Tony thought for a moment, and then tilted his head to get a better look at the lifeless figure. "You're right. We'll have to bury him right here. We sure as hell can't lug him around."

"Lug him around? I didn't have any notion of doin' that. Come mornin' we'll go outside, dig a big hole, and bury him. The plane'll make a good marker. I'll be able to find him when I come back. I'll give him a decent burial, then. Right, Tony?"

Tony remained silent, but out of the corner of his eye, he continued to observe George.

Jack figured the boy to be around 13 or 14 years old. The kid didn't mince words. He said what was on his mind. He liked that in a person.

"So, Tony O'Brien," he said with a sigh, "now that we've decided to bury him in the morning, maybe we should get some shut-eye. We can't do anything in the dark. What do you think?"

Tony leaned his head back on one of the white bundles and relaxed. The package was too hard for his head and he tossed it to one side. He pulled his sweater up around his neck and folded his arms across his chest.

"Careful with that stuff," Jack said, and pointed to the plastic bag Tony had thrown aside.

The boy eyed the package. "Why? What's so important about that?"

"They're bags of flour. See the rest of them? I don't want any to get broken. I'm taking them to Koobi for the cook." He glanced at the boy for a reaction.

Tony picked up one of the bags and brought it to his nose. He gouged his fingernail through the plastic, and then put the white powder on his tongue.

"Sure it's flour, pops," he said with a grin. "Those cats at Koobi are goin' to be in for some mighty strange tastin' bread, man." He hefted the bag and counted the others. "This is a kilo, here. How many you got?"

Jack's face flushed. How could a 13-year old kid be so damned street smart? How did he know what the stuff was? He put his chin in the palm of his hand and stared into the boy's eyes. "I've got about a hundred pounds…forty kilos," he said with a grin.

"Wow!" Tony cried out.

"How does a kid your age know about this stuff?"

"Hey, man, I'm from the Bronx, remember? They have that stuff for breakfast."

"Do you?"

Tony's eyes ignited. "Hell, no!" he shouted, and lowered his eyebrows in a frown. "What do you take me for? I ain't no coke-head." He squirmed, and then continued. "You got one helluva nerve askin' me that, old man."

"Hey, easy, young fellow, I was merely askin' a question. Can't I ask a simple question without you gettin' all huffy about it?" The boy's reaction told him he had hit a sore spot. "Don't be so damn defensive."

"I ain't defensive. I just don't want you thinkin' I'm a coke head, or somethin' worse. I'm from the Bronx, but that don't mean I'm a goddamn coke head, you know."

"Okay, okay, I get the point. Now, can we get some sleep? It'll be daylight in a few hours, and then we'll have to bury George, before we go lookin' for help." With a grin, he added, "Unless you think we should go outside and bury him now. At least you wouldn't have to look at him all night."

The boy's eyes widened and he sat upright. "I ain't goin' out there," he said, and pointed at the darkness through the window. "You can go if you want, but leave me out of it, old man. Too damned many things out there that can eat you."

"Hell, boy, there aren't any man-eatin' critters in this part of the country."

"Then you go right ahead and bury him. I'll wait here."

Jack felt good. It had been a long time since he had a conversation with anybody his age. It was only small talk, but he enjoyed it. He was having a better dialogue with the kid than he could have with most adults. He settled into the pilot's seat and pulled his heavy jacket up to his neck.

"Seriously, how old are you?" he said with a grin. "You reach puberty, yet?"

"Screw you, old man. I told you I was old enough."

Jack closed his eyes, and a smile lingered.

Tony stared at the back of Jack's head for a few minutes, and then put his head against the bulkhead and closed his eyes.

"Jack?" he said, opening one eye.

"Yes, boy."

"What do they do to smugglers?"

"They try 'em, first…then put 'em in jail. Some times they shoot 'em. Why?

"Oh, nothing."

Before Jack fell asleep he committed himself to straightening out a few things he had gathered from Tony's comments: something had happened to his father and it could have to do with smuggling or poaching. At least that's how he read it.

"You must have had a reason for asking," he said. "Why do you want to know about things like that?"

Tony stayed silent for a long time. His eyes filled with tears, as he stared at the roof of the plane.

"Jack?" he said.

"Uh huh."

"Do we have to bury him way out here?"

"What do you mean? We can't take him with us. We'll probably have to walk for miles tomorrow. I haven't the faintest idea where we are." He turned, lifted his cap, and looked at the boy. "Do you?"

Tony ignored the question. "Well, you know what I mean? It don't seem right leavin' him way out here."

Jack laid his head back on the headrest. "Go to sleep or I'll make you sleep outside."

Tony snickered. "You wouldn't do that."

Jack made a lunge for the boy's legs. He giggled and pulled them back under him.

"Jack," Tony said, softly.

"Yes, boy," he answered with a sigh.

"Good night."

Jack turned and lifted his cap high enough to wink. "Good night, you black Irishman."

Tony giggled and turned over on his side. He wiggled and twisted his body, until he got comfortable among the bags of "flour".

Chapter Fifteen

The first light of morning painted all of Lake Turkana with a frosty glow. Two furry lion cubs scampered down to its shoreline to lap up the tepid water. They lifted their heads with a start, when a flock of scurrying flamingos churned the water 50-meters in front of them. Satisfied that the birds posed no threat, they returned to the task of filling their stomachs with the mineral-rich water. Preoccupied by their drinking, they had not noticed a small boy creeping up behind them, with a hand-made spear held high above his head. The cubs looked up in time to avoid the small shaft as it sailed over their heads. They warned the boy with hisses, and then trotted off to a safer distance.

The boy's eyes followed them, until they were a distance down the shoreline. Discouraged by his miss, but accepting defeat like a man, he picked up his spear and inspected it for damage. He watched the cubs until they had rounded a spit of land and disappeared. Emitting a deep sigh, he continued on down the shoreline. Detecting something from the corner of his eye, he raised his spear and attacked another prey, a sand crab.

Smoke from the many breakfast fires circled the village and drifted out over the lake. Women rushed from their huts with heavy skillets to make breakfast for their husbands, before they left for fishing. Elders sat by the fires smoking homegrown tobacco and telling stories about when they were young warriors. *Layanis*, boys three or four years old, brandished miniature spears and played warrior and lion games. *Laibartanis*, young boys who had been circumcised, strapped on their bows and arrows and prepared to hunt for wild foul. Within minutes the aroma of goat, fish, lizard and maize had saturated the dry desert air.

Paul's hut had been situated on the opposite side of a thorn fence from Hussein's. They faced each other, to permit them to sit in their arched doorways and listen to the one radio in the village, their only contact with the outside world...a world far from Loiyangalani.

That morning it was Paul's turn to have the radio. From his hut came the loud blast of a trumpet, desperately trying to keep in synch with a multitude of wind instruments. Villagers, who had been asleep, soon woke to its deafening tempo.

"Paul," Hussein yelled across the fence. There was no answer. He tried again, "Paul. Paul." Still nothing. He made his way through the spiny hedge and looked into his friend's hut. His eyes were closed and he was snoring. He pinched his nose.

Paul's sheepskin cover flew off and he jumped to his feet, rubbing his nose on his way up. "What did you do that for?" he asked. He took a token swipe at his friend's shoulder.

Hussein ducked. "I thought you were gasping for air," he said with a grin. "I tried to clear your nose."

Paul slapped his arm. "That hurt," he said, as he rubbed his nose. He kicked dirt from the hut's floor onto his friend's feet.

Hussein jumped back and forth, trying to avoid the sand, and then kicked the pebbles back at him. For a few minutes bedlam reigned in the hut, as the two boys grappled with each other.

L'empi heard the commotion from her cooking fire. "What's going on, boys?" she yelled. "Paul, come and eat. And get your brother up his food is ready. You know him if he doesn't get fed right away."

"All right, Mother," Paul yelled back. He threw one final slap at Hussein's shoulder, and then raced through the archway, followed by his friend.

"Hussein, have you and N'turi eaten, yet?" L'empi asked, as he raced by. "Are you hungry?"

"Thank you, but we will eat later. When father gets up."

By that response she knew he and his brother would not eat that day.

Hussein's mother had died several years earlier. After that, he and his brother had depended solely on their father, L'Umbo, for all their needs. However, after her death he had provided very little food for the boys or himself. Paul's family and other villagers did what they could, but it was very little; it was a poor village and most *manyattas* did not have enough food for their own use, let alone others. Therefore, sustenance for the boys was on a day-to-day basis.

Before his wife's death, L'Umbo had been a good father and had provider for his family's basic needs. As far as the village was concerned, that was all they could expect from him. However, he began selling their goats to support a drinking habit, brought on by his grief. He only sold one or two at a time, but after several weeks there were very few left. As a result, the family's *manyatta* was left with no food and no way to buy it.

Hussein and his brother, who was three years old at the time of his mother's death, would walk to the fishing club and beg for shillings from tourists. But they could only make enough to buy food for every other day. After a few months L'Umbo stopped drinking, but by then it was too late. He could have asked his brother, G'hambi, but there had always been ill feelings between them. It was a bad time to be proud, but everyone knew he was.

"Come, Hussein. Get your brother and eat with us," L'empi begged. "There's plenty. Etaira fished yesterday and brought us some fresh *tylapia*."

"I'll ask N'turi," Hussein said. "If he wants to have breakfast, we'll come." Hussein went into their hut and asked his brother. He told him he would come if Nathan would let him cut firewood with his new knife. Nathan agreed.

From a large skillet on a metal frame above white-hot coals, L'empi spooned *tylapia* onto dum-palm leaves and handed them to the boys, along with large chunks of day-old bread that had been dipped in *sokotei* tea. As the two small boys ate by the fire, they nudged each other playfully with their knees.

"Boys," L'empi said, and glanced nervously at each of them. "I have bad news." The boys looked up. It was unlike her to tell them news of any kind. Therefore, they knew it must be bad. Nathan and N'turi were also surprised by her comment and stopped eating long enough to look up.

"Son, while you were in Nairobi, many of our goats were killed," she said, trying to hold back tears.

Startled by the news, Paul dropped his bread on the ground. He picked it up and brushed it off with his fingers. "Our goats, mother?" he asked, with a frown.

"Yes." She placed the skillet back on the grate and lowered her aging, arthritic body onto a large piece of driftwood. "The other *manyattas* have only lost several, but six of ours were killed."

"Six?" Paul said. "That means we only have twenty left. Who's doing this?"

"We're not sure but we're fairly certain it's lions. More than one."

Hussein frowned. "If it is lions we must do something about it," he said, and tightened his jaws. "We must hunt them down and kill them."

Paul grinned. "Isn't that how you got into trouble before?" he said. He scanned his friend's long, triangular face and noticed a sudden change come over it. Not long ago, he was his closest friend, but now he acted more like an arrogant warrior, and that frightened him. Their bodies were the same age but Hussein's spirit had gotten much older. When he returned from Nairobi, he had seen Hussein in all his plumage and realized their friendship would never be the same. They would no longer herd goats together, or go into the hills to hunt lizards. They were brothers of the tribe but no longer brothers of the spirit. His friend had lost his adolescence and was now acting more like Ebukut: strong, swift, courageous…and arrogant.

"I don't know what the answer is but something must be done," L'empi said, interrupting his thoughts.

"Something will be done," Hussein said, and stood up. "I'll take my spear and hunt the lions." He turned to leave.

"Hussein?" Paul said, as he walked by.

Hussein turned and gave him a vacant look.

"Don't I get to come? Are you going to kill the lions all by yourself?"

"Of course you can come. I'm sorry I said *I*, I meant *we*," Hussein said, as he turned and headed for the fence. "We must get Ebukut. He'll enjoy the hunt."

Paul thought the invitation seemed weak, but he would come. Maybe this time *his* spear would find its mark.

"There, that ought to do it," Jack said. He threw the last stones on the mound of rocks that covered George's body. "It's a damn shame he had to go that way. But, I guess he didn't feel any pain."

Tony looked down at the burial mound. "Ain't you gonna say something over him?"

Jack glared at him. "What do you want me to say, boy? I'm no preacher. I'll give him a decent burial, when I come back for him." He turned and walked to the wrecked Cessna. "Get those bundles out of the plane. We gotta bury them, too."

"Those ain't my bundles, pop. I ain't goin' near 'em," Tony said. He cocked his head to one side and waited for a reaction, which he knew would surely come.

Jack turned a pair of menacing eyes on him. "Until you get big enough to kick my ass, boy, you'll do as I say. Now get goin'."

Tony hesitated for a moment, but when he saw Jack's icy stare he decided to give him a hand. He carted the bundles from the plane and threw them down next to the hole Jack had attempted to dig in the hard ground, next to the roots of a large acacia tree.

After Jack finally finished digging the shallow trench, he set the shovel down on the fresh mound of sand and stone, pulled out a thin cigar, and lit it. "Gettin' too damn old for this stuff, kid," he said, and sucked in a mouthful of aromatic smoke.

"You're gettin' too damn old to be flyin' this crap around, too."

Jack glared at him. "Mind your tongue, fella. This stuff's always got me what I wanted." He turned his head and pointed a long finger at the bundles. "Now, dump them in the hole and let's get out of here."

"Sure hope you know what you're doin'," Tony said, and dumped an armload into the shallow fissure. "They throw people in jail for this, you know."

Irritated by the boy's comments, Jack threw a piece of broken cowling through a splintered window of the plane. "What do you want me to do, leave the stuff in the plane?" he shouted at the boy. "Then we'd damn sure go to jail. You want that?"

"Not me, pop," Tony said. "I'm only thirteen." He looked up to see if Jack had caught the verbal slip.

Jack glanced over with a grin, but said nothing.

Tony continued. "They kill people for smugglin' this stuff, too."

"No shit?"

"Yeah, no shit."

"Well, I don't think you have anything to worry about. You didn't help me get it or fly it."

"Yeah, but I'm an assessory."

Jack chuckled. "You mean, accessory?"

"Yeah, well, whatever."

"Why are you gettin' so riled up over a little baking flour, anyway?" Jack came back through chuckles.

Tony mumbled under his breath, loud enough for Jack to overhear, "Bakin' flour, my black ass." He threw another armload into the pit.

Jack took his personal items from the cockpit and laid them on the ground. Without looking over he said, "Do blacks really have black asses? I've often wondered about that. When I look at your hands I see white palms, does that mean your ass is like the palms of your hands?"

"Don't be a jerk," Tony retorted with a glare. "Of course my ass is—" He stopped when he realized what Jack was doing. He made a few more trips in relative silence. When he had finished loading the pit with bags, he shouted, "Hey, pops, what if I squeal on you? What if I tell the Feds where the stash is?"

"You'd do that to me?" Jack lowered his eyebrows, menacingly.

"You're white, ain't you?"

"Last time I looked. Why? What does that have to do with anything? I was told there's honor among friends...and crooks."

"I ain't no crook," Tony said. "You're the crook, old man. And I damn sure ain't your friend." After a few minutes of silence, he continued. "I'll bet I know what your gonna' tell the guys you were gonna' give this stuff to. You're goin' to tell 'em when the plane crashed it got lost, or burned up, or somethin' stupid like that. Aren't you? Then you'll come back later and get it for yourself. Right?"

Jack glanced up at the sky, as if to meditate. "Say, I never thought of that. You got a good idea there, boy. What do you say you and me go into business together? I'll fly the stuff and you can be the brains of the operation. How does that sound?"

"You're damned funny for a honky. You know that?"

"What's this 'honky' bit, all of a sudden? You're not in New York now. Your soul brothers here in Kenya look at us 'honkies' as honest, upright citizens." Jack remained silent while he tied his belongings to a shoulder pack. After several minutes, he said, "And when in Rome...you know the bit."

"I don't know what the hell you're talkin' about, pop."

"Never mind. Some day I'll explain it. Now grab that gear and let's get out of here. West, I think."

"West? You think? You mean you weren't kidding when you said you didn't know where we were? How the hell we gonna get to Koobi if you're lost?"

"Don't worry, we'll make it. I gotta get there too, you know." As they walked down what appeared to be a goat trail, Jack glanced over and noticed a gold chain, with a silver key dangling from Tony's neck. He reached over and flipped it with his finger. "Thought you said you weren't a thief. Where did a twelve…oh, pardon me, thirteen-year-old squirt like you get a safety deposit key?"

Tony clutched the key in his hand. "Hey, old man, I didn't steal this. My father gave it to me to—" He stopped in the middle of his sentence.

Jack believed he had finally pieced at least a portion of the puzzle together, and he was pleased. His mind conjured up a plot—Tony's father worked for the DEA, and that was the reason the boy was so set against drugs. He continued—an international dope ring had abducted his father, when he found out something he shouldn't have and he was keeping the information locked up in a safety deposit box. Makes sense, he thought. He continued with his fictitious scenario—before he was captured he gave Tony the key to take to Koobi to give to somebody named John, possibly to expose the ring. "How am I doing so far?" he mumbled, inaudibly.

He thought of a second plot—Tony's father was an archeologist from the states and came here to dig for something. He was fingered as a smuggler and the goons were trying to find out where he hid the stuff he dug up. Jack's mind dwelled on both plots for a half-mile, and then it returned to the situation at hand.

Tony wrapped his jacket sleeves around his waist and tied them in a knot. He held the silver key in his fingers and let his mind drift back to the Bronx. His father had received a letter from the New York Museum. He had no idea if the key was in it, but if it was it unlocked something important. Those goons wouldn't have gone to all that trouble, if it didn't.

He couldn't understand why he hadn't cried out, yelled, or even felt emotion when the goons took his father away, but he hadn't. He wondered if it was because his father never stayed home long enough for them to really get to know each other; he was always too busy traipsing around the world. But he had seemed like a decent guy, when they were together.

He had been with his father several years ago, when he worked with Mr. Anderson at Koobi, but he didn't know if they had worked together since. The one thing he did know, the key was important. When his father was abducted, he had told him no matter what happened he was to get it to John at Koobi. He felt like the kid he had once seen in a Saturday matinee…always on a quest, a dangerous mission to save the world. He tripped on a boulder and went sprawling in the dirt. "Damn it," he yelped.

Jack turned around at the sound. "We haven't gone far enough for you to rest, boy. Up and at 'em. We've got miles to go before we sleep…that's Robert Frost, you know."

"Is he a honky, too?" Tony said, with a chuckle. He got up and raced after Jack.

Chapter Sixteen

After chasing a few lizards away from several weaverbird nests, two lion cubs approached the bottom of a small hill and raced up its steep slope. A huge red-mane lion stood defending a path in front of them. The giant stared at them for several seconds, and then looked back down at the remnants of his meal. He sniffed at the slightly decomposed springbok carcass, then lifted his head and again fixed his large brown eyes on the cubs. Instincts told them to turn and run, that they could be in danger, but instead they darted into a low-lying bush, dropped to their stomachs, and stared wide-eyed at him.

Satisfied there were no edible morsels left on the bones, the lion turned and slowly ambled down a goat path between two large boulders. On short, unsteady legs, the cubs followed at a safe distance. When the huge male crested the next hill, a lioness and two cubs joined him. The cast off cubs remained at the edge of a clearing. They would either be taken in by her, or rejected by the male. Her cubs ran over to the newcomers and chased them up and down the rocky slope, hissing and slapping playfully at them.

The female welcomed the male by licking his ears and rubbing her head up against his long mane. She huffed at her cubs several times, and they stopped in the middle of the chase and ran to her side. She licked their small faces with her rasp-like tongue, and then nudged them over on their sides. The stray cubs stood at the side of the clearing and watched her pamper them.

She lumbered over to the new arrivals and nonchalantly sniffed them. They stood like statues, while they were being inspected. The large male crept up behind her and attempted to take one of the cubs in his mouth, but her vicious snarls and sharp claws turned him away. He jumped to one side, but for the most part ignored her challenge. He lifted his head into the hot, dry air and huffed loudly to a pair of young males resting in the shade of an acacia bush. The yearlings sprang to their feet and joined him. The pride stood quiet as sentinels on the crest of a hill, eying several dozen grazing goats, a kilometer away.

Paul jogged along the path behind his friends, the relentless sun beating down on him. He knew it would be another blistering morning, like the last few, and it wouldn't let up until the evening wind came. However, their bodies would then be pelted with sharp stones and sand, and force them to stop to take cover. He didn't know which was worse the sun or the wind; both were unpleasant. When he discovered he had lagged behind the two warriors he took a few quick steps to catch up.

It was difficult for him to understand why they were on their way to hunt down and kill the raiding lions. The animals were merely hungry, and they had no reservations about hunting and killing to eat. He had considered trying to talk the warriors out of the hunt, but he knew it would have been futile. While in Nairobi, he had witnessed semi-civilized people taking advantage of each other, but he didn't expect his friends to emulate them by killing hungry lions for the sake of a few goats. Regrettably, and under the circumstances, there was only one thing they could do, track down and kill them. On the other hand, for his friends to put themselves back in jeopardy with the rangers didn't make much sense to him. They might not be so lucky, the next time. Previously, they had only been reprimanded, sent home and told not to do it again. But if caught this time they would not get off so easily; they were going after the lions to kill them wantonly, and not in self-defense. He had to be stupid to go along with them, he thought, but they were his friends. Moreover, most of the goats that had been killed were his. He knew he had to go with them, there was no question about it.

The stomping of his *kiatus* on the hot, dusty trail jolted the slippery spear from his hand and it fell against a rock. The metallic clang of its blade frightened a jackal from a nearby bush. The animal sprinted across the dry elephant grass and took refuge in a small cave.

"It's getting too hot" Ebukut said. "We should find shade." He placed his hands on his sides and bent over to suck in more air.

"Yes, it is hot," Paul agreed. "We should stop and rest for a few minutes."

They found shade under a nearby umbrella tree, next to a large boulder. They draped their limp bodies across the huge stone and inhaled the cooler air trapped under its spread.

Ebukut glanced over at Paul, still wearing his school outfit; white shirt, white socks and white shorts.

"You have come unprepared," he said. "Take off your clothes or you'll get sick from the heat."

Paul fingered the mother-of-pearl buttons on his shirt. The big warrior was right; he should not be traveling in all that heat with his clothes soaking up sweat and clinging to his body. He knew he had come ill prepared for the hunt. He had brought his spear, water sack and *sampur*, and even those were burdensome in all that heat.

"I can't take them all off," he said. "I have nothing on underneath."

"You can't run with them on, you can't take them off…what a problem you have, my friend," Ebukut chided.

"Take them off and leave them by this boulder," Hussein said, not raising his head from the coolness of the stone. "We'll pick them up on our way back." He grinned and added, "Are you afraid someone will see your *ume* (oo me)? They won't know what it is, if they haven't seen it before…and if they have, they won't care to see it again."

Ebukut's usual somber expression was replaced by a grin. "Yes," he said. "If it bothers you to be naked, we'll hold our shields in front of you, if we meet some young, pretty *mtoto wa kikes* (toto wa keekees)."

Paul blushed. He knew he shouldn't be embarrassed over his nakedness, but he was. The sisters at the mission school had not allowed them to come to classes even moderately nude. Prior to their arrival the boys had been allowed to wear *ukandas* (ook and as), a type of jockstrap, and the girls *selahs* (se las), fish-skin aprons.

"You're right," Paul agreed. "I'm not a *lmurran,* like you two, but I'm still a Samburu." He tugged at the moist shirt until it slid over his perspiring shoulders, and then dropped the shorts from his hips.

Ebukut looked at his slender, naked body. "There, isn't that better?" he said, and chuckled. "I don't think we have to worry about covering your *ume*, I can't see it anyway." Paul made a mock lunge for him, but he slid across the boulder and out of reach. The big warrior reached into his *sampur* and pulled out a white cloth, which he handed to him. "It isn't much, but it's enough to cover your *ume*." He chuckled.

"Is it time?" Hussein asked. He opened his eyes and pushed his body away from the boulder.

"Yes," Ebukut said. "We must hurry if we're going to get west of the lions before dark. They won't smell us if we come in from that direction."

They raced down the crooked goat path, as the sun was dropping behind the Loima Hills

"He should have been here by now," said John Anderson, the supervisor of Archeological Site 51. He scanned the horizon. "Wonder what the hell's keeping him?"

John was a tall man of medium build. His well-tanned, tapered face housed a pair of penetrating blue eyes set deep behind a long nose that protruded from his face above thin, tight lips. His graying hair had never been parted and flowed haphazardly in all directions. A balding spot on the back of his head glistened with beads of sweat, which ran down the back of his neck and onto the collar of his ever-present Harris Tweed. The Harris was his trademark; he was never without it. In the extreme heat of the outside, or inside away from the chill of the evening, the jacket was always present.

"Is he bringing that foul-mouthed little twerp with him?" said the man standing beside him. "I remember him from the last time you and Robert got together…couple years ago."

"I suppose so, Barry," John said. "Don't be too harsh on the kid. I guess he hasn't had many great times in his life. This is the only way he can be with his father. There's only the two of them now, you know."

"I don't know if I can handle him," Barry said and turned his ruddy face and blood-shot eyes in his direction. "I'm not much on kids."

Barry Wetherford was not known at the site as a man's man. His pudgy face contributed to his pear-like body and gave it the appearance of an over-grown cupid. He wore dark, half-height spectacles that were constantly low on the bridge of his nose. Long, dark brown hair flowed from under a pith helmet and cascaded down each side of his head, and then terminated in thick layers across hunched shoulders. Although he was a top-notch archeologist, the natives at the site never took him seriously. John believed his peculiar appearance had been partially responsible for that.

"He's all right after you get to know him," John said. "He simmers down a bit, after you talk to him for a while."

"Sure hope so."

"What I hope is," John said, "that Robert has either the money or the key."

"Yeah, it would make things a helluva lot easier," said Barry. "I thought he was supposed to be here yesterday?"

"He was."

"Then where the hell is he? It can't be that difficult to catch a plane out of Nakuru, or wherever he's coming from." He scanned the horizon, as John had. "Maybe he ran into trouble. If you remember, we were informed by the museum that there are several guys roamin' around out there who'd love to get their hands on that key…or money."

"Yes, I know," John said, reflecting on the information he too had received. "But I believe Robert could handle them."

"Christ! I would hope so, he's big enough." Barry raised his eyebrows. "What is he, two fifty…six four? I know I'd hate to meet him in a dark alley."

"They'll be here. Just give them a little more time," John said.

"You know time's something we don't have much of," Barry replied. "We have to be finished digging by the day after tomorrow, that's when our licenses run out. As you know."

John dropped his weary body onto one of the many canvass chairs on the patio. "Yeah, I know, you don't have to remind me. We're going to be in one helluva pickle, if we don't get that money. The digging will have to stop. It's those stupid Kenyan regulations…and graft. I wonder why they couldn't wait a little longer for their money? They know it's coming." He poured a glass of lemonade from the ever-present thermos and leaned back against a tent stanchion. "Just when we were about there, too," he added, as an afterthought.

"Yeah," Barry replied with a sigh. "If we don't make it this time, I wonder if the museum will send us back to try again, later?" He thought for a moment. "I'll bet anything that as soon as we get the money the permits will start rolling in like waves on the ocean. Flash a few shillings in front of their damned noses…that's all it takes." His usual placid expression turned to one of disgust.

"Yeah, you're right," John agreed. "I don't even want to think about not finding the rest of it, this time around. And I'll be damned if anyone else is going to dig for it if we can't."

"What would you do?" Barry asked, and poured himself another glass of lemonade. "I mean if we couldn't get the permits re-issued."

"Blow it up," John said, simply.

Barry nearly dropped his drink. "Blow it up?"

"Yes. Under those circumstances, I think it would be the wisest thing to do. Blow the whole goddamn place up."

"Christ, John, we spent the last two years of our lives working on this project. Why would you want to do a thing like that?"

John reached for his drink, but said nothing. He leaned his head back against a tent prop and closed his burning eyes. His mind wandered back to his first days at Koobi. He had been commissioned by the New York

Museum to dig for what they believed was the most important archeological find of the century.

After digging for artifacts night and day for two years, they had run out of money and their permits were ready to expire. Prior to wiring the museum for more money, they uncovered undeniable proof of something of enormous significance buried at the site. They sent proof of its existence to the museum, but only enough information to whet their appetites. After reviewing the specifics, the museum authorities jumped at the prospect of finding more and agreed to send them the necessary funds to renew their licenses.

Robert O'Brien was the museum's trouble-shooter. If they needed something done right away they called on him. He never hesitated because the compensation was extremely good. He was to travel to Nakuru and put the money in the bank, until it could be converted into Kenyan shillings. The bank would then put it in a safety deposit box and give him the key. He would then take it to Koobi for the much needed licenses…and graft.

"But the goddamn key, or money, hasn't arrived!" John cried out, without thinking.

"What?" Barry said, startled by his outburst.

John opened his eyes and turned them on Barry. After realizing what he had yelled out, he said, "Oh, nothing. I guess I was half asleep…thinking".

Ebukut darted behind a large boulder and crouched. "Quick! Hide!" he whispered to the others. "I believe I saw something move behind us. I couldn't make out what it was."

Both Paul and Hussein darted behind the rock and strained their eyes to see if they could detect any movement on the path. They saw nothing.

"What did you see?" Hussein asked. "What was it? I don't see anything."

The tall warrior stuck his head out from his hiding place and squinted in the direction they had just traveled. "I thought I saw something on the ridge, back there." He pointed with his spear. They trained their eyes on the crest of the distant hill, but still saw nothing.

"Are you sure there was something there?" Paul questioned.

The warrior moved out from behind the boulder. "No. I'm not sure," he said. "But we should be alert and on guard. There could be rangers out here."

Still concealed behind the rock, Paul stuck his head out to take another look. For a brief moment, he believed he saw something move on top of a rise. However, the descending sun on the horizon was still bright enough to manufacture shadowy figures, where none existed.

"Do you think it was a person?" he asked.

"I don't know," Ebukut said. "I thought I saw something come over the hill, back there." Again he pointed.

"Should we track it? See if it's the rangers?" Hussein asked.

"Yes," the older warrior said. "If it is the rangers, maybe they'll lead us to the lions. They're probably out here looking for them."

Paul shot him a subtle glance. He was not at all enthusiastic about getting involved with the rangers. Even so, if that was what his friends wanted, he could not refuse. After all, he was only a simple *laibartani*, and they were warriors. He smirked.

"Jack?"

"Yes, Tony."

"You think we'll ever get out of this fuckin' desert?"

"Don't know. And watch your tongue, boy."

As they stumbled along the thorny goat path, Tony worked on their problem; how they could get to Koobi. He realized Jack knew the key was for a safety deposit box, but he couldn't have any idea what was in it...and neither did he. Did it unlock a treasure chest? Did it go to a door? If it did, maybe there would be an ice cold drink behind it. He chuckled. That would sure taste great right about then, he thought. He put his hand on his chest and clutched the key.

"Hey, boy," Jack said between gasps for air.

"Yeah, pops?"

"What did your father do to get you into this mess?"

Tony thought for a moment, and then realized he didn't know, for sure. However, he knew Jack wouldn't believe that. As a matter of fact, he didn't think the aging pilot would believe anything he told him. Nonetheless, one thing was for certain, two men came into the room, put guns on his father and bound his hands in front of him, and then they all left.

Prior to them taking him away, he remembered there was a loud noise outside on the street, possibly an accident. The men rushed to the window to see what had happened and his father took that opportunity to take the key out of his shirt pocket and toss it to him. While the men were still at the other end of the room looking out the window, his father whispered that he was to give the key to a man named John Anderson at Koobi Fora. That was all he had time to say.

"I don't know for sure, pop," he said. "But those guys wanted him real bad. They came to the hotel and dragged him away at gunpoint. I couldn't do a damn thing but take this stupid key he gave me. They were big bastards. Real bad-asses. Mean mothers."

"How did *you* get away?" Jack asked.

"They didn't bother with me. They took him and left me standin' there with my finger up my ass. Guess they didn't give a shit if I squealed or not."

"Did you call the police after they left?"

"Hell no! They wouldn't have done anything, anyway. I found that out before."

"What do you mean? Had you been in trouble with them?"

"Not exactly trouble. Dad had his rental car stolen and they wouldn't do a damn thing about it. They only asked if he had American car insurance, and if he did he wasn't to worry. That's all they said and that's all they did."

"That's it? They didn't try to find it?"

"Hell, no. They prob'ly figured he was a rich American and his insurance would pay for it, anyway. They prob'ly did, too. Right through their damned noses."

Jack chuckled and turned his attention back to the trail.

Tony caught sight of a slight movement on the path ahead of them. "Jack," he whispered. "I think we got company." He pointed.

Jack followed his finger to a spot 100-meters up the path. An imperceptible figure darted behind one of the large boulders and stuck the top of its head out.

Jack dropped his pack and fished through its many pockets, looking for the signaling pistol he had taken from the plane. After finding it, he loaded it with an emergency flare.

"What you gonna do with that stupid looking thing?" Tony joked.

"This isn't a toy, son. Furthermore, it's all we got."

"You mean you've been haulin' that stuff around and you don't even have a real gun?"

"Nope. They're illegal," Jack said with a toothy smile. "What you see is what you get."

"Oh, man. I don't believe this." Tony shook his head. "What would happen if we were attacked by a lion, or something else?"

"He'd have one hell of a hot tail end, if I shot him with this thing. I can tell you that." After inspecting the breach, he snapped the gun closed and put it under his belt behind his back.

Shaking his head in disbelief, Tony continued on down the path.

When they approached the boulder where Tony had seen the hiding figure, Ebukut bolted out from behind it and pointed his spear at them.

Tony jumped back, wide-eyed. He focused his eyes on the spear, and then on the warrior's ocher headpiece.

Jack reached behind him and put his hand on the pistol, but he didn't pull it out.

Hussein and Paul came out from behind the boulder and stood beside the warrior. For a few seconds, they stood staring at each other.

After a long pause, Ebukut walked up to Jack and stared into his eyes. "*Nani wewe*? *Nakwenda wapi*?" he said.

Tony looked at Jack's tense face. "I hope you understand that shit," he said.

"Yes. Somewhat. He wants to know who we are and where we're going."

"Well from the looks of that goddamn spear you better tell him. Right?"

"*Nimepotea*," Jack told the warrior, and then turned to Tony. "I told him we were lost."

"Well, that ain't no goddamn lie," Tony said, still staring at the spear.

"*Jina langu ni*...Jack. *Rafiki yangu*...Tony." Jack clumsily introduced them with a smile.

Paul stepped forward and extended his hand. "I'm Paul. This is Ebukut," he said in English. He pushed the warrior's spear down, and then draped his arm around Hussein's shoulder. "And this is my friend, Hussein. You say you are lost? What are you doing in the desert to get lost?"

Jack looked into Paul's sun-reddened eyes. "It's a long story, son," he said. "My plane crashed...over there, I'd say about four or five kilometers. We're trying to find someplace with a telephone so I can call and report it."

"There are no telephones for many kilometers. But there is a fishing club...that way, at Lake Turkana," Paul said, and pointed in the direction they had just come from. "It's about five or six kilometers. They have a radio but no telephone. I believe they can help you."

"Back that way, huh?" Jack said, and glanced at the smirk on Tony's face. "I guess we were going in the wrong direction."

"If you had continued in this way," Hussein said, and pointed at the trail ahead of them, "you would have ended up in the Chalbi desert. No man goes there on foot. And only a few will go on camel or by truck."

Jack took Tony by the arm and spun him around. "Then I guess we'll head back that way," he said. An embarrassed grin spread across his sun-ripened face.

Tony pulled free and turned his head around to keep his eyes on the warriors.

"Stop staring, it's not polite," Jack said, and with a firm hand turned the boy's head back around. "We don't want to make the natives restless."

"Oh, brother," Tony said under his breath. "Just tryin' to see what my ancestors must've looked like, that's all. In Nakuru they all wear clothes and shoes. Nothin' like them."

Paul overheard him and smiled. "You are black, but not from Africa," he called to Tony, who had traveled only a few steps down the path.

"Fuck no!" Tony yelled back. "I'm from the States, the Bronx."

"I do not know that word, 'fuck'," Paul said with a frown.

Jack chuckled, when he saw the puzzled look on the young boy's face.

"What the hell you guys doin' out here in this fuckin' desert, anyway?" Tony asked.

Paul smiled. "The desert is our home."

"You actually live out here, in all this fuckin' heat?"

"We live in the village of Loiyangalani, on the shores of Lake Turkana...where you will soon be if you go in that direction." He pointed down the path to the east.

"You mean the lake you told us about? Where a fishing club is?"

"Yes. That is our home."

"Well, I'll be damned," Tony said.

"You never would have arrived at the lake," Paul said, "if you had kept going in that direction." He pointed to the west.

Tony continued the questioning. "Why don't you look like those guys?"

"What do you mean?"

"Why do they have those weird hairdos and all that other stuff, and you're not wearing hardly anything? Does that mean they're chiefs or something?"

Paul laughed. He looked at his two friends, and then back at Tony. With their tribal attire and his nakedness, he could understand Tony's confusion.

"No, they're not chiefs," he said. "They're *lmurrans*, warriors. I am not a warrior."

"Why aren't you one, too? You ain't old enough or something?"

"Yes, I am old enough, but—"

"We must go," Ebukut interrupted in Masai.

Paul acknowledged by shaking his head, and then turned back to Tony. "My friend said we must go. If you follow the shadows of the sun they will point you to Loiyangalani. First, you will see the lake. Follow the shoreline south until you see palm trees on a hill. There you will find the fishing club." He stepped back and joined the others. Before they left, he turned back to Tony and added, "Be careful, there are lions here. Do not go by boulders, such as this one, on your way to the lake." He pointed to the large rock behind him. "This is where they will hide."

"Thank you for the warning," Jack said. "By the way, fellows, do you have any spare water? We're thirsty and we don't have much. Probably not enough to get us to the club."

"Oh, shit!" Tony exclaimed, after realizing what Paul had said. "Lions? Man, that's all I'd need to make my fuckin' day...lions!"

Ignoring Tony's outburst, Hussein handed Jack his water bag. "You may take some but we are on a hunting safari and need most of it."

Tony reached for the pouch but Jack pushed his hand down. "No, Tony, we can't take their water if they're going into the desert, it's not right. Thank you, young warrior, but we'll manage. You keep your water; you'll need it more than us. Thank you, anyway."

Tony turned his head around to look at them, but Jack's firm hand twisted it back.

"Why don't we go with them?" Tony said. "They could protect us from the stinkin' lions."

Jack's hand remained on the boy's head until he was certain he was following. "Don't think that would be a wise decision, son," he said. "They're more than likely going after stray goats in the hills, not lions. Either that or hunting for food. They'll probably be gone a day or so. Besides, it's too damn hot out here for us white folks."

"Speak for yourself, honky," Tony chided with a grin.

"We've got to find shade." Jack said. "And we don't have enough water for all this heat."

"I saw you put that beer in your bag," Tony said, with a smirk. "Who the hell you kiddin'?"

"That's only as a last resort. We'd get sky-high drunk, drinking hot beer on a day like this. We'd want more and more…it makes you thirsty as hell. And it would dehydrate you."

"Shit, I wouldn't mind that," Tony said, adjusting his strides to keep up with Jack's long gait. "Sure would like to go with 'em, man. I think I'd like 'em."

"Yeah, but would they like you after they found out what those filthy words meant? These people don't talk like that."

By late afternoon, the oppressive heat had built to the point where it was almost unbearable. It had transported its charring influence to the path in front of them. The white limestone pebbles on the trail had been converted into miniature furnaces beneath their tennis shoes, which forced them to dart from the shade of one prickly acacia to the next. The undulating blanket of heat rose from the desert floor in boiling waves, which made it difficult for them to breathe. Their lungs ached and their nostrils burned from inhaling the fine, super heated air and swirling dust.

As they traveled away from the setting sun, Jack scolded Tony for taking off his shirt and exposing his shoulders to the rays of the late afternoon inferno.

"You're skin might be black, son," he told him, "but you ain't one of them."

Chapter Seventeen

Robert O'Brien had been held captive in a cottage overlooking Lake Nakuru. The building had been situated at the far end of a dead-end road, which had been pitted by rainfall and dried by the sun to the hardness of concrete. Trees around the shoreline concealed the small building, which made it virtually impossible to be seen from the lake.

O'Brien was a big man, 6' 4" and well over 200-pounds. Nonetheless, he was overshadowed by one of his captors who out-weighed him by at least 30-pounds and stood several inches taller.

The second man was smaller by a few inches and weighed around 50-pounds less. He had a stoop to his shoulders when he stood, and a noticeable limp when he walked. His nose looked as if it had been pulled on and then twisted. It was not a pleasant sight and he was self-conscious about it.

"O'Brien," the tall man said. "You know you'll be wasted, when the old man gets here, if you don't tell us where the money is." He glared at him, malevolently, through dark, deep-set brown eyes. He spun the swivel chair O'Brien had been tied to around in circles.

O'Brien could not understand why they had gone to so much trouble, when there wasn't that much money at stake. The lock-box at the bank didn't have over 50 grand in it. A mere pittance for the man he assumed the goons were working for. According to information supplied him by the museum, their boss was a man named Chaka. He didn't believe the man would go to all that trouble for such a small amount he was a millionaire. He believed Chaka had something other than money on his mind.

"Well?" the tall man said, and squeezed the soft fold under O'Brien's chin. "Where is it?"

"You guys are going to an awful lot of trouble for a couple grand, " O'Brien countered. He hesitated for effect, and than continued. "Hell, if all you guys want is money, I'll match whatever you're getting."

The tall man put both hands on the arms of his chair, bent down to eye level, and stared into his eyes. He was not getting through to O'Brien and he knew it. Out of despair, he spun the swivel chair around several more times.

As O'Brien rotated in the chair, he commenced to get sick. He remembered the last time he had motion sickness, it was on the roller coaster at Coney Island. He could not stand sudden movements in any direction. When the chair stopped he lurched forward, as if to vomit. His captor jumped back.

"You don't like that, huh?" the big man said, with a sneer.

"I could do without it."

Crooked nose approached the chair, and with a malicious grin attempted to spin it again, but was held back.

"Don't," the big man ordered. "We want his mind clear when the old man gets here."

Crooked nose's smile dissolved. He turned, glared at O'Brien, and then stomped across the room to a window at the far end that overlooked the lake.

The tall man stood in front of O'Brien for several minutes, as if meditating, then bent down until their noses were inches apart. "You know very well how much money's at stake here," he said, trying to get a reaction. "Hell of a lot more than a couple grand. That's for damned sure."

"It doesn't matter how much," O'Brien said. "You know very well Chaka don't need it, he's a millionaire."

"That is true," the man said. "But that money is our cut. Therefore, as you can see we have a lot at stake here. I'd say about twenty-five grand apiece...if my sources are correct."

O'Brien held the man's stare. He wondered how they had found out how much the transfer was. Only he, the board at the museum, and the bank knew what had been transferred. On the other hand, Chaka had enough money to buy any information he wanted. Why did he want him, if he didn't want the money? He was confused. Another thing, if Chaka didn't want John at Koobi to get the licenses renewed, all he had to do was pay off a few officials.

"I'm confused," he told the tall man. "In other words, all you guys are looking for is the fifty grand. Right?"

"Yes...and no," the man answered. "We want the money all right, but don't think you can give it to us and we'll let it go at that. It doesn't work that way."

"Why not?"

"Do you seriously think Chaka would let us get away with that?" the man said, distorting his mouth in a sneer. "Hell no, he has something else on his mind. This is a cheap way to hire us though; he doesn't have to use his own cash. Clever, don't you think?" He turned and walked across the room to join crooked nose at the window. He called back to O'Brien, "He wants you for some other reason, but I'll be damned if I can figure out what it is. Guess you'll have to find that out for yourself."

O'Brien glanced up at the big man. "What's your name?" he asked.

"It doesn't matter. Call me anything you want."

"How about…big mother fucker? That okay?" O'Brien said, with a snicker.

"Hell, for fifty…I mean twenty-five grand, you can call me anything you want," he answered with a scoff. He glanced over at his partner to see if he had picked up on his verbal slip.

"When will Chaka be here?"

"Whenever he damn well feels like it. Probably tonight sometime."

"Did you let my son go?"

"Why not. We didn't need him for anything."

"Good."

"Wonder where the little shit went," crooked nose shouted across the room.

"Don't know for sure," O'Brien countered, "but I'll bet he's on his way to Koobi, right now. He's got a mind of his own, you know."

"Koobi?" The big man seemed surprised by his remark. He glanced over at O'Brien, as he walked away from the window. "What do you mean? Why would he go there?" He stopped at the swivel chair and glared down at him. "The little shit has our money, doesn't he?"

O'Brien thought for a moment. If these guys believed for one minute Tony had the money, and was on his way to Koobi, they might try to go after him. And he was counting on that. He knew his son could outsmart them. It was a long shot but worth a try.

Crooked nose stared angrily at O'Brien. "That little bastard has our money," he said, "you can count on it. He either has it or he knows where it is. Doesn't he?"

The big man formed a fist and rapped his knuckles hard on O'Brien's head. "Does he have the money?" he asked.

"What?" O'Brien snapped. "You must think I'm crazy. I wouldn't give fifty grand to a thirteen-year-old kid".

"Kevin," crooked nose yelled. "We should go after that little bastard. He has our money. I know he does. If he gets it to Koobi, what do we do then?"

"Shut up, you idiot," the big man said. "He's only saying that to try to get out of his predicament. But it won't work. The kid doesn't have the money, it's somewhere in Nakuru. You can count on that." He hesitated several seconds, and then said, "Besides, Chaka wants O'Brien held here. We couldn't leave him by himself while we looked for the kid. Chaka would have our hides." The big man walked across the room and took crooked nose by his coat collar. "And don't call me by my name, you stupid ass." He pushed the man across the room and he fell to the floor.

Crooked nose got up and brushed the dirt from his jacket. "You're right. Sorry," he said. "I forgot. But I don't see why we can't look for the kid, later. Maybe after Chaka leaves tonight. Whether the kid has the money or not I'll bet he knows where it is."

"Don't be stupid," Kevin said, shaking his head. "In the first place, how would we find him? He's black, along with about six million others his age. What do you want to do, stop every kid that looks like him and ask if he's got fifty grand on him? Don't be an ass, Steve."

Crooked nose walked back to the window and sat on an apple crate, the only other seat in the room. "You called me Steve," he mumbled under his breath.

At that moment they heard the low drone of a powerful engine. Kevin ran to the window and looked out. A long, black limousine twisted and turned its way over the ruts of the washed out road toward the cottage.

"It's Chaka," he said, anxiously.

The limo stopped in front of the door. Steve's face reddened. He rushed to the window, nervously looked out over the lake, and then returned to the other side of the room, not knowing what else to do.

A black chauffeur got out and opened the back door of the limo. A tall, slender black man got out and waited for him to close the door. He deftly stepped on the tops of the deep ruts, as he made his way to the cottage.

Chaka was a distant relative of the infamous Zulu, King Chaka, of South Africa. He was also one of the most powerful and influential men in Kenya. How he had acquired his wealth was a mystery to everyone, including the Kenyan government. However, they were not about to question him; they accepted their grafts and gratuities and let him go about his business.

Before entering the cottage, he stood on the small porch and adjusted the white tie under his black shirt collar. He pulled down on the tail of his white suit coat and fastened the solid gold buttons on his paisley vest. He wore a hat of the pith variety, but instead of brown it was pure white. He glanced down at his gleaming black shoes. Not satisfied with their appearance he lifted his feet, one at a time, and buffed them on the back of his trouser legs. He leaned on his gold-encrusted walking stick and waited for his driver to open the cottage door.

"Mister Chaka," Kevin called out, as the man entered the room. "How nice to see you again, sir." He held out his hand.

Chaka ignored his hand, walked to the swivel chair, and through purple-tinted sunglasses stared down at O'Brien. Without uttering a word he spun around, walked to the window and looked out over the lake. Several minutes later he returned to the chair and bent down until their eyes met.

"So," he said. He clasped his hands behind his back and rocked back and forth on his heels. "You have something we want and you cannot, or will not, get it for us. Is that correct?"

O'Brien stared at his reflection in the one-way glasses. "Let's cut the cat-and-mouse bull shit and get down to business," he said. Chaka raised an eyebrow. "I know you're not concerned with the money," he continued. "So what is it you want from me?" He tugged at the restraining ropes that bound him to the chair, but they would not give.

Chaka turned, walked back to the window and again looked out over the lake. Silence prevailed in the small room. He turned his head and looked back at O'Brien. "This is true," he stated. "I don't want the money." He hesitated for a moment, then looked over at Kevin and Steve. "But I believe these two gentlemen would love to have it. Is that not true?" Neither answered. "But there is something I do want, and its worth a lot more than the money they lust for."

"Get to the point," O'Brien snarled.

"Yes. I will in a moment. Have patience, my good man. All will come in due time, if only you have patience." The half-moon clips on his heels clicked on the hardwood floor, as he made his way from the window to the chair. He bent down, put both hands on the arms of the chair, and again stared into O'Brien's eyes. "I want what they're digging for at Koobi."

O'Brien took a fleeting glimpse at his reflection in the glasses. "I haven't the faintest idea what they're digging for," he answered. "I was hired to deliver the money for their research, that's all. I have no idea what they're digging for, or what they've found. And that's the truth."

"Bullshit!" Kevin yelled across the room.

Chaka held up his hand to demand silence.

With a disgusted grunt, Kevin turned back to the window and mumbled under his breath, "He's not telling the truth. He knows what they're digging for."

Chaka overheard his comment. "What makes you so certain, Kevin?" he said. "Do *you* know what they're digging for?"

"Of course not." He looked back out the window to avoid the man's icy stare. "But it has to be something damned important and worth a lot of money or you wouldn't be involved." He swallowed hard, realizing he could have stepped on the wrong man's toes.

Chaka threw him a glassy stare. "Then if *you* don't know what it is, what makes you so sure *he* does?" he said in a snide voice.

"It makes perfect sense he'd know…he works for them," Kevin replied.

Chaka stood up straight and folded his arms across his chest. "He has no reason to know," he said. "You work for me, Kevin, do you know what I do? But it really doesn't matter. What matters is he has the ability to get it for me."

"That'll be a cold day in hell," O'Brien countered.

"Kevin," Chaka called out.

Kevin turned to face him. "Yes, sir."

"Did you find out about your money? Where it is?"

"No, sir."

"Then I suggest you two go after the boy. I have sources that tell me he can lead you to it."

"See! See!" Steve shouted across the room. "I knew the little shit had the money all along."

Chaka turned and glared at him. "Don't be stupid. He doesn't have the money. It would be foolish on Mr. O'Brien's part to give it to him. And

I'm certain he's no fool. But the boy can lead you to it. He has the key to a safety deposit box. If you can find him."

"O'Brien said he was on his way to Koobi," Steve said.

"This is true," Chaka agreed. "I have been told by my sources the boy has the key for a box here in Nakuru. You have to find him before he gets to Koobi and gives it to John Anderson at Site 51. If the boy makes it there it will be too late, they will have your money, and it will be more difficult to get what I want." With an angry stare he added, "And I always get what I want. Do you understand?" Both men nodded.

"How did the boy get the key?" Kevin said. "When we took O'Brien from the hotel, he had no key on him. We searched him thoroughly."

"Did you ever consider the boy could have been given the key earlier? Or it may have been slipped to him while you two idiots were there."

"Impossible," Steve blurted out. "We didn't take our eyes off those two for a second. He couldn't have given the little shit the key."

"One way or the other he got it," Chaka said. "Why else would he be on his way to Koobi?"

"Are you sure he's on his way there?" Kevin asked.

"Yes," Chaka said, with an edge in his voice.

"But how do you know for sure?" Kevin persisted. "How could he possibly get there?"

"Do not question me or my sources." Chaka raised his voice and his face reddened. "The boy is on his way to Koobi and he has the key. And that's final!"

Kevin's face turned beet-red. "How can you be sure O'Brien will get you what you want, if you let him go?" Kevin asked. "If I were him, I'd get my son and get the hell out of the country."

"God!" Chaka thundered. "I can condone ignorance but not stupidity.

What makes you think O'Brien is going to be set free?"

"But I thought—"

"Don't think," Chaka interrupted. "From now on I'll do that for you." He adjusted his glasses and continued. "By the way, if I remember correctly, you were instructed to get the boy when you picked up O'Brien at the hotel. He was to be our ace-in-the-hole. It would be much simpler if we had him. He was to be our ransom, our hostage. Mister O'Brien would have been forced to do our bidding. But now you must go after him and bring him and the key back, the hard way."

Kevin looked away without saying a word. The back of Steve's neck flushed pink, as he continued to stare out the window.

O'Brien realized what Chaka was up to and didn't like what he heard, but for the moment he could do nothing about it. He knew he shouldn't have told them about his son going to Koobi, but on the other hand he was confident he would make it. The two goons would be sent to intercept him and if they captured him he would be taken hostage. If that happened he would be forced to play along with Chaka's plan in order to set his son free. He finally found out that the plan was to get Chaka whatever they were digging for at Koobi.

"You'll never catch him," he told Chaka. "He's on his way with the key. He's probably there by now."

Kevin rushed across the room and grabbed O'Brien by his collar. "How could you know that?" he shouted in his face. "You didn't even know we were coming for you at the hotel. When we got there your son was in the other room. And you didn't say anything to him or give him anything...especially a key."

"Curious, isn't it?" O'Brien said, looking at him with a grin. "Then how did he get it? And how did he know where to go with it? That Tony's a clever kid, he must have figured it out all by himself."

Kevin slapped him hard across the face. "You black, smart-ass son-of-a-bitch," he shouted, spittle spraying from his mouth. He threw Chaka a nervous glance, realizing he may have offended him by his outburst. He walked back across the room, hoping for no repercussions.

Chaka glared at him for a few seconds, then turned back to O'Brien. "Of course when you men find his son," he told them, without looking over, "which I am confident you will, you will keep him at a safe location. After we have the key, Mr. O'Brien will take it to Koobi."

"But the key is for our money," Kevin complained. "If Koobi gets it, they'll get the money. And that's our money." He looked over at Steve for confirmation.

Steve shook his head.

Chaka's face turned somber. "You idiots!" he shouted. "If they don't get the money they won't be able to continue digging. If that happens I won't get what I want. If I don't get what I want you don't get what you want."

Kevin thought for a moment. "If that's the case, why don't you just let the kid take the key to Anderson. Anderson would be able to continue the dig and as soon as he found what he's looking for you could force him into giving it to you. You have the power." He stopped for a moment, and then added, "So, as soon as you get what you want, we get the money? Right?"

"Of course," Chaka said. "Why wouldn't I give it to you? I said I would. As a matter of fact, that money wasn't for you, anyway. I was planning on giving you the fifty grand out of my own pocket." He stopped and walked to the window. "As far as letting Anderson have the key early, that would be defeating my purpose. I want O'Brien to deliver it with his boy held as insurance. He would be forced to get me what I want…without too many hitches."

As if Chaka's last statement went over his head, Steve said, "That's okay with us, it doesn't matter where the money comes from. But you also said we could have it when we captured O'Brien. Now we have to go after his son and wait while they dig up whatever they're looking for? Is that what you're saying? Before we get our money?"

"If you want the fifty grand, yes," Chaka said. "If we had his son now, as originally planned, I would give you your money. But now you'll have to wait. After listening to you two idiots I'm not at all convinced you'll find the boy, anyway."

They knew Chaka had the upper hand no matter how he played it, and it was obvious they could do nothing about it.

"All right," Kevin said. "We've gone this far we might as well see it through. But I think it's worth an additional ten grand apiece, if we have to go after the kid and then wait for our money…expenses and things, you know."

"Done," Chaka agreed. He headed for the door, and then turned and looked back. "Two men will be here tonight to watch over O'Brien," he said. "When they arrive you go to the Nakuru airport, then on to Nairobi. From there you will go in my private plane to a landing strip near Koobi. After you get there, you will take one of my Rovers, which I have left for you, to the site and see if the boy is there. If he hasn't arrived, you will work backwards until you find him. Understood? If he is there, you will find a way to abduct him and keep him in a safe place. Is that also understood?"

Both men nodded.

Chaka turned toward the door. Before he departed he turned again, and said, "One thing more, to get the boy is of the utmost importance. Without him we have no bargaining power over his father. Even if we could give the key to O'Brien to take to Koobi, we would still have to have his son. Nonetheless, we can work around that, if necessary." He left the porch, stumbled across the ruts, and disappeared into the Mercedes.

Chapter Eighteen

Jack trudged along the goat path, one foot after the other. He knew he had to keep his dehydrating body moving east, where the native boys had said they would find a fishing club. But each step he took became more difficult. He stumbled on the smallest pebbles, fell to his knees, regained his footing, and then continued on down the trail. His heavy pack had become extremely burdensome on his aging back. He informed Tony that if they didn't reach the lake soon he would dump it.

On the other hand, Tony had raced on ahead to inspect each strange flower and shrub he had discovered along the trail. The interminable heat didn't appear to bother him. He still had spring in his legs and a massive amount of energy left in his body. Jack was envious of the boy's vim and vigor. Occasionally, Tony would turn and look down the path they had just traveled, hoping to see the native boys they had befriended earlier.

The sun had dropped behind the mountains, but its soft glow lingered on the low horizon, which made it difficult to see the path in front of them. Jack suggested they stop for the night and continue in the morning but Tony complained; he would have no part of it.

"There's too many hungry critters out there," Tony told him.

On top of a small rise Tony froze in his tracks. "Jack," he yelled back down the trail. "I think I see lights."

"How far?" Jack yelled back.

"Hell, I don't know, man, they're way down there." He pointed down the hill.

Jack's pulse pounded in his ears and adrenalin surged through his body. He lengthened his strides and within seconds caught up. Tony stood in the semi-darkness staring at the lights.

"Down there, man. Follow my finger," Tony said, excitedly, and again pointed.

"By God! I think you're right."

Tony let out a shrill scream of delight, put his arms around Jack's neck, and spun them in a pirouette.

"Tony! Stop that!" Jack demanded. "We're not there yet, son. And there are lots of wild things out here. Don't want to make any more noise than necessary. You understand? This isn't a game. This is for real."

Tony ignored the reprimand and darted down the path that appeared to lead into the valley.

"Tony! Tony!" Jack called after him. Getting no response, he returned to his slow, deliberate march toward the pale lights.

Fifteen minutes later, Jack approached two large boulders with a narrow path cut between them. He walked through the opening and looked out over the valley. Far below, he could make out individual lights.

"Hi, pop," came a shout from behind, fracturing the silence.

Jack jerked his head around. His heart skipped a beat and he grew light-headed. He labored through several deep breaths, before he realized it was Tony standing beside him with an impish grin on his face.

"You little shit!" he shouted at the boy. "Don't do that. You want me to have a heart attack?"

"Sorry, pop," Tony said, and then moved around in front of him.

"How far away do you think they are?"

"A kilometer or so."

"What time is it?"

Jack turned his arm so he could see the radium dial on his watch. "Near as I can tell, about ten o'clock."

"How long will it take us to get there?"

"The way you travel...half an hour. With these old legs of mine...about two."

"You want me to carry you?" Tony planted a broad smile on his face, and his white teeth glistened in the bright moonlight.

"Funny."

"Let's go faster," Tony insisted, and pulled on Jack's arm. "I'm thirsty as hell. And I could eat the south end of a north-bound skunk, right about now." Jack chuckled. They hurried down the almost invisible path, which they believed would take them into the valley and to the lights.

Soon after they left the two boulders, Jack heard a low, guttural growl off to his right. He stopped and remained motionless. He called to Tony and put a finger to his lips, indicating silence. Tony had already heard the sound and had come to an abrupt halt. Jack kneeled, pulled the boy down beside him, and motioned for him to un-strap his backpack. Earlier he had taken the veri-pistol from his belt and put it back in the pack. Now that he needed it he didn't know if he could find it, he couldn't remember where he had put it. Tony checked each compartment and found it in a side pocket. After a quick visual inspection, he handed it to Jack.

Jack checked the breach for a shell and snapped it shut. He held his breath, and with squinted eyes scanned the darkness. Off to his right, no more than 20-meters away, he noticed a pair of green unblinking eyes. Tony clutched his arm with a steel grip and wouldn't let go. Jack spun the barrel of the pistol around and pointed it at the eyes. All of a sudden five more sets stared at them, and were motionless.

"Oh, shit!" Tony said.

"You got that right, kid," Jack said, his voice modulating with a shudder.

Tony moved his head close to Jack's ear and whispered, "How many bullets you got for that thing?"

"Two."

"Two?" Tony hissed, loudly. "But there are six sets of eyeballs out there. What the hell we goin' to do now, Jack?"

For a fleeting moment Jack's thoughts drifted from the green eyes to what Tony had said. He called him Jack, not Honky, not white man, not pops...but Jack. It was a start. His mind returned to the situation at hand.

"Tony," he said, in a whisper. "Why don't you see if you can make it to that tall boulder back there." He pointed behind them. "You'll be safe, if you climb high enough."

"Screw you, old man," Tony came back, loud enough to secure a growl from a pair of eyes. "I ain't leaving you. You got the gun. You tryin' to get rid of me or somethin'?"

"Damn it, Tony!" Jack snapped in a loud, hoarse voice. "Do it!"

Tony turned and faced the boulder, but before he could make a move toward it, a loud roar came from the direction of the eyes. He hurried back to Jack and his weapon.

A shrill scream penetrated the night. Five pair of eyes disappeared into the darkness. One set remained, but it was no longer staring at them. The green eyes blinked several times, turned vertical, and then disappeared.

"What the hell!" Jack cried out.

Tony stared into the darkness. "What happened?"

"Beats the hell out of me."

A dark figure emerged from behind a large shrub, followed by two more. The ghostly shadows walked toward them.

Jack swung the pistol around. As they got closer his finger tightened on the trigger. To his relief it was the boys they had met, earlier.

Tony's eyes widened and an anxious grin spread across his face. He walked up to them and held the palm of his hand out for a fiver. When they didn't return his gesture, he dropped it.

"Hey, bro," he said, and put his arm around Paul's neck. "Thanks for savin' our asses, man." He hesitated, and then added, "It *was* you guys who scared those critters off, wasn't it?"

"Yes," he said, grinning. "It was Ebukut. He speared one lion and the others ran off."

Jack thrust a friendly hand toward Ebukut. The warrior hesitated, and then pumped it once. "That was some display of marksmanship. . . especially in the dark," he said, as he looked the warrior in the eye. "Will the others be back?"

"Yes, they will return," Paul replied. "But now we know where they will be. We'll come back in the morning and kill them. They have been eating our goats."

"Bummer," Tony said. "You guys goin' to those lights down there?" He pointed into the valley.

"We take you," Ebukut said in broken English. "Too late track lions. Come in morning." He spun around and headed down the path, with Paul and Hussein on his heels.

Jack and Tony were left standing in the middle of the path. They picked up their belongings and raced after them.

An hour later they arrived at the cyclone fence of the fishing club.

Ebukut went to the gate and spoke to Kirinyaga. With his beady, bloodshot eyes, the old Kikuyu inspected Jack and Tony. After he was satisfied, he pushed a button on the gatepost. Ebukut returned and told Paul in Masai to tell the Americans someone would be down in a few minutes. Paul told Jack and then left them standing under the floodlights of the gate.

Several minutes later a porter came to greet them. Jack examined him with curiosity. He was a tall, slender boy of Indian descent. He wore a pure white turban wrapped twice, instead of the usual three or four turns, around his head. His larger than average eyes resembled two black olives on both sides of a small, pointed nose. White silk shorts, hanging below his knees, clung to his legs as if charged with static electricity.

"Hello," the boy said in perfect English. "My name is Kobbi. What can I do for you?"

"Hi, young fellow," Jack replied. "How are you?"

Tony waited at Jack's side, while the two held on a conversation. After several minutes, he turned to Jack and said, "Will you hurry up with that nicety nice shit? I'm hungry, tired, and thirsty."

"Patience, Tony," Jack said. "We have to be friendly. We don't know anybody here."

Tony moaned, rolled his eyes, and turned his head away. As he scanned the area with tired, half-closed eyes, dozens of small children converged on them in all stages of dress, naked, ragged, and dirty.

With grubby fingers, the youngest of the lot felt Tony's clothes and dug into his pockets. "Shoo," he scolded. He grabbed the boy's hand and yanked it from his pocket. "Get away from me!" The small boy backed off, but the more assertive continued to pester. He moved closer to Jack and the porter.

Jack turned to Tony. "We're in luck," he said. "The manager told this young man we can stay until we can make arrangements to get to our destination. Isn't that great?"

"Terrific," Tony said, a tinge of sarcasm in his voice. "Where's the goddamn food and water? That's what I want."

Ignoring Tony's remarks, Jack turned back and faced the boy to conclude their conversation. "I must have lost my billfold in the crash," he told the boy. He turned to Tony. "You got any money on you?"

"What the hell do I look like an ATM?"

"Well, we can't stay here for free. We have to pay, one way or the other."

"We almost get killed in a plane crash…travel umpteen miles in the fuckin' desert…almost get eaten by a stinkin' lion, and they want money up front before they'll let us in?" Tony ranted. "How fuckin' considerate of 'em."

"Facts of life, Tony. And watch your mouth."

Tony unbuttoned his shirt pocket and pulled out a plastic card. "Here," he said, and thrust it into Jack's hand. "Don't say I never gave you nothin'."

Jack looked down at the American Express card. "Where the hell did you get this?" he said. "You steal it?"

"Look at the stinkin' name on it, pop.

The card read: Anthony J. O'Brien. "I'll be damned," Jack said. "How the hell did you get this? You're father give it to you?"

"Hell no, they give American Express to all kids in the Bronx. Didn't you know that?

"Is it okay to use?"

"I been usin' it all over Africa. Don't see why it wouldn't be good here."

"I'll pay you back. I have to go back to the plane to get my stuff, anyway."

"Don't worry about it, pops. Let's just get inside where there's food and water."

The porter took them up the red brick path and into the restaurant where Kurt Versteeg, the club manager, had been waiting for them.

Jack greeted him and explained their situation. He described how the native boys had helped them, but the manager didn't appear to be interested in that portion of the story. Versteeg picked up the internal telephone and called the Admission Office for the purser. As soon as the boy arrived, Jack filled out the necessary paperwork. With a forced smile, the porter ran the card through a hand-held state-of-the-arts machine. After the transaction had been finalized, Versteeg turned his back on them and continued his ongoing conversation with a tourist. The porter gave Jack a key to one of the small cabins, and then left them standing in the middle of the room.

"What a rotten fuckin' deal this is," Tony said, loud enough to be heard throughout the lounge. His face flushed. "We now have a room, the same as tourists, but they still treat us like so much shit. Where's the goddamn food and water? Can't we get that with American Express?" He raised his voice even louder, making sure the manager heard him.

Versteeg turned and stared at him. "Is there a problem, boy?" he shouted across the room.

"You goddamn right there's a problem," Tony yelled back. "We crashed our plane fifteen miles from here, walked all that way through the desert, almost got eaten by a stinkin' lion, and when we finally get here you treat us like so much crap. You didn't even ask if we needed medical attention or anything." He lowered his eyebrows and glared at him.

Jack was about to intervene, when he changed his mind. Tony was doing fine on his own, he thought. He remained in the background with a passive grin on his face.

Kurt walked across the room in a deliberate saunter, looked down and fixed his eyes on Tony. "What's your problem, boy?" he asked. "In the first place, we rarely allow blacks in here as guests. In the second place, you're lucky we even had a room for you and your friend."

Jack decided it was time to intervene. He took Kurt by the arm and with a powerful grip that almost crushed it, spun him around.

"I think it's about time you and I had a little chat, Mr. Versteeg," he said. "We better get something straight right here and now." A sinister frown formed above his eyebrows and a wicked smile developed across his twitching lips. "In the first place, I could buy this goddamn place, sell it at a loss and still be happy. Secondly, we expect to be treated like human beings. This is my friend from America." He pointed to Tony. "He's not one of your African *boys*, as you call them. He will be given the same courtesy as any other paying guest." As he glared into Kurt's eyes, he applied more pressure on his arm.

Kurt stood four inches shorter, and about 50-pounds lighter than Jack. He attempted to pull free but his arm was held in a vise grip. His face turned pink. He looked around the room for support but nobody came to his aid.

Jack released his grip, and then smoothed Kurt's lapel with his large hand. "We would like to have something to eat and drink," he said. "If it isn't too much trouble, of course. We haven't had water or food since the day before yesterday." A little deceit could not hurt, he thought.

Kurt snapped his fingers at one of the waiters, and he quickly escorted them into the dining area. Before they entered the large room, Jack turned and glared at Kurt, who was speaking to one of his employees and pointing in their direction. Tony slid into a chair and grabbed the glass of ice water in front of him. He guzzled it down and reached across the table for Jack's.

"Not on your life, kid," Jack said. He reached for the water and lifted it to his parched lips. "I'd probably kill for it." He emptied the glass.

Chapter Nineteen

Steve paced back and forth across the small room. He walked to the window, looked out over the lake, and then returned to O'Brien's chair. He checked the bindings, and then went back to his favorite window.

The two men appeared exceptionally nervous. O'Brien could sense that they were not overly anxious to defy Chaka. Kevin jumped to attention each time he heard a sound outside the cabin, and Steve kept his eyes on the lake.

"Do you think that black bastard's going to honor the fifty grand?" Steve said. He moved to another window and continued his surveillance of the lake.

"He better," Kevin said. He walked over and squeezed O'Brien's shoulder. "This guy is going to make sure he does."

O'Brien winced from the pressure of his hand and raised his eyes to meet Kevin's. "Don't put your life savings on it pal," he said with a smirk.

Kevin released his grip, took a parting swat at his head, and returned to the window.

"When did Chaka say our relief would be here, Kev?" Steve asked. "Wonder who it'll be? You got any ideas?"

"If you don't stop calling me by my name, I'll come over there and twist that goddamn nose of yours even worse than it is."

"Hell, the damage has already been done. What's so important about names, now?"

Kevin trained his eyes on a small motorboat fast approaching the dock below the cabin. He looked at his watch and walked toward the door.

"Where you going?" Steve called after him. "Don't leave me alone with this big bastard."

"I'm going to take a leak," Kevin said, and passed through the door. "Be right back." He found the over-grown path that led to the waterfront and skulked his way down. When he got within 20-meters of the dock, he took out his pistol. A boat pulled up and secured to a makeshift cleat.

He trained his gun on the man, as he came up the path toward him. "Hold it!" he shouted. "There's a gun pointed at your gut. What do you want?"

The other man, who remained in the boat, reached under his coat and Kevin aim his gun at him.

"What the hell you doin', Kev?" the man on the path said. "For Christ's sake put that damned thing away before you hurt yourself."

"Bob, is that you?" Kevin returned. "I thought you were in New York." He looked at the other man. "Who's your buddy there?"

Bob held out his hand. "How you been, Kev?" he said with a grin. "That's Mat. That's all you need to know." Kevin took his hand and nodded at Mat who had jumped out of the boat and headed up the path toward them.

"I've been okay," Kevin replied, as they walked toward the cabin.

"Guess you're the ones we're relieving," Bob said.

"That's right." Kevin turned and looked back at Mat. "He always this talkative?"

As they entered the cabin, Steve recognized Bob right away and greeted him with an enthusiastic handshake. Mat was introduced and he nodded.

"You gonna be our relief?" he asked.

"Yeah," Bob said. "Who were you expecting? The boat's fueled and ready to go whenever you are." He gave O'Brien a brief glance, and then turned his eyes back on Kevin. "Did he give you any trouble?"

"No," Kevin replied. "But don't turn your back on him. He's a big bastard…never know what to expect from him."

Mat walked over to O'Brien's chair and checked his bindings. "He won't give us any trouble," he said in a deep voice. "You guys get going, Chaka wants you to have the kid by tomorrow night."

"Tomorrow night?" Steve complained. "That's impossible! It'll take us that long just to get to Koobi. What if the little shit isn't there? We'll have to backtrack 'til we find him. Tomorrow night? That's impossible!"

"Suit yourself," Mat said. "But I wouldn't want to be the one that tells Chaka you can't find him." He looked over at Bob. "Would you?"

Bob grinned. "Not on your life." He pointed to the door. "You'd better get going. The plane is at the strip waiting for you. And you better not keep it waiting. Things like that have a habit of getting back to Chaka. You know what I mean?"

Steve started for the door then stopped and returned to O'Brien's chair. "See ya, buddy," he said and slapped him hard across the face. "We'll take real good care of that little bastard of yours, when we find him." They left the cottage and walked down the path to the dock.

As Mat and Bob stood by a window watching the small boat disappear across the lake, O'Brien sized them up. The one called Bob was above average in height and girth, and had long, muscular arms with large calloused hands attached. He had black wavy hair, and dark piercing eyes that constantly darted back and forth. He was the type found in most gyms, he thought.

Mat, on the other hand, was smaller…maybe five foot eight but with the arms of a weight lifter. He could not help but notice the man's biceps; they were several inches larger than his. He wore a T-shirt with the words "white power" emblazoned on its front. A menacing frown and a pair of dark-set eyes informed him he would be the one to reckon with, should anything happen.

While the two men continued their surveillance through the window, O'Brien made good use of his allotted time. In his younger days, he had played football for the New York Giants. The large diamond ring he wore was a payoff for one of their championships, which he now put to good use. The ring had sharp knobs on its sides to secure the diamonds to the setting, and the protrusions were sharp enough to cut into the cheap hemp rope binding his hands. The operation had taken longer than anticipated, but it was slowly getting the job done. He had no idea what he would do after the rope severed.

Bob left the window, walked over to O'Brien's chair and stood in front of him. He bent down until their eyes met.

"Well, now," he said, and glanced over at Mat with a grin. "We're looking after this nigger for two hundred a day, while Steve and Kev are going after his son and will probably make fifty big ones." He turned his eyes back on O'Brien. "Wouldn't you say the ratio and proportion is a bit out of whack here?"

"You got that right," Mat said with a sneer. He left the window and joined Bob. "I'd say we were getting the short end of the stick, to say the least."

"Two hundred a day?" O'Brien said, and shook his head. "You gotta be kidding." He looked up and smiled. "Hell, man," he continued, "I'd be glad to pay you guys your wages if you let me go. How's that sound? In fact I'd even throw in a bonus."

Mat lifted his arm to strike him but it was held back by Bob's strong hand.

"Don't do that," Bob said. "He still has to go to Koobi. Once Chaka gets the kid, and after this nigger delivers the goods, you can do any damned thing you want with him."

Mat walked back to the window. "What the hell's so important in Koobi anyway, nigger?" he called across the room, not turning his head.

"The name's O'Brien…Robert O'Brien. Niggers are the ones that burn down houses of white trash. I don't do that…anymore."

Mat turned his head from the window and eyed him, contemptuously. "As I was saying, 'Robert'," he said with a snicker, "what are they looking for up there? What the hell's so important up there that it makes Chaka go to all this trouble?"

"Beats the hell out of me," O'Brien came back. "I wish I knew. Maybe I could get in on some of the action." He was happy for the banter; it took their minds and eyes off his bindings, which were almost severed.

Bob slid the apple crate across the room and sat next to O'Brien. He pulled out a cigarette, lit one, and offered it to him.

O'Brien shook his head. "If I can light it myself," he said with a grin.

"Let's get serious, Robert," Bob said, and stared into his eyes. "I really want to know what they're looking for at Koobi. Doesn't it make you the least bit curious? Aren't you at all excited by the possibilities?"

"No," O'Brien said. "I don't give a damn what it is. They pay me to travel, and that's all. They don't confide in me about their projects."

Bob jumped up from the crate and flipped his cigarette across the room. "Damn you!" he shouted. "I'm trying to have a serious, civilized conversation, and all you do is aggravate the hell out of me."

"Then stop talking about it. I can't help you." O'Brien glared at him. "Besides, it wouldn't do you or me any good to know what it is. Chaka's the one who wants it. Moreover, he'll more than likely get it. Either way, I don't give a damn."

The remainder of the half-cut strands on O'Brien's bindings finally gave way and he felt them hanging against his wrists. The rope started to fall to the floor, but he caught it in time and pulled it back into his hands. One stumbling block out of the way, he thought. Nevertheless, his legs and chest were still bound to the chair. Cautiously, he glanced down at the swivel legs. They were made of oak or similar wood and attached to the bottom of the seat with angle irons, reinforced with several strands of rusty bailing wire. If he could distract them long enough, he knew he could break the fragile legs by standing up and falling backwards with all his weight on them. Nevertheless, if either the chair didn't break, or the remainder of his bindings didn't fall free in the several seconds he would have, he would be in serious trouble.

"Listen," he said, cocking his ear toward the window. "Is that those two idiots coming back? I thought I heard a motorboat."

Bob joined Mat at the window and looked out over the lake.

O'Brien's move was swift. With the chair still strapped to his back, he pulled his hands free from the bindings, stood up and fell backwards with all his weight on the flimsy legs. The plan was flawless, the legs broke as expected. He untangled the rope from his chest and legs, jumped to his feet, and without hesitating raced for the unlocked door and bolted through it.

Mat was the first to turn. He reached for his gun but realized it was in his holster hanging on a nail on the opposite wall. He darted across the room to retrieve it, but he couldn't get it out of the soft leather. In that amount of time, O'Brien had already traveled 50-meters down the rutted road and had turned into the sanctuary of some tall acacia bushes.

Bob didn't have time to draw his gun before it was all over. He stood by the window half paralyzed watching his friend wrestle with the holster.

Mat finally ripped the gun free from the holster and made a dash for the door.

"Wait," Bob shouted. "Don't go out there. You can't find him in the dark."

Mat stopped at the door. "I got a gun and a flashlight, idiot," he yelled back. "He doesn't have either."

"He probably doesn't need one," Bob replied. "Did you see the size of that guy? I'm not going after him. Let's see how far he gets in the underbrush, with all those critters out there."

Mat stood motionless on the small porch. "What should we do?" he yelled back. "Chaka's not going to like this."

"Chaka don't have to know," Bob replied. "Kevin and Steve are on their way to Koobi to get the kid and the key. That's all Chaka cares about." He hesitated long enough to consider their situation. "Chaka will get the kid and the key. Everything will be okay."

Mat walked back into the room, holstered his gun, and strapped the remnants of the black leather harness around his shoulder.

"Guess you're right," he said. "But what the hell are *we* going to do? We're a long way from Nakuru with no means of transportation."

"We got our feet," Bob said. He switched on his flashlight and headed for the door. "And we got guns in case those critters out there get restless."

They left the room and secured the door, ignorant of the fact that Chaka needed O'Brien to complete his mission.

At six o'clock in the morning, Ebukut lifted the flap to Hussein's hut and shook him until he opened his eyes.

Hussein threw his blanket to one side, stood up in the middle of the hut, and yawned. He scratched himself from top to bottom, while on his way to light a small fire. He placed a black, cast-iron kettle filled with *sokotai* tea on the coals, and then went through the thorn gate to Paul's hut. He found him awake and sitting on a blanket in the middle of the dirt floor weaving back and forth still half asleep. Satisfied that he was awake, he went back to his own hut.

Paul washed his face with several handfuls of tepid water from a goatskin bag, and then left to join Hussein, who sat with Ebukut by the fire struggling to ward off the morning chill. Hussein went into his hut and returned with a loaf of *maize* bread. They downed the tea and sweetbread, and then remained by the fire for another few minutes. Without saying a word, they picked up their spears, water bags, and the remainder of the *maize* bread and left the village.

A half hour later, they reached the trail they had traveled the previous night. As they walked down the goat path, Paul lagged behind; his mind was filled with many thoughts. He still had trouble justifying a need for the hunt. It didn't seem right to hunt down and kill the rest of the pride. For one thing, they had no way of knowing if that pride was the one responsible for raiding their herds. However, it was too late to worry about it, Ebukut had killed one and they were on their way to kill the rest.

He glanced at his friends a few yards up the path. They were walking side-by-side, their spears slung over their shoulders in typical warrior fashion. As he watched their slender bodies bob up and down in cadence, he wondered if he would ever change his mind about becoming a *lmurran*. Or would he return to Nairobi for another shot at civilization? He didn't know.

Hussein looked over his shoulder. "Come on, Paul, let's go," he called in Masai, trying to hurry him along.

"Why do you rush me? We'll find the lions soon enough…or they'll find us."

"By the time we get where we were last night," Hussein yelled back, "they could have eaten more of your goats. Do you want that?"

Paul didn't answer. He was in no hurry to get in trouble with the rangers; they might not be so lucky this time.

Jack had been up since pre-dawn. He had not slept most of the night, trying to find a way to get them to Koobi. He had checked with the Land Rover drivers at the club, but they would not accept American Express. He could not ask Versteeg he was not up yet. Even so, he doubted if he would help, especially after the previous night's confrontation. He returned to the room and woke Tony.

"Let's get something to eat, kid," he said. "As soon as Versteeg gets his ass out of bed we'll see what we can do about getting to Koobi. Assuming he's still talking to us."

"That Honky?" Tony said with a snicker. "I wouldn't trust that asshole as far as I could throw him."

"We've got to get to Koobi, son," Jack said. "He might be our only chance."

"Okay. Let's go for it." Tony said, and rushed for the door.

Robert O'Brien had made his way into the deep underbrush and huddled all night at the base of a large banyan tree. When the light of morning came, he was cold, tired and hungry. His body ached from the many cuts received while thrashing through the acacia thorns in the dark. His shoes were scratched and caked with red dust and his cloths half-torn from his body.

With all his remaining strength, he pulled himself off the huge root of the banyan and threaded his way through the needle-like thorns to a spot not far from it. He glanced in all directions. Seeing no danger he walked into a small clearing.

He sat on a nearby log to consider his dilemma; he was in the middle of nowhere, a long way from the cottage and lake, with no idea how to get back to civilization. He put his elbows on his knees and dropped his face in his hands.

All of a sudden, a deer raced by and almost knocked him off the log. It ran only a few meters and collapsed on the ground, with a spear sticking in its side. Its stomach lurched up and down for a few seconds, and then stopped.

He quickly scanned the area. He believed he heard Swahili voices and headed in that direction. He had traveled only a few steps when three men bolted out of the underbrush and almost collided with him. Surprised by the sudden encounter, they rushed back into the bushes.

"What are you doing here?" one of them yelled to him in Swahili, and came out from behind an acacia bush. "That's our deer. We killed it. You are not welcome to it."

O'Brien knew some Swahili but not enough to understand what the man had said. He held up his hands, as if holding a white flag in surrender.

"Do you speak English?" he yelled at the now visible man. "I don't understand you. You speak too fast."

"Yes," the man said. "I speak your language." He emerged from behind a large bush and approached O'Brien. "You are black, but you are not African."

"No. I'm from the United States," O'Brien said. "I'm lost. Which way do I go to get back to the lake? Or to a telephone?"

The three men studied him while they circled his tattered body. After a final inspection, a man in a chopped off T-shirt said in Swahili, "Have you met a lion?"

"No. Not a lion," O'Brien returned in the same tongue. He reverted to English. "But it was just as bad. I was held captive by two men in a cottage by the lake." He glanced at each of them. "I have to find a telephone, or a way to get to the Nakuru airport. Can you help me?"

The three men huddled together and an animated conversation ensued that lasted for several minutes. When the meeting was finally over, the tallest man turned toward O'Brien.

"We've discussed your problem," he said, and glanced at his friends. "We can help you."

O'Brien's face beamed. "I would be grateful," he said. "It's important I get to the airport."

"Yes," the man said. "We can help. But I'm afraid my friends want payment for their services." For a fleeting moment, his dark eyes met O'Brien's, and then he looked down at the ground, as if embarrassed. "It's not for me, but their time is valuable. Do you understand?"

"Yes, I understand perfectly." O'Brien gave him a crooked grin.

"After we get our impala we will take you to someone who can help you with your problem," the tall man said. "He will get you to the airport."

One of the men climbed a nearby tree, examined the area, and then slid down. Two of the men yanked the spear out of the carcass, picked up the impala, and lifted it onto the tall man's shoulders.

"You have been out here all night?" the tall man asked.

"Yes. I have been hiding under a tree, over there," O'Brien said, and pointed to the large banyan. "How far are we from Nakuru?"

"Nakuru? Nakuru is on the other side of the lake."

"Yes, I know. How do I get across without being seen by the men that are after me."

"Don't worry," the tall one said. "They will not find you in the direction we are going. You can trust me on that."

Paul had forgotten his thick-soled sandals; he had only his *kiatus* with him. Because of their leather toe bindings it made it difficult to keep up with the others. From time to time he would have to stop to extract a stone from between his toes. The first few times his friends waited, but after that he had to run to catch up.

"We are about where we were last night," Ebukut said, and pointed to the left of the trail.

"I don't see the lion you speared," Hussein said, searching the area with his eyes.

"The hyenas have taken him away," Ebukut said, after he had examined the tracks around the area. "There will be nothing left. I'm certain of that."

"Do you think the other lions will come back?" Paul asked.

"That's what I'm counting on," Ebukut said. He turned off the trail and headed for a group of large boulders a few meters away. "They are not like elephants; they have no concept of death. They will sense that he is still here and return."

They had found boulders to hide behind and within minutes the hillside was completely silent. By positioning themselves downwind, they were confident the returning pride would not detect them.

The noon sun bore down on them like a furnace and made their bodies glisten with sweat. As much as they wanted to wipe their eyes and foreheads, they remained motionless. They knew that if the lions returned the slightest movement would spook them or trigger a charge.

Not long after they had concealed themselves they detected a faint disturbance in the nearby bushes. From their hiding places they could not see what had made the sound, but they assumed it to be the pride returning.

Paul had hidden at the bottom of a ten-foot tall boulder. He had wedged himself between it and a smaller one. He heard a scuffing sound behind and above him. He didn't dare look up for fear of being detected. Nonetheless, he knew a lion was standing on top of it; drool from its panting mouth had fallen on his shoulders. His heart pounded. Salty sweat from his forehead ran into his eyes and burned them. All the lion had to do was look down from its perch and he would be discovered.

Hussein was not over four meters from Paul, and concealed behind two boulders of equal height. He had positioned himself where he could see Paul's dilemma, but was unable to move for fear of being seen by the pride.

Ebukut had hid in the middle of a patch of large acacia bushes, with a huge rock in front of them. He was unaware of the episode between Paul and the lion.

They heard what sounded like padded feet and a small pride of lions paraded past their hiding places. The lion above Paul's head inspected the back of the boulder, searching for an escape route down its slippery slope.

The rest of the pride had moved ten meters in front of it.

The pride stopped in a small clearing in front of the boulder and sniffed the ground. After urinating on several bushes to mark their territory, they stood in a tight group and sniffed for signs of the missing yearling.

The young male on top of Paul's boulder began to slide stiff-legged down its steep incline, but halfway down he tripped and tumbled end over end onto the hard-packed ground. He landed with a resounding thud, shook his head, sneezed several times, and then joined the others.

Paul wiped the dripping perspiration from his forehead, making as little movement and sound as possible. He pulled a cloth from his *sampur* and slowly wiped his burning eyes. As he put it back in his pack, a movement caught his eye to the right of the boulder. He parted the leaves and sneaked a quick peek. One of the cubs had discovered him. It hissed, meowed, and then backed away. The pride turned their heads toward the sound. They stood motionless, examining the bushes in front of the boulder. Trying not to make a sound or move a muscle he held his breath as long as he could. When his lungs were about to burst, he slowly exhaled through thin, pursed lips.

The cub hissed several times, and then ran back to the security of the pride. Before it had reached its mother's side, it tripped and went sprawling on the sand. For several minutes, the pride stood rigid as sentinels, staring in Paul's direction. After a few tense moments the pride dropped their heads and continued to snuffle the ground.

Paul was aware of Hussein's hiding place behind the two boulders, but could not see Ebukut's. He made several questioning hand gestures to Hussein, and the young warrior pointed to the bushes where he had last seen him.

He detected a movement in the bushes several meters beyond the pride. It believed it to be Ebukut. If it was he had concealed himself upwind from the pride, the one thing a warrior should never do. With a pride that size, one grown male, a huge female, and a yearling, not counting the cubs, they would attack if they picked up his scent.

The female raised her head and huffed. Both the male and yearling lifted their heads and stared at her. Except for the playful antics of the cubs, the pride stood motionless. The male pointed his head upwind and again sniffed the air. He huffed several times, and then growled in a low, guttural baritone. The lioness woofed and the cubs ran to her side. She paced back and forth in front of the two large boulders, every few seconds lifting her nose to sniff the wind.

Paul was certain the pride could smell Ebukut, but they appeared confused. He wondered what the warrior was up to. He glanced over at Hussein who stared wide-eyed at the lions.

He believed Ebukut might have been considering an ambush, while the lions were still confused by the smell. If that were to happen they would spook and run in *his* direction. It was a good plan; when they tried to escape through the opening between the boulders he and Hussein could spear them. It might be their only chance.

They had two spears between them, but there were two adult lions, and a yearling almost as large. Their only hope for success would be if Ebukut could spear one when he charged. If not, they would be outnumbered. Even if he did spear one, he and Hussein would have to make perfect throws at the other two. If either missed, they would be lion food.

Paul studied the underbrush upwind from the lions. The tip of a spear slowly parted the tall, brown elephant grass and waved from side to side, signaling. He glanced over at Hussein. He had also seen it.

Ebukut was no more than six or seven meters from the lions, buried in the tall grass flat on his stomach. The lions appeared confused by the unidentifiable smell, and returned to nervously sniffing the ground. As he continued to whiff the dirt, the large male moved closer to Ebukut. He ambled to within five meters of where the warrior's spear had parted the grass.

Ebukut suddenly jumped from his hiding place and stood at full height, yelling and waving his arms about. He aimed his spear at the large male and threw it with all his strength. The spear caught him behind the right shoulder and passed through his body. With a loud bark and a look of surprise the male leaped high into the air, and then landed on all four feet. Both the female and yearling stood glued to their spots. They watched as the big male twisted and turned, in an attempt to grab the shaft with his mouth. His attempt had failed and within seconds he dropped to the ground and lay motionless.

Ebukut stood at the edge of the tall grass, frozen with fear. His spear was gone and the other two lions had not spooked, as planned. He knew he could not run or they would attack. His eyes sent a plea to the boys. The lioness spotted the warrior, lowered her body, and prepared to charge. His face flushed and filled with anguish.

Paul jumped out from his cover, raised his spear, and ran at the female yelling Masai epithets. The lioness raised her body to full height and spun around to meet him. Before she could get set to charge, his spear had plunged into her chest below the neck, and she fell lifeless to the ground.

A split second after Paul's charge, Hussein closed in on the yearling. The young lion appeared confused, but stood his ground. It was obvious; he didn't know what to do. He looked over at the dead male, and then at his mother lying at his paws. Somehow, he could sense he no longer had their protection.

Hussein was several meters away when he threw his spear. The instant he let it go, the yearling jumped to one side. Nevertheless, he was not quick enough to avoid being hit on his hindquarter. He leaped into the air and screamed in pain. When he landed, he darted into the elephant grass on a collision course with Ebukut. As he ran into the thicket, the shaft of the spear caught the high weed and broke in half, but the blade and part of the shaft remained in his hindquarter. He raced through the field and disappeared, leaving only his painful cries behind.

The cubs ran into the tall grass and disappeared, but their meows and hisses could be heard for several minutes after they had vanished.

Chapter Twenty

Robert O'Brien hurt all over. He and his rescuers had managed to thrash through the thick underbrush for two kilometers and end up at the lake. When they arrived at the shoreline, two men in khaki uniforms met them. According to his calculations, he was about half a kilometer from the cottage where he had been held.

His liberators stopped to talk to the rangers.

"What does the man want?" the ranger in charge asked in Swahili.

"He says he has to get to the airport in Nakuru," replied the tall native.

"Did he tell you what he's doing here?"

"He said he was held captive in the old cabin at Lookout Point, up the shoreline."

"And what was the reason for that?"

"I'm not sure. Maybe you should ask him."

The ranger glanced over at O'Brien. "What is your problem, sir," he asked in English.

"Problem?" Robert said, eying the man contemptuously. "My problem is that I was abducted by two men, taken at gun-point from my hotel, tied up and held hostage in a cottage by this lake." He pointed up the shoreline.

"What did they want from you, sir?" the ranger asked.

"They were trying to rob me."

"Rob you? What did they want, your money?"

"No. They were holding me because they wanted something they thought I had."

"Did you give it to them?"

"No. I didn't have it."

"Then they did not rob you. Did they?"

O'Brien stared angrily into the ranger's eyes. He knew it was a set-up. He realized the ranger was not going to help him. At that moment he wished the natives had not helped him at all.

"In other words you don't believe a word I told you," he said to the ranger. "You're not going to help me, are you?"

"I didn't say that, sir."

"If that's the case, why can't we get in that boat of yours and head across the lake to the Nakuru airport? I'll pay you, if necessary."

"I must wait for instructions, sir."

"And where might those be coming from?"

"Mister Chaka."

O'Brien's face turned ashen. He was being fed to the wolves. Chaka even had the rangers under his thumb. He saw no escape.

"Chaka?" he said, eying the ranger in disbelief.

"Yes. Do you know him?"

"Uh…no. But I've heard of him.

"Then you might appreciate what he can do for you, sir."

"Yes, of course," O'Brien came back. "I'm sure he can do a lot for me." Of all things, he didn't want them to know of his dealings with the man, or his connection to him.

"I should hear from him within the hour, sir," the ranger said, and glanced down at the boat tied up to the pier. "As soon as he arrives and gives permission we'll take you to the Nakuru Airport…but not until then. Do you understand?"

"Perfectly," O'Brien replied.

He knew he would be in for a rough time, if Chaka arrived. His only chance of staying out of captivity was to get away, and fast. He looked down the waterfront and saw a 12-foot Boston Whaler tied up to a cleat. Somehow, he had to get to that boat. But he knew it would be extremely difficult with all the rangers around. There were four rangers, two at his side and two on the pier smoking cigarettes and drinking beer. The only option he could think of was to overpower them, or at least cause a distraction long enough to escape.

The beeping of a cell phone broke the silence. A short, black ranger standing beside him answered. "Yes, sir," he shouted into the mouthpiece. "Yes, sir. He's standing beside me." There were several moments of silence, and then he continued. "Yes, sir. We will not let him leave." He looked over at Robert. "Yes, sir. We have no reason to believe he will leave." He hung up.

O'Brien heard their conversation and it didn't sound good. He wondered if he should attempt his escape at that moment or wait for a more opportune time. He didn't have much choice, he either had to go immediately or suffer the consequences. He glanced down at the boat, again. The two men guarding it were still sitting in deck chairs smoking cigarettes and drinking beer. It was the opportunity he had been waiting for. It was then or never. He shoved the two men next to him down an embankment and into a tangle of thorn bushes. With the speed of a gazelle he rushed down the path to the pier. The two men sitting on the dock drinking were not paying attention to what was going on around them. He jumped onto the boat, took the helm in his hand, and turned the ignition. The engine sputtered and hesitated for a few anxious seconds, then fired.

The half-drunk men finally realized what had happened and drew their pistols. They both staggered aboard firing wildly into the air. It was not difficult for O'Brien to shoulder them into the cold lake water. After the second man had fallen overboard, he pushed the throttle to its limit. The boat tore free from the rotted out cleat and sped into open water. The two rangers, who had been standing next to him on the path, thrashed their way out of the bushes and rushed down to the pier. They arrived in time to watch the boat disappear across the lake.

The other side of the lake was several kilometers away. O'Brien had been there many times and knew the shoreline well. He could not pull up to the more popular piers on the water's edge; he was certain Chaka had already called his men and they would be waiting for him if he landed. He had to find a cove, or an out-of-the-way dock or mooring. He had the advantage; they didn't know where he would make land and they couldn't be everywhere at once.

When he approached the rocky shoreline, he strained his eyes for a place to pull the boat into, or get close enough where he could swim ashore. He noticed a lighted sign next to a paved strip of road at the water's edge and pulled up close enough to read it. The sign read: NAKURU AIRPORT 1km, with an arrow pointing to the right. He spun the boat around and headed in that direction.

Within minutes, the silhouette of the control tower appeared on an elevated site. He noticed a small cove close to the tower and made a beeline for it. When he made ready to cut the engine and glide through the 50-meter opening in the channel, he noticed a black limousine parked on a small jetty near the landing. Several men got out and made their way to where they had anticipated he would land. He spotted them in time, swung the boat around, and headed back to the middle of the lake.

He had not gone more than a few hundred meters, when he looked back at the cove and noticed the limousine speeding down the road parallel to him. After dodging several small fishing boats, he found another inlet that looked safe. He headed into the cove, but found the same limousine parked and waiting. Again, he turned the helm toward open water. A few hundred meters out, he stopped and cut the engine. Perplexed, he slouched down behind the wheel, took in a deep breath, and sighed. As he examined the shoreline, he noticed several small speedsters leaving one of the docks. He watched for several minutes, and then realized they were heading toward him.

He started the engine and pushed the throttle all the way to the dashboard. The Boston Whaler's bow lifted out of the water and shot forward, leaving the two speedsters in its wake. He had no idea what he would do next, but he knew he had to make land and get to the airport.

Several loud reports broke the silence. He turned and looked back at the two speedboats several hundred meters behind, coming on strong and shooting at him. He didn't believe Chaka would have given them orders to kill him he was too valuable. But, if their bullets hit the boat at a critical spot it would be dead in the water and he would be captured. He had to think of something fast; the two speedsters were just a few dozen meters away.

A thought flashed through his mind, and a smile came to his face. If it worked for James Bond, perhaps it would work for him. He slowed the whaler until the speedsters were only 10-meters behind and lined up in his wake. When everything appeared to be in place, he pushed hard on the throttle and spun the whaler180-degrees. The two speedsters were caught off guard and veered to one side of the wake to avoid a collision. As they jumped over the huge rooster-tail, they were jettisoned into the air and landed upside down. O'Brien turned the boat around and headed back in the direction of another small cove he had seen earlier.

When he arrived at the cove, he noticed the black limousine parked several meters from the water's edge. He shoved the throttle all the way forward and made a beeline for it. Its occupants looked surprisingly like Steve and Kevin. They got out and watched, as the whaler headed toward them at full throttle.

While O'Brien held the bow in a direct line to the car, he reached under the dash for a life jacket. He could see that the two men were nervous by their jerky reactions, but they didn't move away from the limo's side. He was 50-meters out and moving toward them at full throttle. He located a signaling pistol beside the seat and found that it had four flares attached to its side. He loaded one flare and put the others in his pocket. When the boat was no more than 20-meters out the men on shore drew their pistols and scurried behind the limo. The speeding boat remained on a collision course. Before it left the water, he jumped over-board. The boat skidded across the small rocks on the shoreline, still on a collision course. He lifted his head from the water in time to see the whaler's sharp bow penetrate the side of the limousine, and then splinter into hundreds of pieces. The two men that had crouched behind the limo were thrown across the small jetty and landed in the water on the other side.

O'Brien swam to shore and checked on the two men stretched out in the water. After pulling them ashore, he discovered they were only unconscious. If they had been killed, he would have had more of Chaka's wrath to contend with. He didn't want to get on his bad side anymore than he already had.

He knew he wouldn't have much time before Chaka came after him with a passion. Especially, when he discovered the mess he had made of the man's limo, the two speedsters and four men. Nevertheless, he had to find a place to hide, until his clothes dried. After that, he would take the next step getting to Nairobi, and then on to Koobi. When he walked by the remains of the limo he noticed gas pouring from its tank. He pointed the flare gun and pulled the trigger. A thunderous explosion shattered the quiet of the lake, and metallic pieces flew high into the air, forcing him to race up a small path to the sanctuary of a gravel road at the top of the jetty.

By the time he had reached the road, natives were already converging on the scene. He took off his wet shirt, tied it around his waist, and headed in the direction of the airport. There were natives all around him. He thought perhaps Chaka's men would not be able to single him out. A native with a reed basket balanced on his head walked alongside him. He asked the man if he would sell him his merchandise, along with the basket. The man agreed and accepted a soaked American twenty-dollar bill. After a few attempts, he balanced the basket on his head and continue on down the road to the airport.

Chapter Twenty-One

Jack still had not found them a way to get to Koobi. He had tried several times to get the drivers of the Land Rovers to take American Express, but they were not allowed the manager only wanted cash. Versteeg had not yet arrived on the scene, and he was their last resort. He went to the lounge and relaxed in a wicker chair. He believed that Versteeg would show up, sooner or later. From what he had heard, the man frequented the bar.

Tony rushed up the sidewalk and vaulted the steps to the lounge. "Hey, old man," he said. "What's happening?" He slumped down in a nearby chair. "Have you found a way to get us to Koobi, yet?"

"No. But I'm working on it. I'm waiting for Versteeg to get his ass out of bed."

"That asshole," Tony said, making a sour face. "I wouldn't trust that guy to walk my dog." As an afterthought, he added, "I'll bet he could get us there if the price was right."

"Probably. However, we'll have to wait for him to get up, before we can even talk price."

"Don't they have a telephone in this friggin' place?" Tony said. "They don't even have a TV."

"That's the least of our worries," Jack said, and looked over. "I know you've got to get to Koobi, son, but you have to understand I've got a lot at stake up there, too. I've got to get to my contact to tell him what happened. I damn sure don't want him to come looking for me. It wouldn't be healthy." He hesitated, then added, "However, I don't even know who he is...he's supposed to find me."

"See. What'd I tell you about haulin' that stuff? You're gonna' get yourself killed, if you keep truckin' it."

"Well, what's done is done," Jack said. At that moment, he looked up and spotted Versteeg entering into the lounge.

"Morning," Kurt said, and displayed a broad smile. "Did you and your little friend sleep well?"

"Good morning," Jack said. He was taken back by the man's good-natured greeting, after the previous night's confrontation. Jack stood between Kurt and the bar, making it difficult for him to get to his favorite seat. "There's something I want to talk to you about, Mr. Versteeg."

Kurt slithered by him and got a cup of coffee from a silver dispenser. "Yes? What is it? What can I do for you?"

"Mister Versteeg, we have to get to Koobi Fora, right away."

Kurt stirred in several spoonfuls of sugar and swirled it around in his cup. "I see. And what's so important up there? There's nothing up there but camels, scorpions and lizards."

"Site fifty one," Jack said, dryly. "They're digging for something important up there and Tony has to get there right away. It's urgent that he gets there as soon as possible."

"And you want me to get you there, right?"

"I'd appreciate it. We'll pay you of course, assuming you'll still take American Express."

Versteeg slurped his coffee and stared at Jack. He turned his head and eyed Tony sitting in the lounge area. "I could probably do that," he said. "But I don't know about the card. They charge us a lot to use it, you know."

"Naturally, you can add any extra charges. The thing is we have to get there right away.

"The fact is…I got you fellas by the balls. Don't I?" Kurt said with an impish grin.

Tony overheard their conversation and got up from his chair. Before he could walk across the room, Jack held up his hand and yelled, "Tony, you stay right where you are. I can handle this." The boy saw the fire in his eyes and returned to his chair.

Kurt observed the exchange with humor. He walked over to Tony, who had slouched down in the chair like a child waiting to be reprimanded, and said, "I guess he got the best of you that time. Didn't he?"

All that Tony could say was, "Funny. Ha, ha."

Kurt returned to the bar and poured a fresh cup of coffee. He took a note pad from his jacket pocket and started scribbling. "Well, let's see…it's quite a few kilometers up there, and the driver will have to wait for you to return…several hours, I would imagine." He jotted down some figures and handed the pad to Jack.

"Holy Christ!" Jack exclaimed. "Is this what you charge your guests?"

Kurt grinned. "No. I'm giving you a discount. You're new guests."

Jack went over to Tony and showed him the figures. "Can your card handle this?"

"Holy Christ is right!" Tony said, and blew a stream of air through pursed lips. "What the hell do I look like, the mint? Christ, I could buy half of the Bronx for that amount." He looked up at Jack with a grimace. "I guess it'll be okay. Dad said I had an unlimited account."

"What are they digging for at Koobi, anyway?" Kurt asked. "The last I heard they were no longer allowed to dig...government regulations, licenses, etcetera."

"Be damned if I know. But whatever it is it's important enough to send the kid to meet with John Anderson to give him something he can't do without."

"John Anderson?" Kurt said, raising his eyebrows.

"Yes. Why?" Tony intervened. "I'm supposed to give him something."

"I know John very well," Kurt said. "He's a good friend of mine. We go way back...even before Koobi."

"Well, ain't that a big friggin' deal!" Tony said, using his best slang. "Do you charge *him* this much when he needs something?" He pointed to the pad.

Kurt laughed. "Okay. Now you've got *me* by the gonads. Tell you what I'll do. I'll get you up there for nothing, because John's a friend of mine. All you have to do is pay for the gas. How about that?"

"How much is the gas...a hundred bucks?" Tony said, sarcastically.

Kurt let the comment pass and picked up the house phone. He spoke into the outdated device for several minutes. "Okay," he told Jack. "It's all set. Get whatever you're taking with you and go to the main gate. Look for a truck with the number four printed on its side. The driver's name is Waldo. He'll take you there and wait 'til you're ready to return.

"Waldo?" Tony said with a grin. "Don't sound native to me."

"We call him Waldo because we can't pronounce his tribal name," Kurt said with a grin.

"Can we eat first, Jack?" Tony asked.

"Yes, but make it fast. We've got to get up there as soon as possible. Okay?"

Chapter Twenty-Two

The trip to Koobi had been nothing but bumps and dust, with an occasional washout, which had to be circumvented. Several times along the way, they had been forced to stop long enough to replenish the radiator. Waldo had not been the most talkative person in the world, and Tony made a big deal out of it. However, after several hours driving, he loosened up and started talking, and then they couldn't shut him up.

When the Rover pulled into Site 51, it was early afternoon and the sun was at its hottest. John Anderson and Barry Wetherford met them. After introductions all around, they all moved to the sorting tent, sat on the ever-present chairs on the patio, and tapped the bottomless container of lemonade.

"Well, Tony," John said. "Where's your father? He was supposed to be with you."

"It's a long story, Mr. Anderson," Tony said. "Let's just say he was detained. I'll explain it all later, it's complicated. But I think I have something you want." He took the key chain from around his neck and handed it to him.

John looked at the number stamped on its side. "God! Can we ever use this!"

Barry eyed Jack from across the patio, and then went over and sat next to him. "So, Jack…it's Jack, isn't it?" he asked.

Jack nodded.

"What are you doing in this part of the world? Pleasure trip?"

"Tony hired me to fly him up here," Jack said. "We had trouble with the plane and crashed…somewhere in the saw-tooth mountains. Had a bitch of a time gettin' here."

"Well, I'm certainly glad you made it," John said.

"Mister Anderson, there's something you should know," Tony said, interrupting him.

"Yes, Tony. What is it?"

"There are some goons out there looking for this key. I don't know if they'll come this far to get at it but I wouldn't be a bit surprised. Be on the lookout. They're mean mothers."

"Thank you, Tony. I'll put my men on alert. They won't get past them, if they value their lives."

Barry left Jack, shuffled his pear-shaped body across the room, and sat next to Tony. He put his elbows on the arms of the chair, bent forward, clasped his hands, and turned his head so he could stare into his eyes.

"So, Tony," he said. "Where's your father? Now would be a good time to explain what happened…we usually close the diggings when the sun is at its hottest. The men won't work this time of day…too damned hot. Now's a good time to explain things…and we've plenty of that."

Tony fixed his eyes on the swirling sand blowing across the patio. "Ain't much to tell," he said. "Some ass-holes with guns came into our hotel room, took dad away, and left me standing there." He returned Barry's stare, and then continued. "Before they left, dad had a chance to toss me that key. He told me to get my ass up to Koobi Fora and give it to Mr. Anderson." He turned his head and stared at John.

"Did he tell you what the key was for, Tony?" John said.

"No. But he said it was damn important and that I was to get it to you, no matter what."

"Good man," Barry interjected.

"Just so you'll know, Tony," John said, "this key goes to a safety deposit box in Nakuru. It's got lots of money in it for our licenses so we can continue our dig."

"If you don't mind me asking," Jack said, "what are you digging for that's so important?" He hesitated for a moment, and then added, "Somebody's gone to a hell of a lot of trouble want you to keep you digging, while at the same time it seems somebody's trying to shut you down. The thing I don't understand, when those men took Tony's father why didn't they get the key then? If they had it they would have the money and you couldn't continue your dig. I don't understand. If there's something valuable at this dig it seems to me they'd *want* you to continue."

"Confusing, isn't it?" John said. He rose from his chair and walked to the entrance flap of the sorting tent. "Come, let me show you something." He turned and stared at Barry.

Barry frowned. "John!" he said. "Do you think it's wise to show them?"

"Look at it this way, Barry," John said, stopping at the flap, "everyone seems to know about the money, the licenses, and more than likely what we're digging for, anyway." He unlocked the flap, and then turned to Jack and said, "Come with me, I'll show you something that'll knock your socks off."

They went into the back area of the tent and John stopped in front of a long table. For several moments he stood motionless beside it. Finally, he pulled down a long canvas that covered a large object on the table. His face beamed. The skeletal remains of a huge figure had been reassembled down the length of the table. It was at least eight feet long and three feet wide. There didn't appear to be a bone missing.

"Holy Christ!" Tony exclaimed. "That's one big mother—"

"That's right, Tony," John said. "We measured him from head to toe and he's eight foot two inches tall." He reached across the table and pointed his finger at one of the ribs. "That's not all, there's a piece of metal stuck in between one of his ribs, all the way to his spine…there." He moved one of the bones so they could see it.

"Looks like the head of an arrow," Jack said.

"It's not an arrow. It's the tip of a spear, or knife…we can't be certain," John said.

"How old are the bones?" Tony asked.

"Here's the fun part," Barry said, with obvious excitement. "The carbon dating puts them at well over two million years. Can you believe that?"

"Is that piece of metal an integral part of the skeleton, or was it put there later?" Jack asked.

"The tip passed between his ribs and lodged in the backbone where it broke in half, which makes it an integral part of the skeleton," Barry said. "And here's the kicker…there were no metal weapons or anything like that two million years ago. At least that we know of."

"Especially this kind," John added. "We broke off a small piece and had it analyzed. It's an alloy unknown to science. That's not all, a medallion of the same metal hung around his neck. There was an inscription on it, but to my knowledge no one, at least up to now, has been able to decipher it. That's what we sent to the museum and that's why they sent the money to keep us digging."

"You're sure it's two million years old?" Jack asked.

"Yes. We had the bones carbon dated by two different facilities," Barry said. "There's no question about it, they're over two million years old."

"I'll bet that really set the archeologists back on their heels," Jack said.

"You can bet your sweet ass it would have, if they had only known about it," Barry said. "You can see now why we need the licenses to keep digging. We're fairly certain more bones are out there, just like these. And who knows what else."

"Wow!" Tony said, blowing a gust of hot air. "I read something about...who was it, Lucy? But she was only about four feet tall. And she damn sure didn't have a metal necklace. But I guess she was about the same age."

"They only found a partial skeleton, though. Not like this one," Barry said. "This one is perfect...everything's intact. It's as if it had been preserved for all eternity. Even the teeth are all there. And the strangest thing, those teeth are perfect not a single cavity, not one missing."

"Does the Kenyan government know about your find?" Jack asked.

"We tried our best to keep it a secret, but you know how that goes. Word somehow leaked out. It's impossible to keep something this big a secret, when you have over a dozen natives working for you." He looked over at Jack and smiled. "Of course Kenya is going to get the brunt of it. I'm sure some kind of a deal will be made through the museum in New York, but we should get credit for the find...and a little of the booty. Money talks, you know."

The sun had dropped halfway down the western sky and the heat of the afternoon had eased. Most workers had already returned to their respective spaces to continue digging.

John covered the skeleton and lowered the flap to the locked room. He led them back to the patio and drew more lemonade. "Well, Tony, what do you think?" he said, and dropped his aging body onto a canvas chair. "Have we uncovered the find of the millennium, or what?"

"I don't know about that, but I guess dad knew what he was doin' when he told me to get this fuckin' key to you guys," Tony said, in his own unique way.

Barry glanced at John and cringed.

"By the way, Jack," John said. He pointed across the compound to an old Piper Cub they had purchased from a local flying school. "You're a pilot, right?" Jack shook his head. "Do you think you could handle that old relic over there?"

Jack squinted across the compound. "Piper J5, huh?" He looked back at John. "Hell, that's what I learned to fly in, fifty or so years ago." He grinned. "What do you have in mind?"

"Well, I know she flies, but I don't have anybody here that can fly it. We have to get this key to the bank in Nakuru. I imagine by now they've converted the dollars into shillings."

"So, you want the old man to fly that thing?" Tony said. He glanced over at Jack and grinned. "Hell, he couldn't even fly the one he had."

Chapter Twenty-Three

In the early afternoon, O'Brien arrived at the Nakuru airport. He lifted the basket from his head and pulled the wet shirt from around his waist. He found a bathroom and draped the saturated clothes, along with his shoes, over the top of a stall. He checked his billfold and found that his American Express card was dry and undamaged, but that was about all. After spending the better part of three hours in the bathroom, waiting for his clothes to dry, he grew impatient and put the semi-dry clothes on over his damp underclothes.

He was hungry and he had seen a snack bar in the lobby when he first arrived. Nevertheless, before he headed for it he checked out the terminal for signs of Chaka's men. When he was certain the coast was clear, he made a beeline for it.

After eating several sandwiches, he went to the terminal counter to check on local flights. He realized he might need his passport but Chaka's men had taken it, another way to keep him from escaping. But there was no alternative; he had to get on a plane.

The person behind the counter was a beautiful native girl. She looked up and smiled. "*Nakuenda wapi?*" she said.

He hesitated, trying to remember his basic Swahili. "*Kujaribu, Nairobi,*" he said.

She looked at him with amusement, and then smiled. It was obvious she had seen through his attempt at Swahili, but she put her fingers on the keyboard of the outdated computer and started typing. Several minutes later she slid a printed ticket across the counter.

"*Ahsante*," she said, and scanned the ticket for charges. "*Mia mbili, tafadhali*."

He made a quick calculation in his head, 200-shillings. After that long breakfast, he didn't know if he had that much left. He took out his billfold and checked the bill compartment, 100-shillings and change. He figured the ruse was up, unless she took plastic. Even then, if she noticed that the card was assigned to the Museum of Archeology the game might be over, anyway. He figured she was on Chaka's payroll, along with everyone else in Nakuru. He handed her the card and threw a casual glance across the terminal; a feeble attempt to appear casual

Without hesitating, she swiped the card through the machine, pulled the receipt out, and handed it back for a signature. He noticed indecision in her eyes, but she said nothing. Moreover, she never asked for a passport. More than likely she didn't want to be embarrassed if he turned out to be a Kenyan.

He signed the receipt and left the counter. But he had a strange feeling she was still eying him as he walked across the lobby to the gate for Nairobi. He looked back and detected a smile.

The plane lifted off the runway and made the required circle around the airfield, before it headed for Nairobi. He breathed a sigh of relief. Halfway through the turn he looked out the window and saw a long, black limousine parked at the opposite end of the runway, next to a small Cessna.

"Mister Chaka," the ranger responsible for O'Brien's escape shouted into his cell phone. "What do you want us to do? We were informed that your man was on the plane when it left for Nairobi. The airline officials said they could have picked him up at the airport, but they didn't know what you wanted them to do."

"Tell them to let him go," Chaka's metallic reply came back. "Don't bother with, him for the time being. It's the boy I'm interested in."

Kurt Versteeg sat at his usual watering hole at the end of the mahogany bar, sipping his first martini of the afternoon, when he heard the sound of loud footsteps on the patio stairs. He glanced over and noticed a tall ranger about to enter. He sat his drink down and squinted to get a better look. His face flushed and his mouth dropped open.

"My God!" he said, and walked across the room to meet the man. "We all thought you were dead!"

"Not quite," Sergeant Mandeli said with a smirk. "Wishful thinking, I assume?"

"No, really. We heard the crocks got you."

"I don't wish to discuss it," the sergeant came back with a sneer. His eyes were threatening, as he examined the lounge. His uniform was not the usual spit and polish it was dirty, crumpled and torn. He took his eyes off Kurt long enough to walk halfway into the dining room, where he noticed a few tourists having their evening meals. Satisfied with the inspection, he returned to the bar. "Have you seen any rangers?" he asked Kurt. "Were there any here looking for me?"

"Not to my knowledge."

"How about the Samburu boys? Did they come back here?"

"Not here. They're probably at their *manyattas*."

Without saying a word Mandeli turned, rushed down the stairs, and disappeared around the corner of the building.

Kurt held his martini high in a salute to his departure. When he was certain he had left, he called Jonathan over and whispered in his ear, "Tell George to call the barracks at Marallel and inform them Mandeli is still alive, and to come and get him. Also, go to the Samburu village and tell the boys he's back. You know what boys I'm talking about." The boy smiled and darted from the lounge. He took a swig of his martini, and then mumbled, "The son-of-a-bitch has nine lives."

After standing outside the window of the radio room for several minutes waiting for the purser, Jonathan got impatient and left without delivering the message. He figured he would tell them about Mandeli, when he returned.

He raced across the barren desert to the Samburu village, half a kilometer away. When he arrived, he lifted the flap to Paul's hut and shouted in Masai, "Paul! Paul! Get up! Sergeant Mandeli is looking for you guys!"

Paul rolled over from his short nap and rubbed his eyes. After he realized what the boy had said he stared at him for several second, and then jumped up and raced through the opening in the thorn fence to Hussein's hut. He was also asleep.

"Hussein! Quick, get up!" he shouted, and shook his shoulder.

Hussein rolled onto his side and looked up with half-closed eyes. "What? What is it?" he mumbled.

"The sergeant isn't dead! He's after us! Get up! Hurry, we have to get Ebukut and go into the desert and hide."

"What do you mean? Everyone said he was dead. Even the helicopter pilot couldn't find him."

"Well, he isn't. Jonathan just told me. He said the sergeant came to see Mr. Versteeg at the club, and he's looking for us, too. Come on, get up."

"Get your things," Hussein replied, as a command. "Get everything you need for the desert, and plenty of water. I'll get Ebukut and meet you back here in five minutes." As he turned to leave, he grabbed Paul's arm. "Don't tell *anyone* where we're going."

"I don't know where we're going. How can I tell anyone," Paul answered.

"We'll discuss it with Ebukut when we meet back here," Hussein told him. "Now, go!"

Jonathan raced back to the club, vaulted the steps to the restaurant, and sat for a few moments in one of the wicker chairs, trying to catch his breath. He had forgotten about stopping at the radio room to inform them of the sergeant, as Verteeg had instructed.

Mandeli skulked about the compound for nearly half an hour, before he found a Rover with a napping driver inside. He pulled the man from the cab and ordered him to hand over the keys. It was official business, he told him.

As he sped down the dusty road in the confiscated truck toward the small Samburu village, his mind mulled over his past few days. K'eti's spell had taken him to within a few hundred meters of the island of no return then something snapped inside his head and he found himself no longer under her spell. He had discovered a small cove on the island's shoreline, and the sound of a helicopter prompted him to pull in and wait until it had passed over. A few hours later, when darkness had flooded the area, he paddled back to the shoreline north of the El Molo village and waited in the cold, early morning hours until Eric and the others had left for the club. He then returned to the village. The Site 51 vehicle he had commandeered earlier was still parked up against a sand dune and he made a run for it. As he left the village, he noticed Kibbi standing beside a hut. He charged out of the vehicle and confronted him. Kibbi told him everyone thought he was dead, because the helicopter couldn't find him.

He had waited until the villagers returned to their huts, and then sped up the goat path onto the main road to Loiyangalani. When he arrived at the outskirts of the small town, he waited until he was certain no one had seen him, then abandoned the truck in the heavy bushes and walked to the fishing club.

He believed that if everyone thought he was dead he could use that to his advantage. As far as the rangers were concerned, they had already declared him dead. Therefore, he was no longer a wanted man. With that in mind, he knew it would be much easier to capture and punish the boys. After he had dealt with them he would consider going back to the El Molo village to take revenge on the old woman who had put him under her spell. He had too many harrowing experiences on the lake not to retaliate.

He approached the thorn fence that surrounded the Samburu village and slid to a stop in front of a *manyatta.* He leaped from the cab and looked for an entrance through the acacia-thorn barrier. Finding one, he went into the compound and looked for someone to command.

A small boy approached. He eyed the sergeant's soiled and wrinkled uniform and said, "Are you a ranger?" He stuck a dirty finger up his nose and twirled it around.

"Yes. I am," the sergeant said, and glared down at him. "Where can I find the warrior Ebukut, and the one called Hussein?"

"They have left the village," the boy said, tilting his head up to look at the tall rangers face.

"Where have they gone?"

"I do not know. They did not tell me."

"This is official business! Find someone who knows…right now!"

The boy held an intense stare. "They will not tell me," he said. "I am too young. Besides, Hussein said not to tell anyone where they were going."

"Go get your father or mother," he told the boy. "Tell them I am here on official business, and they must tell me where the boys went." The boy turned and skipped one foot after the other back to his hut.

Several minutes later, a tall, slender man holding a long fishing spear walked toward the sergeant. "Can I help you?" he said.

"Do you know where the two *lmurrans* are, the ones who killed the lions a few days ago?"

"I don't know. They left about an hour ago and haven't returned."

"Which way did they go?"

"I don't know, I was not watching. I just know they left…in a hurry."

Mandeli reached out and slapped the man hard across the face. "You will go to every *manyatta* and ask if they saw them leave, and which way they went. Go! Quickly!"

The man put his hand to his burning face and gave the sergeant a defiant scowl. "They will not tell me. You have my word on that."

Mandeli drew his pistol and pointed it at the man's stomach. "They will either tell you or I will shoot you," he said, looking at the man with menacing eyes. "Now, go ask them."

Seeing the gun and the fierce look, the man turned and slowly walked away.

The sergeant figured it was pointless to expect them to tell him, but he had to try. There could be someone in the village that might inadvertently give them away.

Hussein's father came out of his hut and approached Mandeli. He was as tall as the ranger and slightly heavier. He was not used to having his friends intimidated by rangers and did not appreciate it. He stood nose-to-nose with Mandeli and glared into his eyes.

"What do you want my son for?" he said. A furrowed scowl formed above his dark eyes. "He has done nothing wrong. Your own rangers have forgiven him for killing the lion in self-defense. What do you want him for, now?"

"His pardon was not justified in my eyes. He must beg for my forgiveness, and pray that I'll be compassionate."

As the two men stood glaring at each other, a dozen men approached with hunting spears in their hands and *rungus* hanging from their goatskin belts. L'Umbo could tell by the sergeant's eyes that he sensed them coming and was becoming extremely nervous.

Mandeli turned his eyes toward the approaching men. They did not stop. His face flushed. No village had ever challenged him before. He had always been in command. He didn't know what to do. His shoulders slumped and his legs started to buckle. He knew he should leave. It was ridiculous for him to stick around and be brave and assertive. He turned, slowly backed toward the opening in the fence, and then sprinted for the truck.

As he drove away L'Umbo let out a war whoop, and the villagers joined him. For them, the incident had turned into a celebration, but not for the sergeant.

Chapter Twenty-Four

O'Brien's short flight to Nairobi landed at the local airstrip adjacent to the International Airport. He left the plane and was immediately escorted into the Quonset hut that housed the custom's office. The man at the front desk asked for his passport. He fumbled around in his pockets, knowing he didn't have one. He had to come up with something, and fast. When the girl in Nakuru hadn't ask for it, he didn't think they would ask in Nairobi. He was wrong. The man at the desk showed his impatience and instructed him to go across the room and check in at the main customs desk. The waiting room was filled to capacity with tourists returning from local flights. He approached the long line, but before he had reached the official's desk, he spotted an open door that led to a small tarmac. After checking the room for police or rangers, and not finding any, he walked through the door and onto a small plane parking area. A man in coveralls stood beside a two-passenger Piper, with a pad and pencil in his hand.

O'Brien approached him. "Hi," he said with a pleasant smile.

Startled, the man jerked his head around. "Hi. Don't sneak up on a man like that. You scared the hell out of me," he said in English.

"Sorry. I was admiring your plane. Piper Tomahawk, isn't it?"

"Yep. The best plane Piper had to offer. . .years ago." Then he added,

"And probably the hardest to fly."

"What's the shortest takeoff and landing for that thing?"

"Oh, about five, six-hundred feet takeoff, with a good wind…if I put the pedal to the metal, so to speak. It'll land in about the same."

"Is she for hire?"

"What you got in mind?"

"Have you ever flown to Koobi Fora?"

The man eyed him, with a suspicious sideways glance. "Koobi Fora?"

"Yes. You know, way up north, by Lake Turkana."

"I know where it is. But why do you ask. You're not thinking of going up there, are you?"

"The thought had crossed my mind."

"I've taken supplies up there. They only have a short landing strip. Taking your life in your own hands when you land there. It's rocky as hell."

"Let's get down to business, shall we?" Robert gave him a toothy smile. "It's worth quite a bit to me to get up there…right away."

The man put his pad on the low wing of the plane, stood upright, and stretched. "What are we talking about?"

"I don't know," Robert said. "What do they pay you up there to bring in supplies?"

"Well, I never took passengers before."

"Give me a ballpark figure, and make it worth your while."

"If I was to consider it, I'd probably ask for about five hundred…American." He gave O'Brien a crooked grin.

"You take American Express?" O'Brien grinned back.

The pilot glanced up at the sky, as if pondering. "Hell yes." Then he added, "Let's make it six…credit card, paperwork, you know." He gave him a smug glance.

"Done," O'Brien said. "When can we leave? I have to get up there right away. It's very important."

"Hell, I'm all gassed up, checked out, and ready to go right now." The man turned and headed for the Quonset hut.

"Where you going? I thought you said right now?"

"Hold your horses, I've got to fill out a flight plan or we don't go any place."

"Do you have to tell them you have a passenger?"

The man cocked his head to one side and gave him a curious look. "Do you have something to tell me that I should know about?"

"It's a long story, but they lost my passport and I've been having all kinds of trouble without it. I don't want to make my life more difficult than it is." He stared at the man with a determined look.

The man went to the storage compartment of the plane and pulled out a pair of coveralls. "Here, put these on and look like you're working. I'll be right back." Again, he headed for the hut. Halfway across the tarmac he turned and yelled, "By the way, I'm Mat. What's your name?"

"Robert."

"Okay, Robert, I'll be back in ten minutes. Look busy."

Chaka's Cessna 270 approached an abandoned airstrip, several kilometers from Koobi. Kevin and Steve buckled up and waited for it to land on the hard-packed, rock-strewn strip.

"Hope the little shit's at Koobi," Kevin said. "I'd hate like hell to chase him down."

"Yeah, but what if he *is* there?" Steve came back. "How the hell we gonna get in the compound with all those guards around. And there must be dozens of natives working the dig."

"Stop worrying. Chaka will get us in…somehow."

"Did he say that? That he'd get us into the site?"

"No, not exactly. But I'm sure he'll find a way. He has too much at stake not to help us."

When the plane touched down it nearly ran off the strip, which had baseball-sized rocks, and eight-inch-wide heat-breaks caused by previous rains and intense sun. It sprinted to the end of the short runway and stopped.

"Okay," the pilot shouted above the roar of the engine. "We're here. There should be a vehicle waiting for you on the other side of that little rise." He pointed to a bush-covered hill, 50-meters from them. He waited while they got their gear and disembarked then revved the engine and spun the plane around. Before he left, he opened the cockpit window and yelled, "I'll be back for you tomorrow about this same time. Be here." Then he added, "Unless you want to drive all the way back to Nairobi. Whatever you decide let Chaka know."

Before they could respond, the plane shot down the runway and climbed into the hot afternoon sky. They stood for a few minutes at the end of the short runway and watched it disappear over the horizon.

Steve turned to Kevin. "Now what?" he said. "Do you have any plans on how we're going to get the kid?"

"Play it by ear," Kevin said. "Come on, let's get to the vehicle. It's only a couple kilometers to the site, from here. We can wait in the truck until it gets dark."

They strapped their backpacks across their shoulders and trudged over the hill. There stood a blue Rover with a Site 51 logo painted on both sides. Kevin pulled down the sun-visor and the keys fell into his lap.

By the time the Piper Tomahawk had landed at Site 51 and taxied up to the sorting tent, it had started to get dark. When Tony discovered that the passenger was his father, he bolted from the tent and ran to greet him.

After a short reunion, Tony said, "Hey pops, it sure took you long enough to get here. What happened?"

"It's a long story, son. One I'd just as soon forget."

"How did you manage to get away from those goons?"

"I told you it's a long story. I'll fill you in later. Right now I want to sit and have a cold drink." He put his huge hand on Tony's bare neck and gently squeezed it. When he felt no chain around his neck, he said, "I see you made it here with the key." A shocked look spread across his face. "You *did* give Anderson the key, didn't you?"

"Certainly. Would I let you down?"

"Of course not. I can always count on you." O'Brien grinned and ruffled Tony's hair. They walked to the sorting tent and sat in chairs next to the ever-present thermos of lemonade.

Anderson walked out of the tent. He had a smile on his sunburned face. "Robert O'Brien, I presume," he said with a twinkle in his eye and an outstretched hand. "I haven't seen you in a coon's age. You must have had quite an adventure...according to Tony."

"I could have done without it."

"Well, never mind, it's over with now," Anderson said, and drew him a glass of the sweet nectar. "We have the key and Jack is going to fly either you or me to Nakuru to get the money." He called Jack over. "I'm sorry, I don't think you two know each other. Jack's the one who got your son here in one piece," he told O'Brien. "We owe him a bundle of thanks."

They shook hands, and again tapped the lemonade jug. After a second glass, the pilot of the Tomahawk looked at his watch and told them goodbye. He got in the Piper, revved the engine, and spun it around to face the strip. They watched, as it raced down the runway, lifted gently above the desert, and disappeared over the low-lying mountains to the south.

"Well," Barry intervened. "I guess those goons, as Tony called them, didn't get the key or the money. That's damn good. Now we can continue our dig."

O'Brien looked over at Barry and grinned. "Don't put you're life savings on it. Those guys work for Chaka, the one who held me captive. I guess you've heard of him. He had the notion that if Tony was held captive he could force me into stealing the relics you're digging for. I'm sure it's not over. Keep your guard up, they might still be after Tony."

"Over my dead body," Anderson said. "We have a dozen guards here at the site, and they're all loyal to me. I pay them enough, they should be."

"Still, I'd keep my guard up, if I were you," O'Brien said. "Chaka has enough money to do, or buy, anything he wants, and he wants what you're digging for. He'll go to any length to get it."

"Let's take it minute by minute, hour by hour," Anderson said. "We're not about to give up the 'golden goose' without a fight. Barry and I have worked too damned hard for too many years to let it slip through out fingers."

"Hey pops, let Mr. Anderson show you what you went through hell for," Tony interrupted. "You won't believe it…trust me."

Anderson took O'Brien into the locked sorting tent. He showed him the skeleton and explained everything he knew about it. After a few minutes they returned to the patio and replenished their lemonades. O'Brien seemed impressed with what he had seen, but he displayed little emotion or interest; it was not his forte, he told them.

The Samburu warriors had found a small cave several kilometers from the village where they could hide. They would stay there until dark, and then resume their trek through the desert before the first light of morning. They realized the sergeant would go to no end to capture them. They were unaware that he had already been to their *manyattas* and voiced his threats.

"Paul! Hussein!" came a shrill voice from outside the cave. Startled, the boys looked at each other with blank stares. It was obvious someone had found them, although they were certain no one had seen them enter the cave.

Paul stuck his head out and saw a young boy standing a few meters from the cave with an awkward grin on his face.

"Jonathan. What are you doing here?" he said. "How did you know where to find us?"

The boy's grin turned into a full-faced smile. "You're not the only ones that know about this cave. I've been here many times. It's a good place to hide."

"Why have you come? You might have given us away."

"I came to tell you your friend from Nairobi is here."

"You mean Somerville? He's here?"

"Yes, William too. They just arrived at the club. When they got there, I guess they found out that the sergeant was still alive. They said they wanted to see if there was anything they could do to help you guys. They gave me fifty shillings to find you." He looked at Paul with another broad grin. "That was easy money. I knew where you'd be."

"Is the sergeant still looking for us?"

"Yes, but he won't find you. Everyone in the village is against him. Nobody will help."

"Go back to the club and ask Mr. Somerville if he will come and get us," Paul said. "Maybe he can take us back to my aunt's village."

"Okay," the boy said, and then disappeared into the thorn bushes.

Chapter Twenty-Five

It had been a long and dusty trip to Koobi, much longer than Dan had anticipated, and they were still not there. The interminable sun had not made it any easier. He had muscled the Rover through centuries-old ruts and around large needle-sharp bushes, until his hands grew weary and occasionally slipped from the steering wheel. He had never traveled that far before in such heat. It was never like that in the south. Sweat poured down his forehead and ran into his burning eyes. After several hours, he pulled the truck to the side of the road. His four passengers welcomed the respite and raced from the cab to empty their bladders behind the first acacia bushes they could find. When they returned, they slid back onto the hot leather seats and closed the windows. Dan switched on the air conditioner, which had not used to save fuel. It was not long before the cool air had begun circulating throughout the vehicle.

"I was told William was here too, Mr. Somerville," Paul said, breaking the silence.

Eric turned to face him. "Yes, he is. But he was in no condition to take this trip, especially on a goat path like this. We left him at the club with Versteeg."

"Is he in much trouble with the safari company?" Paul asked with a frown.

"He could be. The company was not at all happy with him." He turned his head back to concentrate on the road. "All things considered, he'll make out okay. He's too valuable for them to let him go."

Hussein reached across the seat and touched Eric on the arm. "We thank you for rescuing us," he said. "We don't know what we would have done. We had no place to go, other than back to the El Molo village. That would have taken us days. The sergeant would surely capture us."

"Don't worry about Mandeli," Dan said, and looked over his shoulder. "We'll take care of that problem when it arrives."

The cab remained silent for several miles. "Where are you taking us?" Paul finally asked. "You are headed toward Koobi. Are you not?"

Eric turned and looked at him. "Yes, we're going to Koobi. We have something to give to John Anderson, which I believe he will find quite interesting." He turned his eyes back to the road, adjusted his sling, and continued. "An International courier service was in touch with me in Nairobi and gave me a letter to give him. They said it was quite important, but they didn't know how to get in touch with him. Somehow, they found out I was going to Loiyangalani; their service doesn't go that far north. After I got to the club Kurt told me about Mandeli, and I wanted to see if there was anything I could do to help you boys."

"Do you know what the letter says?" Paul asked, out of curiosity.

Eric glanced over at Dan and grinned. "Well, the courier service had to open it for security reasons…at least that's what they told me. As long as it had already been opened, my curiosity got the best of me. Nevertheless, I don't think I should tell anybody about it. I'll let Anderson explain it, if he wants to."

"We'll be there in an hour or so," Dan interrupted. "Hold onto your kidneys." They all laughed.

They had traveled to within a few hundred meters of the site when Kevin pulled the truck to the side of the road and parked behind a large bush.

"I don't think we should go any farther, 'til it gets dark," he said. "I damn sure don't want to go into that place with all those guards around, while it's still daylight."

Steve reached behind his seat and retrieved a bottle of scotch from his pack. "Then let's have a drink," he said. "It'll be a while before it gets dark. Might as well enjoy it."

For several minutes, Kevin looked out his window, deep in thought. He turned to look at Steve and saw the bottle in front of his face. He reached for it and took several sips, then handed it back and opened the cab door.

"Where you going?" Steve asked.

"Can't I take a piss?"

"Oh, sure. Sorry. Thought you were going someplace without me."

"I've got to have time to think things over, anyway."

"What's there to think over?" Steve said, and took another long swig. "All we have to do is sneak into the site, get the little shit, and high-tail it out."

"That easy, huh?"

"Well, there might be a few minor hitches. But we can handle them."

"Think so?" Kevin yelled back, as he walked behind a small termite mound. After relieving himself, he went back to the truck and slid behind the wheel. He took the bottle from Steve and gulped down a mouthful. "Assuming we do get the kid, what do we do then? We're supposed to take him someplace and hide him. But where? Chaka didn't say."

"I'm sure he'll get back to us on that," Steve answered. "He has so damned many contacts, someone will get in touch with us. I'm sure."

"They better. I don't want to baby-sit that kid," Kevin said, and reached for the bottle.

It had been a long, miserable day for the sergeant, and it had not gotten any better. He returned the confiscated truck to the parking lot in front of the club and slipped out of sight behind a building. The vehicle he had commandeered from Site 51 was parked in a grove at the edge of town. When he got to the truck, he jumped inside and sat motionless, deep in thought. He had no idea what he should do next. He thought he knew where the boys were headed, but he was not sure enough to take a gamble. He knew he had to do something; he couldn't just sit there. He had to find the boys and make them pay for their sins.

"Koobi Fora!" he shouted, breaking the silence in the cab. "That's where they're going! I'm sure of it." After several fruitless attempts the truck started. He put it in gear, spun the wheels on the loose gravel, and set out for Koobi and satisfaction. "Anderson!" he continued his thoughts out loud. "If they're not there, he'll know where they are."

He realized he had to be careful. More than likely the club had already informed ranger headquarters of his whereabouts. If that were the case, he was no longer a missing person; he was once again a wanted man. It would take him several hours to get there and it would be dark before long. Nevertheless, he had to go. It was his only option…and his duty as a ranger. He smiled

As Dan fought the Rover on the makeshift road toward the site, he finally spotted the lights of the old generator. He muscled the truck through the unguarded main gate and pulled up to the sorting tent. Anderson and Barry greeted them.

"Hi...again," Anderson said. "To what do we owe this honor?"

The truck unloaded and they all headed for the patio in front of the sorting tent. Barry went inside and brought out several more canvas chairs. When they were seated, Anderson offered them lemonade, which they readily accepted.

Hearing the commotion, Tony rushed from his newly acquired tent and greeted them. He noticed Paul sitting on one of the chairs.

"Hi, buddy," he said. He held out his hand for a fiver, but drew it back when he remembered Paul didn't know its meaning.

"Hello, my friend," Paul said with a broad grin. "I see you and your friend made it through your little adventure."

"Little adventure, my ass!" Tony said, returning the grin. "The last two days were the longest and scariest of my life."

After listening to their banter for several minutes, Anderson looked over at Somerville. "Well, Eric, what brings you here?" he asked, interrupting the boy. "You get homesick for the old farm?"

Eric reached into his safari jacket and pulled out the letter. "I think you might be interested in this," he said. "It's been opened, but not by me...customs, I think. But I did read it. Hope you don't mind. However, I didn't understand much of it."

John reached for the envelope and pulled out the letter. After reading it once, he read it again, and then again. When he had finished, he handed it to Barry.

Barry lost no time reading the short paragraphs. As John had, he also read them several times. When he had finished, he folded the paper and put it back in the envelope. His face turned somber and blood slowly drained from it.

"My God!" he cried out. "What the hell we got here? A Martian? Was he a man from outer space? What the hell was he, when he was alive?" He handed Anderson the envelope and stood like a statue in front of him. "Did you come up with the same conclusion I did?"

Anderson fondled the envelope for several moments, and again pulled out the letter. He motioned for Barry to sit next to him while they both read it. With heads inches apart, they thoroughly examined its contents.

The men sitting on the patio remained silent. They seemed to realize the importance of the document and remained quiet and motionless. Occasionally, they would glance at each other, and then look back at the two archeologists.

"Look at that long line of zeros and ones," Barry said, pointing with his finger. "That looks like binary?"

"Yes, I believe it is," John said, squinting to see the small characters. "What the hell is modern binary doing on a medallion two million years old?"

"Good question," Barry returned. "But are you sure it's binary? They could just be characters that look like it."

"It's binary, all right," Eric interrupted. " I saw it when I briefly read the letter. I can read that stuff. I didn't have four years of computer science for nothing."

Anderson handed him the sheet. "Then what does it say?"

"I believe it tells you at the bottom of the page."

"I know, but I want a second opinion…doctor. It's hard to believe what I just read."

"It'll take me a few minutes. I need a pencil and paper. It's been some time since I did this. I might be a little rusty."

Barry went into the tent to get the necessary items. When he returned, his hands shook when he handed the items to Eric. "You sure you can come up with the same message that's written at the bottom of the page?"

"Don't know. But we'll soon find out," Eric said, displaying a comical grin.

Site 51 had always been a place of spontaneity, activity, and the hustle and bustle of many diggers. However, the entire camp had somehow found out about the letter and it suddenly became as quiet as the bow of an ocean liner. The diggers in the field had apparently realized the importance of the letter, although they had not been officially informed of its contents. It was a tense moment for all.

To the men on the sorting tent patio the wait had seemed interminable. Nevertheless, it had only been a few minutes before Eric put his pencil down and handed John his findings.

John read the scribbled words. "Do you know what those strange words mean, Eric?" he mumbled almost incoherently.

"What does it say? What does it say?" Barry asked, and attempted to grab the letter from his hand.

"The letter from the museum," Anderson began, "said that on the medallion they had found the inscription 'warrior of the wind'." He thought for a moment, and then added, "But Eric, what you wrote down doesn't say that. It's a hodgepodge of strange words, which make no sense to me."

"That's right. What I translated is in another language. No idea what kind. The cryptographers at the museum must have cracked the code. That's why they sent you the message in English. They're pretty clever, those cryptos."

Barry grabbed the paper from John and held it in one hand and the letter from the museum in the other and compared the two. "Regardless, it's still impossible!" he stated. "We had those bones dated and they're definitely two million years old. This letter infers that they're modern—the last few decades. Only then did they start using binary."

"Did you ever consider that if those bones are that old, they're probably from a civilization a million times more advanced than ours?" John said. "From a time never recorded, but one we may have evolved from."

"Or from outer space!" Barry interjected with a guffaw.

"Quite possibly," John said. "Some people, including myself, think all life came from the stars...or space. The impacts of asteroids or comets could have dropped microbes here. At first they may have been microscopic, but then evolved into life forms we now know." Everyone on the patio appeared wrapped up in his own thoughts and images of what John had just said.

Kevin pulled the truck from its hiding place and drove to a side road a few meters from the main gate. Kevin jumped out, and like a trained dog Steve followed. They stood beside the truck and relieved themselves, then pulled their packs out of the back. After strapping holsters around their shoulders, they slid .45s.into the soft leather. Their expressions remained sullen, as they draped the backpacks over their shoulders. Kevin locked the doors and they trudged down the path toward the cyclone fence.

The sun had completely vanished below the horizon, and overhead the stars twinkled brightly. The perpetual wind had not yet arrived, but they could sense it was coming—the calm before the storm.

"Wonder where the little shit is?" Steve said, as he stumbled on one of the many large rocks hidden between the acacia bushes. "Maybe he's not there yet. But if he is, they probably have him hidden someplace. I'm sure by now they realize we're after him."

"Doubt that. I don't think they know at all," Kevin came back.

Steve stumbled several more times on the raised ridges manufactured by thousands of goat hoofs. He turned on his flashlight.

"Turn that damn thing off!" Kevin yelled, breaking the deathlike silence. "For Christ's sake, you want us to be discovered before we even get there?"

"Sorry. But I can't see in this damned darkness."

"I know, life's a bitch, ain't it? Suffer through it; we've only got a few meters to go. We gotta get there before that damned wind picks up. If we don't, we won't be able to see or do a damned thing."

"What are we going to do when we get there?" Steve asked, stumbling again and almost falling.

"Play it by ear."

A few minutes later, they arrived at the cyclone fence that completely surrounded the site. Kevin dropped to the ground at its base, and then retrieved a pair of wire cutter from his backpack. After several attempts, the heavy-gauge metal gave way and made a hole large enough to crawl through. They shimmied under the small cutout, and then dashed toward the only visible light they could see. The dim glow appeared to come from a structure on the edge of the tent complex. They made their way to the back of the first tent and looked through its clear plastic window. In the light of a 40-watt bulb, they could see a figure lying on a canvass cot.

"Is it him?" Steve asked in a loud whisper.

"Don't know. Can't make out who it is," Kevin whispered back.

"That would be too easy, anyway," Steve came back. "If it isn't him, he'll be in one of the other tents. There must be a dozen on the site."

Ignoring his comment, Kevin shined his light on the figure and held it there until Steve pulled his arm down.

"You crazy?" Steve said. "What if he wakes up? We'll be in all kinds of trouble."

"I can see it isn't him, anyway...he's too big," Kevin said. "Let's go to the next one."

They searched the outlying tents and only found native workers asleep on their cots. The search brought them to a well-lit tent, somewhat larger than the others. They looked through the window and saw a half-naked black man standing over a smaller figure lying on a cot.

Kevin grabbed Steve's arm and pulled him back several meters from the tent. "Bingo!" he whispered. "I think we found him. But we still have a problem. His old man is with him. I think the kid's asleep, but O'Brien's standing over him like a guard dog."

"What'll we do?" Steve said, and then moved farther from the tent. "We can't get at him while that big bastard's in there."

"Got an idea," Kevin said, and dropped his backpack to the ground.

"What's that?"

"You'll see," Kevin said. "Bear with me. Get back there and keep an eye on O'Brien. Let me know if he leaves."

He rummaged through his pack and pulled out a half-stick of dynamite. He put it on the ground, while he fished through its pockets for a lighter. Without telling Steve what he was up to, he walked to the front end of the tent with the stick in his hand.

O'Brien shook Tony's shoulder, attempting to wake him from a sound sleep. Getting no response, he shook him again. "Wake up, son. I'm going to the sorting tent. I've got to talk to Anderson."

Tony stirred, and then opened his eyes. "Okay. Don't be too long," he said, sleepily, then rolled onto his side and went back to sleep. O'Brien headed for the large tent, which was fully lighted and guarded by several men.

"Okay, O'Brien's gone," Steve whispered loud enough for Kevin to hear. "He's headed for that big tent, over there." He pointed where several 100-watt bulbs flooded the area.

Kevin skulked his way back to Steve, who still stood by the window. "Alright," he said. "Listen up. You get over by the front flap. When I start a commotion, you wait for the kid to come out then you grab him. Understood? Before you do that, get some duct tape from your pack and have it ready to cover his mouth."

As Steve searched for the tape, his face flushed with excitement,. Finding it, he unwrapped a few inches and tore it free from the roll. It wrapped around his wrist and clung, but he quickly untangled it and rushed to the front flap, where he waited for the signal.

Kevin moved back to the other side of the tent and lit the fuse. He waited until it had burned nearly down to the charge, and then threw it far from the tent. It took several seconds before it exploded, but when it did the entire area lit up. The diggers, who had been sound asleep, woke up and rushed around in a daze. They bumped into each other and tripped over tent stanchions in an effort to run from the unknown danger. Anderson and O'Brien emerged from the sorting tent and watched, as the workers ran around in circles.

With tape in hand, Steve stood at the open flap and waited for the boy to come out. When he didn't show, he looked inside and discovered he was still asleep. He ran to the cot, covered the boy's mouth with the tape, picked him up and rushed back through the open flap. Around the corner of the tent, Kevin waited with the two backpacks and a small throw cloth.

He put the sheet over the boy's head and ran toward the hole in the fence.

When they had arrived at the fence, Steve dropped Tony to the ground and held his arms and legs while Kevin wrapped tape around his wrists and ankles. After sliding him under the fence they made a beeline for the truck. When they arrived, they shoved Tony in the back seat and sped down the dark rutted path.

When O'Brien returned to the tent he discovered Tony was missing. He assumed he had gone outside to investigate the disturbance and rejoined Anderson at the sorting tent.

"What the hell was that?" he asked.

"Damned if I know," Anderson replied. "One of the workers may have accidentally detonated a stick. We use a few to uncover hard to get at bones."

"Did you see Tony come out of the tent?" O'Brien asked.

"No. I was kind of involved with the explosion. Didn't see a thing."

"Wonder where he disappeared to?"

Anderson stared at him. "Maybe we should try to find him. Didn't you say this fellow Chaka may be after him. Maybe that explosion was a diversion."

O'Brien ran to where the explosion occurred and called out several times. With no success he returned to the sorting tent and rejoined Anderson.

"You may be right," he said. "That son-of-a-bitch would stop at nothing to get what he wants; grabbing Tony would be his first objective. If he does have him, he'll try to use him as a pawn to get me to do his bidding. But he's got another think coming, if he thinks he can use him to get at me. I know my son, and if that bastard has him he's in for a rude awakening. You can trust me on that."

Barry came out of his tent, rubbing the sleep from his eyes. "What happened? Didn't I hear an explosion? What the hell was it? What's going on?"

"Must have been some digger getting careless with dynamite," Anderson said. "Go back to bed, we'll talk about it in the morning." Barry gave him a thumbs-up and returned to his tent.

"I'm going out to look for him," O'Brien said, and turned to leave. "I don't think I'll find him, but it's worth a try."

"I'll stay here and wait," Anderson said. "If he shows up I'll whistle."

O'Brien headed for the point where the fence came closest to the sorting tent. When he arrived, he discovered the cutout section and noticed that it had been freshly cut. He then realized he wouldn't find Tony. He had to assume Chaka's men had taken him.

He returned to the sorting tent and slumped down in a lawn chair next to Anderson. After several minutes, he looked up and said, "John, I think he's been taken by Chaka's men. Your fence has a fresh cutout and from the looks of it, it was done recently. Maybe we should wait 'til morning to do anything more about it. Even if he were still out there we'd never find him in the dark. If Chaka's men do have him I don't believe they'll harm him. He just wants to use him for a while. He'll be in touch, I'm sure."

"You don't think something else might have happened to him?" Anderson said, glancing out of the corner of his eye. "There are lots of hungry critters out there, you know. This is a bad time of night to be wandering around in the dark."

"With this fence all around the property, I doubt if there's any danger of that," O'Brien said. "Besides, I pity any 'critter' that would have to deal with him." They both chuckled.

The Rover raced wildly down the dark, deserted road. Kevin's knuckles had turned white from his tight grip on the steering wheel, and his eyes burned from the swaths of light radiating from the sealed beams.

Something didn't add up for Kevin, about their arrangement with Chaka. Nonetheless, they had to trust him; they had no other choice. On the other hand, maybe they should find out more about what was going on before they turned the kid over to him. He had heard the man was notorious about screwing people, and they were no exception. However, they had the upper hand; they had the kid. For Chaka to fulfill his plan he needed him. Even so, he had doubts whether the man really *did* need him. Chaka had enough money to buy anything he wanted. Why did he need the kid? All he had to do was bribe a few officials and he could get anything he wanted from Anderson, without the boy or O'Brien's help. He was confused. Nevertheless, he figured things would eventually work out for the best.

"Take the tape off the kid's mouth," he told Steve. "Nobody's going to hear his foul mouth way out here." Steve reached in the back and yanked hard on the duct-tape.

When the tape ripped off, Tony let out a yell and threw his head back against the seat. He glared at Steve. "You ugly bastard! Why'd you have to be so goddamn rough? You could have pulled it off slow. Bastard!"

Steve took a swipe at the boy's head, but he ducked in time to avoid contact. "Don't 'bastard' me, you little shit. I'll take you outside and feed you to the animals." He looked over at Kevin and grinned.

"Why don't you untie my hands and feet?" Tony asked. "You know I can't do anything to you guys, you're too damned big and ugly."

Steve glanced over at Kevin. "You think it'll be okay? I locked his door with the remote lock. He ain't goin' anywhere."

Without looking over, Kevin nodded. "Yeah, I guess it can't hurt. But keep an eye on him. He's a clever little shit…at least that's what his father said." They chuckled. Steve took his knife and severed the bindings.

Tony slid across the seat to the window on the driver's side. He tested the door handle, while nonchalantly looking up at the stars. It was locked. He leaned back in the seat and continued to view the stars. Several minutes later, he noticed Steve's silhouette against the dim light reflected off the front windshield. "God! You got one ugly nose. What happened? Did it get caught in a meat grinder, or something?"

Steve's face flushed. His blood pressure rose and pounded feverishly in his ears. He was accustomed to people talking about his nose behind his back, but never to his face. He wanted to reach around and slap the kid, but he let it pass. He knew it was just an attempt to aggravate him. He turned his head and glared at the boy.

"Why did you guys grab me?" Tony asked, looking out into the darkness. "You don't need me. I don't have that stinkin' key you were after. I gave it to Anderson."

"See," Steve said, looking over at Kevin. "I knew all along the little shit had it. There goes our money…right down the old shit-chute."

"You know what Chaka said," Kevin replied. "He told us he'd give us the money out of his own pocket…if necessary. So shut up about it." Steve turned his concentration back on the road and remained silent.

"If Anderson has the key and he gets the money what does your boss need me for?" Tony said. "I'm confused." He thought for a moment, and then added, "You guys are in for a rude awakening when my dad finds you. He'll have your balls on a platter."

Kevin glanced at the boy in the rear-view mirror. "Chaka needs you," he said. "That's all he told us. We're going to hang onto you until he tells us otherwise. Get it?"

Tony turned and gazed up at the stars. Silence filled the cab. Moments later, he started to sing: "Twinkle, twinkle, twisted nose, how it got there no one knows. High above that ugly snout, two black eyes dart all about. At the bottom of his face, lips look like they're out of place—"

Kevin turned and grinned at Steve. He chuckled when he noticed his sullen expression.

Steve turned to say something, but when he saw the boy's expression he broke into laughter. "You little shit," he said, grinning.

As they made a sharp turn around a bend in the road, a set of high beams materialized in front of them. Kevin stomped hard on the brakes, causing the truck to slide sideways and come to a stop only a few feet from them.

"Jesus Christ!" he yelled. "What's that ass-hole doing stopped in the middle of the road? He could have killed us!" He jumped out and approached the immobile truck. When he got to the driver's side window a .9 mm pistol was pointed at his face.

"I am Sergeant Mandeli from the ranger station in Maralal," the shadowy figure behind the wheel said. "What are you doing out here? Where are you going?"

Kevin looked at the barrel of the gun, then at the sergeant stripes on the man's sleeve. "We're on our way to Nairobi," he said. "We have to deliver something from the diggings at Koobi." He stared into the sergeant's eyes. "What's wrong? Did something happen to your Rover?"

"Yes. I ran out of gas."

"I have a spare can in my truck. Can I offer it to you?"

Mandeli pushed the door open, forcing Kevin to back away from the truck. "No. I will come with you," he said. "But we're not going to

Nairobi. You will take me back to Koobi." He held the gun against Kevin's spine, while he forced him back to his truck.

"We can't go back to Koobi, we have something to give to—" Kevin stopped in the middle of his sentence.

"What do you have that's so important?" the sergeant interrupted. "It's more pressing that I get to Koobi. I am after two criminals. They must be captured." He held the gun on Kevin until he slid behind the wheel, and then got into the back seat. When Tony saw the gun he cringed and slid up against his door. The sergeant gave him a quick glance, then focused on the two men in the front seat. He had not bothered to search them for a weapon that was the last thing on his mind; he had to get to Koobi. "Turn the truck around and head for the diggings," he continued. "It's well past midnight and I want to get there by first light, before the workers wake up. I don't want to contend with those idiots."

Kevin turned and eyed Mandeli. "Can I make a call to Mr. Chaka, tell him we've been delayed? He'll be angry if we don't check in."

"You work for Chaka?" the sergeant asked, lifting an eyebrow. "So do I…in a round about way. Occasionally, he pays me for services rendered."

Kevin and Steve glanced at each other, and then grinned.

"Yes. Go ahead," the sergeant said. "But tell him I'm helping you. He will appreciate that."

"You can put the gun away, sergeant," Kevin said. "We're all friends here."

The Rover bounced up and down on the deep ruts, as it sped on its way back to Koobi. Kevin dialed a number on his cell phone and put it to his ear.

"Yes?" Chaka answered. "Do you have the boy?" There was a brief pause, while he listened to Kevin. "What do you mean your taking him back to Koobi? I want him here." Several moments passed while he listened, and then he continued. "Sergeant Mandeli?" he questioned. "Don't trust that maniac. He's on some sort of vendetta. He'll stop at nothing to get what he wants. Don't turn your back on him." He remained silent for several seconds, and then said, "Don't let that boy escape. Tie him up, if necessary. Take him back to where the plane dropped you off. Stay there until you hear from me." He thought for a moment, and then added, "Do you still have your weapons? Did the sergeant take them? No? Good. At your first opportunity get rid of him. Understand? I don't care how…just *do* it. He'll only cause you to fail in your mission, Kevin, and I'm counting on you. Don't let me down. You know what's at stake."

At 5 o'clock in the morning, the sun had already climbed over the tops of the highest mountains to the east and had spread long, gray shadows across Site 51. It had already begun to paint the landscape far into the Chalbi desert to the west. Workers dug into their plates of curried rice and *tylapia*, while they sat by campfires waiting for the bell to inform them to start digging.

Anderson emerged from his tent and headed for the patio, where breakfast had been waiting on a long table. The aroma of bacon wafted throughout the camp and Barry didn't hesitate to follow its scent to the source. He walked leisurely from his tent and sat beside the largest portions of bacon and eggs. After washing sleep from his eyes, O'Brien joined them. Eric and Dan, still groggy from sleep, wandered over and sat in the two remaining chairs.

Ebukut, Hussein and Paul sat on their haunches in front of their own campfire, a distance from the others. They had been offered portions from the table, but it was refused. They told Anderson they would eat their own food.

A peal of the bell told the workers it was time to leave for their respective locations. Although still sluggish from sleep, they boarded several vans and left for the day's work.

When they had finished eating, Anderson rose from the table and walked to the sorting tent. "Barry," he called out. Barry looked up, his mouth still full of bacon and eggs. "I think we should do something about our friend in there on the table. What do you think?"

Barry wiped his mouth on his sleeve, rose from the table, and joined him at the tent flap. "Think you're right," he said. "I got the strangest feeling something's going to happen today. You got that feeling, too?"

"Yes, I do."

"You think someone's going to try to make off with him?" Barry asked, and raised his eyebrows. "I think we should collect all his bones, put them in a sack, and hide them someplace. At least until this is all over."

"Good idea," Anderson agreed. "We'll wrap them up and label them."

Eric overheard their conversation. "I'll help," he said. "I've got to have something to do. Besides, I'm not leaving as long as you might be in danger from that Chaka character."

They all spent the rest of the morning tagging and wrapping the bones. Occasionally, they would break from their work to visit the lemonade jug, and then return to the sorting tent. When the last bones had been wrapped and tagged they placed them in a gunnysack and took them to a van where they were gently loaded. Cantu, a trusted digger, was elected to drive them into the desert to a location only he would know. He was to dig a hole, bury them, and then flag the spot. Only when he returned was he to tell Anderson where he had hid them.

After Cantu left, Jack drove a utility Jeep across the barren field to the old Piper. He walked around it several times to inspect its functionality. Satisfied that it was air-worthy, he climbed onto the lower wing and hoisted himself into the cockpit. He sat for several minutes refreshing his knowledge of the instruments and controls. It had been over 50 years since he had flown such a derelict, and the J5, according to Anderson, had not been airborne in several years. He had no idea if it would even start, let alone make it off the ground. He checked the fuel level and scanned the various instruments for any defects or possible problems. However, first things first, he had to start it. With the throttle in one hand and the choke in the other, he adjusted the levers where he thought they should be. It was fortunate that the school where Anderson bought the plane had upgraded it to an electric start, no spinning the prop by hand. He turned the key and after a few revolutions the engine caught and began to sputter and backfire. With a fine tune of the choke the cylinders fired smoothly and the plane inched forward. The J5 was a lightweight "tail-dragger" and it didn't take much to get it moving. He held down on the brakes, while he sat in the cockpit admiring his handiwork. After a few minutes he shut it down and hopped out. He felt triumphant. For the first time in 50 years he had fired up an antique. From his previous experiences with a J5 he was certain it would make the trip to Nakuru. All he had to do was locate a landing strip away from the main airfield. If he landed on the major runway he would have a lot of explaining to do, and he didn't need that. It would be a big enough adventure just to make it to Nakuru in one piece.

Weary from driving, Kevin pulled the Rover to the side of the road close to the perimeter of the compound. He closed his eyes and dropped his head on the steering wheel.

Mandeli had been catnapping. When the vehicle stopped, he opened his eyes and looked around. "Why are we stopping?" he asked. "Where are we?"

"We're outside the compound at Koobi," Kevin said. "We can't go any farther without being detected. And I'm sure you don't want that."

"What time is it?" the sergeant demanded. "How close are we to the camp?"

Kevin looked at his wristwatch. "It's a little after five. We're a couple hundred meters from the fence. What do you want us to do?"

"Stay with the boy. I'm going to the tent area to see if I can locate the Samburu boys."

"It's daylight out there, you know," Steve said. "You'll be seen by the guards. Then we'll all be in trouble." He turned and looked at the sergeant. "We cut a hole over there." He pointed to a section of the fence.

"Good. Don't worry," Mandeli said. "I have a plan. Wait in the truck until I return. That's an order!" He opened the door and disappeared into the underbrush.

The large boulders, which had been placed in the middle of the runway earlier, had been pushed aside for the Piper Tomahawk, but now it was ready for use, again. Anderson gave O'Brien the key to the lock-box and he and Jack headed for the J5. After several attempts, Jack charmed the plane into starting. As the engine caught it billowed black smoke, coughed multiple times, and then smoothed out to a purr. He taxied from the parking area and spun it around on the gravel strip. After checking the mags at 1700 rpms, he applied full power. The plane balked for a few seconds then sped down the rocky runway. After catching sufficient warm air across its wings, it lifted and gained altitude. The diggers gave it a salute as it flew over the camp and headed for Nakuru.

Cantu had arduously dug a hole below the limbs of the only drooping sausage tree in the area, and then gently placed the sack of bones in the pit, which he then covered with a sheet of plastic. He filled the hole with the dug up dirt and rocks he had found alongside the road. To avoid sunstroke, he sat down and rested a few minutes under the shade of the tree. He was certain he could remember the location of the tree, but to be on the safe side he marked the spot with a piece of cloth tied around one of its limbs. He rested for a few minutes in the cab, and then headed back to camp.

Several kilometers down the road he rounded a sharp turn, and standing in the middle of the road staring at him was a dark-mane lion. He spun the wheel sharply to avoid hitting it, but by doing so the truck hit a patch of loose gravel, slid off the road and vaulted down a steep incline. The driver's door flew open and he was thrown onto the hard ground, and then catapulted end-over-end into a large acacia bush. The truck freewheeled to the bottom of the slope, and then came to rest on its side. He tried to free himself from the bush, but one of his arms had been broken. With only one good arm, he did not have enough leverage to free himself. The lion stood on the road like a sentinel staring down at him.

"Oh, my God!" he shouted, and stared back at the lion. He made another fruitless attempt to get free of the needle-like thorns, but with only one good arm he was not successful.

The huge animal eyed him for several minutes, and then lumbered down the embankment toward him. It stopped no more than a meter from him and crouched, but did not take its eyes off him. He could feel the heat of the lion's breath as it moved even closer and dropped on its belly a foot in front of him. Its large, light brown eyes stared hypnotically at him, as it crept even closer and licked his face with its raspy tongue. The man remained motionless. He did not dare move a muscle or blink an eye. If he had, he knew the animal would attack.

Several minutes later, the animal appeared to lose interest in him as a meal and turned to leave. Cantu exhaled a long sigh of relief, but in doing so he emitted a moaning, gargling sound. The lion turned, and with a ferocious snarl sunk its long fangs into his shoulder. He screamed and struggled to get free but the lion re-gripped and dragged him across the desert to its lair. For a few minutes, his screams filled the silent void of the valley, then all was quiet.

"Where the hell is Cantu?" Anderson said, to no one in particular. "He should have been back by now. I'm sure he didn't go too far into the desert…it wouldn't serve any purpose."

Barry overheard him and commented, "Do you trust him? I know he's been with us for a long time, but there's a lot at stake here. If he's seen, or if he says anything to anyone, we may be in for a lot of trouble."

"I trust him. He's always been loyal to us. He won't say anything. And I'm sure nobody will see him, we're too far out in the boonies."

"Sure hope you're right," Barry came back. "Those bones are our claim to fame…so to speak."

"Stop worrying. Even if something did happen to them there's more out there…someplace. All we have to do is find them. And we'll soon have enough money to do that."

Mandeli slid under the cyclone fence and crawled within a few meters of the first tent. He had no idea where the boys were located in the compound but he told himself he would search until he found them. He figured they had to be somewhere in the camp and there were not many places they could hide. He figured Anderson would do his best to conceal them, if he thought they were in trouble. But he was just as determined to locate them. He had to make them pay for the suffering the Samburus had inflicted on him and his family.

After searching several tents he realized they were all empty. He believed they were all at the diggings. However, the boys were not diggers. Therefore, they had to be at another location in the camp. He sneaked behind the largest tent and saw a man holding a rifle. He peeked around the corner and noticed three boys beside a dead fireplace. He knew it had to be them. He could not capture them now, not with the guards around; they had rifles and he had a .9 mm pistol, which would have been useless against their firepower. He had a plan before, but now it wouldn't work, not with the guards around. There would be another time, he was certain of that. He inched his way back through the acacia bushes to the fence, crawled under it, and then located the Rover hidden in a grove of large shrubs.

Kevin rolled down the window. "Did you find the boys you were looking for?" he asked. "Were they in the camp, like you thought?"

"I don't want to talk about it," the sergeant said, sarcastically. "Go back to the air strip where we were before. We'll park there until it gets dark, then I'll come back and capture them."

Kevin could not resist a quiet chuckle.

"How are you men doing?" Anderson said, as he walked toward the warriors standing by the dead fire pit. "Would you boys like to have something to do, other than stand out here in the hot sun? I'll pay you to work for me. How does that sound?" The three boys put their heads together and discussed the proposition.

Several minutes later, Paul told Anderson they would be happy to work for him, but they would not take money. All they needed was food and a place to sleep at night. They had no need for money; there was nothing to buy in their village anyway, he told him.

The boys followed Anderson back to the sorting tent. He handed them buckets, shovels and screen filters and explained how to use them. He poured them several glasses of lemonade, and then pointed to a location where they were to dig. They slung the digging equipment and their spears over their shoulders and left for the area.

John Anderson had never been a person to worry about much of anything. He was humble, sincere, and laid-back. Nevertheless, he *was* worried. Cantu had not returned and it was approaching late afternoon. He had no idea where the man had taken the bones or even which way he went when he left. If he had become lost, or if anything had happened to him, they would never find the bones; the desert was too enormous.

He had one option left, to get in touch with Jack in the Piper by cell phone. The plane did not have a radio, but Barry had loaned Jack his cell-phone in case of an emergency. He slumped down in a canvass chair, poured a glass of lemonade, and dropped his head in his hands. He was extremely troubled by the situation.

Barry sat down beside him. "What's on your mind, John?" he said, and poured a glass of the cold, sweet drink.

"I have a feeling something happened to Cantu."

"Why? What makes you think that?"

"Just a feeling. He's been gone too long."

"We could try to contact the plane," Barry said. "You know I gave Jack my phone. Maybe they could come back and search for him. I don't think they've arrived at Nakuru yet, as slow as that old plane is."

"I was thinking the same thing. I'll get my cell and give it a try," Anderson said.

As Jack brought the plane over the last ridge, prior to the sparse desert to the north of Nakuru, the ring of the cell phone sounded sharply. He looked over at O'Brien.

"Is that the phone Barry gave you?" O'Brien questioned. "Better answer it, it could be important."

Jack searched for the phone in the pockets of his safari jacket. After finding it he held it in front of his eyes and attempted to read the small print on its face. Even after squinting, he could not focus on the small words and numbers. He handed it to O'Brien. "Here," he said. "I can't figure this thing out. You answer. Okay?"

O'Brien took the instrument and pushed a button. A tinny voice blasted through its miniature speaker, "Jack, this is Anderson! If you read me, please answer."

"This is O'Brien. We read you. What's the problem?"

"There might be one," Anderson yelled into the phone. "We sent a man into the desert to hide the artifacts so Chaka couldn't get them, but he hasn't returned." There was a pause, and then he continued. "He's been gone over four hours. That's too long. He should have been back by now. He was only supposed to go into the desert a few miles to find a place to hide them."

"What can *we* do, John? We're a couple minutes north of Nakuru looking for a place to set this thing down where we won't be spotted." He glanced over at Jack and shrugged.

"If at all possible, could you turn that thing around and maybe make a few passes over this area to look for him?" John pleaded in the speaker.

Jack grabbed the phone. "The bank closes at five, you know," he shouted back.

"Yes, I know," Anderson said. "But this is more important…at least for the time being. You could always go to the bank tomorrow." He paused to gather his thoughts. "Our man went alone to bury them. If he doesn't return we won't know where he hid them. Those bones are all we have to prove our case…except for the item we sent to New York, and if that gets lost we'll have nothing. Do you understand? Nothing!"

Robert O'Brien snatched the phone out of Jack's hand. "What do you mean you don't know where he buried them?" he yelled into the mouthpiece. "How can that be?"

"Security!" John said, raising his voice. "He and I were to be the only ones to know where he hid them. If we can't find him, or if something happened to him, we'll never know their location."

Jack glanced down at the gauges on the dash. They had enough fuel to get back to the camp and make a few passes over the area, but that was the extent of it.

"Okay," O'Brien said with a sigh, "we're on our way back. Which direction did he go?"

"We don't know," John replied, irritably. "Nobody saw which way he went."

"Terrific!" Jack said, and looked over at Robert. "That makes our day!"

Several hours later they arrived back at the site to start the search. Using circular patterns, expanding outward with each revolution, they ended up 20-kilometers from the camp, but with no sign of Cantu or the truck. Jack held the plane close to its stalling speed, while O'Brien searched with binoculars. After several more passes they spotted the Jeep lying on its side, but still no sign of Cantu.

"I'm going to make a short-runway landing on that level spot a half-kilometer from here," Jack said.

"You gotta be kidding!" O'Brien erupted in protest. "We might make it down but how the hell could we take off? We'd never make it. It's too damned rocky down there, and that clearing is too short. And you know it!"

Jack grinned. "Just kidding," he said. "I'll make a couple more passes over the Jeep and you take a bearing with the GPS in that cell phone. It'll help when they come with a search party." He looked over and added, "It does have a GPS, doesn't it? Barry said it did."

"Hell, I don't know. Let me check." O'Brien held it up to his eyes. In the dim light of the afternoon sun he could barely read the small characters under each button. "Yes, it does. All I have to do is figure out how to use it."

"Well you better hurry. We don't have much daylight left and we're running low on fuel."

"Okay," O'Brien said. "I think I've got it. All I have to do is push this button…right here." He pressed down on the small key and within seconds the screen sprang to life with longitude and latitude figures. "Got it!" he said, and looked over at the old pilot. "Let's head back. We'll still have enough daylight left to make a couple more search passes. The Jeep's only a few kilometers from the camp." The Piper made another pass over the Jeep, and then turned and headed for Koobi.

When they arrived at the compound they noticed a blue, six-passenger Cessna parked alongside the sorting tent. The old J5 floated down the length of the strip like a feather. It made a perfect landing and taxied up to the tent. They jumped out of the cockpit and joined Anderson, who was having a conversation with a well-dressed black man leaning on a gold-handled walking stick.

"Chaka!" O'Brien shouted in a venomous tone. "The son-of-a-bitch has balls enough to come here, after all he's put me through? I think I'll kill the bastard!"

Just then two men walked out of the sorting tent. O'Brien recognized them immediately as the two he had escaped from back at the cottage. As soon as they recognized him smirks spread across their faces.

"Robert," Anderson said. "I guess you know Chaka."

"Yes. I know the bastard!"

"He's here to make a deal."

"Don't make any deal with him, he's a no good skunk."

Chaka smiled, displaying gold-crowned teeth. "Mister O'Brien, how can you say that about me? Especially after what you've cost me in cars and boats. I'm the one who should be angry." When he saw Jack he held out his hand. "I know you but I don't think we've had the pleasure of meeting in the flesh, so to speak."

Jack glared at him, but didn't extend his hand. "It wouldn't be a pleasure if you really got to know me," he said with a smirk.

Chaka dropped his hand and smiled. "One of the reasons I came was to pick up my shipment, which you were supposed to deliver to me, Mr. Emerson." His dark eyes flashed. "But I've just been informed your plane crashed somewhere in the saw-tooth mountains. Is that correct?"

"What do you mean, *your* shipment?" Jack said. "I had nothing on the plane for you."

"Oh, yes you did. There were a number of packages to be delivered to me, here," Chaka said, raising one eyebrow.

"You mean those were yours?" Jack looked at Chaka with a shocked expression.

"Yes."

"No one told me you were the one that ordered them. If I'd known I wouldn't have accepted them."

"That's no way to talk, Mr. Emerson…Jack," Chaka said. "I paid well for that delivery. Whether you like me or not, a deal's a deal. Now, where are my packages?" His face turned surly, as he stared into Jack's eyes. "I came all this way to pick them up and found out you didn't deliver them."

"I thought you had a secret network working for you," Jack said with a sneer. "I was told you always knew what went on around you. How come it didn't know about my crash, until now? Is that any different?"

"No one is perfect. I certainly am not. And, neither is my 'network'."

"Your 'packages' are buried at the crash site…as if you didn't already know."

"Sorry. My network either didn't know, or didn't inform me. Do you know the plane's location?"

"Not exactly. However, it's visible from a helicopter or plane. It's west of Loiyangalani about five kilometers, I think. It was night…dark as hell outside."

"I'll get my men right on it," Chaka said. "If they find it and everything is all right, you'll get the other half of your money." He paused, and then added, "Those items were to be used for the possible purchase of Mr. Anderson's relics. If we don't find the items, we might have to revert to our original plan."

"Which is?" Jack said.

"I think everyone knows. Mister O'Brien certainly does."

O'Brien's face turned beet red and he made a lunge for Chaka. One of the bodyguards caught his arms and held him back. "Where's my son, you son-of-a-bitch?" he shouted into Chaka's face. "Why did you need him, if you were going to buy the stuff anyway?"

"Your son is fine," Chaka said. "My men, and Sergeant Mandeli, have him at a safe location. You will get him back if Mr. Anderson agrees to sell me what I want."

Standing at the far end of the patio, Somerville overheard their conversation. "Mandeli?" he shouted. "What the hell's Mandeli got to do with this?"

Chaka turned and looked at him. "Ah," he said. "You must be the American photographer I've heard so much about."

"Yes, I am," Eric said. "What's this about Mandeli? I didn't know you had him on your payroll, too."

"Isn't everyone?" one of his bodyguards said with a sheepish grin. Chaka turned and glared at him.

Ignoring Eric's comment, Chaka turned back to Anderson. "My other reason for coming was to make an offer to Mr. Anderson…in person." He paused long enough to adjust his coattail, and then looked John square in the eye. "I am prepared to offer quite a sum of money for what you have already dug up. In addition, much more for anything you may find in the future. I'm sure I can beat any offer you could possibly get from the museum."

"What on earth would you want with a bag of old bones," John said. "They're useless to try to sell. Their only value is to a museum."

"I have my reasons," Chaka returned with a smirk. "What I want them for is no concern of yours. You must believe me; I will go to great lengths to acquire them, as Robert already knows. Right?" He looked over at

O'Brien, whose arms were still being held by the burly bodyguard.

Anderson glanced over at Barry, who had drifted away from the group to watch at a safe distance. "Barry," he yelled at him. "Will you tell them why we can't accommodate them?"

Barry's face turned pale. After a slight hesitation, he slowly walked toward them. He paused for a long moment, and then said, "Are you sure you want me to tell them, John?"

"Yes. Of course I'm sure."

Without looking at Chaka, Barry began, "The bones are somewhere in the desert. We had a man take them there to hide. But he never returned. We don't know where he buried them…truthfully." He let out a big sigh, caught his breath, and continued. "Our only hope to find them is to send a search party to look for the man…and pray he's found alive."

"He's telling the truth," Anderson said. "If we don't find him alive, we've lost the only artifacts we have."

"What about the medallion?" Chaka asked. "Bones were not the only thing you found."

"You know about the medallion?"

"Yes, of course. As a matter of fact, I have a man working on 'acquiring' it from the museum, as we speak."

"That's impossible! Nobody can get anything out of the museum without the board's approval. And I'm sure they wouldn't give that to you."

"Whatever you say, John," Chaka said with a grin. "See what you can do about getting those bones back, while I make a trip to the crash site to get my goods." He turned and walked toward the plane. Chaka's bodyguard released O'Brien's arms and followed. As he was about to enter the plane, he turned and yelled back, "John, think about Robert's son, before you do anything rash. But *do* make a decision before too long."

O'Brien's face flushed. He made a dash for the plane, but the cabin door slammed shut and was locked before he got there. He pounded on the side of the plane, as it spun around and headed for the makeshift runway. As the Piper turned, its tail assembly slammed against him and knocked him to the ground. He got up and shook his fist at the plane. It picked up speed and slowly lifted into the hot, dead air.

Diggers in the field had stopped their picking and brushing long enough to wave at the plane as it sailed overhead. The evening was fast approaching, and they would soon be back at camp eating and dancing by the large open-pit campfire, completely unaware of what had transpired. In most cases they wouldn't have cared anyway, they would get their day's pay and a full stomach; that was all that mattered.

Anderson called the three Samburu boys up from the site and asked if they would help in the search for Cantu. They agreed. Barry went to the mess-tent and brought back ample supplies of water, food, and flashlights. He figured they might be in the desert for a while and he wanted to be prepared. They pulled two trucks up to the tent and loaded the men and supplies.

Eric searched his Rover for the .22 John had loaned him and found it under the seat, along with two boxes of ammunition. When asked what he planned to do with the "elephant" gun, he smiled and said he would shoot any critter in the eyeballs, if they messed with him. Less than a half hour later they left camp and headed for the coordinates the GPS had established.

"Hey! Ugly one!" Tony shouted at Steve. "What the hell do you plan on doin' with me? I ain't no good to you. I'd sure hate to be you guys when my dad finds me."

Steve turned and glared at the boy. "Shut your yap, you little monkey," he said with a slight grin. "He's not going to find you. Not way out here. If you don't shut up we might just decide to feed you to the lions, after all. Let them take care of you and your mouth."

"Ha, ha."

Mandeli had been catnapping beside Tony and woke when he heard the bantering. "Shut up! Both of you," he shouted. "I can't hear myself think." He looked out the window; it was getting dark. "When did you say that plane was supposed to be here?" he asked Kevin. "You did say they were sending one, didn't you? We can't keep the kid in the truck forever."

"It was supposed to have been here by now," Kevin replied. "Maybe something happened. Maybe Chaka had a change of plans when we told him we were on our way back to Koobi. Who knows? He told us to wait here until he contacted us. So we wait."

Tony was big for his age, five-foot seven and 150 pounds. Although shorter than the sergeant he outweighed him by several pounds, and from all appearances much stronger. The sergeant was tall and frail; he intimidated by his gun, not his size. Mandeli took the gun from his holster and laid it in his lap. He looked out the window at the stars, which had already begun to illuminate the dimly lit horizon.

Tony saw his opportunity and took advantage of it. He grabbed the gun from the sergeant's lap and with a vicious blow to his head knocked him unconscious. Before either Kevin or Steve had realized what happened, Tony had climbed over Mandeli's body, opened the door on the sergeant's side, which Steve had not locked, and rushed into the darkness. The suddenness of the attack left the two men stunned. Before they could gather their wits, Tony had darted into the underbrush and disappeared.

Steve opened the door to go after him, but Kevin grabbed his sleeve. He yanked his arm free and glared at him. "What did you do that for?" he yelled. "We've got to go after the little shit. Chaka isn't going to like this."

"Don't be an idiot!" Kevin said. "You would never find him in the dark. Let him go."

"Let him go?" Steve questioned with a frown. "I don't want Chaka to find out we don't have him. We gotta get him back!"

"Use your damned brain, Steve! He's out there in the dark, with the sergeant's gun, and he's from the Bronx. Do you want to go after him under those conditions?"

"But, Chaka—"

"Fuck Chaka!" Kevin exploded. "He's probably not going to pay us, anyway. You should have realized that by now."

"What do you mean? He promised us the money and I intend to get it!"

"Clear your head for a minute and think. Chaka set us up—he makes us wait here with the kid and doesn't send a plane in for us. He doesn't give a shit what happens to the kid, or us. Even if something *did* happen to the kid, O'Brien wouldn't know about it for some time, and Chaka could still use him as a pawn to get his old man to do his dirty work."

"What about the sergeant?" Steve said.

"I don't know. Shall we dump him out here and go back to Nakuru?"

"I don't think so," Mandeli said, as he slowly regained consciousness. With both hands, he held his throbbing head. "We're going after the kid. I've got a score to settle."

"No! We're not going after him," Kevin said, firmly. "We're going back to Nakuru. You can either go with us or get out and go after him yourself." The sergeant reached for his gun, but felt an empty holster.

Kevin drew his own gun and pointed it at the sergeant's head. "Well," he said. "Which will it be, Nakuru or the desert with all those critters out there?"

The sergeant leaned back in his seat and glared at him. "Loan me one of your guns and I'll go after him myself," he said, sarcastically.

Steve ejected the clip from his gun and handed it to him. "If you're stupid enough to hunt him down in the dark, be my guest."

On his way out, the sergeant kicked the half-open door with his foot. He stuck his head back in and with a sheepish grin said, "Do you have a flashlight I can borrow? And the clip for the gun?"

The moon was exceptionally bright that evening, which helped Tony find the cutout in the fence. He crawled through it and made his way to the sorting tent, where Anderson, his father, and Jack sat under a string of lights polishing off a bottle of scotch.

Jack was the first to notice the boy and rushed to him. "Well, look what we have here," he said to the others. "The wayward son returneth."

"Tony!" his father shouted. He ran over and wrapped his arms around him in a bear hug.

Tony was embarrassed by his father's overt actions and pulled away. "Dad!" he said. "For God's sake, contain yourself. I'm not a little baby anymore."

"Sorry," O'Brien said and dropped his arms. "What the hell happened? Did those bastards have you all this time? Did they hurt you? How did you get away?"

The barrage of questions was too much for Tony to handle. He sat down on a chair and poured a cold drink. After a long pause, he said, "I'll tell you all about it later, Dad. But right now I think Mandeli and the other two ass-holes are probably still after me. I had to cold-cock the sergeant to escape." He handed the gun over to his father. "Here, you might need this."

O'Brien took the gun, cocked his head to one side, and said, "How the hell did you get this?"

"I told you I'd tell you later. Right now you guys better be on guard. They still have guns, and they're probably pissed off."

With the aid of a powerful battle-lantern, Barry spotted the wrecked truck. He jumped out of the Rover and raced over to it. "Hey, guys," he yelled. "I found it!"

The search party joined him. They walked around the truck and checked it for damage. Other than being on its side, it appeared to have no major damage. They got on one side and hoisted the vehicle upright. One of the natives got inside and tried to start it. After several attempts it fired and roared to life. He backed it up the embankment and onto the road. They all cheered.

"Okay," Barry said. "We've got this far, let's go find Cantu. He can't be too far. Hope nothing serious happened to him."

After a few sweeps of the area they found him lying face down at the mouth of a small cave, with his shirt partially ripped off. They turned him over and saw that his face had been eaten away. He had also been disemboweled.

"Simba!" Ebukut said in Masai, pointing to the man's stomach. "Not many animals attack like that."

"Look at this!" one of the natives said, and pointed with his flashlight.

"Here, on this flat rock. It looks like something is scribbled in his own blood—*mti.* Wonder what that means?" They gathered around the rock. The word was faint but legible.

"*Mti*?" Paul said. At first he was puzzled by the word. "Correct me if I'm wrong, but I think he was trying to tell us something. Cantu spoke Swahili and in that language I think *'mti'* means tree."

"Are there any trees around here?" Hussein asked. "Maybe that's where he hid the bones. Let's see if we can find one in the area. It's probably a big one or he wouldn't hide it there."

"Yes, there is a tree," said one of the native. "I have been here before. There is a big sausage tree, less than half a kilometer west of here."

"Okay," Barry said. "Let's wrap him up, put him in one of the trucks and go look for it."

Minutes later they found the sausage tree and stopped beside it. With the aid of flashlights, they found a cloth marker tied around a limb, and what appeared to be a freshly dug grave directly below it.

They had started the process of removing the rocks from the burial mound, when Barry shouted for them to stop. "Maybe we shouldn't disturb the bones," he said. "They're well hidden where they are. Let's leave them there. If we don't tell anyone they're here, they'll be safe." He eyed each person, and then continued. "Do I have your solemn promises you won't tell anyone their location?" He stared at each man for several moments, examining his face. They all nodded.

"Should we go back and look inside the cave?" Paul asked. "If the lion is in there we should kill it."

"We don't have time," Barry said. "Besides, what good would it do now? The damage has been done. We'd be killing an animal that was just hunting for food."

They milled about the tree for a few minutes, to get acquainted with its location in the dark, then returned to the trucks and headed back to the site.

When they arrived, Barry took Anderson aside and informed him of their discovery. A broad smile spread across the old man's weathered face…a smile of relief. He couldn't imagine what it would have been like to work for so long and so hard on a project, only to have the fruit of his labors disappear. He was almost certain there were other relics out there, somewhere in the digging fields, but to him a "bird-in-the-hand" was worth more than the likelihood of finding others.

It had approached midnight and the night air started to get chilly. Anderson pulled the Harris Tweed tightly around his chest, sat beside the insulated lemonade container, and began to think about his situation. The museum had always played square with him in the past. But would they continue to do so if they received very little in return? If they didn't get any artifacts, would they discontinue their support? He wondered. Those were questions that had to be considered, before he could come up with an answer. Chaka said he would give them a substantial amount of money to keep digging, but only if most of what they found was turned over to him. Was it worth pursuing? He wondered that, also. Or, should he take his chances with the museum? And, to top it off, it was doubtful that Chaka would live up to his agreement, low-life that everyone knew him to be. He put his head in his hands and closed his eyes.

Barry sat down beside him. "What's up, John?" he said. "You got the same thing on your mind that I have?"

John looked up. "And what's that?"

"Oh, I don't know. I guess I have reservations about turning those bones over to the museum. I've been thinking about the deal Chaka made us." He turned a pair of nervous eyes on John and continued. "Maybe it would be wise to do something right away. I doubt if the location of the bones can be kept a secret for very long...from our dealings with the diggers in the past."

"You don't trust them? You don't think they'll keep their mouths shut?"

"No. As a matter of fact, I don't. But then I don't trust Chaka either. It's kinda like a catch twenty-two, isn't it?"

"Well," John said, glancing over. "I guess we both have the same reservations. I was thinking along those same lines." He dropped his head back in his palms and again closed his eyes. "I can't think straight right now. Let's sleep on it and worry about it in the morning. I don't think anything is going to happen to our cache tonight." They got up and headed for the sleeping tents.

Sergeant Mandeli thrashed his way through the thick underbrush until he had reached the cutout in the fence. He shimmied under it and made a beeline for the first row of tents. Bypassing the first few, he headed for the tents closest to where he had seen the boys standing beside the campfire, earlier. One particular tent was set back from the others and could not be easily seen. By the brightness of the moon, he had no trouble making his way to the front flap. He pulled the gun from his belt and loaded the clip. Holding the flap to one side, he scanned the inside. The three Samburu boys appeared to be sleeping.

He had to think of a way to tie their hands without waking them. An idea came to mind; he would knock them out, tie their hands, cover their mouths, and *then* wake them. Another troubling thought flashed through his mind...where would he take them? His ride was probably on the road to Nairobi. Even so, he knew he would think of something.

He had no trouble with Paul and Hussein. He slammed the barrel of the pistol down on their foreheads, tied their hands and gagged them. The big Samburu warrior was his major concern. If he didn't knock him out on the first attempt, he would have to shoot him. He didn't like that thought at all; he wanted him alive so he could suffer along with the other two.

As he crept toward Ebukut's cot the warrior rolled over, opened his eyes, and stared up at him. When their eyes met, Mandeli froze. With the speed of a charging bull, the warrior jumped up from the cot and collided with him. The sergeant swung his gun around but the warrior knocked it out of his hand and it flew to the other side of the tent. The two men grappled violently, almost knocking down the tent. Before Mandeli could get to his gun, Ebukut had located his spear and charged. With all his strength, he thrust it into the sergeant's chest.

The sergeant's eyes opened wide and rolled upwards. He gasped for air, but none came. Thoughts of his dead family raced through his head. Images of the three Samburu boys momentarily clouded his vision. A long, white tunnel drifted across his mind's eye and he felt at ease, almost peaceful. He was surprised the blade didn't hurt; he felt no pain or anguish. He reeled backwards and grasped the spear in an attempt to pull it from his stomach. His thoughts slowly drifted to a green pasture with trees lining a calm, blue lake, and then his mind went blank. His limp body crumpled to the dirt floor and remained still.

Paul was the first to regain consciousness. He sat up in his cot and looked around. The first image he saw was Ebukut standing over a prone figure.

"What happened?" he asked, still sitting on the edge of the cot. "Who is that?" He pointed to the figure on the floor, that was barely visible in the subdued light from outside.

"The sergeant attacked me. I had to defend myself. I had no choice."

"Sergeant Mandeli?"

"Yes. We no longer have to worry about him."

"Is he dead?" Paul asked. The warrior shook his head. "Now, we have to leave the camp. The rangers will be looking for us." He looked over at Hussein, still lying unconscious on his cot. "What about Hussein? Is he hurt?" He went over to the cot and shook him.

After several slaps in the face, Hussein opened his eyes and stared up at him, still dazed. "What happened?" he asked. He lifted his hands to his forehead and rubbed it. "Why do I have this terrible headache?" he added, confused by what had happened. He noticed them standing over the prone body. "Who is that?"

"Sergeant Mandeli," Paul said. "We'll tell you about it later. Right now we have to leave. We have to go into the desert so the rangers can't find us."

Ebukut pulled his spear from the sergeant's body and turned to face them. "Wait! Why do we run? The rangers believe he's dead. If we bury him they will never know about this."

"What if someone contacted the rangers, when he showed up at the fishing club?" Paul said.

"That's a chance we have to take. We don't know if they were informed, or not. Even if they were, I'm sure they don't know he's here at the camp."

After thinking it over, they agreed and carried the body to an area that had already been excavated. They found shovels and dug a deep hole in the soft, section of the refilled pit. They slid the body into the makeshift grave and covered it over with dirt and stones.

When they returned to their tent, Ebukut cleaned the blood from his spear and wiped it down with lemonade left in a glass beside his cot. "No one must know what I have done here tonight," he told them. "It is something I alone have to live with for the rest of my life." He looked into their eyes. "I did not want this, but it would have happened, sooner or later."

The two boys rubbed their sore heads and stretched out on their cots. Ebukut sat on the edge of his, deep in thought. When he realized there was nothing more he could do about the tragic situation, he leaned back and closed his eyes.

Before he fell asleep he believed he heard a faint flapping sound, along with what appeared to be a powerful engine. He opened his eyes and cocked his head toward the sound, but didn't hear it again. He closed his burning eyes and fell asleep.

The early morning sun triggered a flurry of activity in the camp. The cook had already prepared the long breakfast table for the diggers that had lined up beside it, plates in hand. Anderson and Barry left the wash-up area and joined Jack, Robert and Tony at another table in front of the sorting tent. Eric and Dan joined them. They greeted each other and sat down beside the bountiful table.

Anderson looked up and down the table. "Where are the Samburu boys?" He asked.

"You know how they are," Barry said. "They're probably eating by themselves at their campfire."

"More than likely," John affirmed. "But I think you should ask them to join us. I have something to tell all of you and I don't think it fitting to leave them out." He looked over at Barry sitting at his usual spot beside the largest platter of bacon and eggs.

The hunched over figure dropped his knife and fork noisily in his plate, got up from the table, and stormed toward their tent. When he arrived at the dead campfire, he entered their tent. They were not there and nowhere to be found. He returned to the table and sat down. He loaded his plate with another large portion of bacon and eggs, and then looked over. "They're not there," he said, and began to eat.

"Where are they?" John asked.

"Hell, I don't know!"

"Don't you think we should try to find them?"

Barry gave John a defiant glare. He slammed down his utensils, and started to get up.

"After breakfast," John said with a grin, and looked over at him. "Jack," he continued. "Are you and Robert ready for another flight to Nakuru? We need that money, badly."

Jack was silent for a moment, and then looked over and said, "Sure. Why not? Maybe this time we'll make it all the way there." He threw John a wry look, followed by a grin.

After filling his plate, John looked up and said, "All of you should know that one of our diggers is missing. He's one of our 'trusted' men. One of the men who accompanied us on our search for the bones."

Barry looked up from his plate and stopped eating long enough to ask, "When did you find this out? He was with us last night, he couldn't have gone far."

"Eboni came to me early this morning and told me he never showed up last night. They sleep in the same tent."

"Did he know where he might have gone?" Barry said.

"No," John answered. "He didn't know. He also said he wasn't to be trusted. He was having financial problems back in his village. If that's true, we might have a problem...he knows the location of the bones." And then he added, "I'm certain Chaka would pay a great deal for that information."

"Hell," Barry said. "Chaka probably already knows, as wired as he is here in Kenya."

"It would be impossible for him to know, unless one of us gave him that information," John said, thoughtfully. "Assuming that's what happened, how the hell could he get the information to Chaka? It's over fifty kilometers to the nearest civilization. And to my knowledge all vehicles are accounted for...at least none have been reported missing."

"I'll check it out," Barry said and stuffed another egg in his mouth. "Right after breakfast."

"Oh, by the way, Barry, when Jack leaves this morning for Nakuru you better give him back your cell phone, he might need it again."

"Hope we don't need it for the same reason as before," Jack said with a grin.

Barry finished eating and went to his tent to get the phone. A few minutes later he returned empty-handed. "I can't find my phone," he said. "I know I put it next to my cot last night, but it isn't there." He frowned and stared hard at John. "You don't suppose that digger got hold of it, do you? If he did, he could easily call Chaka and tell him where the bones are."

John leaned back in his chair and looked into the morning sky. "You're sure it's not there?" he said. "You don't suppose you misplaced it...like you sometimes do?" He looked disdainfully at Barry. "We could have a problem, though. I thought I heard a chopper last night, about midnight. You don't suppose it was Chaka going after our bounty, do you?"

To avoid his derisive stare, Barry turned his eyes away, and said, "You know, I thought I heard the same thing last night. But I was half asleep…in never-never land." He chuckled, attempting to break the tension.

"We better get someone out there to see if the bones have been disturbed," John said.

"I'll get right on it. Right after breakfast," Barry said with a grin.

The Piper was halfway to Nakuru, when Jack spotted a black and silver helicopter a distance from them heading north. He made a comment to Robert, and then dismissed it and turned his eyes back to the controls. A half hour later they landed in a clearing he had used many times before, a kilometer outside the city and where knew the owner of the field.

After helping Jack secure the plane, Robert went to the man's house and asked for a ride into town. The man was quite accommodating, especially after he was handed a 500-shilling note. It took no longer than an hour for him to make the transaction at the bank. After he had finished, he returned to the plane and they took off on the return flight to Koobi.

"You mean the bones are not there?" John bellowed in Barry's face. "Oh shit! Now we really have a problem. The museum isn't going to like this! I can assure you."

"That must have been Chaka, last night," Barry said, looking down at his feet to avoid the man's glassy stare. "I guess we were right. That digger got to him by way of my cell phone."

They sat beside the sorting tent deep in thought, drinking ice cold lemonade. All of a sudden, they heard the flapping sound of a helicopter. They got up from their chairs and moved from the tent to where they could see the sky. Several kilometers away, whirling blades were silhouetted against the morning sun, and heading directly at them.

"That's got to be Chaka," John said. "No one else could afford one."

"Wonder what the hell he wants?" Barry said. "He probably wants to gloat over his newly acquired treasure. He has it all right, there's no question in my mind."

The diggers ran for cover when they saw the big aircraft come in low and make a dusty landing beside the sorting tent. After barely missing the tent the chopper settled down beside it.

Chaka's bodyguards, Bob and Matt, jumped out of the plane, dropped the metal stairs, and held the door open. Chaka stood by the open door for a few second waiting for the dust to settle, then climbed down the steps and strolled nonchalantly over to Anderson.

"Good morning," he said. "Beautiful day, isn't it?"

Without a word, Anderson glared at him, and then turned and walked into the sorting tent. Chaka's bodyguards followed him in and stood a few feet behind him.

A few seconds later, Chaka made his flamboyant entrance. As he walked through the flap his huge diamond ring caught the rays of the early morning sun and flashed multiple colors around the tent. He adjusted his Italian wrap-around coat and tugged on his paisley vest.

Anderson stood hunched over a workbench of old relics and didn't look up. Barry followed Chaka in, walked around him, and stood beside to Anderson.

"Well," Chaka started to say.

"Wait!" Anderson interrupted, and turned to face him. "Before you say anything you might be sorry for, why did you take my bones? We might have made a deal with you. But now, you can go screw yourself!" He glared into the man's eyes.

"I had a feeling you wouldn't make a deal, so I did what I had to do," Chaka replied, with a sarcastic tone. It was the only sure way of getting what I wanted. Now, they're mine. Possession is nine tenths of the law, you know." A devious grin spread across his face.

"Even if you steal them?" Barry cut in.

"Ah, that's such a laughable word…steal," Chaka was quick to answer. "Nobody steals things. When a person drops his guard you take advantage of it, especially when there are circumstances and situations involved that you have little control over."

"We trusted one of our workers and he let us down," Anderson said, still staring maliciously at him. "I guess you could say we were the ones who 'dropped our guards'."

As the two men stood eye to eye, Tony rushed into the tent. "Mister Anderson," he shouted. "One of the diggers told me the man with you last night is in the helicopter. The one they said was missing."

Anderson broke off his confrontation and left the tent. Barry followed him closely, and then Chaka and his bodyguards joined them. He looked in the window of the helicopter and saw the digger staring at him.

"That bastard!" Anderson said under his breath. He made a move toward the chopper, but the bodyguard held him back.

"I see you found your Benedict Arnold," Chaka said with a wily grin. "Don't blame him, he was only interested in money, and I gave him plenty…enough to buy his whole village."

"Money solves everything, doesn't it, Chaka?" John said and yanked his arms free from the bodyguard's tight grip. "Discovering the find of the century doesn't mean a thing to you, does it? You're only interested in its monetary value." He turned and walked back to the patio, sat down and dropped his head in his hands. His years of work had gone down the drain. His only hope was to find more relics. On the other hand, if he uncovered more Chaka would find a way to get them, as he had the others.

Chaka sat down beside him, his diligent bodyguards not far away. "Tell you what I'll do," he said. He cocking his head and looked sideways at him. "Now that you've lost everything, I'll pay you to keep the dig going. Furthermore, I'll give you a good bounty for anything you find in the future. How does that sound?" He put his elbows on the arms of the canvass chair, leaned forward, and continued. "You don't have to mess around with the museum. Screw them; they're only looking to get their name in the papers. They don't care about the monetary value—but you and I do."

Before John could answer, the popping sound of a plane's pistons filled the quiet desert air. Long before it was visible, he knew it was the J5 returning from Nakuru with the money they so desperately needed. He smiled. "I don't think we'll need your money now," he told Chaka. "I believe the museum came through."

"Don't count on any more money from them, John," Chaka said with a sneer. "When they find the medallion missing, and now the bones, they'll give up on you...especially if you can't produce anything more."

"You bastard!" John erupted. "You *did* get the medallion!"

"Of course."

"Then you have both the bones and the medallion?"

"Yes. However, I want you to know something...if anything happens to me, it would be fruitless for you to try to find them. I have secured them in a safe place. Only I know where they are."

John was about to make a lewd comment, when the plane's engine became louder. He ran from the sorting tent in time to see the J5 make a perfect three-point landing. It taxied down the crude strip and stopped alongside the tent.

O'Brien climbed out of the cockpit. When he saw Chaka and Anderson standing together, he rushed over. Bob and Matt started to move in to protect their boss, but before they could get there O'Brien had his hands around the man's neck.

"You bastard!" O'Brien shouted at him. "What the hell are you doing back here? Haven't you done enough already?"

The bodyguards grabbed O'Brien's arms and pinned them behind his back. He tried to get free but he was being held too tightly. The only thing he could do was glare at Chaka.

Chaka stepped back a few feet and grinned. "What are you so pissed off about, Robert? Your son is all right, you're a free man, and I got what I wanted. So, what's your problem?

"You're the problem!" O'Brien shouted, his voice quivering. "You think because you have more money than God you can get anything you want. Well, it doesn't work that way." He relaxed his body and the bodyguards let go of his arms. "Even if you had my son, I wouldn't work for a slime ball like you!" He backed up and pulled out the gun Tony had given him. He pointed it at Chaka's bodyguards and they backed off. He spun the gun around and aimed it at Chaka's chest.

"Let's talk about this," Chaka said, as he moved back several paces. "We don't have to go this route. I've offered John a deal and I'm certain I can make one with you. Money does talk, you know that."

"Bullshit!" Robert yelled, and pulled back on the .9 mm slide. "I'm not making any deals with you." He was facing Chaka, with his back to the bodyguards. When Bob noticed O'Brien had turned, he reached for his gun and pointed it at him.

Tony saw the gun and screamed, "Dad! Look out! He's got a gun, behind you!"

O'Brien swung around, but before he could get off a shot, Bob had pulled the trigger. O'Brien had anticipated his move and jumped to one side. The bullet grazed his shoulder but hit Chaka in the chest, barely missing a solid gold button on his paisley vest. Chaka gasped, clutched his chest, and crumpled to the ground.

O'Brien spun around and leveled his gun at Bob. "Drop it!" he commanded. "Kick it over to my son!" Without hesitating, Bob dropped it to the ground and kicked it over.

Matt's face flushed, when he saw what had happened, but he made no attempt to get involved. O'Brien motioned for him to put his gun on the ground, which he did. Tony picked up both guns and tucked them in his belt. O'Brien lowered his eyebrows and threw Tony a quick glance, but said nothing.

Anderson rushed over to Chaka to check for a pulse, but there was none. "Oh, my God!" he said, and looked up at O'Brien. "He's dead! Do you know what this means?"

"Yeah! One less scum bag to deal with." O'Brien's voice reeked of contempt

"It means all our work was in vain," Anderson shot back. "We have nothing to show for all our years of labor."

"What do you mean?" O'Brien said. "You should be able to get your bones back, now that he's out of your way." He pointed to the bodyguards. "Just ask those guys where they are. If they won't tell you, I have ways to make them."

"It's not that simple. He was the only one who knew where they were hidden. Moreover, he has both the medallion and the bones."

"Oh, shit!" O'Brien said. "You serious? He's the only one who knew?"

"Yes. At least that's what he told me."

The pilot of the helicopter saw what had happened and jumped down from the plane and rushed over.

"Is he dead?" he asked.

"I'm afraid so," Anderson said. "One of your boys shot him…Bob, I think it was."

The pilot looked down at Chaka, lying in a fetal position. "The son-of-a-bitch owed me big bucks," he said.

"Join the crowd," Matt said, as he went over and looked down.

"Will you take care of him?" Anderson asked the pilot. "We had nothing to do with this. He'd still be alive if he hadn't been in the wrong place at the wrong time." He looked over at Bob, who was standing behind them with a shocked expression on his face. "And you," he shouted, "you're going to have one hell of a time explaining this when the officials get here." Bob's body went limp. He slid down a tent stanchion to the sand and put his head in his hands.

O'Brien kneeled down beside him. "Your sure you don't know where he hid the stuff?" he asked, like a father to a son. "If you can tell us anything, we'll make sure it goes easier on you when the officials arrive."

Bob stared into his eyes. "Honest to God, I don't know…neither does Matt. Chaka told you the truth, nobody knew but him."

Anderson overheard the conversation and looked over at O'Brien. "Well," he said. "We're definitely out of business now…if he's telling you the truth."

Bob's eyes opened wide and he looked up. "Why would I lie?" he said. "What would I have to gain? We won't even get paid for what he owes us…Matt and me."

"Sorry to hear that," Anderson said. "But you guys made your beds now you'll have to lie in 'em." Tony rolled his eyes at the cliché.

The pilot went back to the chopper and made a call to the police in Maralal. When he returned to the tent, he told them they would be out soon, and that they were not to move or touch anything until they got there.

Eric and Dan had been standing in the background when the action took place. They wanted no part of it. Earlier, they had talked about returning to the fishing club with the Samburu boys, if they could find them. However, no one had seen them since the previous night. They figured they would go back, with or without them.

"Mister Anderson! Mister Anderson!" someone shouted. John turned and looked in the direction of the voice. A digger raced toward them flailing his arms and stumbling over acacia bushes as he approached. When he arrived at the sorting tent he bent over and took in several deep breaths. "Mister Anderson," he finally yelled out, and pointed at the digging fields. "You'll never believe what we just found!" Anderson's face turned pale.

Chapter Twenty-Six

The old Rover bounced up and down erratically, as it made its way to the fishing club. Every few seconds it would hit a pothole and Eric would grab his shoulder and swear. His injured arm was much better, but it had not completely healed. It was late in the afternoon and the sun's rays on the horizon were all but unbearable. Every few minutes Dan would have to stop and replenish a leaky radiator from the water can attached to the front bumper.

Eric had asked Robert and Tony to join them. For some unknown reason Tony was silent, and his father was dumbfounded. He had never known him to be that quiet. Sweat trickled down their foreheads and dropped onto their shirts, where it dried within seconds. Eric asked Dan to slow down but he said they had to go fast or the dust would catch up and eat them alive.

O'Brien wiped his forehead for the third time. His shirt clung to his broad shoulders and his khaki shorts stuck to his bottom. "Don't you have air conditioning in this thing," he asked. "I thought all Rovers had it."

Eric glanced in the rear-view mirror. "Yes, we do. But it takes so damn much gas to run it I don't think we would make it to Loiyangalani."

"How much farther?" Tony asked.

"Oh, about a hundred kilometers, I'd guess," Dan replied.

"What's that in good old American miles?" Tony asked with a scoff.

Dan snickered. "I'd say about sixty miles...couple hours."

The cab was quiet until they came to a sharp turn in the road. Dan suddenly stomped down hard on the brakes to avoid hitting another vehicle directly in front of them. He slid to an emergency stop a few feet from its bumper.

"What the hell!" he said.

They all came to full alert, when they saw the truck in the middle of the road. Three people were inside the cab, apparently asleep. The sound of the Rover sliding to a halt caused their heads to materialize in the windshield.

"That's the boys," Eric said. "I'd know them anywhere."

As soon as the dust had settled, Dan went to the truck and looked inside. Ebukut sat behind the wheel; Paul and Hussein in the back.

"What are you boys doing way out here?" he asked. "We were looking for you guys. We're on our way back to the fishing club. We were trying to find you to see if you wanted to come with us."

The big warrior rolled the window down and looked at him. "We leave last night," he said in broken English. Sweat poured down his cheeks and dropped onto the beads around his neck. "We return to Loiyangalani."

"Then why are you sitting in the truck? Where did it come from?"

"Truck no gas," Ebukut replied. "This truck sergeant take from Anderson. Is pleasant to rest in."

"Do you boys want to come with us?" Dan said. "We'll be at the fishing club in a couple hours." Then he added, "We'd put gas in that thing, if we had any to spare, but we barely have enough to get to the club."

"Yes," Hussein said, and opened his door. "We will join you…my feet are tired." Tony cried out in delight, when he saw Paul and the others walking toward them.

After they had settled down in Eric's truck, Dan turned to Ebukut and said, "Weren't you guys afraid the sergeant would come back for his truck and find you?"

"The sergeant is—" Paul started to say.

Ebukut interrupted him by holding up his hand. "We not worry about sergeant," he said. "He far from here." Dan snickered, and then turned his sight back on the road.

"Dan!" Eric shouted, after they had driven several kilometers. "Can't you be a little more careful with those damned bumps?"

"Sorry," was Dan's only response.

Several hours later, the truck pulled into the fishing club. Kirinyaga stood at the gate, and after a mock interrogation let them pass. They all hopped out of the truck and rushed for the lounge. The Samburu boys and Tony remained outside on the patio; warriors were not allowed inside the restaurant. Robert, Eric and Dan ordered large, stiff scotches.

Kurt was at his usual watering hole at the end of the bar. "Has anyone seen Mandeli?" he asked. "He was here yesterday, you know. But he left in a hurry and I haven't seen him since."

"Does anyone care?" Dan said.

"He has a duty to perform," Kurt said, dryly. "But, sometimes he gets a little overenthusiastic."

Sitting in a wicker chair on the patio, Ebukut overheard Kurt and glanced over at Hussein and Paul. They all smiled.

"So," Kurt began. "I heard you had quite an adventure, up at the site." He took a sip of his drink, and then eyed them.

"You know what went on up there?" Dan questioned.

"Of course. Between scuttlebutt and Chaka's grapevine, I'm quite well informed."

"Then you must be on Chaka's payroll, too," Dan said, with a slight grin. "It seems like everyone else is."

Kurt took a long sip of his martini, and then lifted his glass in a toast. "Here's to the most powerful, the most arrogant, the most cunning, the most dangerous, and the richest man in Kenya." He downed his drink in one gulp, and then looked around the room. Noticing all eyes on him, he poured another martini from a pre-mixed container. "Of course I'm on his payroll," he said with a grin. He turned his head and looked at Dan. "Who the hell in their right mind isn't?"

"He's dead, you know," Dan said, bluntly.

Kurt's eyes turned glassy, as he stared at Dan. "What did you say? What do you mean 'he's dead'?"

"Just what I said...he's dead!"

"What happened?"

"One of his bodyguards accidentally shot him. But in any case, he's dead."

"But that's impossible! He has the best men money can buy. They wouldn't shoot him, accidental or not." He laid his arms across the bar and dropped his head on them. "He owned part interest in this club, you know. Now there'll be all kinds of legal proceedings...paperwork and the likes." He raised his head and looked at them. "Oh well, the son-of-a-bitch had it coming, I guess."

Dan thought for a moment. "When the man's alive he's a rich angel from heaven, but when he's dead he's a poor son-of-a-bitch. Is that it?"

"Kurt," Eric said. "It's getting late and we're all tired. Do you have a place we can spend the night?"

Kurt gulped down the rest of his drink. "I don't have a vacant cabin in the place." He looked up at the ceiling, and then added, "Maybe you could stay in Mr. Emerson's hut. He never relinquished it when he went up north. I'll have them bring in some cots."

"Terrific!" Eric said. "That'll do just fine." Then he added, "Who the hell is Mr. Emerson?"

"I guess it's Jack, to you. The pilot who crashed a few days ago."

O'Brien joined the boys on the patio. "Tony," he said. "We're going to stay in Jack's hut for the night. We're leaving now."

"I'm not staying with you guys," Tony said. He pointed to the warriors. "I've been invited to stay with them tonight. They want me to go with them in the morning to hunt for a wounded lion...one that's been eating their goats." His face beamed. "Isn't that cool! They're giving me a spear and everything."

O'Brien raised an eyebrow. "You don't say. Will you be okay? Will they take good care of you?" He looked over at the warriors.

"Yes, he will be 'okay'," Paul said. "We will take *very* good care of him." He snickered.

"Okay. I'll see you tomorrow, sometime. You'll be careful out there in the wilds, won't you?"

"Didn't Jack and me live through a plane crash and a walk on the wild side, a few days ago?"

His father grunted, turned and left.

Tony got very little sleep that night. Between the small, large, and very large insects that had invaded his hut and sleeping blanket, and the howling, freezing wind that had shook the hut for several hours, he had been up most of the night.

When morning came, Paul found him huddled in the corner of the hut, eyes wide open and shivering beneath his flea-infested blanket.

"Tony," he said. "Come get something to eat. We'll be going into the hills, soon."

Paul's mother had already lit a fire and it was going strong. A pot of tea was bubbling and spewing steam, and *tylapia* was cooking in a large pan above the flames.

"Hello," she said in English. "You must be the one they call Tony. I am L'empi, Paul's mother. I was asleep when you boys came in last night and did not get a chance to welcome you. Forgive me."

"Hi," Tony said. "What's that stuff you got cooking in the pan? Smells great."

"That is *tylapia*, a fish."

"Fish for breakfast," Tony said with a grin. "I never heard of that. But then, what do I know."

L'empi frowned, but said nothing. She spooned a whole fish onto one of the only glass dishes she owned and handed it to him, along with a cup of tea. He waited for a fork but none came.

Paul looked on with amusement. "We do not have utensils," he said." They are too expensive to buy. We use our fingers. It tastes the same."

"Mmm," Tony hummed his approval, as he bit into the flesh. "This isn't bad. Tastes like fish." They all laughed.

"The warriors will soon be here," Paul said. "When you finish eating I will give you my spare spear and show you how to use it."

Tony downed his fish in a hurry and got up from the driftwood log he had been sitting on close to the fire. He followed Paul into the third hut of their *manyatta*, where they kept a small amount of stores. Up against the far wall was a seven-foot spear with a lanceolated blade. He walked over and looked at it. The shaft was smooth as silk. He pulled it away from the wall and lifted it over his head; it was extremely heavy. He was not sure he could throw such a weapon; he could barely lift it over his head. Paul showed him how to hoist it up to his shoulder and keep it there until ready to use. Then, he demonstrated how to lift it from his shoulder with the palm of his hand and hold it over his head.

The two boys took their spears and left the thorn barrier of the compound. When they were well outside the fence, Tony spotted a bush and flung the spear at it.

"No!" Paul said, raising his voice. "Do not throw the spear. Its two meter shaft is for stabbing, not throwing. Its length will keep the animal away until you can spear it."

"Oh," Tony said, embarrassed. "Sorry. I thought a spear was for throwing."

"You will notice my spear…it is lighter and shorter. It is for throwing. I gave you that spear so you could kill the lion, once we wounded it."

"How many lions are there?" Tony asked in a concerned voice.

"There is only one. The one we wounded before. It will have a broken spear in its side, unless it is already dead from the wound." Then he added, "Of course there are several cubs…the ones that ran off. You were there, don't you remember the cubs?"

"Oh, those," Tony said. "There were three of them, weren't there?"

"Yes."

"Are you going to kill the cubs, too?"

"If we can find them, of course. We will eat them."

"Bummer," Tony said. He thought for a moment, and then added, "What does lion meat taste like? And don't say chicken."

"It is very good...tender and sweet."

Ebukut and Hussein joined them outside the fence. "Are you ready to go?" the big warrior said in Masai. "We must get to the big boulders before the sun is high in the sky. The lion will not come out if it's too hot."

They left the village and headed up the first hill toward the familiar goat trail that had directed them to the two large boulders where they had seen the animal before. Halfway up the trail Ebukut turned to Paul. "He must take off his clothes," he said in Masai. He will wilt in the morning sun. Or is he afraid he will show us his '*ume*', too?" They both laughed.

Paul giggled. "I don't know about that," he answered. "But I will mention it to him."

"What's so funny," Tony asked. "Is he making fun of me, or something?"

"He made a joke."

"About what? About me?"

"Only that you should take off your clothes because of the heat."

"What's so funny about that?"

"He also said, maybe you were afraid to show us your '*ume*'"

"My what? What's an '*ume*'?"

"It's what you pee with." Paul giggled. "But you should at least take off your shirt and shorts. It will soon be unbearable. You could collapse from the heat, if you don't take them off.

Tony slipped his shirt over his head and tucked it under his belt. "That's as far as I'm going. I ain't goin' to show you my '*ume*'." He grinned, and they all laughed.

An hour later they had arrived at the two large boulders that overlooked Loiyangalani. Ebukut instructed them to spread out and creep slowly through the acacia bushes, their spears held in readiness. He told them to go slow, if the wounded animal were still alive, it would attack if they got too close.

Tony had been carrying the heavy spear on his shoulder ever since they left the village, and he was about to collapse from its weight and the intense heat of the morning. He lifted it off his shoulder and carried it in his hand by his side. An hour passed and still no animal was in sight. Exhausted, he sat down to rest on a large rock and laid his spear down beside him. He was quite a few meters from the others and could not see or hear them. As he sat on the boulder regaining his strength, he heard rustling in the bushes several meters from him.

"I hope that's one of you guys," he called out in a quivering voice. There was no response. The sound stopped. "Oh, shit!" he mumbled. He picked up his spear and cautiously headed in the direction of the sound. He parted a large acacia bush and discovered a young lion lying on its side, with a broken spear protruding from its hindquarter. When the animal saw him, it made no attempt to rise or run. Panting and gasping for air, it looked up at Tony with what he believed were pleading eyes. He saw no danger and approached it even closer. As he moved within a couple meters of the yearling, it attempted to get to its feet but fell back onto its side. Tony jumped back and almost dropped his spear. Again, he inched toward the animal. With a gurgling sound and wobbly legs, it stood upright and attempted to charge. Terrified, and not knowing what else to do, he hefted the long spear and raced forward. With all his strength he forced the blade deep into its chest below its shoulder. The yearling screamed in pain, looked at him as if pleading for its life, and then collapsed at his feet.

Hearing the lion's cry, Paul rushed in the direction of the sound. He parted the bushes and saw Tony standing quietly at the other side of the small clearing. Tony pointed at the ground and Paul looked down at the dead yearling.

"Ebukut! Hussein!" he shouted. "Tony has killed the lion. Come quick!"

The two warriors rushed over and saw the lion lying lifeless at Tony's feet. "It is the one we were after," Ebukut said. "My broken spear is still in its side." He went over and kicked the animal to make sure it was dead. "The elders will make you a *lmurran*, Paul," he continued. "And tonight we will feast."

Paul turned and gave the warrior a hard look. "But I did not kill it, Tony did. It was his spear."

"Then you don't want to become a warrior?" Ebukut asked. "I thought because you could not live with the white man you wanted to come back to our village and become a warrior."

"But I—"

The big warrior interrupted him by yanking the spear from his hand and thrusting it into the side of the lion. "Now it is your spear that killed it." He glanced at Tony with his dark, menacing eyes. "You will both become warriors. Nobody knows whose spear killed it…if we don't tell them."

Hussein's thoughts flashed back to when he and Ebukut had hunted each other with one spear. He had said the same thing to the warrior.

"What did he say?" Tony asked, interrupting his thoughts. "Tell him to speak English."

"He said you and Paul will become warriors. That is, if you want to become one. And they will have a big feast, tonight."

"Bummer," Tony said. "I've already been circumcised. That's as far as I go."

"Then you don't want to become a warrior?" Paul said.

"I think I'll stick to my way of life. I couldn't handle any more of those gigantic bugs you've got here…or that damned cold wind. Think I'll stick to getting shot at in the Bronx. It's safer there. Not so many wild animals." He thought for a moment, and then added, "Though we do have a few."

"What about the three cubs?" Paul said. "They must still be here, somewhere."

"Let them go," Ebukut said. "In a few months they will be big enough for us to have another feast."

When they arrived in the village with the carcass, word about the kill had already spread throughout the village, and people from every *manyatta* came to greet them. How they found out so quickly, no one seemed to know. They already had a roaring fire going and a long pole set aside for roasting the lion. Etaira had brought her famous sweet bread and L'Umbo his *pombe* beer. There would be another *lasar le ntoruto* tonight and Paul would become a *lmurran.* L'Umbo said they would have many more feasts, if Mandeli didn't catch them. However, the boys knew that was impossible.

Robert O'Brien and Tony were invited to watch Lnuie prepare Paul for his rite of passage. Several hours later, after she had finished, the ceremony began.

Paul knew exactly what to expect, after watching it for so many years. He didn't mind when the warriors put him through the ceremony of manhood, because his mind was on Lnuie and the way she had looked at him when she said, "I can touch your soul, Paul. I can feel it flowing through your body."

The feast lasted well into the night. When the last of the carcass had been devoured, and all villagers had returned to their *manyattas*, Robert and Tony said their farewells and left for the club. When they arrived they found Jack Emerson sitting at the end of the bar in Kurt's favorite spot downing a scotch.

"How the hell did you get here?" Robert said. "I thought we left you at the site."

Jack grinned and held up the drink. "Yes, you did. But John was nice enough to take me to that truck that ran out of gas, halfway between here and Koobi. He filled it up and loaned it to me."

"How the hell did he know it was there?" Robert asked.

"Like Chaka had, he has a grapevine, too…and people with cell phones."

"What are your plans, now?" Robert asked.

"Strange as it may seem, John offered me a job at the site."

"Why would you want to go back to that God forsaken place? There's nothing there but camels, lizards and heat."

"Most of that's true," Jack said, as he motioned for the bartender to refill his glass. He offered Robert a drink, but he shook his head. "Well," he continued. "If you believe in sheer luck, John has it."

"What do you mean?"

"Do you remember just before you guys left, a digger came running up the hill to John yelling that he would never believe what they just found?"

"Yes, but we had to leave at that time. I thought it was just some more old bone they found."

"'Old bones' is right!" Jack said, and grinned. "They found the mate to the skeleton they lost. And that ain't all, this one's a female. And to top it off, she had the same type medallion around her neck!"

"I'll be damned!" Robert said. "And the museum doesn't know about this one?"

"Not yet, anyway. But I wouldn't trust too many of his diggers not to tell anyone."

"Hell, there's nobody left to sell the information or bones to…now that Chaka's dead. Is there?" O'Brien said.

"There are people out there, other than the museum, who'd pay a premium for them," Jack said. He stopped long enough to take a healthy sip of his drink. "That's what he wants me for, to keep an eye on their finds and get things moving toward possible sales. He thinks because I was in Viet Nam I'm tough enough for the job."

"Are you?" Robert said, and grinned.

"Hell, I don't know. But I'm willing to give it a shot." He looked down at his glass and whispered so only Robert could hear, "Besides, Chaka never got around to picking up his packages from my plane. And I know exactly where they are. And, to top it off, Chaka's helicopter pilot made a deal with me. He'll fly me out to the crash site, if I pay him what Chaka owed him…plus a little bonus. Those 'items' will go a long way to finance John's venture. Maybe we can be partners." He took a long swig, and then laughed.

"Well, Jack, good luck with whatever you decide to do," Robert said. "I've only known you a short while but I think you'll do okay." He thought for a moment, and then added, "By the way, what happened to Chaka's bodyguard? Did the officials come and get him at the site?"

"Yes. But after waiting for hours for them to show up only Matt could be found. Bob, the one who shot Chaka, had somehow disappeared. No one knows when, how, or where, but he was gone. They have a nationwide manhunt out for him. It's only natural they would, with all the graft the police took from Chaka over the years." By the way, he continued, "What are your plans? You and the little squirt, there." He pointed to Tony, who stood at the end of the bar devouring devil eggs the bartender had put on the counter.

"Eric and Dan are heading back to Nairobi in the morning. I think they'll be good enough to give us a lift. From there, home sweet home."

Tony overheard. "Bummer!" he said, with his mouth crammed full of eggs.

—The End—

LaVergne, TN USA
30 August 2009
156446LV00003B/131/P

9 781607 039761